A Wildflower in the Wind

Book One of the Magic of the Wildflowers Trilogy

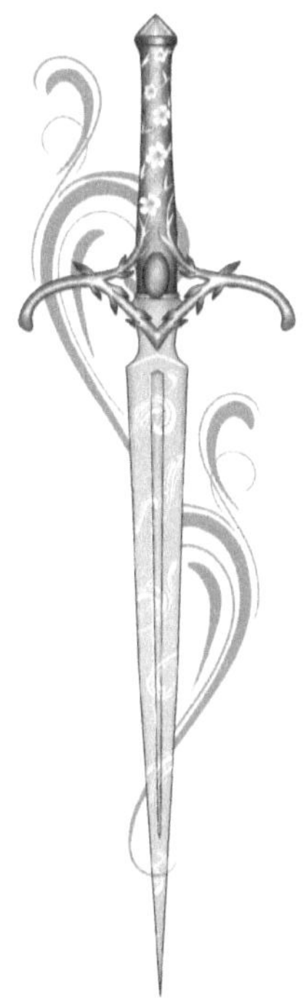

By Megan Shade

Published by: Shade Made Publishing LLC

First Edition

ISBN: 9798987832400

Editing by Sara Coombes: https://saracoombescom.wordpress.com/

Interior art by Brianna Strahsburg: @busybri.art on Instagram and Tiktok

Cover Art by SeventhStar Art Services

Authors note: This is the first book in the Magic of the Wildflowers Trilogy and ends on a cliffhanger. It includes adult themes including language, severe physical assault, and sexual content, and is intended for readers 18+.

CONTENTS

To Andrew,

Who, instead of questioning me when I told him I wanted to write a
book, bought me a laptop and made sure I had time to write.

I love you.

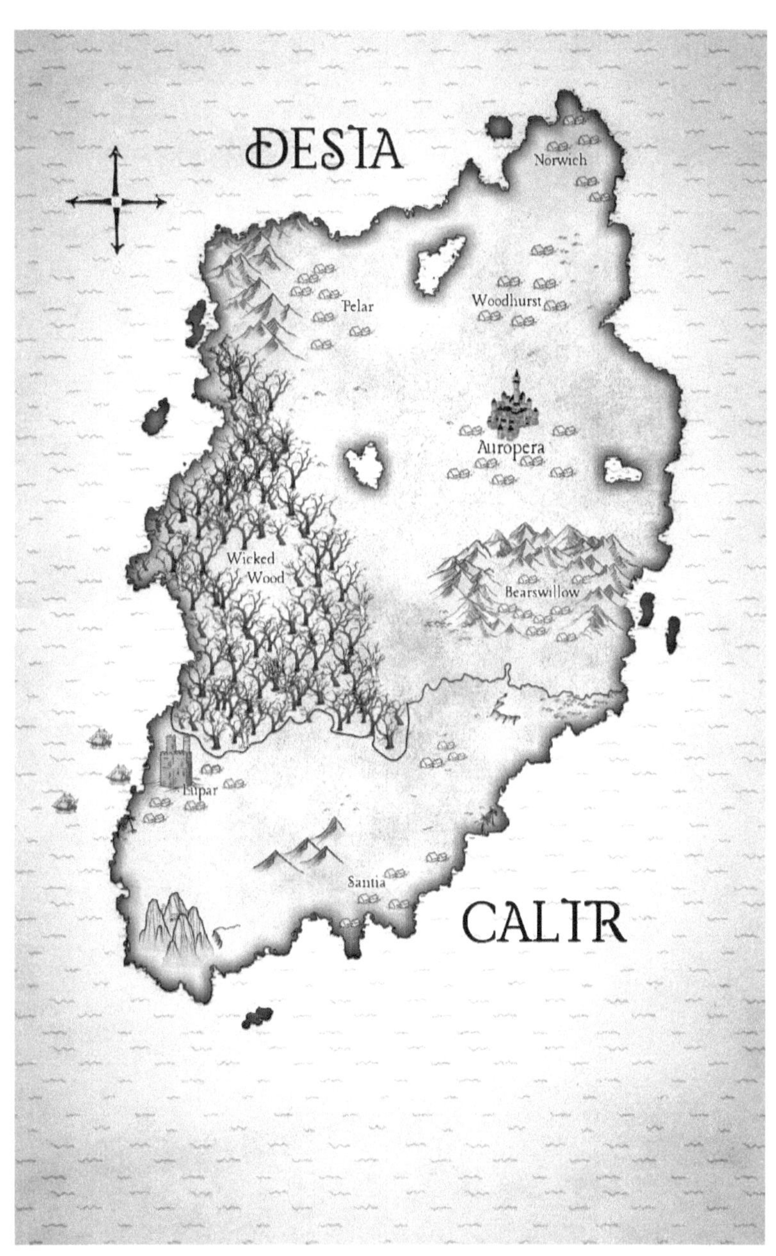

ĐESIA
Norwich
Pelar
Woodhurst
Auropera
Wicked
Wood
Bearswillow
Lupar
Santia
CALIR

PROLOGUE

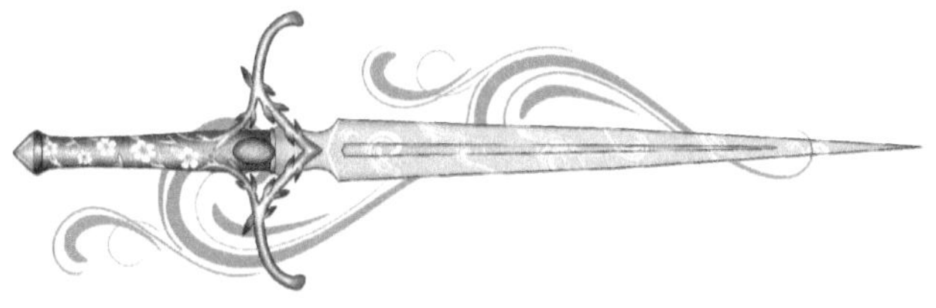

Rain drenched the ground as the cloaked woman picked the pure white petals from the dark, thorny vine. A smile crossed her face at their beauty, only for a moment, before the blade of betrayal sliced silently across her throat. The gods' own blood pooled from her neck under the glow of the moon, the magic within feeding the roots of the moonflowers she'd waited on through the night.

Death left only a moment to see who had ended her life—a man with familiar green eyes that swirled with darkness, so similar to the shadows she ruled. He escaped into the night as the petals floated softly toward the ground, falling from her hands and dropping into the puddle of deep red blood. As her soul severed itself from her earthly body, preparing for its journey beyond the veil, she watched as the petals turned black and rotted into ash, taking with them all hope that remained of bringing peace to her people.

At the very moment the flowers and the woman ceased to live, a seer in a kingdom far away woke from her slumber, eyes glowing white as the words of the gods were pulled from her throat.

"With the blessing of the goddess, evil will fall at her feet, and death will follow where she commands."

CHAPTER I

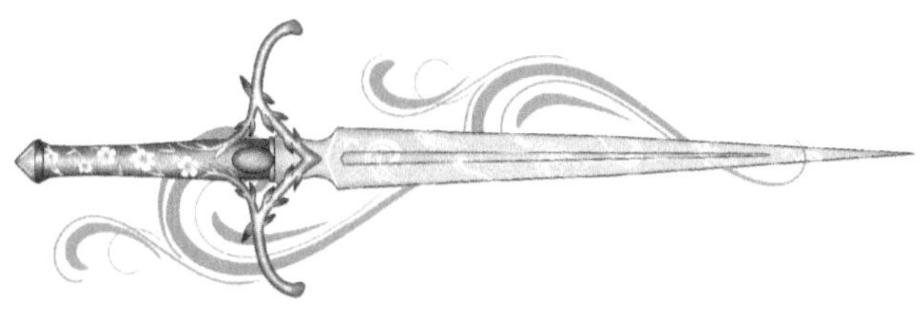

Lea needed death to wait. But it had never been considerate enough to give her time before. Time to say goodbye, time to make amends, time to take even a single breath before it ripped away pieces of her soul and dragged them back to wherever anger and pain and sorrow dwelled. Its greedy fingers had taken enough from her village in the past year—snatched away innocence and joy, deprived children of the peaceful dreams they'd once had as they slept safely in their beds, stolen mothers away from their daughters... her mother.

She crouched in the soft, tilled soil of her garden, rubbing her arms as shivers racked her body and goosebumps rose along her skin in the cool, spring air. She should have brought a sweater, but tonight she'd been pulled from her dreams, summoned, something drawing her to the darkness like the tides to the moon. Lea had known without a doubt as she'd raced into her garden in her nightgown and bare feet what had called to her—what had caused the sense of urgency that had floated in through her open window and woken her from her dreams.

The moonflowers—her only hope at saving the boy who had been infected three days ago—were close to waking from their slumber. She'd planted them the moment she heard the news, had pressed the small crescent-shaped seeds deep into the dark, damp soil with a prayer that they would grow quickly enough to stop the Lonely Death. Lea couldn't believe the illness had found her village again so soon, and a cry wrung from her throat at the thought of her young neighbor locked inside his room, dying alone to prevent the contagious disease from spreading. The wind whistled off the mountaintops surrounding her village as she waited for the small buds to unravel, the low chirping of crickets and melodic croaking of frogs a harsh juxtaposition against the erratic pounding of her heart.

These moonflowers will bloom in time, she thought. She would make them.

There wouldn't be much time to pick the petals and deliver them to the boy once they bloomed. Minutes—if she was lucky—that the small white flowers that bloomed only once would be free from their prison of fibrous leaves before turning a deep black and dissolving into ashes along with the magic held inside them.

"Wait until they're ready, *Wildflower*," her mother, Adelaide, had told her. "They must bloom fully... You'll know when to pick them. Picked by the right person with the right intentions, at the right time, the flowers from these seeds can stop death himself." They'd been some of the last words her mother had spoken to her, with a tight smile and a kiss on her cheek before she had barricaded herself in her room to protect her only child from death's selfish grasp. While Lea held all the memories of her mother close to her heart, she wished that, in this particular instance, she'd been more specific with her instructions.

Adelaide had used this very garden's bounty to create potions and salves. The herbs and spices swaying in the wind around her that were as familiar to Lea as the mountain air she breathed could speed up healing and cure most illnesses. All, actually, except for the Lonely Death. It was this very disease that had killed her mother; the petals of the moonflowers failing to open before she took her last breath, and Lea refused to let it happen again.

Lea's eyes were dry as she stared at the flowers—three long vines that twisted and climbed up the old metal trellis she had planted them beneath. Each dark, waxy leaf protruding from the thorny vines had a pointed tip, sharp enough to draw blood if one wasn't careful when handling them. Every few inches, the acorn-sized white florets she was waiting on sat stagnant, taunting her. She was afraid to blink, afraid to move anything at all as she crouched next to them. Her legs were shaking and her toes cramping from gripping the ground, but she remained still. She wouldn't miss the chance to pick these petals in time to help the boy.

Lea finally rocked forward onto her knees, unable to hold herself on the balls of her feet any longer. She brought her nose inches away from a tiny blossom that stubbornly refused to emerge. "Please," she whispered to the plant, her voice cracking as she begged for it to bloom. Little Anthony Coughlan didn't have much time; she could feel it, could somehow feel his frail body growing weaker, his breaths growing shallow along with her own. "Please!" she cried again, louder this time, as she ran her trembling fingers along the buds. She waited, tears streaming down her face as she sent a prayer up to the gods. The wind picked up a bit, the strong breeze blowing across her shoulders as if comforting her, but still, the flowers remained tightly coiled.

"Gods dammit, bloom!" she screamed, pounding her fists into the ground as her voice echoed across the large hill she knelt upon. "Fucking *bloom*! I'll do anything! Please..." she begged to the flowers, to the gods, to the wind and the sun and the sky above. Still, the flowers refused to obey as she watched the tips of the vines curling themselves tighter around the metal frame.

Bells rang out from the center of town, a simple melody that played throughout the day and served to either mark the time or alert the town of news. She immediately looked at the sky, *still dark*, she thought as she counted the dings. *Please, just be the time. It must be 4:00 by now... It has to just be the time.* Lea felt like she might faint as she listened, breaking out in a cold sweat, her stomach twisting into knots. "Please!" she screamed, uncertainty filling her tired, hoarse voice as her eyes darted back to the moonflowers. Her fingers shook as they hovered less than an inch above them, ready to pluck them and run.

Ding...

Ding...

Ding...

Ding...

The bells stopped, and Lea remained as still as the flowers before her, holding her breath and biting her lip so hard she tasted blood. She prayed with all her might that she wouldn't hear another bell as a drop of sweat ran between her shoulder blades. Blood rushed through her ears, the roar of it so loud she almost didn't hear what came next.

Ding... An extra bell. An announcement. Death hadn't listened. Once again, it hadn't waited.

CHAPTER 2

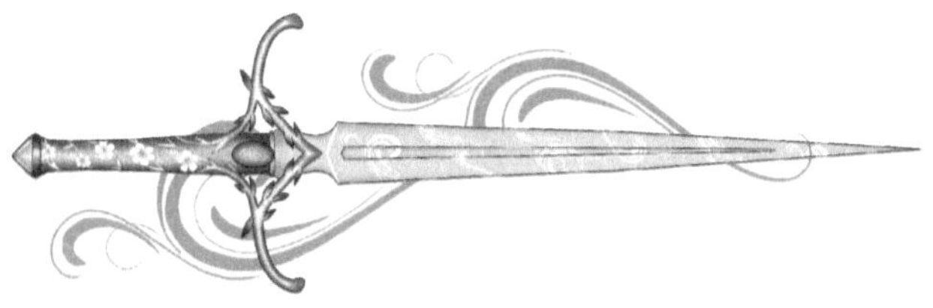

Lea wasn't sure how long she stayed there, watering the ground with the salty tears that had streaked down her dirt-covered cheeks. How was she ever going to beat the Lonely Death when the petals only remained alive for minutes? When they grew too slowly to emerge before the sick took their final breath? She sat in the moonlight, numb, as she calculated in her head how many moonflowers remained in the wreath above her bed. Her mother, Adelaide, had given it to her—dozens of dried moonflowers, their delicate seeds in tight spirals at their centers. Adelaide had never revealed how she had preserved the flowers so perfectly, insisting they had been a gift from an old friend. Yet the petals looked only days old despite the twenty-three years Lea had slept beneath them.

Lea had tried desperately, when her mother fell ill, to save her with those very same flowers. She'd ripped one from the wreath and planted every single seed from inside it, refusing to leave the patch of dirt where the flowers grew. Like a dutiful daughter, she'd stayed there day and night, but her mother's illness had been swift, and death had left no time for the flowers to bloom.

Over the last year, Lea had tried repeatedly to grow the moonflowers more quickly to allow her to harvest the petals before the ill were taken beyond the veil, but each time the Lonely Death found her little village, she failed—again and again.

Her mother, even as the experienced healer she was, had never had success using the flowers. But Lea had hoped, with the moonflower-shaped birthmark on the inside of her left arm, a stark white against her tan, freckled skin, that she'd be able to do what no one before her could. She knew it was a sign from the gods as surely as she knew her own name, so why the hell couldn't she get it right?

She looked back at her moonflowers through tears, watching as their petals finally unfurled from their tightly wrapped bundles. The petals were small, about the size of her thumbnail, and were a white so bright they almost seemed to glow. Lea ripped a vine from the trellis in anger, hot tears burning her eyes. They had bloomed minutes too late... She'd been so close.

She watched as the flowers began to turn black in her hand, a dark shadow creeping from the heart-shaped base and spreading until the petals were as dark as the night outside. She stood, throwing the dead vine on the ground as she screamed at the sky. *It's not fucking fair!*

Her mind drifted to the Coughlins, to the pain she knew they were feeling at this exact moment. She had failed them. Shame burned her cheeks as nausea rose from the pit of her stomach. The wind whistled in her ear, a sweet melodic sound that triggered a memory of her mother's voice as she'd walked through this very garden and picked flowers for the families of the departed. It was a ritual her mother had never missed, one that Lea had taken over in the year since her mother's passing. One that she would now perform for the Coughlins.

She hurried along the same path, pulling her rust-spotted shears from her apron pocket. Her hands trailed along the flowers before her as she sang her mother's recipe for a gift of healing. As a child, she had thought that the flowers her mother picked for the grieving families held magic like the moonflowers, but as she'd grown, she'd learned that the only magic they held was reminding those who were grieving that they were loved.

Lilies for peace. *Clip.*

Poppies for sorrow. *Clip, Clip.*

Peonies for hope for a better tomorrow. She let her fingertips find the space just above the junction where the plant would blossom again. *Clip.*

Astrantia for strength. She breathed in the sweet scent of one of the flowers her parents had named her after, wishing she could live up to the strength and courage it represented as she used her shears to gather the largest and most beautiful blooms from the plant. *Clip, Clip, Clip.*

Jasmine to heal. She pulled a long strand of her Jasmine vine to hold the bouquet together. *Clip.*

Orchids for remembrance of a love that was real. *Clip.*

Lea placed the bouquet on a nearby stump and walked deeper into the garden to find her most beautiful blooms to add to it, hoping to see bright pops of color from the flowers that had already burst from their deep winter's rest.

Stepping over a discarded watering can, she walked to the buds of lavender she had recently planted, rubbing them softly in encouragement as she saw just a hint of purple emerging. They would be popping into fragrant purple tufts within the day. She picked a few, hoping the scent would help the boy's family to sleep.

She took a deep breath... *Delphinium.* She clipped a light blue flower, turning her thoughts to her mother and the name she had given her. Azalea Delphinium Astrantia, though she had always gone by Lea. It was a name she had never felt like she could fully live up to—Azalea for eternal beauty, Delphinium for an open heart, and Astrantia for strength, power, and courage—the qualities her mother had hoped for her to hold one day, ones that Lea wished she possessed *more* of... always feeling that something was missing.

Lea wandered quickly through the garden, picking different colored flowers here and there as she thought about what that could be. She rubbed her chest, wondering what could fill that tiny pocket of emptiness that she felt nestled next to her heart.

Walking to the center of the garden where the vegetables grew, Lea stepped over the bright red tomatoes to peek at the onion and garlic that had grown through the winter. Crouching down, she was pleased when the powerful scent of garlic hit her nose. They were nearly ready for harvest, *thank the gods*. King Nestruir would be expecting at least four baskets within the month, despite the fact that the village also depended on her for food. *Not that the Black King cares.* They had missed their quota by three bags of grain once, years ago, when the mountains had blocked the rain from watering their fields. In response, the king had sent soldiers to slaughter their cattle and sheep. Bearswillow had survived the winter, but not without growling bellies and shivering bodies.

It was one of the reasons that her father was never home. He was always away hunting—trading furs and meat to feed and clothe their village. Anger twisted sharply in her chest at the thought of her father and the other villagers pulling wagons through the harsh terrain to deliver food and goods to Auropera, the capital city of Desia. They risked their lives for nothing more than to avoid the king's vindictive punishments, as well as his help controlling the spread of the Lonely Death by removing the bodies of the affected, and only after it had run its course through the village.

Finishing up, she grabbed the bouquet to return home. As she closed the gate to her garden, she looked up to see the sun beginning to crest the horizon. A beautiful pink-orange glow had begun to spread across the hill and the valley below. Lea tilted her head back and allowed the accompanying rumble of magic to pass through her, the familiar, shimmering rush of power-filled air that raced away from the horizon to mark sunrise and sunset—the magic of the night transforming into magic of the day.

She looked down at her hands and imagined having magic of the sun. Maybe she could have used it to help the moonflowers grow more quickly, giving Anthony a chance. Maybe those powers could help her find a way to escape the cycle she seemed to be stuck in. Wake up, grieve, attempt to find solace within her garden walls, try to fill the hole the loss of her mother had carved inside her, fail at beating death, try to sleep, toss and turn, repeat.

Her thoughts were interrupted when the wind suddenly picked up, whipping her hair violently around her face. She heard a low growl as the wind met her ears; the sound running along her spine and causing the hairs on her neck and arms to stand on end. Lea froze. The only movement was the rise of her chest and the thump of her heart. The wind carried the faraway sound to her once more, the snarl of something *hungry*.

She looked around, searching the tree line and the woods behind it for what could have made the noise, but her search was met with only the rustle of leaves in the trees and an occasional bird flitting from branch to branch. And while she was fairly certain she was alone, a distant memory nagged at her mind. That growl; it was so familiar. She was certain she had heard it before. *It's just my lack of sleep, death winning again… It's nothing.* Lea tried to convince herself that it was just the stress of the morning causing her imagination to run wild, but the noise sparked a memory of the hum of worry that seemed to permeate her home in the evenings as she was growing up. Her mother constantly double-checking the locks on the windows and doors during the night. Always cautious, always careful. And still, death had found her.

"Enough," she said aloud as she took the final steps into her house, closing the door firmly behind her and placing the flowers on the table. Enough of the fear, enough of the hiding and grieving. She went to dress for the day, pulling on a light blue dress that flowed down to just above her knees and a cream-colored sweater on top. She walked to the mirror, pulling her thick honey-blonde hair away from her face and braiding it across her shoulder, the long plait reaching nearly down to her navel. There was little of her mother in the reflection in front of her. Lea's eyes were the color of bluebells, while her mother's had been a rich chocolate brown. Her tulip pink lips were a bit larger, her cheeks spattered with freckles from the sun—a stark contrast to her mother's fair skin. But within her eyes, she could see the same look of determination.

Her mother had refused to believe that life wasn't worth living. She'd thought that every hardship was an opportunity for adventure. Lea glanced at her soil-covered nightgown in the basket near her closet and thought of the dreams she had at night that always urged her to wake. Dreams of vast blue oceans, forests so dark the trees turned to black in the distance, and cities bigger than even the mountains surrounding her small cottage in her small village. She couldn't continue to let herself dream of finding what was missing from her life if she was unable to walk through her grief and take hold of it. *Death has taken enough from me.* She grabbed the bouquet off the table and walked to the front door. *It's time to live.*

CHAPTER 3

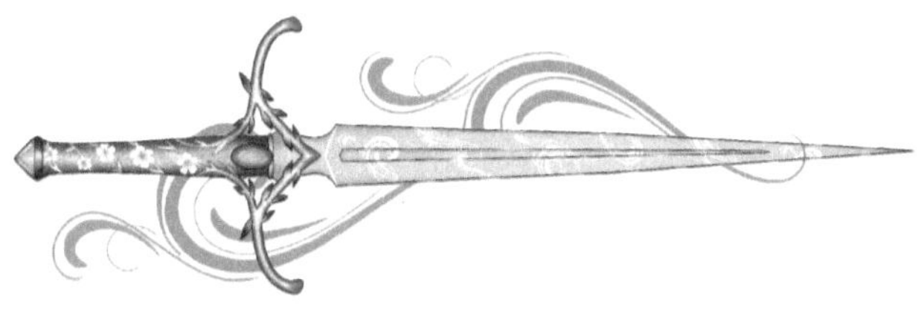

Lea's feet were heavy as she walked the worn grassy path to the Coughlin's home. She stepped onto the front porch, pausing when she saw the grief-stricken faces of Anthony's parents cast in the glow of the day's new light streaming through their front window. It felt like looking into her own memories as she took in the devastation on their faces, their arms clinging to each other as the life they had previously known slipped away.

Lea cringed as Anthony's mother ran to the entry of his bedroom, slamming her flat palms against the wooden door that separated her from her son's body. Her grief was so palpable that Lea had to turn away from the window, unable to watch their sorrow unfold as she thought about what would come next for this family. Soldiers from the Royal Army would be arriving soon; Fae who were blessed with magic that made them immune to all diseases. It would be their job to take the boy to an unknown grave far enough away from civilization to prevent the Lonely Death from spreading even further. No plot to visit, no stone to mark that he had existed at all.

Lea placed the bouquet on their doorstep, not wanting to disturb them, before wandering toward the center of town. Her pain was too potent to go back to her house or her garden right now. She needed to find Thomas. He was her best friend and always seemed to find the words that could soothe her grief.

As she turned the corner around the meeting house to find him, she was hit with the smell of roasted meats. She looked up to see colorful tables filled with sweets, fabrics, pelts, and other goods lining the sides of the stone street. Men with large barrels served ale and wine to those passing by, while other tables held roasted birds and boar. There were always people in the village square, but today the crowds were a bit larger, the stands fuller and more decorated.

"Lea!"

Thomas strode forward through the crowd. His height and broad stature caused the crowd to part around him as he moved, like a ship cutting through the sea below. She ran toward him, wrapping her arms around his waist and pressing her face into the rough fabric of his shirt as a sob burst from her throat. He leaned down and immediately wrapped her in a hug, his large body encircling her far smaller one in comfort, a sigh leaving his chest as he kissed the top of her head.

"It didn't work, then?" he asked solemnly.

She looked up at Thomas, her neck straining to meet his eyes as she shook her head, unable to say the words as shame filled her belly.

"I didn't think you'd be here or I would have come to find you sooner. It's not your fault, Lea. You have to know that." Thomas grabbed her hand and pulled her out of the crowd and toward his booth; a wooden table covered with knives, swords, daggers, and shields. Lea was grateful for the privacy his booth offered as she wiped at her eyes with her sleeve. Thomas reached up and cupped her face, wiping her tears away with his thumbs. "You did your best. You tried. I know that you're going to do it one day, Lea."

Sincerity filled his every word, every touch, and Lea knew that he believed what he was saying. She finally met his eyes, her brow immediately creasing in concern as she reached up and ran her fingers across the dark bags bruising his fair skin.

"Have you slept?" she questioned worriedly, taking in his untucked shirt and dirty hands.

"I worked through the night to prepare for the market today. We needed to forge extra stock with the Royal Army passing through town." He ran a hand through his shaggy brown hair, clearly exhausted.

It hit her then, the differences she hadn't noticed in the market before. Too enticed by the sounds and smells, she had missed that the banners hanging from various buildings were stitched with the royal insignia—a black background, a moon surrounded by shooting stars, and a sun with long, thick, wavy tendrils surrounding its center that reached toward the moon as if to eclipse it completely. She looked around the square and realized that Thomas was right, there were Fae everywhere; a race very similar to humans, except for a few differences. They were huge, for one, more powerful than ten humans together. Always beautiful, always cunning, and sometimes, magical. Her eyes caught on a group of four Fae males standing behind Thomas, all several inches over six feet tall. Their muscular builds hinted at their enhanced speed and strength, with sharp features and a wildness about them that reminded her of the visions from her dreams at night.

Lea's eyes darted to Thomas, and she watched as his shoulders stiffened. It wasn't safe for him to be selling his weapons here, among the Fae who were likely loyal to the Black King. Looking back toward the soldiers ambling across the streets, her worry only grew.

Her eyes bounced between her fellow villagers working at their booths and the large creatures who had long ago lived beyond the *Fe Fiada*—the wall between the human and Fae worlds that had been destroyed centuries before when the stars themselves had fallen from the sky and shattered it. While many of the merchants appeared unbothered, others seemed as wary of the soldiers' presence as she was. She turned toward the stand where her mother's friend, Sarah, was selling beaded jewelry, her smile tight and not quite reaching her eyes. Behind her, the baker's son was staring wide-eyed and alert as Fae soldiers walked past his crusty breads and sweet rolls. He was hardly blinking, and Lea wondered if he felt like the Fae were going to steal from him.

"What can I help you with?" she turned and asked Thomas, craving a distraction and wanting to help her friend. He looked truly exhausted, and despite the risks of him selling his weapons here, Lea wanted him to have a successful day at the market. Thomas sold more when the Royal Army was in her village than in two full months without them visiting, allowing him to provide for his mom and seven siblings. It was something Lea had tried to dissuade him from time and again, but money had been tight lately. Lea knew that his sales today were crucial to keeping food on the table for his brothers and sisters.

"Just spending time with you is helping, Lea." He patted her arm sympathetically.

"Stop it. Don't feel sorry for me. I need something to *do*, Thomas. Let me help you."

He studied her face for a moment, then handed her a soft cloth covered in oil. "Okay. Help me polish the weapons I made last night. I want them to shine as we sell out," he said with a wink. But under Thomas's smile, she could see lines of worry bracketing his eyes.

"Done." Lea picked up the closest sword and began to polish it. "Where's Joe?" she asked, wondering why Thomas was manning the booth alone when he was only the apprentice to the Blacksmith.

Thomas nodded across the street to the tavern. "Halfway to the wind, I'm sure. He knows I'd rather not be the one selling the weapons..."

Lea was well aware of what could happen if the soldiers realized his weapons were *too* good. Though anyone could tell he had worked hard at his trade based on his callused hands and arms scarred from the heat of the blazing forges he used to melt metal, his success wasn't just from his skill with an anvil and a hammer. Thomas also possessed magic. It was a secret he had only shared with Lea and the blacksmith, who cared more about money than turning Thomas in for treason. Magic was still strong within the royal line, but outside of this, very few were known to be blessed with it, and to wield it without alerting the king of your abilities was illegal. Without a drop of Fae blood inside him, it should have been out of the question for Thomas to have magic, yet the swords he created seemed impossibly sharper and more durable than those the blacksmith made. The magic he used to create the blades had so far gone undetected, but Lea could tell that Thomas felt the risk far more acutely whenever the Royal Army was passing through.

"It'll be okay, Thomas." Lea brushed her hand against his in solidarity as she picked up a small jewel-encrusted dagger. But would it? She placed a smile on her face and continued to work, unsure if Thomas was convinced by her facade of bravery. Could he sense the ache in her chest and the way her heart pounded when she thought of him in danger?

He gave her a tight smile, lowering his voice. "I know it will, but I can't serve the Black King, Lea. My family needs me. If I were to get caught..."

Anger sparked in Lea's chest at the thought of Thomas leaving to serve King Nestruir, who viewed all magic in the kingdom as an extension of his own and, therefore, property of the Crown.

"You won't, because I won't allow it. You know you can't get rid of me, so leaving me behind as you go to Auropera is out of the question. I'd never allow you to have an adventure like that without me, and seeing as I have no—" she wiggled her fingers, her poor attempt at a code word for magic, "I'm not allowed there. So, you'll just have to stay hidden and stay with me." She kept her voice light, but her stomach dropped at the familiar pang of worry she always felt when she thought about Thomas's magic. "Did you make this last night?" Lea changed the subject, reaching out to trace her fingers along the swirling patterns on the blade Thomas was holding. It was already shiny, and Lea was certain Thomas had polished it at least twice in an attempt to work out his nerves.

"I did." He pulled the sword from her hands. "Do you like it? It was the last one I made as the sun was coming up. I worried I wouldn't have time to finish it before my magic weakened."

"It's perfect," she replied, bumping her hip into Thomas's as she ran her hand along the carvings in the hilt. It looked like the wind. Lea wished she had enough money to buy it herself. She knew he would gift it to her if she asked, but a weapon that beautiful would bring a good sum, and she couldn't take that away from him, no matter how beautiful the sword was.

Lea had moved on to polishing a silver sheath when her stomach grumbled. Leaning into Thomas, she eyed the sweets lining the table across the street—small cakes with pink and cream frosting with tiny flowers on top, chocolate tarts with berries, and fruit coated in a hardened candy coating with powdered sugar on top.

Thomas leaned down so that his head was even with hers and followed her drifting eyes. He laughed before placing his overly polished sword onto the wooden table in front of them, grabbing her arm, and pulling her toward the sweets-filled booth. "Take your pick," he said. "Though, truly, how you have any teeth in your head with all the sugar you eat, I'll never understand," he teased while elbowing her in the ribs.

Ignoring his jab, she ordered two of each dessert with no intention of sharing. The plump, balding merchant wrapped all but one—which was already halfway into her stomach—into a pretty parcel with a sage green ribbon. Lea licked the syrupy chocolate off her fingers, feeling a bit more like herself now that sugar was coursing through her veins.

"Let's bring the rest to Nora later." Lea handed the box to Thomas, thinking about his sister, who was too young to be part of the festivities that would be happening this evening.

Thomas nodded and slid his arm loosely around her shoulders as they walked in familiar silence back toward his booth. The warmth of his arm combined with the sun beating against her skin made her feel almost as if she was glowing. Content, she tipped her head up toward the sky, soaking in the sun's rays that always seemed to energize her and calm her at the same time.

As her eyes closed and she took a deep breath of spring air, she felt a prickle along the back of her neck. A tingle of awareness that something was coming, or a gut feeling that something was amiss? She wasn't sure, but the sensation lurked there, a buzzing undercurrent that *something* was very different, and *someone* was watching her.

Lea looked around for whatever was causing the feeling, scanning for anyone who could be looking in her direction. Thomas's brother was walking toward the ale booth, and the seamstress was following her daughter toward a little girl who had fallen and torn a hole in her stockings, but she didn't see a single pair of eyes looking in her direction. She continued to scan her surroundings when a small child suddenly darted between Thomas's legs as he chased a spinning top, crashing through the crowd on his singular mission to find his toy. Thomas jumped backward, pulling his arm from around her shoulders as he tried to remain upright. Lea was knocked off balance and stumbled, nearly falling to the ground.

She watched as Thomas pulled the boy to the side of the street, gently scolding him. He patted the boy she now recognized as a friend of Nora's on the head before turning to find Lea and gesturing for her to join him back at his booth. She pushed through the crowd back in the direction they had come from but paused when a brush of cool air touched the back of her neck, sending shivers down her arms as the feeling of being watched increased tenfold. A strange sensation in her chest caused her to rub her hand against her sternum, but the ache only grew. *What's happening?*

She looked behind her, searching for whatever was causing her body to react in such a strange way. Was it the beast whose growl she'd heard this morning? Distracted, she bumped into a large Fae soldier, causing him to spill the ale he held all over her shoes.

"I'm so sorry." She looked up to apologize, only to see a look of fiery anger on the Fae she had knocked into. He was huge, definitely taller than Thomas, with a shaved head and tattoos peeking out from under his black uniform and up the base of his neck.

"Are you blind or stupid?" he asked her as he stepped forward and shoved her backward into the wall behind her. She winced as she felt the irregular surface of the stone press into her back.

"Neither, I... I was distracted. I just didn't see you." Her voice got progressively quieter as she spoke, her fear closing her throat tight around her vocal cords. "I'm sorry–"

"I find it hard to believe those big, pretty eyes could miss me." He paused, looking her up and down slowly as a disgusting grin grew on his face. "Did you run into me on purpose then, sweetheart?" He pressed himself up against her, and she recoiled further into the wall, the chill of the stone seeping through her clothing.

"What? No! It was an accident. Just let me go!" She pushed at his chest as she strained to look behind the Fae for help. Where had Thomas gone? She tried to duck under the man's arm as he pressed himself against her, grabbing her shoulder and shoving her roughly against the wall, tearing the sleeve of her sweater.

"You made me drop my ale, you know. You'll have to repay me somehow. A beautiful girl like you... I can think of a few ways." His words felt oily as they left his mouth and slid against her skin, and nausea filled her belly as she tried unsuccessfully to move out of his grasp.

"No!" she screamed as the soldier covered her mouth with his hand, muffling her cry. Bile rose in the back of Lea's throat as she began to fight, pounding her fists against the soldier's dirty uniform. She was trapped and felt as if she might vomit as he pressed himself more firmly against her.

A deep, rumbling voice growled from behind them. "You *will* let go of her." The sound reminded her of the roll of thunder before a storm. "*Now.*"

The calm, commanding tone lacing the man's order made her shiver. There was no room for argument between his words; it was a demand that simply had to be obeyed. The soldier immediately jumped back, his face turning white as his pupils doubled in size.

She stepped back from the soldier who had trapped her against the wall. A blush bloomed across her cheeks as her eyes met the largest man—no, Fae—she had ever seen. He was at least six and a half feet tall, with olive skin and a muscular build apparent even beneath his dark clothing. His dark, wavy chestnut hair was pulled back into a bun with several loose strands hanging around his face. At least a week's worth of stubble peppered his cheeks and chin, but even his facial hair couldn't hide the sharpness of his cheekbones or the strength of his jawline. A dagger was strapped to a belt around his waist and a sword that had to be as tall as she was hung across his back. Her stomach flipped as she took in the danger radiating from the Fae, but she wasn't afraid of him. She felt... Well, she wasn't sure what it was.

His heated gaze was fixed on the tear in her clothing, exposing the skin of her arm almost down to the elbow. His eyes finally left her shoulder and moved to her face, the look of murderous rage in them so potent she wondered if the man touching her would leave this encounter alive.

"Commander, I apologize. I was simply speaking with the lady," the soldier sputtered. The enormous Fae Commander took two slow steps forward, the heels of his shoes clicking on the cobblestones.

"You were *simply* assaulting her," he seethed, taking a step closer and holding his right palm out in front of him. Shadows emerged from his fingers, small tendrils of darkness that were blacker than the night sky. The Commander flicked his index finger toward the soldier and the shadows followed his command, darting toward the terrified Fae and wrapping themselves firmly around his throat. "If you were smart, which you obviously are not, you would get back to camp and pay attention to your post, at which I believe you are due in ten minutes."

Lea's jaw dropped as she took a step back and watched the display of night magic before her. Most who held magic were gifted with a specific skill, but this Fae had elemental magic, the purest form of magic. It wasn't just rare; it was a wild, raw power that allowed him to manipulate the fabric of the world around him. Something she had heard of but never seen with her own eyes. *This man is dangerous...*

She pressed her back against the wall as she watched the shadows coiling tighter around the soldier's neck. His face turned red, then purple, as the man known as the Commander continued to hold his hand up, silently ordering the shadows to twist and writhe tighter around his subordinate's throat. His furious eyes never left hers, and she was suddenly struck by their color. *What a peculiar green*, she thought. So familiar... Had she met him before as the Royal Army had passed through town? Surely she would have remembered the handsome giant with bright green eyes if they had crossed paths before?

The offending soldier attempted to pull at the shadows still holding tight to his neck, but his hands passed right through them.

"You should know struggling is useless." The Commander wrapped the shadows impossibly tighter. "Do we touch things that do not belong to us? Do we touch anyone, let alone a defenseless human woman, without their permission?" He spat the words at the now purple soldier.

The man shook his head again, faster this time, and the Commander released his soldier from the shadows, allowing him to sag toward the ground.

"Yes or no?" he roared. The soldier didn't respond as he sucked in deep, hungry breaths, starved of oxygen for too long.

"You will answer your Commander. *Now!*" His voice held venom as he raised his palms again, and the soldier's eyes lit up in fear as he scrambled to answer, but no sound came out as he continued to gasp for air.

The Commander's eyes flashed black. "If you can not gather the strength to speak, perhaps I should cut out your throat. Or better yet, I should take your hands for touching what does not belong to you."

The man's face turned from a ruddy purple to a pale, almost white, in an instant, and Lea took a step back at the sight of the shadows once again expanding around the Commander. Cringing, she watched as the soldier placed his hands behind his back as if hiding them out of sight would save them.

"Please. You can't take my hands, Commander." The scent of urine filled the air as the soldier begged for mercy.

"Hmm… And why not?" the Commander asked coldly, picking at his fingernails.

Stuttering, the man searched for a reason. "I'd be of no use to the army—the king!—if I couldn't hold a sword."

Leaning casually against the wall, the Commander crossed his arms and looked away as if pondering the soldier's words. "Perhaps you're right; scum like you are of no use to me if you can't wield a sword in battle. But, seeing as I have trained you, I would expect you to be proficient enough with one hand…"

Scrambling forward, the soldier dropped to his knees. "You can't take my hand! Please!"

"Then you do it," the Commander said casually as he leaned down and pulled a small, sharp dagger from his boot.

"What?" the cowering man sputtered, his mouth opening and closing like a fish searching for air.

The dagger gleamed in the Commander's hand as he drug it along the rough stone wall, sparks flying off the metal with each slow stroke. Nausea rolled in Lea's stomach as she watched the dagger's smooth edge grow jagged, small pieces snapping and crumbling with the force of the Commander's movements.

Looking down, the Commander studied the dagger, slowly turning it, taunting, as he examined the now uneven, ragged blade from every angle. Satisfied, he tossed it to the ground in front of his soldier.

"I said," he leaned down, voice deadly, "You. Do. It. Left or right, it doesn't matter, but you will do it before sundown, or that dagger will be used to carve you piece by piece to be fed to the horses."

The soldier had no words… How could he, with the threat of this terrifying man hanging above his head? He was the Commander of the most evil king in the history of Desia, and Lea had no doubt in her mind that, to have assumed this role, he must be equally vicious and unforgiving.

With shaking hands, the man picked up the dagger, staring at it as it lay in his open hands.

Shadows snaked from the ground up his legs and body, wrapping in tight coils around the man's arms before climbing up his chest and pushing his head back, forcing him to meet the Commander's eyes. "I will know if you use a different blade. And I will know if you numb the pain with drink, or ask for help from another. If you don't believe you can do it, tell me so I can kill you here and now."

"No, please," he whispered. "I'll do it." He kept his eyes downcast as he replied, despite the darkness holding his head in place. Lea suspected that, were she to look closer, she would see tears gathering behind the terror he was trying to hide.

"Then go," he ordered. A demand, and Lea could not decide if it was meant for her or the soldier shaking in front of her.

The soldier turned and ran, and Lea noticed that some of the shadows followed behind him as he sprinted toward the camp. Several steps away, the Commander looked at her with furious concern. "Are you okay?" he asked. She looked down to see that she was shaking, an after-effect of the adrenaline that was pumping through her body.

"I think... yeah. I'm okay. I just. I think I need to find Thomas?" she whispered as she tried to calm her mind.

"Is that the name of the coward who ran off?" he growled angrily.

"We were separated. He didn't run off," Lea replied defensively. How did this man know she'd been with Thomas moments before?

"Regardless, he wasn't here, and you almost got hurt. Let me walk you home." The Commander took a step toward her when she suddenly heard a commotion behind him. Thomas turned the corner at a run followed immediately by her friend, Solomon, then three of Thomas's brothers. One of them, Sam, jumped on the Commander's back and hooked his arms around his neck as Solomon held up what looked like a small branch from a tree over his head.

The Commander flipped Sam easily onto the ground at his feet before turning around and positioning himself directly in front of Lea, shadows bursting from every inch of exposed skin and blocking her friends from view.

"Stop!" Lea cried out, peeking around the large waist shielding her. "He's gone. Thomas, the one who attacked me is gone! Solomon!" Her voice was firm, like a mother scolding her child. "For the love of the gods, put down the stick!" Solomon looked at her before dropping it to the ground.

"It's bigger than a stick, Lea, it's like... A battering ram or something. Don't make it sound so wimpy..." Solomon pouted.

"Okay... Thank you for putting down the very manly stick weapon thing," she teased him before pushing past the Commander. A cold pressure wrapped around her waist and tugged her backward, just a bit, as she walked toward Thomas. She paused. *How odd...* She began to turn in the direction she was being pulled when Thomas pushed himself between Lea and the Commander, nearly severing the connection she had been feeling with him. She rubbed at the spot in her chest that still quietly buzzed from his proximity to her. *What the hell was that?*

"I'm so glad you're okay," Thomas said, grabbing her hands and holding them tightly.

"No thanks to you," a deep voice rumbled behind them.

"Excuse me?" Thomas turned around, and Lea saw the Commander look at their clasped hands in disgust. "I was across the square... I got help. What else should I have done?"

"I see how you look at her, just like I saw how the man assaulting her looked at her. If she's so precious to you, you shouldn't have let her out of your sight. You should have been with her and fought to protect her. Not taken precious time to find your friends and a stick, leaving her alone with a man who had every intention of violating her."

"Thanks for your input, but you have no idea what you're talking about. I'd never let Lea get hurt, and I had it handled. Let's go." Thomas said to Lea, pulling her by the hand away from the Commander and back toward the marketplace. Shadows immediately grabbed the back of Thomas's shirt, halting his movement forward.

"If you want to keep your tongue, then you will not use it to order her around. Do you understand me?" the Commander spat, stepping forward, clearly seconds away from not-so-gently removing Thomas's hand from around hers.

Lea let go of Thomas and looked toward the Commander, offering him an apologetic smile as she tried to de-escalate the situation. He was just doing his duty, making sure she was okay after his soldier had acted out of line. "It's okay. I'm okay. Thank you for your help." She reached out and touched his arm, jumping back as a shock zapped her fingertips.

She looked up at him, her eyes widening in surprise, only to notice that he was staring at the exact place she had touched him, his eyes locked firmly onto the patch of skin just below his elbow where the electric current had crackled between them. She looked at her fingertips, the aftershocks of electricity still spreading up her arm. He took a step toward her as she met his gaze, the look on his face deadly serious. She was about to ask him what had happened and if he had felt it, too, when she was pulled away quickly by Thomas dragging her behind him.

She turned back to the Commander as she followed Thomas, locking eyes with him and giving him a small wave before mentally kicking herself. *He doesn't care about you*, she thought, dropping her hand and cringing in embarrassment as he stared after her with a scowl on his face that caused heat to rise to her cheeks. She didn't know that man. The Commander of the Royal Army, pledged to the king who took from her village until they had nearly nothing left. The king who stole away children with magic, never to see their parents again, to serve him for the rest of their lives. If the Commander was the leader of the Royal Army, then he couldn't be trusted, and with any luck, he would forget her as soon as she walked away.

So, why did she feel that odd tug in her chest—a deep, intense need to run back to the Commander and apologize for Thomas's behavior?

CHAPTER 4

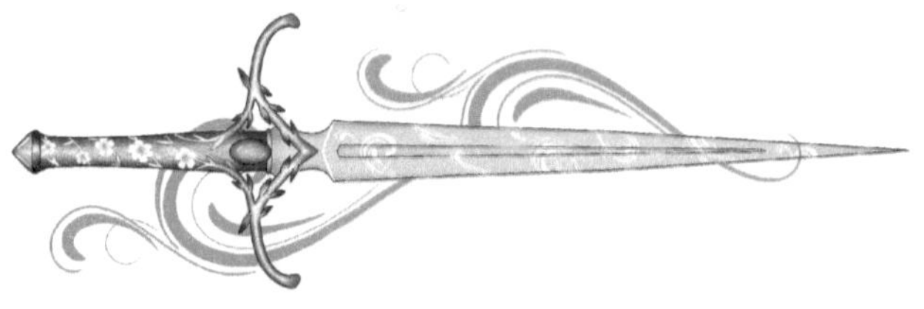

As the sun set and the marketplace grew quiet, the woods came alive as they did in this part of Desia each night. The fireflies danced as the sky turned a deep pink, a dazzling display to accompany the first Ignis Nocturno of the season. She could smell the beginnings of spring in the air, the scent of growing grass and budding honeysuckle, as it mixed with the earthy smoke from the torches that would soon light the many fires spread across the field.

Lea and Thomas remained arm in arm after cleaning up his booth as they walked toward the woods in the throng of villagers to join their friends for the Fire Celebration. It was a tradition in the spring months that celebrated the beauty of light and dark together, bright fire against the black night, just like the magic that, though scarce, ran through their kingdom itself. Tonight, and every night for the next several weeks, would be filled with wine and dancing, women wearing bright spring colors and intricate braids in their hair. There would be tales of magic and couples disappearing amongst the trees to return hand in hand later with flushed cheeks and hushed whispers.

They continued climbing up a small hill of long grass and sleepy wildflowers toward the large, unlit pyre where her friends sat. Solomon, the dopey-eyed boy who had run to her rescue with a stick, stood and waved, and Janelle and Danielle followed his lead.

"Took you two long enough. I was beginning to worry you'd lost yourself in a giant piece of cake down in the market," Janelle said with a laugh as she pushed her light purple hair, dyed from berries from Lea's own garden, away from her pale face. Lea had met Janelle when she was eleven, when a boy had kicked dirt in Lea's eyes during a game of ball, angry that she was winning. Janelle had run over and punched him straight in the nose, telling him that only jealous wombats cheated before grabbing Lea by the arm and cleaning her eyes out with water. She was small, but fierce, and often outspoken. "Or maybe you got lost in something else..." Her words were teasing, but her eyes bounced between the two of them suspiciously.

Thomas blushed but quickly turned his head. "We were just browsing the booths, Janelle. I'm surprised I didn't see you there, *sampling* the wines."

Lifting her glass slowly, she looked him dead in the eye while taking a long sip. "If you had seen me there, I wouldn't be much of a thief, now would I?" Janelle had a penchant for swiping things that weren't likely to be missed. Though she never took anything of importance, she had a knack for remaining undetected and enjoyed the thrill of trying to sneak what she could without getting caught. So far, her record was flawless, and she would usually repay whoever she stole from in some way or another without their knowledge. She had no ill intent and did not wish to harm anyone with her thievery. She was, quite simply, bored.

"You really shouldn't get into the habit of stealing when the Royal Army is here. You know they are always looking for reasons to punish us," Solomon said. "Though, I do enjoy watching you pull the wool over those bastards' eyes." Solomon had hated the Royal Army for years, ever since two of them had beat him in a game of dice, one of them using his day magic to force the wind to flip his die over to a five, giving him three-of-a-kind and a new dagger that Thomas had crafted as a gift for Solomon.

Danielle, a fair-skinned, willowy girl with strong opinions but a quiet demeanor—though that quiet demeanor only extended to strangers—huffed and stood, grabbing the matches from the ground. "Gods above, we have a celebration to get to! Are we just going to stand around saying what we think of each other? We get it. Janelle steals. Solomon thinks the Royal Army is full of idiots. *I think* Thomas is an idiot, and Lea is as clueless as they come. Can we get to the party now, please? The sun is about to set." She held out the matches impatiently to Thomas, who obligingly took the matchbox and walked toward the pyre. Danielle followed, her brown ponytail swinging behind her with each step.

"Wait! What am I clueless about?" Lea yelled after Danielle. Janelle simply stared at Lea with raised eyebrows for several long moments before joining the others.

Lea sat alone for a few minutes as she watched her friends gather around the fire, speaking together in hushed voices. Between the five of them, they were as close to a family as she'd had since her mother's passing. Her father had seemed to take longer and longer trips since her mother went beyond the veil, and while it stung to see him leave and await letters with small words of affection that were soaked in ale and layered with grief, she was content with her family of friends. When she was under the stars with all of them on nights like tonight, she *almost* felt like it was enough.

"Lea! Come over here! It's time for the Fire Rite." Danielle turned and waved her over.

She came to stand by the fire that was identical to the ones nearby, each pyre encircled by people holding hands. She threaded her fingers with Thomas and Danielle's just as the rite began and the last bit of sun dipped below the horizon. A ripple of power rumbled across the land, quickly passing through each fire and blowing sparks into the night sky like dancing stars. The rush of magic caused the wind to blow their hair around their faces and the ground to shift, the limbs to bend in the trees, and a flood of magic to pass along their skin as it raced away from the sunset.

Lea tried to catch the magic as it passed through her, tried to pull it into her body, into the hole in her chest, but it was like a feather in the wind, dancing wildly through the air before disappearing altogether. It was a tradition that on the first night of the Fire Celebrations, a prayer would be offered to the gods, and the magic that passed through would carry your deepest wishes and hopes to their ears. She thought of this morning and all the nights that had come before that she'd spent in her garden, screaming at the sky as she failed, again and again, to stop death from taking from her village. With a pang of pain and a glimmer of hope, she exhaled, sending up the prayer that she held most deeply. She would beat death. She would not let it claim another innocent soul.

When the magic passed, and the rumble stopped, she opened her eyes and again felt the awareness of someone's attention on her. She turned her head to see Thomas looking at her, a mix of trepidation and excitement on his face. Before Lea could ask him what he'd wished for, Janelle grabbed her arm and pulled her to the table filled with spirits, handing her a glass of sweet pink wine. Lea took a small sip, the tart, sugary alcohol bringing an immediate warmth to her belly.

The flames grew taller around her as they were fed more wood and brush, growing so high that the one nearest to her was now dancing above her head. As the fires rose, a vibrant melody floated across the field as instruments started to play. Straining her ears, she tried to identify the tune. It was a folk song, one she had heard hundreds of times since she was a child, that was fast and cheerful and made her bounce on the balls of her feet. She sipped on her wine as Janelle jumped into Solomon's arms and began to dance with him, smiles on their faces that flickered in the firelight. She wasn't sure why; maybe it was the energy of the stars above her or the presence of her friends all together and safe, but Lea felt truly happy in that moment—a feeling that had been rare and fleeting for her these days.

A breeze danced across her skin as a shiver ran down her arms, and she tipped her head up toward the sky, looking up at the stars and taking a deep breath of fresh night air. Despite the wine, and the dancing, and the whispered wishes shared only with the stars and the breeze in the trees, Lea still couldn't shake the feeling deep in her bones of someone's eyes on her. Lea spun in a circle, looking past the fires into the inky black night for whatever was causing the odd sensation, but as she searched for whoever's eyes had found her in the dark, it wasn't fear that she felt. It was anticipation. Maybe it was the spirits of the forest watching over her after hearing her prayers. Maybe it was her mother calling to her from across the veil to tell her she knew she had tried, and that she was proud of her for it. Or could it be her father, finally home from his weeks away and coming to find her? She felt a stab of pain in her heart. No, of all the people it could be, she was certain that it was not him.

Whoever it was, she could feel that they were here to keep her safe. After being on her own for so long, her constant fight against death, and the ominous growl she'd heard this morning, it was nice to feel protected, like someone or something out there would take the burden from her, even if she didn't know who it was.

She finished her glass of wine and returned to the fire, settling down next to Thomas, who refilled her glass as Solomon told a story involving a runaway donkey and sack of flour that had all of them giggling until their drinks shot out their noses.

As the evening passed, the fires around her filled with people whose faces she did not recognize. Soldiers from the Royal Army. Men and Fae who, when mixed in among the people she loved, did not seem so different to her. They brought gifts of flowers and whiskey, with crooked smiles and crinkles around their eyes when they looked for a woman they hoped would spend the evening with them under the stars. She suspected the army timed their trips through the village to allow them to attend the

Fire Celebrations, a time when all lines between those of the Crown and the villagers, the Fae and the humans, blurred, and for an evening, they could all just *be*.

The wine and ale flowed, and the music continued to grow louder, a rhythm humming through her arms and into her chest. She tripped over a small stick as she stepped back into the glow of her friend's fire toward a giggling Danielle and Janelle, an *oof* leaving her throat as the air knocked from her lungs when she hit the ground. She felt the cool stalks of grass tickle her cheeks as she rested her forehead against the hard ground in embarrassment. Her friends descended in a fit of laughter at her expense, tears pouring from their eyes as they held their bellies and moved to help her up. Rolling over onto her back, warm from the wine and the fire, a familiar hum filled her chest. She gave herself a moment for the air to return to her lungs as she looked at the stars. The hum grew deeper; electricity vibrating against her breastbone. *How much wine have I drunk tonight?*

She was rolling over to stand up when her eyes flicked to the fire next to hers. *Shit.* The Commander, who she definitely had not been hoping would be here tonight, sat on the ground next to a large log facing them. Lea thought about earlier today and how her body had buzzed in response to his touch as she looked at him through the glow of the fire, his shadows reaching toward her and weaving through the flickering flames in between them. He had one hand placed on the log and one leg bent underneath him as if he'd been about to stand, but he settled down onto the grass again as Lea rose to her feet. Had he been coming to help her again? Why would he choose now, of all times, to make his appearance? He kept his gaze locked on hers as a blush crept up her cheeks, her nervous hands busying themselves with dusting off her dress and picking the leaves from her hair.

She stared at the very handsome, abnormally large man who had saved her that afternoon. Had he been this attractive in the light of day? This... rugged? He had certainly seemed dangerous, terrifying even, but seeing him sitting so casually by the fire, Lea couldn't help but recognize the flutters she felt in her stomach as she drank in his muscular body. She normally didn't like long hair on men, but the Commander looked like a warrior poised for battle–manly in a way she had never experienced before. He looked like he could easily pick her up with one arm, and she wondered what it would feel like to be pressed against his very muscular, firm body.

A booming laugh rang out from a tall, blonde Fae sitting at the Commander's side, knocking her out of her trance. The Fae was oblivious to the Commander's lack of attention as he gesticulated with his hands, telling some sort of outrageous tale to the other soldiers around the fire, and his radiant energy was contagious enough to bring a smile to Lea's lips.

She swore she heard a snarl come from the Commander's chest, a ricochet of anger stealing the grin from her face and pulling her eyes back to his as if by a magnet. The soldiers sitting around him paused their conversation before standing one by one. The blonde man's eyes flicked to Lea with a knowing smile before he walked away, patting the Commander on the shoulder as he left the fire. The Commander's eyes never left Lea's, and she met his gaze once again, the flames from the fires and the wind moving the trees ebbing away until all she could see was the intensity of his stare as they held eye contact.

The rhythm of her pulse changed, slowing in pace but beating harder, as if it was someone else's heartbeat entirely. Her hand floated up toward her chest, rubbing at the spot where her blood pounded under her skin. The Commander followed her hand with his gaze, his eyes darkening as he watched her try to soothe away the odd sensation. *What was happening?*

Someone called her name from behind her and Lea turned on instinct, subconsciously recognizing Thomas's voice as the spell was broken. With their eye contact severed, she was able to breathe easily again as she turned toward her friends. Her heart returned to its normal rhythm as the buzzing in her chest subsided a bit. Why did it feel like her body was vibrating? Was it the wine? The thrill of the attraction she so clearly felt toward this Fae?

She glanced over her shoulder to look back at the Commander, who was now speaking to a soldier she hadn't seen before. His eyebrows were lowered, creating a look of intensity on his face, different from the usual stern expression he wore. She could sense his awareness of her movements, that he was tracking her even without looking at her. She wasn't sure how she knew, but she could *feel* it, like a string tugging in his hand as she moved around. The sensation of his eyes caressing her body fueled her movements as Lea allowed the sound of the violins and drums to thrum through her body. Glowing flames around her danced to the rhythm of the woods as the music played, and she swayed back and forth, arms above her head toward the stars above while spinning in a slow circle. The warmth of the fire eased the chill of the air from her skin as she peeled off the torn sweater she wore, looking down at her dress that billowed as she twirled. Why wasn't he coming over to her? Was it because she was human? Some of the Fae seemed to consider themselves superior to humans, but he had saved her today. He certainly wouldn't be the first Fae she had danced with around the fires on nights like these, though that was only as far as she'd ever allowed things to go.

Every so often, as she spun, she met eyes with the Commander, who now held a goblet in his hand and the same stern expression on his face. His eyes were always so serious, so *angry*... Could she make his expression change? She took another deep gulp of her wine and turned back to him, deliberately holding eye contact this time as she once again raised her arms above her head. She wasn't sure it was possible to break through his stony exterior, but gods, something inside her begged her to try.

Lea felt, rather than heard, a low rumble rip from his throat before whispers of a touch danced along her arms as if imaginary fingers were tracing patterns along her skin. She leaned into the feeling as she swayed her hips, unable to resist the way her body sang as the sensation flowed across her shoulders, her stomach and neck. Raising her fingers, she followed the lines she felt being drawn across her skin and watched as the space around the Commander turned impossibly darker, inky black fingers jutting out around him and pushing against the black of the night. His hand was clutching the goblet so tightly she thought it might bend from the strength of his grip. Maintaining eye contact, she twirled. Slowly. A dare to join her, to dance with her under the blanket of stars and find out what this need pulling her toward him was telling her.

Her bold display of attraction was broken with the lively beginnings of the ritual dance of the Anhi. It was ancient lore that the pounding of feet during the dance awoke the spirits of the forest, reminding them to wake from their winter sleep and protect the village from danger in the year ahead. Lea looked back to the Commander and tilted her head toward the fires, silently asking him if he'd like to perform the dance with her. She felt his mood darken before he turned his head away.

Embarrassment twisted in her gut with the rejection, her face heating as she looked down. Had she misunderstood his attention as attraction? Was the sensation of light touch ghosting across her skin just a combination of the wine and her imagination? Lea turned to look for Thomas, knowing without a doubt he would dance with her, only to find Jamie, a kind boy who had grown up three houses away from her. He held his hand out in a request, and they began the steps of the dance, stepping forward, backward, then a step to the side as they turned beneath their arms and spun away from each other, grabbing onto the next partner. As the music moved faster, the rumbling of feet grew louder, and Lea moved from partner to partner, the stars spinning above her head. With each spin, her smile grew, and her tension eased. She hadn't remembered how much she loved this dance until her feet were moving beneath her. The music crescendoed as she was passed one more time, landing in familiar arms.

She looked up at Thomas, his brown eyes staring at her flushed cheeks and breathing hard from the dance. He pushed a damp piece of hair from her forehead and tucked it behind her ear before cupping his hand along her jaw and tilting her head to meet his eyes. She reached up and smiled as she traced under Thomas's eyes, the bags from earlier now replaced by smooth skin, rejuvenated by his night magic.

"You seem to be enjoying yourself." He smiled down at her and Lea leaned into his touch, butterflies dancing in her stomach at the intimacy of the moment.

"These Fire Nights—I'd forgotten how alive they make me feel. The warmth of the fire, the stars... It's like I'm closer to mom somehow; like she's here with us. Have you ever seen anything more beautiful than this?" Her voice trailed off, her eyes turning toward the heavens. She felt the magic from the stars on her face, small tingles that called to her skin and pulled her eyes toward them.

Thomas paused before speaking, still searching Lea's face, one side bathed in the orange glow of the fire, the other in the silver light of the moon. "The stars are not nearly the most beautiful thing here tonight," Thomas said in a near whisper. His hand returned to her cheek, his thumb brushing across her lips. She turned in surprise to look at his face, which was suddenly very close to hers. The air was stolen from her lungs. The way he was looking at her... It made her want to pull herself closer into his embrace.

"Lea, I—"

A piercing scream broke through the night. A scream of pure and utter terror.

CHAPTER 5

The world went still. The instruments that had been playing so happily before scratched into silence as those dancing turned toward the sound.

"Please, No! Help me, please! Mommy!" The voice sounded so small, but the fear inside those screams permeated through every inch of the field they stood in. Thomas's eyes met hers, terror causing his pupils to dilate, the fire from the pyre in front of him mirrored in the large black circles.

"Nora!" Thomas shouted, turning from Lea and quickly scanning the surrounding woods. He assessed for threats before looking toward his house at the top of the hill where his baby sister was home alone, too young to join the Fire Night festivities like her older siblings. Thomas brushed a quick kiss across Lea's brow with trembling lips. "Stay here, Lea!" he shouted over his shoulder as he turned and ran.

A noise in the distance caused the hair on the back of Lea's neck to rise as she watched Thomas go, a low growl that met her ears as if carried to her on the wind along with the echo of screams. It was the same growl from this morning, which had itched at the back of her mind as she'd tried to place where she had heard it before. She recognized the sound now. It sounded just like... But, no, that was impossible. Thomas's house was too far away, the sound too quiet to travel so far.

Lea's heart pounded in her ears, adrenaline pulsing through her body as she looked around for something she could defend herself with. Next to a soldier's jacket by the fire, a small, bronze-handled dagger had been pushed down into the ground, the hilt sticking up to prevent someone from injuring themselves on it. Without hesitating another moment, Lea sprinted toward the dagger, brushing the dirt off the blade on her leg before she raced after Thomas. Her legs were too short to keep stride with him as he pulled farther and farther in front of her.

She came to the base of the hill but couldn't see Thomas anymore. With no time to waste, she raced up the steep incline, her legs and lungs burning with exertion. Footsteps thundered behind her, likely other villagers running to help, but she was in too much of a hurry to look back. She had kicked her shoes aside while dancing, and now little bits of rubble and jagged rock that jutted from the soil as the flat ground became uneven and rugged tore at her feet.

As Lea neared the top of the hill, terror spiked through her chest at what she saw. She stopped, her heels digging into the dirt to slow her momentum. *Shit*! Her fears were confirmed; that growl was more than a figment of her imagination. At least two dozen fenrir, an ancient species of wolves the size of grown men with fur as black as night, stood on the slope leading up toward Thomas's home.

Lea froze, the courage she wished she had more of caught in her throat. She had trained in basic weaponry with Thomas as he was learning his blacksmith trade and testing his creations to see what worked the best in battle. She'd learned how to hold a sword and throw a dagger, but she had only ever struck wooden posts... inanimate objects that did not move or have teeth the size of her hand or eyes that told her they were hungry for flesh.

Lea couldn't remember how the men of her village had killed the fenrir before. There hadn't been an attack in years. The mountains usually kept them far away, though she could remember a few rogue attacks by a single fenrir as she'd grown up. She had never heard of more than one entering their village at a time and had been taught that they were no longer pack animals since losing their bond with the Fae, so how were there so many of them standing in front of her now? And why were they on this hill? Had they sensed Thomas's power? The fenrir had once been bred to serve those with magic, but that had been hundreds of years ago when magic was still plentiful. Was it just a coincidence that they'd chosen his house to attack?

"Shit!" she cursed again, breathless. She shifted her weight back and forth on her feet, her arms at her sides as she racked her brain for a way she could help him without getting anyone killed. *Maybe screaming would distract them? Or maybe, it would cause them to attack.*

Lea pulled at her hair as she watched Thomas tuck Nora behind his back with his left arm, holding a sword in his right toward the large black wolf stalking toward him. The rest of the wolves remained at a further distance and had spread out, almost as if searching for something. Lea crouched down and crept toward Thomas, making herself appear as small as possible, dagger in hand. *Maybe I can sneak up behind the wolf, make it turn around long enough for Thomas to strike...* She was about halfway up the hill when a howl that could rattle the trees themselves erupted from the wolf in front of Thomas. The fenrir crouched down before lurching forward, nipping at Thomas's sleeve.

A scream erupted from Lea's throat, though she wasn't sure how she could make such a loud noise with no air in her lungs. She stood from the shadows she'd been hiding in, ready to run toward Thomas, to try to get the fenrir to follow her and allow him to escape with Nora.

Three pairs of eyes swung toward her at once, one pair filled with tears and tight with fear, one enormous pair that looked feral, otherworldly, and *hungry,* and one familiar brown pair that locked onto hers and filled with panic.

Thomas's eyes darted toward the other fenrir, who had stopped their searching and turned, along with their leader, to look in her direction.

"Run!" Thomas yelled, pleading with his eyes for her to get as far away as she could. She could read his expressions, could feel his emotions without him saying a single word, and right now she was confident he was furious at her for following and, especially, for staying.

Her blood heated in anger at the absurdity of his silent request. She gripped the dagger tighter in her fist. She would not leave him... He knew better than that. Below her, she could hear more people approaching, the clank of metal against the rocks telling her they were armed. She just needed to create a distraction. The wolf that had been cornering Thomas slowly stalked toward Lea, his foaming mouth open as his tongue lolled out to the side.

Lea twisted to face down the hill to see some of the villagers now locked in battle with the fenrir. She stepped closer toward them, anger and terror immediately flashing across Thomas's face as he realized her intent. She raced diagonally toward the fighting below, placing herself in between the fenrir in battle and their leader above. Thomas shouted to her as she ran straight toward the battlefield, but his words were lost to the roaring in her ears.

She held the small dagger in her hands, unsure what to do, where to strike most effectively to bring down a wolf the size of a bear.

Thomas's screams echoed through the chaos around her, the wolves below her snarling as the sound of their teeth crashing against metal rang out. She strained to hear his panicked words through the deafening growls and the pounding of her heart in her ears. A fenrir with gray-tipped ears, who was slightly smaller than the leader, circled her—slow circles that spiraled closer as he stalked toward her.

"RAISE YOUR BLADE!" Thomas roared, and she finally heard his command. She lifted her dagger up in the air and immediately felt a ripple of magic vibrate through the hilt. Lea's eyes met Thomas's in a panic as the dagger grew heavier. She watched in awe as it glowed a dark, navy blue and doubled in size, sharpening to a deadly point. Lea looked around frantically. The Royal Army was here. If they had seen him... Lea looked down to see her body glowing faintly along with the dagger, the blue outline extending from the weapon to wrap around her skin. Lea suddenly felt stronger, her pulse slower, and her attention sharper.

The wolf circling her, initially startled by the sight of the magic, but now several feet closer than it had been before, crouched onto its back legs, poised to attack. She heard Thomas fighting above her, yelling for Nora to run inside and hide, screaming for Lea to fight, that he was coming.

Distracted by Thomas's words and the glowing sword in her hand, the wolf closest to her leaped forward, teeth bared as it latched onto her left forearm. Pain seared through her as she let out an inhuman scream, blindly stabbing with her dagger in her right hand toward the wolf's head. She felt her dagger meet flesh, hot blood squirting against her palm holding tightly to the hilt. The wolf yelped in pain, causing his hold on her to loosen slightly. As she pulled the dagger back, ready to plunge it once again toward the wolf's neck, she felt the pressure release completely as the giant black wolf was ripped from her arm. His body flew back, crashing into the ground with a sickening *thud*. The wolf tried to rise, but before it could even roll to its belly, a sword cut through the air at an impossible speed, slicing through sinew and bone, decapitating the monstrous beast in front of her.

Lea attempted to take a step back, holding her arm close to her body as she slipped on the bloody grass. Pain shot through her entire body as her ribs knocked into the rocky earth. Her own blood ran down her arm, mixing with the fenrir's as it slid between her fingers and pooled onto the ground. *I'm losing blood too fast...* She looked away, queasy from the sight of the blood, and closed her eyes as a wave of dizziness caused the world around her to spin. She felt a hand cup her cheek and opened her eyes to see the Commander through her eyelashes, his green eyes once again angrily locking onto hers. Her vision went blurry around the edges as the

Commander felt for her pulse, growing weaker and slower as her limbs went numb.

"Stay with me, Little Flower." He grabbed her chin with one hand, forcing her to meet his eyes as he placed his other hand over her chest. She felt a pulse of magic as his calloused fingers touched her skin, a shock delivered straight to her heart that caused her pulse to speed up and become regular again. The Commander broke their eye contact to look over his shoulder at the exact moment a wolf launched at him from behind.

With a single step, a movement so quick she almost missed it, the Commander attacked, killing the wolf flying through the air toward them with a single swipe of his sword before whirling between the other fenrir that had been just behind it and striking them down as if they were small dogs. His weapon was an extension of his arm, his eyes fierce as they darted between his targets. Large clouds suddenly moved in front of the moon, blocking nearly all its light as the wind blew fiercely. It seemed to bolster him, almost carrying him, helping him to move more quickly as he raced across the hill. Lightning flashed above her, an unusual gray color that somehow still glowed against the darkness, so different from the lightning storms she'd watched across the ridge that so rarely made it through the mountains surrounding her.

As the wind whipped and the lightning strikes grew angrier and more rapid, the few remaining wolves raised their heads to the sky and howled, quickly turning to disappear into the woods as one. They escaped into the night, leaving behind the whip of the wind and the moans of the injured. Tears pricked her eyes as she lifted her gaze toward the top of the hill, desperate to see if Thomas was okay... if Nora was okay.

She tried to rise onto her hands and knees, blood still pouring from her arm as the clouds moved away, allowing the soft light of the moon to once again glow across the hill. The wind and thunder ceased. Lea swayed as the world tilted on its axis. Her arm felt heavy, her bones cold. She tried to stand, but her legs wouldn't hold her up. Before she could fall back to the ground, Thomas was at her side, cradling her into his chest and lifting her from the blood-soaked ground.

"You're hurt. Where's the blood coming from, Lea?" His voice cracked as he patted around her body, still holding her close as he searched for the source of the blood. Lea winced when his hand found the bite on her arm. Thomas immediately clamped pressure on the wound as he hurried toward his house. "Stupid girl, I told you to run. Barely five feet tall and throwing yourself in between the wolves. I had it handled. You should have run." He lifted her higher in his arms and picked up his speed. "I can't lose you, I can't... I... I told you to run! Lea, why couldn't you just listen?" He was repeating himself, saying the same things over and over again and making less sense the more he talked. Lea tried to respond, to tell him she wouldn't have left him, that he should have known better, but the words became thick on her tongue, a coldness sweeping through her limbs.

"You listen to me! Stay awake, do you hear me? Lea, open your eyes. *Dammit, Lea!*" His words became frantic. "I can't lose you. I need you to understand. You're everything. You're *everything*, Lea. Please." He kicked open the wooden door to the home he shared with his family and stormed through the hallway, laying her gently on his bed and quickly pressing something against her wound, holding pressure tight against her arm.

Lea tried to open her eyes, but the heaviness only grew. Her vision darkened, the edges turning black, when she saw a furious, bloody Fae run through the doorway—the enormous Commander, with stern, green eyes that filled with pain as he took in Lea's injuries and watched her slip into the darkness.

CHAPTER 6

Lea awoke to the singing of birds and a pain in her head so severe she cursed the light streaming in through the windows. Closing her eyes, she rolled over, breathing in the clean scent of the bed she lay in. *Smells like Thomas,* she thought absently as she snuggled deeper into the thick covers. *Thomas!* The events of the night before flooded back to her as she attempted to sit up, the room spinning around her. She remembered Nora's scream, Thomas racing toward her, checking her wound as he'd carried her up the hill...

"Thomas!" She tried to scream, but her voice came out in a dry whisper.

"He's not here. No need for dramatics." A rumbling voice came from the side of the room.

She startled, looking in the direction the voice had come from. The Commander sat in an armchair far too small for his large frame. He was relaxed back with one ankle crossed over his knee, both hands loosely resting off to the sides. He still wore his uniform—head to toe black with a blue moon and stars covering the left breast pocket, signifying that he held night magic. Leaning forward in the chair, the Commander placed his elbow on his knee and his chin on his fisted hand. In the light of day, he was somehow even more attractive. His piercing green eyes seemed to look right through her, and Lea pulled the covers higher over herself. Panic filled her chest as she wondered why it was the Commander who was sitting beside her and not Thomas.

"Where is he? Where is the rest of his family? And why are you here?" Her voice grew a little stronger, but it was a struggle to get the words out. He stared at her with a stoic expression on his face, then stood and left the room with long, slow strides.

"Wait!" she croaked. Seconds passed as she looked around the room for any clue as to where Thomas might be, and her panic began to rise. The small room looked exactly as she remembered. The fireplace held ashes that still flickered from a dying fire. The window was closed, and the dresser stood against the wall where it had always been, drawers shut, and all of Thomas's belongings exactly where he'd left them. The only thing missing here was Thomas. *He should be here...* she thought. He wouldn't leave her here with this stranger, alone, especially if she were hurt. He'd be right here, waiting for her to wake up...Sure, the stranger in question was a Commander in the Royal Army, but Thomas didn't know that. Something was wrong. And why had the Commander bothered to help her, anyway? She was only a human, after all. The Fae didn't care about them. Not once had she heard of a Fae risking their life to save a human.

She looked down at her arm to see a bandage wrapped tightly from her fingers to just above her elbow. She had been bathed, her body now free of the blood and mud that had caked her from head to toe the night before. She looked frantically around for a washrag, praying to see a bucket of water or something to indicate how she'd ended up so clean. Footsteps pulled her eyes back to the doorway, and the Commander walked in, a glass of water in hand. He gave it to her without a word, then remained standing stiffly by her bed.

"Where is he?" She tried to ask again, taking a sip of water.

His eyes bored into her, searching for some answer to a question he had not asked before he finally answered.

"Awaiting trial. Did you know about his magic?" he asked, his voice low, shadows dancing around his fingertips.

Panic rose from the pit of her stomach and spread through her chest, down her arms and into her fingers. Thomas had used his magic to save her–out in the open. He had risked his and his family's lives and livelihoods by using his magic to give her a fighting chance against the wolves. And his repayment was imprisonment? Maybe if she'd just listened to him and stayed back at the fire, he wouldn't have had to use his magic. He'd be sitting here with her right now. Lea started to truly panic. *What would happen? He couldn't leave his family... They needed him, she needed him.* Her thoughts bounced around her mind, one question after another, filled with uncertainty.

"When?" was all she could say.

"Four days." He hesitated before continuing. "The Crown Prince of Desia will come here for the trial."

Alaric, the eldest of the King's two sons.

"The Prince of Day is coming here?" she asked, relieved when her voice came out more easily. "Isn't he busy with more important things, like... drinking ale and sleeping with women?" Lea snapped her mouth shut, covering it with her hands as her eyes went wide. She couldn't trust this man who worked for the prince and the royal family, and she definitely couldn't gossip about the Crown Prince with him. "I'm sorry... I didn't mean that."

The Commander turned to sit, shifting uncomfortably in his chair and rubbing his large hand along his scruffy jaw and neck. He pinned her with a glare, and Lea shrunk down on the bed, pulling her blanket slightly higher as if it could protect her from his ire.

"I'll excuse your outburst, and blame it on your blood loss. But it would be in your best interest to keep your judgments of the royal family to yourself," he answered with a rumble laced with anger.

She looked away, her cheeks growing red from his scolding.

"Will the Night Prince be coming as well?" she asked tentatively, referring to Evander, the younger brother who was feared nearly as much as the Black King. Lea's stomach dropped as she waited for his answer, hoping with everything she had that Prince Evander wouldn't be joining the Crown Prince for Thomas's trial. He had a reputation for having a calloused heart and a lack of mercy, and Lea feared that Thomas's sentence might be far harsher if he were the one determining it.

"No. Neither will King Nestruir," he confirmed, and Lea's shoulders dropped in relief.

"And the princess?" She immediately bit down on her lip. *Shit*. She shouldn't have said that.

The Commander's eyes darkened, fury crossing his face as shadows burst from his hands. "That's enough questions. There is no princess. Something you should be aware of as a subject of this kingdom." Lea knew that the rumors of the Princess of Desia might not be true, but it didn't change the whispers that spread throughout the kingdom of a girl born into the royal family who had never been seen. Some inferred that she was born disfigured, an embarrassment to the king and queen, who were known for their beauty. Others questioned if there had ever been a Princess Nestruir at all, if maybe the story was a ruse to entice Calir, the kingdom to the south, into a truce with the prospect of a marriage contract.

They sat in silence for a moment before the Commander stood, striding across the room toward the window with the firm *click* of his boots.

"The Royal Army will stay in Bearswillow until after the trial. We can't afford to leave this village unattended with the fenrir so close. Without this stop on our way to and from the palace, we have no food, no weapons, no place to rest and water our horses."

"Are you saying that the only reason you're staying to protect us is that you need our village as a stopping place on the army's travels? You don't care about the lives here? The children who run through the fields and the men and women who work and laugh and gather round the fires at night? The people you are sworn to protect, that are loyal to your king and queen?"

"It's irrelevant why we care about this place." He bit back with a sharp tone, his voice loud enough to make her lean away from him. "The fenrir will still be close, and we can't leave Bearswillow with no magic to defend itself against them." He took a deep breath. "Prince Alaric will travel here to determine your... *friend's* fate." He said the word as if tasting something bitter.

"Please," she whispered, pleading. "Please let him go. He's not powerful enough to be of service to the king. His father died of the Lonely Death... His family needs him." Lea's tongue felt thick and dry in her mouth, her throat choking down in fear on the words.

"It's too late. There were witnesses, and the prince is already on his way. He *will* stand trial." He leveled her with a look. "As I suspect you were aware of his magic, you could be called as a witness, put on trial yourself for treason to the Crown."

Lea's stomach dropped. *Who would tell her Father that she was gone? Would she ever see her friends again?* The Commander sighed, clearly exhausted from her panicked questions.

"If you will listen to me, you won't be called as a witness. The boy will be fine. But you are still weak, and your wounds will take time to heal completely. It would be prudent of you to stay here and rest. I will assume that you knew nothing of his magic. Do not take this kindness lightly. Stay away from the trial and let the next few days pass. You can return to your life once the prince leaves." His words held a finality to them, as if closing the lid on the matter tightly. She tried to sit up as he turned to leave, but the room spun, and a stabbing pain shot through the base of her skull. He paused, taking a quick step back toward her, worry flashing across his face.

Lea leaned back onto her elbow and closed her eyes as she waited for the room to go still. "I have to see Thomas. Please... I have to talk to him."

She couldn't just stay here, wondering how Thomas was doing as he sat alone in the army camp awaiting trial. "I just need to see if he's okay."

The air seemed to shift in the room, the heat from the remaining embers of the fire suddenly suffocating her as she waited for a reply. The Commander did not move a muscle from inside the doorway, his hands fisted at his sides, knuckles white. He stood as still as stone, the only movement his chest rising and falling–a snake poised to strike.

"I will not repeat myself again, human. You *will* obey my orders. You *will* stay here. And you *will* heal. What you will not do is meddle in the affairs of a criminal hiding from the Crown. If I see you step one foot outside of these walls, I promise I will personally drag you by your hair before the prince and tell him of your treason."

"It's my fault he's there! Can't you just bring me to him, just for a few minutes to—"

"Stop!" Shadows began to float toward her as anger radiated from his massive body. "Do not test me on this, Little Flower. I assure you, I always keep my promises." Without waiting for a response, he turned and walked out of the room, closing the door firmly behind him.

Lea sat speechless. *Little Flower?* Did he think she was so weak she was nothing but a dainty flower he could pluck from her home and place her in a vase to sit uselessly? Why wasn't he charging her with treason when he had to know that she was aware of Thomas's magic? He was saving her from a lifetime of servitude or execution, while at the same time threatening to bring her to the prince himself if she left the house. *Why does he want me here?*

As soon as she heard the front door slam, shaking the foundation of the house, the bedroom door flew open. Lea felt herself deflate at the Commander's absence as little Nora ran through the door with red, swollen eyes and a runny nose. How would she get answers if he wasn't here? Nora crashed onto Thomas's bed, the impact sending searing agony through Lea's wounded arm and back. She ignored the pain and hugged Nora tightly, rubbing between her shoulder blades as she attempted to soothe her.

"Where is he, Nora? Where is Thomas? Where are your brothers and sisters, your mom?"

Nora sobbed, unable to speak through the sobs tearing from her throat. The girl looked tiny as she curled into Lea, with her dark long hair falling around her face, hiding her striking blue eyes that were now swollen and puffy from her crying.

"Nora. I need you to breathe. Where are they?" Lea smoothed Nora's hair from her face, tucking it behind her ear as she continued to rub small circles on her back.

Nora took several deep breaths, clutching Lea's hand like it was the only thing saving her from dropping off the edge of a cliff into her grief.

"Thomas is in the Royal Army's camp. So is the rest of my family. My mom was working a shift at the tavern. The soldiers went and got her." Lea winced as Nora squeezed her tighter. "They wouldn't even let her come back here to see me." She took several shuddering breaths between words, her whole body shaking. "The soldiers said they're in trouble, too, that they have to testify about my brother's magic or we could all be sent away and punished. I only got to stay here because I'm too young to be charged with treason and that scary Fae said you would need someone to help you recover." She strengthened with those last words, focusing on having a task and distracting herself with a purpose. Lea pulled Nora closer, avoiding her injuries and smoothing down her hair.

"I love them so much, Lea." Nora sniffled. "Thomas was just protecting me."

"I love them too, Nora, and I love you. This is not your fault. Look at me." Lea gently grabbed Nora's chin and forced her to meet her eyes. "I swear to you, we will bring them back home. This time next week we'll be gathered around the table, laughing and trading our tales from the time we were all held prisoner by the Commander of the Royal Army." *I really need to learn his name*, she thought as she held Nora tighter. "I promise you, Nora, the Commander is not the only one who keeps his promises."

Lea drifted off after Nora brought her some soup and bread—still tired from the blood loss from her wound—and awoke hours later to the ripple of magic marking sundown. She felt sharp pain from the injuries to her ribs as she slowly slid to the side of her bed, sitting with a wince and placing her feet on the cold wooden floor. A wave of nausea overwhelmed her, and she leaned forward onto her knees. It didn't matter how bad she felt, she needed to get out of this house and somehow, into the royal camp. She had to save Thomas. He'd been there for her so many times, and she was not about to let that fact go unreciprocated. They had both lost too much this year.

She slowly stood, testing out the strength of her legs. Though she was still slightly wobbly, she was able to remain standing on her own. She was glad, with Thomas not here to help hold her up. He had been the one to catch her on her worst days. Held her when she'd collapsed on the floor after returning home the day she lost her mother to a barricaded door and a note on the table, next to her solemn father.

She was not going to let him down. She needed to get to the camp and figure out a way to get him out of there. They could go south to Calir, or hide in the woods until the Royal Army moved on... She wasn't sure. But she had to do something.

Making her way through the bedroom and across the hall, she stopped in the room Thomas's sisters shared to find a change of clothing; something to help her blend into the dark night. She opened the window to let out some air from the stagnant and stale-smelling room, before turning to the closet. She breathed in the sweet, jasmine-perfumed air wafting from the open window as she picked out some trousers. They were long, and she would have to cuff the bottom if she didn't want to trip over them. She opened the top drawer and pulled out a black tunic top, pulling it over her head and tucking the necklace her mother had given her close to her heart. As she left the room, a soft *thud* sounded behind her, causing her to pause. Turning her head toward the closet, she noticed a thick, dark green cotton jacket that would be too small for Thomas's sisters had fallen to the floor. Had she knocked it off somehow when she'd walked by? A shiver ran through her at the chill creeping in through the open window, the temperature dropping quickly now that the sun had set. Grabbing the jacket, she tied it around her waist, then combed and braided her long, golden hair in a style popular in the village—both to blend in and to keep it out of her face. She laced up a pair of boots that were at least a size too large for her feet, wiggling her toes and wondering if she would get blisters in them. Satisfied that she might blend in with the other women ambling around the fires for the second Fire Night of the season, she walked out into the living room. A pang of loneliness hit her as she took in the empty space. She'd spent so much time here; she could see Thomas's siblings playing on the staircase and hear his mother clanking about in the kitchen.

She could see Thomas's father, could remember when he noticed a wound appearing on his upper arm, just days after her mother had passed. He'd simply stood and walked upstairs, closing the door behind him as the house went silent. Lea had spent the following days either in her room with her mother's herbs and plants or kneeling next to the moonflowers she'd planted in her garden, desperately trying to find a cure to prevent her best friend from feeling the unspeakable pain of losing a parent. Thomas had sat with her in a chair at her table as she tried to outsmart death: willow bark and turmeric for inflammation, holy basil for its ability to kill bacteria, elderberry for vitamins, as well as flaxseed, pomegranate, and lemon balm. She tried every combination of every herb she could think of, but nothing helped, eventually resorting to a simple tea from her mother's stores with camomile for rest and sleep. Thomas's father did sleep that evening; a sleep so deep he did not wake. Three others in the village died that week, the largest outbreak of the Lonely Death in decades, and Lea hadn't been able to help a single one.

She squared her shoulders and slowly opened the door, peeking out into the darkness. The sky was cloudy, hiding the stars and dimming the light that she had been hoping she could use to navigate her way to the camp. She hoped, if nothing else, the lack of light from the moon would help shield her from unwanted eyes.

She crept down the side of the hill, her torn-up feet stinging with each step, though not as badly as she'd expected. She avoided where the attack had happened the night before, unsure if it would still be sticky from the blood soaking the ground and not wanting a visual reminder of what she could have lost if last night had gone differently. A pit formed in her stomach, hard and painful as the guilt settled deeper under her skin. Shaking the thought from her head, she continued on.

Lea snuck through town, her feet crunching against the dry grass as she hid behind the edges of buildings and trees, darting through the dark. It was mostly empty, with only a few villagers going to and from the tavern or taking a night stroll.

As she reached the border of the village, the encampment just on the other side of the trees before her, she steeled herself for what might come next. Edging around a particularly large redwood, she caught her first glimpse of the army camp. Hundreds of tents were set up in groups of four, a fire in the center of each quadrant that bathed the whole camp in an orange glow with men casually gathered around them. Some walked between the fires talking amongst themselves, while some remained seated with mugs of ale in their hands. There was no air of concern among the men. Their faces were clear of worry, youthful in the firelight as they laughed and joked amongst themselves. She'd expected tension in the air, patrols in organized lines with alert eyes scanning for threats, but they appeared unconcerned about the prisoners hidden somewhere within the camp.

Lea continued to circle within the tree line, grateful for the soldiers' lack of awareness as she looked for where Thomas and his family were being held. In the very back of the camp, there was a break in the layout of the tents. Instead of groups of four, there were several smaller tents in rows of three, all with one entrance and one guard standing in front of it. As she looked between them, she squinted her eyes to look at a small flag, no larger than a book, flying at the top of one of the tents in the middle. It bore the symbol of night magic—a moon and stars–identifying the type of magic of whoever inhabited the tent. The rest of the tents were bare, with no clues as to who might reside within them. Lea's heart lurched in her chest, her feet turning toward the tent with the flag. Thomas had to be in that tent. He was the only one in his family with magic.

Her heart began to race as anticipation heated her blood. Closing her eyes, she listened, willing her body to relax and her mind to open. Within moments, she felt the wind urging her forward, pushing against her back and pointing her straight toward the flag-topped tent. With little choice and little time, she crouched down and prayed to the gods to help her succeed.

Lea waited, searching for an opening. She couldn't run straight into the soldier's view without an excuse, and it was naive to believe they hadn't been made aware of what she looked like—the Commander didn't seem like one to take chances. She was certain every soldier within the camp would know exactly who she was.

Moving to stand, the wind suddenly shifted, pushing her down flat into the dry grass. "Who's out there?" a deep, calm voice called from behind her.

Shit! The voice wasn't close... but it was closer than Lea would have preferred. She twisted on the ground to look behind her, moving as silently as possible to avoid detection. She couldn't see anyone... So how could someone know she was out here? Lea had heard of Fae soldiers with magic of the hunt, an ability to track and find whatever they were searching for with uncanny speed and ease. *Please, just be a magicless Fae. Or one with stupid magic, like a talent for baking,* Lea thought as she searched for an escape, her heart rattling against her ribcage.

"I can smell you, human... I sense your fear," the voice was closer, calm in a way that made her blood run cold. Whoever he was, he knew she was here, and he was getting closer.

Lea tried to stand, but the wind pushed her back to the ground, her head flat against the dirt. "Let me up!" she whispered, before wondering who exactly she was speaking to. She could feel the soldier getting closer. She swore his footsteps were reverberating through the ground with each soft step he took. The wind only pushed harder, blocking her view of everything behind her. *Was the wind trying to show her something?*

Scanning around, she looked for a weapon. There was nothing on the ground, nothing in front of her but fires and soldiers. *Fire.* Lea thought of the dry grass she had walked through on her way here, how the spring rains had barely just begun.

"It will be easier if you surrender. The prince will be arriving soon, and after such a long journey, I'm sure he will be itching to punish someone. Your attempts at entering our camp must not be noble. Are you a thief then? Or are you a rebel, come to slaughter us all?" The man laughed, so much closer now she was certain that if she only turned around, she would see someone walking through the trees toward her.

Focusing on the fires, Lea began to pray. To the gods... to the wind, too afraid to say the words out loud. A gust of wind blowing an ember into the dry grass... that's all she would need as a distraction. It would spread until it reached the tree line. The soldiers would have no choice but to put it out. *Please, gods.*

The wind released her, and she turned on instinct, a tall, skinny Fae appearing in her vision no more than thirty yards away. Grateful for the trees and bushes to cover her, she sidestepped quietly, still crouched as close to the ground as possible. She stared at the fires, willing them to move, willing a spark to fly out into the kindling stacked nearby, a pile of straw that would surely ignite in a second.

"I can smell you, little girl." He was closer now. Maybe twenty yards away. There was no time.

Lea imagined having day magic as she prayed with all her might. She tried to picture what it would feel like for her hands to warm, for magic to leave her fingertips and the light to obey her. *Please,* she begged as the Fae grew closer. *If you never grant me another prayer, let it be this!* She stared at the fires before her, willing them with all her might to grow, to leap from the circles of rocks that contained them. She imagined them igniting the ground, spreading a fire so wild that every soldier in the camp would be forced to attend to it.

An enormous gust of wind erupted around her, the orange and blue fires roaring to impossible heights. The heat was so intense she could feel the warmth through the fabric of her clothing. The fires lept and reached, twisting and turning, until they bent as one, the tips of their flames tickling the dry grass, the piles of kindling.

"What the fuck?" the soldier behind her exclaimed, only feet away from her at this point on the other side of a large tree.

Lea didn't have time to look at him as small fires began to race across the camp, soldiers suddenly scrambling from their tents and racing toward barrels of water and ale. Anything to put out the fires. She heard the Fae who had been pursuing her curse before running away. They'd need his abilities to hunt out a water source, for a fire this big wouldn't be tamed with only their supplies. Guilt nagged in her gut, just a bit, but Lea shook it away. There was a stream nearby, and somehow the fires seemed to be avoiding igniting the tents. It wasn't as if she wanted anyone to get hurt.

Lea watched as the flames raced across the grass and imagined the fire parting for her, the wind pushing it away so that she would have a clear path into the tents. As if obeying her will, the wind picked up again, parting the flames. Seeing what might be her only chance, Lea sent up a thank you to the wind and ran. She ran without looking sideways, without knowing for certain who was in the tent with the night magic symbol she was running full speed toward, but praying that her hunch was right. Launching herself inside, she suddenly found herself plunged into complete darkness.

Lea didn't have time to be afraid, because immediately, she felt familiar arms wrap around her waist.

"Lea?" Thomas almost cried. "Oh Lea, you're okay... I'm so glad you're okay."

"Thomas! You're actually in here!" She wrapped herself around him, pressing her face into his chest. She couldn't see a thing, the tent so dark her eyes couldn't even make out Thomas's face, but she recognized his touch immediately. He held onto her so tightly it would have been painful if she hadn't been so relieved to see him. She felt the stubble on his face tickle her forehead as his rapidly rising and falling chest pressed against her, his racing heartbeat causing hers to pick up in response. He was holding her to him like she was the breath he needed to survive, and Lea was unsurprised to find she felt the same. He was her best friend, after all, the boy she hadn't spent even a single day without seeing in years. She'd been so worried, and a sob burst from her throat as relief that he was alive and in front of her crashed down on her.

"How are you here? Why—Lea, what's happening out there?" He looked toward the outside of the tent with concern etched on his face where the fires still raged, though they appeared to be maintaining a considerable distance from Thomas's family's tents, due to the lack of heat she felt.

Not wanting to concern him, Lea brushed off his question. "A distraction, nothing more."

Thomas pushed her back from his chest, his hands tight around her arms as he looked straight into her eyes. As her vision adjusted to the dark, she was able to see Thomas's face, his searching eyes, only for a moment before he pulled her back to him as if the few inches between their bodies had been far too much.

"You have to leave, now. It's not safe for you to be here." His voice grew more fierce, his mouth telling her to leave while his arms pulled her closer to him.

"Slow down. I'm okay, Thomas, look. See?" She held up her bandaged arm in front of her, wiggling her fingers to show him that she wasn't as injured as they'd initially thought.

"They can't know you're here. They know about my magic, Lea, they saw me." He swiped away a tear that she hadn't realized was running down her cheek. "They know about me, but they can't prove you know anything. My family didn't even know; they can't prove otherwise. You have to leave."

"Then come with me, Thomas. We'll leave together, hide till the army is gone." She pulled at his arm, her feet digging into the grass under their feet, but Thomas remained still.

"Don't you think I've tried? There's nothing I've wanted more than to get to you and get us away from here, but I can't leave. There's some sort of magic keeping me here, Lea. You have to go."

"Thomas–" she grabbed onto his shoulders, about to shake him for believing for a second time that she would leave him behind.

Before she could object that there was no way she was leaving the tent without him, she felt his lips crush down upon hers. His hands found her waist, her back, and pulled her flush against him. The tent spun around her as she froze in shock for a moment before returning the kiss. Her heart raced as her lips began to move, her breaths becoming shallow as she grabbed his arms. The pressure of his mouth was firm against her lips, and he broke away, only for a moment, to take a ragged breath while looking desperately into her eyes.

Lea stared at him, unable to speak. She *had* been a stupid girl, just as Thomas had said, but not for running into the line of wolves, and not for coming here tonight. She couldn't believe she had missed what everyone else had so clearly seen. Janelle's jokes, Solomon ribbing at Thomas whenever she was just out of earshot. He was just Thomas, the only constant in her life. Someone she loved fiercely, but had somehow missed that his love for her was *different.* Her stomach flipped, and she tried to breathe, unsure if her racing heart was from the adrenaline of sneaking into camp, Thomas's sudden declaration of feelings for her, or the fact that she had just kissed her best friend.

"Lea, you have to go... But I have to tell you. Before I'm taken away, you need to know..." He leaned in closer to her, grabbing her face between his hands and rubbing his thumbs across her cheek.

The flaps of the tent flew open, moonlight illuminating the sparse canvas tent in a soft glow.

"Yes, *Azalea,*" said a familiar voice, a rumble of thunder on a cloudy night. "You have to go."

The Commander's broad shoulders filled the entire opening of the tent, a fog of black surrounding him. Small, wispy tendrils spread out from his hands and reached out toward her, floating through the air as if they wanted to wrap around her neck and tear her away. Lea's hand itched to reach out and touch the smoke, but she pulled it quickly back to her side.

Instinctively, Thomas pushed her behind him, attempting to hide her from the Commander's accusing eyes. With Thomas's touch, the Commander's murderous expression deepened.

"I believe I made a promise of what I'd do should you try something foolish like this." His angry voice was terrifyingly quiet, but somehow filled every inch of space with the tent.

Lea pressed herself into Thomas's back, trying to make herself as small as possible. "Turn me in, then. I'm not leaving without him. Or, just let us go. No one has to know." She spoke into Thomas's shirt, her words muffled as she tried to press herself further into him.

"No! They'll kill her if you send her to trial! Just let her go. I'll stay." Thomas said firmly, anger lacing his words as he reached around his back to touch her.

Thomas and the Commander made eye contact, staring silently at each other for what felt like an eternity. The crickets chirped and the frogs sang as the quiet in the tent grew deafening, a silent conversation passing between them as Thomas's arm wrapped around her protectively.

The Commander's eyes flicked to the arm around her before his darkened eyes rose to meet Thomas's. He gave Thomas a small nod, barely noticeable.

"Why are you nodding? What are you agreeing to? Thomas?" Lea's voice shook with panic as she tried to look around him to see what his face might reveal, but he held her firmly against his back. "Thomas! I'm staying with you!"

"You'll let her go? You'll take her back and keep her away from here? Away from this whole thing?" Thomas asked, motioning around the tent, one hand still holding onto her as if she might disappear.

The Commander held his stare for a long moment before speaking in a low voice. "Agree to cooperate with the proceedings and accept whatever punishment Prince Alaric sentences you to. Agree to confess and yes, I will let her leave. I will take her back to the safety of the bed you left her in, and I will keep her away from the trial. That is the most I can promise you."

"No!" Lea shouted, clutching onto the back of Thomas's shirt as she attempted to turn him around to face her, but she was swiftly cut off by Thomas's words.

"I'll confess to everything. I'll confess to my magic and go wherever you tell me, to the palace or the executioner's block, but you have to keep her away, keep her safe."

Words failed Lea. Her mouth opened in shock but sound refused to leave her lips. How could he give up on her, on his family? He pulled her around to his front, brushing the tears from her cheeks. She tried to speak, but what words could be said to make this right? His eyes, as they met hers, told her that he felt the same. With a final kiss to her temple, he let go of her and walked to the back of his tent.

"NO!" Lea finally heard her voice through the ringing in her ears as she rushed toward Thomas, but he held up his hands, pushing her away as he stepped backward.

"You have to go, Lea. You have to live. You have to stay far away from me, from this trial. Help my family, if you can." Tears filled his eyes as he let the Commander grab her around her chest, pulling her backward.

Disbelief hindered her reactions, making her sluggish, unprepared. *This can't be happening.* "I won't go! Thomas, I won't!" She began to kick, fighting to get back to her best friend. They had too much to talk about, too much still unsaid for her to leave like this. She couldn't fail in saving him, not when she'd made it this far.

"Get her somewhere safe, please," Thomas said, his voice soft, but full of determination. It was clear from the tension in his body language that he wanted to reach out to her, to pull her back and allow her to stay, but instead, he turned around, avoiding looking in her direction as the Commander grabbed her arms with firm hands.

Tears streamed down her face as she reached out for Thomas, her fingers extending as she tried to close the last few feet between them, but she wasn't strong enough to escape the Commander's grasp. "No! Thomas, please! I won't leave you, I won't!" She tried to kick out toward the Commander, but he sidestepped her attempt at escape and grabbed her tighter. "I'm not leaving!" she screamed louder as she was pulled outside the tent. She watched the tent flaps close behind her, barely able to move between the pain in her body and the pain in her heart. Salty tears dripped from her cheeks, and she swore the wind once again carried quiet words into her ears—"I'll love you, always, Lea."

The words gave her strength, and she tried to fight back, tearing at the Commander's arm, reaching back toward the tent as if she could bridge the gap between herself and her best friend. Before she could say another word, Lea felt a brush of magic run through the Commander's hands where he held her. The zap of electricity was so sharp, she cried out in pain before slumping backward against the Commander's chest. As dark spots began to dance in her vision, her limbs becoming heavy like just before a deep sleep, she sent a prayer to the gods to help her find a way back to the boy she was leaving behind.

CHAPTER 7

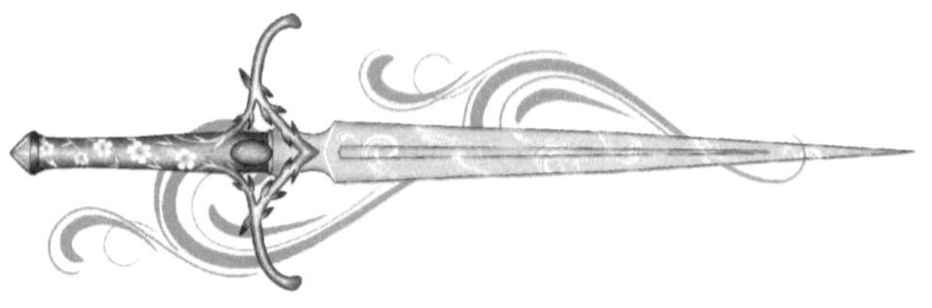

S he woke up, once again in Thomas's bed, feeling like she had drank too much wine the night before, her tongue thick and dry in her mouth and her head pounding behind her eyes. This time, she didn't have a few moments after waking to forget that her whole life appeared to be falling apart. No, she was acutely aware that she'd been unsuccessful based on the buzzing she felt dancing across her skin that pulled an invisible string within her to look toward the small chair next to the bed. Refusing to give in, she rolled to face the opposite wall where Thomas's dresser sat, the top covered with trinkets she recognized from over the years.

"You can leave," she said aloud, too exhausted to worry about why she had felt *his* presence in the room before she'd even opened her eyes. "I know you're sitting there."

A slight shuffling sounded behind her, the springs of the too-small chair groaning with the movement.

"There is nothing you can do for him, Azalea," he said like it was an obvious conclusion she should have come to herself. "At least thirty of my men saw Thomas use his magic. The king and Prince Alaric were notified almost immediately. This is out of your hands."

She remained silently facing away from the Commander, pulling her blanket up further around her as her eyes stung with tears she refused to shed in his presence. She stared at the grape-sized marble sitting atop Thomas's dresser, trying to focus on the blue and green swirls in the glass to prevent herself from turning toward the large man behind her.

"You can hate me all you want. I don't particularly care, but you *will* stay here. You can leave this room, but you'll remain in this house. Agree to comply, and I will make sure that Nora is safe here with you. Think about her. Think beyond your... *boyfriend*," disgust colored his tone, "and think of that little girl eavesdropping in the hall. Consider those other friends you sat around the fire with... If you just do as you're told, I will make sure that they are *all* kept away from the trial."

The intent behind those words was clear. Make a choice. Listen to him, and her friends would be safe... She would be safe. Ignore his warning, and no one would be. But why did he care to keep them safe? Was it some misguided sense of duty to protect her since he had saved her at the market? *Is he threatening my friends now, too?* "They weren't even there. You'll never be able to prove otherwise."

"No, they weren't." He sighed. "But you'd be surprised at the influence I have as the Commander of the Royal Army. An accusation from me that they were involved would be all it takes to ensure they are taken away as traitors. Think carefully, Little Flower." He leaned forward, his words and tone implying he could crush her under his boot like one of the small wildflowers on the hill. "Do you truly wish to risk all your friends' lives to save only one?"

She finally turned to look at him, expecting to see the large imposing man she had met in the days before. Rather, he sat with his chin in his hands, looking so very... tired. His beard was unkempt, but he had at least changed into a fresh black shirt. The first two buttons were undone at the top, and a sliver of a black tattoo peeked out of the neckline. He met her eyes, brows furrowed and bracketed with fatigue.

"Poor Commander," she spat. "Must be so difficult holding a tiny and defenseless human captive."

He groaned, leaning back in his chair with ungraceful, exhausted movements. "Make this easy, Azalea. Three more days. Stay in this house and protect your friends. The prince will not grant you the same kindness I am showing you."

He waited for an answer from her, a confirmation that she would comply, but he was met with stony silence. With a sigh, he stood and handed her the glass of water that was sitting on the table next to his chair.

He sure seems concerned with my hydration for someone who hates me enough to hold me prisoner, she thought sarcastically. Anger ignited instantly in her chest, and without thinking, she grabbed the glass from his hand and threw it against the wall opposite her bed, shattering it into a hundred shards. "Just. Get. Out!" she screamed, turning back toward the wall.

"Fine. Act like a spoiled brat, human. I'm sure Nora will be happy to clean up this mess, just like I'm cleaning up the mess you made for the rest of her family." He turned away and walked to the door, footsteps heavy, before pausing. "Please, Azalea. Just listen, for once. Stay here. You will not enjoy the consequences you will face if you disobey me again." And with those words, the door closed firmly behind him.

Lea paused—*how does he know my name?* She was certain she'd never told him... that it hadn't come up in the few encounters they'd had so far, especially because no one in the village called her by her full name. Her ears were hot, filled with a buzzing noise that threatened to drive her mad. She knew what he had said was true; she should have listened to Thomas. This was her mess, her fault, and there didn't seem to be a thing that she could do to save him–the boy who loved her. He *loved* her.

She turned the thought around in her mind. Of course, he loved her. The same way Janelle and Solomon loved her. And Danielle... honestly, she wasn't completely sure about that last one. But did he really feel more? She thought back to all the times he'd grabbed her hand, holding it as he pulled her through the streets to his blacksmith shop or toward the fires at night. The times he played with her hair absently while they lay in the field beyond her house, telling stories and watching the stars fly by. Maybe it was because her father had been so absent on his hunting trips since her mother had died, and she was craving love and a family so much that she'd missed his intentions, just grateful to feel a gentle touch from someone who cared about her. She had let him down, and her chest ached at the knowledge that had she just paid attention, she could have loved him, too, and they could have been happy.

Finally gathering her strength, she stood from the bed and attempted to carefully pick her way through the glass shattered along the floor to go find a broom.

"Gods dammit!" Lea cursed as a sharp pain shot through the inside of her foot. Looking down, she examined the long gash in her skin, blood pooling on the floor where she had stepped on a jagged piece. She reached down to remove it, continuing to curse under her breath, when she realized that, aside from the one deep cut she was now inspecting, the rest of her foot was almost free of injury. Moving to the other foot, she rocked onto her heel to look at the bottom. The deep lacerations she knew she had given herself just two days prior while running up the rocky hill to help Thomas had healed into small scrapes, tiny scars that crisscrossed where each rock had torn through her skin.

Impossible... Removing the piece of glass and tossing it closer to the wall to clean up later, she walked backward and sat on the bed. She inspected her arm, which had been so severely injured just the day before, and noticed that her bandage held no fresh blood, only the rust-colored remnants from when it had first been cleaned and dressed. She removed it, unwinding the gauze slowly and methodically. Along her arm ran a series of raised pink scars, roughly two inches long each, starting just below her thumb and running to the inside of her elbow. She prodded them gently. They were sore, but surely they should be far more painful.

Thomas had healed her in the past, only minor cuts and injuries, but she had never been injured like this before, and usually, it took several minutes for him to heal something as shallow as a scrape from her gardening shears. Lea definitely hadn't been in his tent for long enough for him to heal her like this... so who did? She remembered the Commander shocking her heart before the fenrir had launched at her, but could he have healed her injuries as she'd slept? She didn't know of anyone else with magic, but why would he bother?

Deciding she couldn't waste time asking questions without answers and grateful for her lack of pain, she returned to cleaning up the glass.

Once she was confident every last piece had been picked up, she opened her door and walked into the hallway. Nora sat on the floor, her back against the wall just outside her bedroom door. Her eyes were pressed into the tops of her knees and she was rocking forward and backward the slightest bit.

"Nora... What's wrong? What happened?"

"I want my mom," she sobbed, not lifting her head.

Lea rushed toward her, dropping to her knees. She felt her heart breaking as she watched Nora's little body shake.

"I know Nora, I know you do. We'll get them back... I already promised you that, but I need your help to do that, okay? Do you think you can help me?" Lea kept her voice gentle, smoothing down Nora's hair.

Nora dried her eyes on her sleeve, unable to speak as her breaths shuddered in and out, but she grabbed Lea's hand and shook her head *yes*.

"I need you to get Janelle. Tell her I need a change of clothes. Tell her that in my room, there is a crate in the back of my closet filled with scarves. Have her grab the box underneath them and tell her the bottles inside are fragile. There's another bottle in the washroom, purple with a cork stopper. Tell her I'll need that as well."

Nora rose, but Lea grabbed her hand, looking her in the eye.

"And Nora, tell her to be careful."

Lea watched out the window as Nora left the house, turning toward town to find Janelle. She was to tell anyone who asked that Lea had asked Janelle to get a tonic to help her rest and heal her injuries from the fenrir attack, though the villagers were likely too loyal to allow any suspicion to fall on little Nora to begin with. Turning back toward the kitchen, she noticed a familiar parchment-covered package with a sage ribbon sitting on the kitchen table. A note was sitting on top of it. *Stay put,* the note read. No signature, no other explanation.

Her package of treats had been destroyed in her encounter with the soldier in the alley. How could it be here? She opened the box to see that it was new, filled to the brim with different cakes and candies from the ones she had picked. Next to the box of desserts was a stack of her clothing, two pairs of pants and undergarments, as well as a tunic and dress, both navy blue. The Commander had clearly left the note, a reminder of his promise to Thomas to keep her locked up until the trial was over. Did he buy her new sweets after he'd saved her and brought the clothes as well? *It couldn't have been him*, she decided. She was his prisoner; why bother with her comfort?

Putting one of the chocolate tarts on a plate, Lea walked to the seat by the window. There was a bluebird sky outside, the sun beaming down on the tall green grass as butterflies flew from wildflower to wildflower. It was a complete contrast to how dark her world felt at this moment. She picked up the treat but placed it back down almost immediately, pushing the plate of chocolate to the other side of the table. There was no way she could eat when she was this worried and wondered why she had even grabbed it, to begin with. Trying to calm her mind, she settled into the chair to watch the grass blowing in the slight breeze. She leaned forward and cracked the window, only a few inches, attempting to keep out the heat of the day but needing some fresh air. She longed to step out into the sun, but worried that there would be consequences for her plans to save Thomas if she went outside and was caught. Surely the Commander had guards outside if he wasn't out there himself sulking on the front porch. A surge of anger filled her belly. He had no right to sulk, to act so frustrated. He was the one causing all this–keeping her prisoner. And for what?

The wind picked up a bit, pushing warm air through the crack in the frame.

"*Lea...*" She heard her name spoken on the breeze, almost a whisper. It was impossible, but the voice sounded like her mother's... a sweet memory of her calling to her from their garden.

Lea jumped, startled, when a noise sounded above her head upstairs. Jumping to her feet, she heard another *thump* a little further down the hall. She looked around for some sort of weapon and was in the process of reaching toward a heavy book nearby when Janelle appeared on the landing.

"What the fuck is happening, Lea?" Janelle ran to her, her purple hair tied into a haphazard ponytail atop her head. "Why can't you leave? Where is Thomas and why is every gods damned soldier in the village acting like we're all a bunch of thieves?"

Lea's mouth opened to answer, but Janelle cut her off.

"I know I'm a thief; that's not the point. What happened?"

Lea tried to speak again, but instead of words, a sob wrenched from her throat. She shed the tears she had been holding inside as she told Janelle everything that had happened since they'd heard Nora's scream ring out from the top of the hill and ending with the Commander dragging her back home, unconscious.

She finished her story and looked up at Janelle, eyes wet. "Where were you all?" Lea softly cried, not realizing until this moment that she resented her friends for not being there by her side to help Thomas fight off the fenrir.

"We tried to follow you after you ran off, I swear. We were right behind you, but that Commander started shouting orders for his army to keep us all back. He was terrifying, Lea." Janelle led them to the couch to sit.

"He sent a group after you and Thomas before tearing off toward the hill himself, and I swear all the darkness from the woods around us, it just... *followed him.* There are guards everywhere now, outside your house, the market, this house."

Lea deflated immediately. "So you couldn't—"

"I swear to you, Lea Astrantia, if you finish that sentence, we are most definitely not friends anymore. Doubting my abilities... I'm in here, aren't I? Of course, I got in. Of course, I have what you asked for." Janelle's words were angry, her tone offended, but the crease between her eyebrows and bags underneath her eyes showed that her anger was a thin disguise for her worry.

"How did you even get in here if the house is guarded?" Lea questioned.

Janelle pointed toward the back corner of the house, where there were no doors. "There's a trellis underneath the oak. It's mostly hidden from the road. I might have used it once or twice, sneaking in to see Joseph."

Lea's jaw dropped. "Joseph, as in Thomas's brother...? Tell me you didn't sleep with Thomas' brother? Janelle! Does Thomas know?" *Seriously*, Lea wondered, *have I been oblivious to absolutely everything?*

"Do you really think that's what's important right now?" Janelle shouted incredulously, standing and gesturing toward the staircase. "Come on, let's go upstairs. I left everything by the window."

As they walked up the stairs, Lea's legs felt unexpectedly strong, considering she'd barely eaten today, along with the injuries she'd had. She followed Janelle into an upstairs bedroom, recognizing it as Joseph's. Janelle walked quickly over to the window and grabbed an over-the-shoulder satchel. She handed it to Lea, who immediately dumped the contents onto the bed. Lea almost wept when she saw everything she had asked for. Opening her mother's box, she was relieved to see all its contents right where they belonged. Reaching forward, she picked up the large purple vial filled with a gel-like medicine inside, rolling it between her fingers.

Lea set the vial aside and pulled out the letter her mother had left her, words that she'd read so often that they were imprinted on her soul like words pressed into the pages of a book. Words that made less sense the more they spun in her mind.

My sweet girl.

I am sorry that I was not more careful, that I took a risk that allowed me to be taken from you before we could speak of things that need to be said, before I could tell you the truth. I know you have always felt different, my darling, and that truth that I have hidden from you is this: You are different, and your father and I hid it from you the same way we hid it from the world. All we wanted was to protect you, and I pray to the gods we made the right choice. Wear this necklace always; it will keep you safe if you let it. Amethyst for protection, a rough cut that is as wild as the spirits that I know call you outside of these mountains. Jasper that I have carried in my pocket since before you were born, smoothed over the years by my fingers, rubbing it in times of stress. It will calm your mind and ground your spirit when you feel worried. I hope it helps your heart to heal. I've left you a bit of magic, and should you ever need it, the wind will guide you... let it. There are answers you may someday seek to questions you do not yet know—the stars will guide you to them. Let them. I promise no distance will keep me from protecting you, loving you, even beyond the veil. Remember who you are-why I named you. It will remind you that you have everything you need to change the world.

I love you, my Wildflower.

Lea pulled her necklace from beneath her shirt, a gift that had accompanied the letter. It was beautiful, a slim golden chain with a rough cut of amethyst that cut into her palm when she squeezed it and a piece of jasper so worn she could imagine her mother's fingers rubbing it smooth.

Between the two familiar stones, there was a rough piece of black rock, wild like the mountains that surrounded her, but darker in color with small flecks of something that shimmered when touched by the light. It was roughly the size of her pinky nail, hanging right alongside the stones that had adorned her mother's neck for as long as Lea could remember.

"I'm assuming you have a plan, based on the random things you asked for?" Janelle interrupted her thoughts, eyes questioning.

"The trial is in two days. We have to pretend nothing is different, aside from the fact that I'm a prisoner here until then. I can't tell you my plan, Janelle. I already made this mess for Thomas. I'm not pulling you any further into it."

Janelle looked at her with wide eyes, her face pinched in annoyance as she grabbed Lea's arm.

"If you're going to do something stupid, Lea, then I plan on being stupid with you. You're not the only one who loves Thomas. And he's not the only one who loves you."

Tears filled Lea's eyes. "But I love you, too, and I want to protect you just as much as Thomas. Just let me do this. I'll be fine."

Janelle stood on her tiptoes and crossed her arms. "I won't. If you won't let me help, I'm going to go get Samuel and Danielle, and anyone else I can find to help me. And we will probably ruin all your plans because we'll come up with our own. So it's pointless for you to argue. I'm helping whether you let me or not."

Lea sighed. "Fine. I'll let you help. I'll let you all help, I promise. Keep your ears open for any information you can gather. If you find anything out, come tell me. You can bring me something, a book to pass my time maybe, as an excuse for why you're here. I can't leave, but no one said anything about visitors."

The front door slammed below them. She heard doors begin to open and close downstairs, along with the familiar grumbling of a furious Fae.

"I was gone for an hour. I swear to the gods, if you left again, Azalea, I will execute you myself!" the Commander roared.

Lea swore she felt the floor shake as the vibrations of his enraged voice traveled through it.

"Be careful," Janelle whispered, slipping out the window with the grace of a cat. Lea watched her leave and hoped her friend had nine lives like one, too. Lea shoved the satchel under a pillow and grabbed a blanket off the chest in front of the bed.

She quickly shuffled down the steps, her shaking hand steadying as it trailed along the smooth handrail. The stairs squeaked beneath her feet as she hurried down, coming face to face with the Commander's wrathful gaze. Determined to seem unsuspicious, she continued walking past him without acknowledging his presence. He gave her a questioning look before turning on his heel and following her.

"Feeling chilly in the balmy eighty degrees?" he asked without an ounce of humor as he bolted around her, stopping her in her tracks as she came face to chest with the Commander blocking her way.

She pushed past him roughly, immediately feeling an electric current run through her shoulder where it had bumped into his arm. "Damn magic," she muttered under her breath.

He followed her down the stairs as she placed the blanket on the couch in the living room.

"What do you want, Commander?" The last word came out sarcastically as she placed the blanket down on the couch.

"Gray," he said, not looking at her, but instead unbuttoning his jacket and placing it over the back of a chair.

"Excuse me?" she asked, turning to look at him.

"My name... It's Gray. No need to call me Commander. You're not one of my soldiers."

She continued on to the couch, keeping her back turned to him. *Gray... what a simple name.* So much less intimidating than what she'd imagined in her mind. "And why would I need to call you anything? I plan on spending as little time with you as possible." She unfolded the blanket and hung it over the arm of the couch, busying herself so she would not have to look at him.

"That might be difficult, Little Flower." Her stomach clenched as his deep voice wrapped itself around her body at the same time his hand wrapped around her arm. Lea didn't fight against him as he turned her to face him. "Last night showed me you can't be trusted to follow commands." He took a step closer, pressing himself against her, sending a shock straight to her chest that made her heart pound furiously as he stared down at her. "So I'll be staying here to make sure you do. Until after the trial, I'm not leaving again."

CHAPTER 8

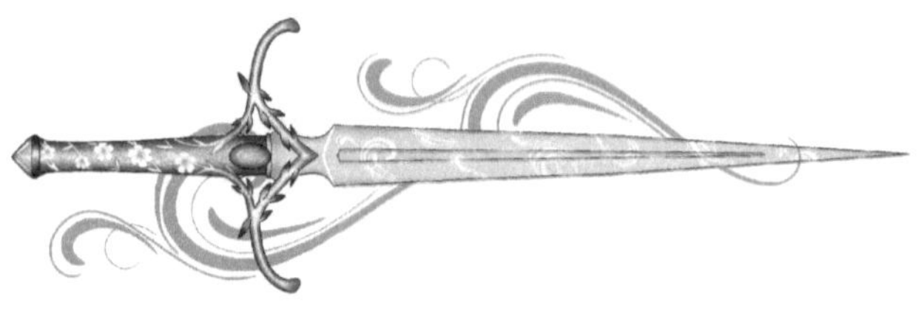

"Y ou're staying here... The Commander of the Royal Army, staying... here?" she said in disbelief. "Do you not have hundreds of men who could be here instead? You have nothing more important to do?"

"Oh, I assure you, I have far more important things that need my attention, but I don't trust you." He shrugged, looking pointedly toward the blanket on the couch, before turning toward the kitchen and walking away. She heard dishes clanking in the kitchen and wondered if he was getting her more water and how she could drown him in it.

He walked back through the kitchen doorway with two bowls. "Here. I brought dinner."

"You brought dinner?" she asked, wary.

"Yes, soup. Do you want to sit?"

"Sit?" She was so confused. Why was he being so nice when he was keeping her as his prisoner? The Commander had sent her best friend to a trial that would likely end in his death. Did he think she'd let one small act of kindness—which wasn't even that kind, honestly; he had to eat, too—overshadow everything else he'd done? He thought she'd happily sit and share a meal with him?

"Or, you can just repeat everything I say for the next two days," he said. "Imitation is the highest form of flattery, after all." He walked past her toward the table and set both bowls down.

"Here's some flattery for you. You have the largest nose and the worst manners of anyone I've ever met. And... you're weirdly tall..." She turned and walked over to the table where he sat, his bowl of soup halfway gone already. He *was* weirdly tall, with strangely enormous muscles... some of the features that made him so wildly attractive, but she'd never admit that. "If you hate me so much, why are you bringing me dinner? Actually, why are you bringing me anything, for that matter?" She gestured toward the table where her clothes and box of desserts still sat.

Commander Gray didn't respond, as if he didn't know the answer to the question himself, tension rolling off his shoulders. He took several spoonfuls of soup, looking toward her bowl expectantly.

"I'm not eating your hate soup." She pushed the bowl toward him roughly in anger. "Just tell me why you despise me so much."

Commander Gray stopped eating, placing his spoon down into the bowl as if his appetite was gone.

"As positive as I am that you won't believe me, I don't hate you, Azalea. I have a job to do, a job in which my success determines the fate and safety of the entire kingdom. Like I said before, I don't trust you, and I will not stand by and let you undo everything I have been working toward. So I brought soup, and now I'm trying to be patient with your stubborn attitude and find a way to make the next two days more tolerable for us both."

"And how does keeping me from Thomas and the trial change the fate of the kingdom!?" she shouted, frustration causing her hands to shake.

Commander Gray leveled her with a look, his mouth remaining firmly closed.

Lea sat down and looked at him pleadingly. "You don't need to stay. I promise I won't leave. At least let me go to my house." She looked away, unable to meet his eyes and beginning to feel panicked by his proximity.

He felt too large for the table, the room, and the chair he sat in. It felt wrong to have him in Thomas's home, looking so casually domestic.

"It makes no difference to you if I stay or not. You will be *here* either way," he said pointedly. "Besides, a bed here is more comfortable for me than a cot in the camp." He paused, leaning forward toward her across the table. Lea's heart suddenly raced as he came closer to her. "I'm not a fool, Little Flower. I know you will try to save that boy. I can't let that happen, so you can argue until your tongue falls out, but I'm not going anywhere."

"That boy?" She felt her anger rising again, as it did so often in his presence. "That boy is a hundred times the man you are. He cares about everyone in this village, and he cares about me. He doesn't knock people unconscious with his magic and carry them off to be imprisoned along with a terrified twelve-year-old girl." She looked around for Nora, her heart seizing in her chest when she realized she had not come home yet from finding Janelle.

"The girl is no longer here, if that's what you're worried about. I told her she could come and go to see you as she wishes, but she is going to stay with her mother in our camp for the next few days until the trial. I gave them my tent until then so they'd have extra room."

Lea paused, shocked by his moment of thoughtfulness. Her heart calmed at the thought of Nora being back with her mom, her panic easing.

"And," he continued, "you just admitted the boy has magic. So you did know?" he asked, ruining any goodwill he had garnered by allowing Nora to stay with her mother. Her brief moment of thinking that maybe somewhere inside of him, he actually had an, albeit small, heart, ended before the thought could even be fully formed. Fury bubbled in her stomach at the reminder that it was his direction that was causing Thomas to face trial in the first place.

Lea stood, leaving her untouched bowl on the table. Her anger was so hot she was certain fire would shoot from her mouth with the next words she spoke, so instead, she stormed off toward Thomas's room and slammed the door behind her.

"Goodnight, Little Flower!" the Commander called. She heard him clean up the dishes before walking into the room beside hers and closing the door, loud enough to make sure that she knew he would be just next door.

Great, of course that's the room he chose. Gods forbid he gives me space to breathe. Lea was, at least, grateful that he had not chosen the upstairs room where her satchel hid beneath a flimsy pillow, her only chance of saving Thomas mere feet from where the Commander now slept.

Lea went to the washroom to scrub her face but quickly realized there wasn't any water. She stood, wondering if going to the well would piss off the Commander just enough to ruin his night, or enough to tie her to the bed until after the trial. Though it would be satisfying to see his anger, she decided it wasn't worth the risk. Saving Thomas was her priority.

She walked out of the washroom and directly into the room beside hers, pushing the Commander's door open without knocking. If he was going to stay here without her permission, she would not be treating him with the usual manners that came along with being a house guest.

Commander Gray, though she did not much care to call him by his given name, paused and swung his head toward the door. He was in the process of undressing, his shirt now folded neatly on the foot of the bed, his hands at his waistband, now rebuttoning the trousers hanging loosely around his v-shaped waist.

Lea's mouth ran dry at the sight of the shirtless Fae before her. He was gorgeous, his brawny chest and corded arms accentuating his defined abs. Lea shuffled uncomfortably, refusing to admit that the sight left her feeling aroused, intrigued... How was it possible for him to look even more gigantic, more imposing, when wearing less clothing?

The Commander scanned her body quickly, then glanced down the hall, assessing for threats as he took two long strides toward her.

"What's wrong? Are you okay?" he asked her urgently, reaching out and touching her arm with a zap.

She took a step away, alarmed at how her body responded to him standing so close with his chest on display. Heat pooled in her core, her belly warm and her heart beating erratically in her chest.

Gray searched her face for a long moment before his eyes landed on her hands. "I don't see a weapon, so I assume you're not here to stab me." He stepped back. "So, to what can I owe this unwanted intrusion? Are those the rules of the house? No knocking required before walking in on someone undressing in their bedroom? I assume it goes both ways." He smirked.

Lea didn't know where to begin, her breathing still erratic. She planted her feet firmly on the ground, trying to channel the anger she had been feeling for him just minutes ago rather than the nervous heat that seemed to have taken over her body. "No promises on the whole stabbing thing. And this is not *your* bedroom," she reminded him. "I need water. I assumed that if I went to the well, you'd do the whole troll routine again, and I'm too exhausted for your anger tonight."

He stood there staring at her, bare-chested. She maintained eye contact, trying to fight back a blush while pretending that she had not noticed his enormous arms and his defined, hard stomach. She could see the black of a large tattoo across the left side of his chest, climbing up to his collarbone, right where his night magic symbol had been on his uniform. However, she refused to allow her eyes to stray to study it further.

"Troll routine?" His eyebrow raised.

"You know..." She lowered her voice an octave and added as much gravel to it as she could. "*You shall not pass. You must pay the toll or stay here and rot forever. I'm an abnormally large angry trollish Fae asshole who eats the bones of little humans without magic.*" She nodded, satisfied with her impression. He might be a hot troll, but he was a troll, nonetheless.

"There is no toll to pay, and you'll stay here no matter what." He stared at her blankly. "The metaphor doesn't stand."

"For the love of the gods," she rolled her eyes, "I am just letting you know I am going to get some water to wash my face. I'm not running away. Feel free to watch me." She began to turn toward the door.

"Stop." He told her sharply. "It's too dark, and I sent my soldiers home for the night." He sat and began putting his shoes back on. "We haven't found the other fenrir who attacked your village, and they clearly know a way of bypassing the main roads. I'll go, you stay here."

"Stop telling me what to do, *Commander*." She emphasized the last word.

"I told you that you can call me Gray. You're not one of my soldiers." He stood again, taking a step closer to her, his eyes gentle.

"Well, you're ordering me around like one." She stood on her tiptoes as she said this, attempting to look imposing.

He laughed quietly, his face *almost* breaking into a smile, as he placed his hands on her shoulders and pushed her back onto flat feet. That same shot of electricity flooded into her shoulders where he touched her, taking her breath away. She was about to tell him to turn off his magic when he answered her.

His eyes flashed, shadows swirling against the vibrant green of his irises. "Trust me, Little Flower. You would know if I was ordering you around." Lea's stomach clenched in response to his threat and the Commander stiffened, taking a deep breath as he started over. "I don't think it's safe for you to walk to the well alone at this hour. Would you allow me to come with you?"

She stared into his green eyes, so earnest in this moment. She liked this softer side of him, the one she'd only seen a couple of times—when he wasn't busy being an asshole. *He's keeping your best friend prisoner; you are a hostage.* Snapping out of her misguided moment of weakness, she lifted his hands from her shoulders, putting some space between them. She didn't want to give him the satisfaction of getting what he wanted, but he was likely right. It wasn't going to be safe at night until they found the rest of the wolves, and she couldn't save Thomas from inside the stomach of a fenrir.

"Fine, you can come. But I want you to put your shirt back on."

"Your racing heart says otherwise, Little Flower, but if this is the game you want to play…" He shrugged, turning around to reach for the folded shirt on his bed.

"My heart is beating at its usual speed, but thanks for your concern." Lea retorted. "You're not even touching me, you have no idea how fast my heart is beating…" Lea trailed off, trying not to notice the thick muscles that ran along his back, the way his waist narrowed as it disappeared below the waistband of his pants. She turned around and walked toward the front door, not waiting for him to follow. She was angry at herself for staring, but he was a half-naked, almost seven-foot-tall monster. His chest practically took up her whole visual field. What was she supposed to do?

Lea opened the door and stepped across the threshold to the outside world, wondering if she should have grabbed a jacket. She closed her eyes and took a deep breath in, holding it for several seconds before exhaling. The night air calmed her, and she realized just how jittery she had been. She did not do well locked inside, unable to touch the grass or breathe fresh air. She kicked off the house shoes she had been wearing inside, not caring about the chill of the grass, and walked forward toward the trees.

Knowing that she would only have a few moments alone before Commander Gray caught up with her, she kept walking forward, stepping around the small stones that dotted the ground and allowing her face to tip up as the tree branches swayed above her. A few fireflies flickered above her head, and an owl hooted nearby.

She soon felt a presence behind her, a pulsing energy that told her Commander Gray had finished dressing and was now walking with her to the well. They didn't speak as they walked, and she was grateful for the silence, the energy between them so loud she wasn't sure she could handle it if he spoke.

They soon reached the stone structure that held all the water they could possibly need to help them wash up before bed. She'd visited this well hundreds of times over the years and felt a sense of comfort when she placed her hands along the familiar moss-covered stone.

As she picked up a bucket and walked to the well, a firm hand folded around hers. *Zap.* Her body filled with warmth, and she sucked in a small breath at the feeling that was becoming more and more familiar. The weight of the bucket lifted from her tired hands, and without a word, Commander Gray walked toward the well, filling up the bucket before grabbing and filling another. With just a quick glance toward her, he turned and walked back toward the house. Lea stared at him for a long moment. Then, deciding to pick her battles, she followed behind him, rubbing her arms as the chill of the evening caused goosebumps to rise.

They reached the house, and he carried the buckets into her washroom to set them down, one on the floor and one on the counter, before turning and silently leaving the room. She washed her face quickly and walked back into the bedroom, still shivering and thoroughly exhausted.

The door swung open without a knock, and Commander Gray strode in with a blanket in his arms–the one she had brought from upstairs earlier in the day. He unfolded it and tentatively took a step forward before wrapping it around her shoulders. It trailed along the floor as she subconsciously stepped toward him—only the tiniest step. He gave her one last lingering look before leaving, not a single word spoken between them.

Lea waited for the sound of his bedroom door closing behind him, but it never came. She wondered where he had gone before walking to the bed with the blanket still around her shoulders, lying down on top of the soft mattress, and falling into a deep, restful sleep.

CHAPTER 9

Lea jumped in surprise when she walked into the living area to see a strange, smiling man drinking tea with a plate of food before him at the table.

She stepped back and wiped the sleep out of her eyes, trying to see him more clearly. After a moment, she recognized the man with blond hair who had sat next to Commander Gray on the night of the fire celebration. She remembered his warm, friendly laugh and felt the tension in her shoulders loosen.

"Morning," he said gruffly, shoveling a spoon full of eggs into his mouth, barely looking up at her.

"Good morning." She approached the man tentatively. "Where's Commander Big Nose? Did he need to go search for the stick up his ass?" Turning toward the cabinet, she walked to make a cup of tea.

The stranger choked on his bite, and Lea turned to look at him in alarm. He was laughing so hard she was worried eggs might come out of his nose.

"Sunshine, that stick is so far gone, there's no chance of him ever finding it." He beat at his chest, trying to clear the food from his throat.

The man's eyes were kind, and a layer of her distrust slipped away as he stuck out his hand. "I'm Erik."

She took a moment to assess him. He had at least three days' worth of whiskers on his face and crinkles around his eyes. His skin was tanned beneath the same black uniform Commander Gray always wore, and she was certain he spent a lot of time in the sun. He looked far nicer than Commander Gray and decided to give him a chance. She reached out and took his hand.

"Lea." She gave him a small smile. "So, are you my jailer today?"

He laughed loudly again, bringing a smile to her face, and she decided that as far as royal soldiers go, she liked this one.

"You can say that. Gray has... business to attend to, so I guess you're stuck with me. What should we do?"

"Do?" she asked in shock.

"Yeah... Do. I'll go crazy cooped up in this house all day. I'm way too big for this furniture and it's so hot in here with all the windows closed. I feel like I'm suffocating, Lea." He held his large hands at his throat dramatically.

"You know, Commander Gray's head will explode if he finds out you let me step foot out of this house," she said, weighing her options.

Erik gave her a broad smile, his eyes mischievous. "All the more reason to get out of here."

Seeing an opportunity, Lea scurried up the stairs, shouting over her shoulder. "Wait for me. I need to grab a change of clothes!" She rushed to get the leather satchel, thankfully still hiding underneath the pillow on Joseph's bed. Lea grabbed it, and, with Erik still mercifully in the kitchen, she scurried to Thomas's room and quietly closed the door. She shoved the satchel in the bottom drawer of the dresser under Thomas's clothes and changed quickly, not wanting to raise any suspicions.

Lea looked outside. The sun was shining through the tall peach trees out the window, and there was little to no breeze—it would be warm today. She opted for the navy sundress and a pair of brown sandals that wrapped around her ankle and slightly up her calf. Eager to feel the sun on her face, she brushed her hair and teeth and washed her face before running back into the kitchen so fast that she collided with Erik. Lea flew backward into the table and tipped it over, sending his plate crashing to the floor.

Erik ran to her, looking over his shoulder toward the hall and pulling her to stand.

"Gods! What are you running from?" He continued glancing between her and the doorway, hand on his sword.

"I'm running *toward* getting the hell out of this house! Let's *go!*" she grabbed his hand, pulling him after her. Lea would clean up the mess later, she thought with a smile as she raced toward the fresh air just outside the front door. She ran through the doorway and immediately turned her face up to the sky, her energy building and her heart rate slowing. She spread her arms wide and spun in a slow circle before stopping and taking several deep breaths, just standing in the sun and letting its rays fill the empty spaces inside her. When she finally turned around, Erik was looking at her with both questioning and concern in his eyes.

"I'll tell him he can't keep you locked up inside." He said simply before patting her on the shoulder. "Come on."

They walked in the opposite direction she would have expected, away from town and toward the Southern part of the mountain range that surrounded them. They continued on until the streets of her village disappeared behind them, her muscles warming at the exercise of climbing up and down the hills she was so familiar with.

A rustle met her ears from behind the trees and Lea paused, looking over her shoulders toward the sound.

"Something wrong?" Erik asked gruffly, placing his hand on the sword at his hip.

She shook her head. There was nothing prowling the woods, likely a bird taking flight or a fox playing in the long grass in the field behind the treeline. *You're just on edge after the attack,* she told herself. Lea took off her sandals as they neared the stream that snaked through the valley and into her village, leaving them in the grass. Walking into the icy water up to her calves, just barely brushing the hem of her dress, Lea felt as if she was glowing. She had always loved walking in this stream, the water melting down from the mountains in the spring that had carved a path in the rough stone over hundreds of years. Erik looked at her with raised eyebrows and an odd expression on his face, but didn't question her as he picked up her shoes and walked parallel with her toward the mountains on dry land.

The water was brisk but felt heavenly after only washing in tepid well water the past few days. A small smile crossed her face as she let the shock of the cool water calm her nerves, realizing how anxious she had really been. The heat of the sun kept her from getting too cold, and so she continued walking in the stream, enjoying the sensation of the smooth pebbles underneath her feet, grounded for the first time in days. Feeling stronger, more confident, Lea decided to try to get some information from Erik, anything that could help her to free Thomas.

"So..." she began, unsure where to start. "What does Commander Gray do for the Royal Army? Why does he care so much about a single human with magic in a village so far away from the palace?" Lea couldn't help the frustration she heard in her voice as she asked the question.

Erik's steps remained steady as he pondered her question, brow furrowed and fingers tapping against his leg. "I know it looks like this is all about one person to you, but it's not. It's about protecting thousands of other people who don't even know they need protection. It's about doing the right thing, Lea."

"Thousands of people? How can making Thomas stand trial help thousands of people?" she questioned.

"There is far too much you don't know to answer that. I know you don't know me, or Gray, for that matter, but I have known him for well over a hundred years, and I'll have you know that I trust him implicitly. If he told me I needed to chop off my left hand to help protect the people of this kingdom, I would do it without hesitation. Gray makes hard decisions, and not always popular ones, but he somehow always makes the right ones."

Lea continued on, eyeing a wild blackberry bush in the distance that she had eaten from more times than she could count. A small fish darted past her leg, and she smiled as she dissected what Erik had just said. They were nearing the base of the mountain, where the river turned slightly, and the rocks changed from small pebbles to large, flat pieces of boulder that had long ago broken away and settled into the ground. Lost in thought, Lea stepped on a slippery rock covered in some sort of algae. Unprepared for the loss of balance, she swung her arms in circles before falling into the water, hitting a stone and crashing into the rocks.

A hiss of pain escaped her as she looked down to see a trickle of blood running through the water from her elbow, her dress torn at the hip on the same side. *Great,* she thought. *More injuries.*

Lea attempted to stand but slipped again as her feet tried to find purchase on the rocks. She laughed as she fell once more, avoiding injury this time.

"Gray warned me to not trust you." Erik laughed, "But I didn't know that extended to trusting you to walk without hurting yourself." He reached down and took her hand, pulling her to stand as if she was a bag of feathers.

"Come on, you'll freeze like that, and Gray will kill me if he knows I let you hurt yourself. Let's get you back home." He shrugged off his coat and placed it over her shoulders. It was warm from the heat of his body, and while she didn't particularly want to wear part of the uniform of the Royal Army, or go home, her teeth were chattering from the chilly water, and she wasn't willing to lose her life to a cold when she had more important things to focus on, like saving Thomas.

They walked toward the cottage, turning their backs on the jagged mountains. After a few minutes, Lea felt the hair prickle along her spine—a warning. She rubbed at the base of her head, pulling her hand away to find blood smearing her fingers. Cursing under her breath, she realized that Erik had stopped walking in front of her. The woods were silent, not a single birdsong floating through the air as there had been just moments before. She paused, following Erik's lead, when behind her, far closer than she would have liked, she heard a low growl—one that sounded suspiciously like the growl of a fenrir.

CHAPTER 10

Lea felt the fenrir's hot, wet breath across her neck and arms, the growl reverberating straight into her bones as fear gripped her heart and adrenaline pumped through her veins. She didn't have a weapon, not a single thing to defend herself.

"Do not move. Don't breathe. Don't blink. I need you to stay calm," Erik said, rather coolly for the situation, as he slowly reached for the sword at his side.

The growl rumbled again, closer this time. She jumped, turning toward the noise on instinct, locking eyes with a massive wolf. Her sudden movement caused him to attack, teeth bared as it lunged for her neck. Erik shoved Lea to the ground as he thrust the sword forward, striking the fenrir in the throat. Blood spurted from the wound, and the black wolf stumbled. Before he could attack again, Erik pulled his sword free and, raising it over his head, sliced downward with all his strength, severing its head from its body.

"Now we really need to get you home..." Erik stepped forward quickly, reaching toward her.

"Do you guys have to go for the head every time?" she replied. "It's so gory." She motioned toward herself, splattered with thick red blood, as she tried to wipe her hands on her dress. Erik grabbed her arm and once again pulled her up from the ground. As she tried to wipe the blood from her face, she noticed the sky darken around them. It happened so quickly that she would have missed it had she blinked—day turning to night in the span of a second. A boom of thunder so loud it hurt her ears cracked through the sky, the strange lightning she had seen on Fire Night returning overhead.

"Well... Shit," Erik said, not appearing overly concerned. He crossed his arms and looked around.

She grabbed his arm, unsure why he wasn't moving with the lightning growing closer. "We need to go... *Now!*" She tried to shout over the thunder, but her words were swallowed by the ear-shattering booms. The wind picked up and dust flew into her eyes, making it hard to see as she tried to pull him back toward the house.

"He'll find us either way. There's no point in running." Erik sighed before turning to the tree line and waiting.

She looked around, confused, as the storm above them grew more furious. The wind blew her hair in front of her eyes, causing it to stick to the blood on her face. Within seconds, a hulking figure emerged through the trees from the direction of the cottage. He moved so quickly that her eyes struggled to keep up with his form as it came barreling toward them. Before she could blink, Erik was being held against the trunk of a tree by an enraged Commander, his arm pushing against Erik's chest as a dagger kissed his throat.

"What part of staying inside did you *not! Fucking! Understand?!*" he roared as another boom of thunder rattled her insides. Commander Gray's eyes were nearly black, all traces of green disappearing in the dark, swirling smoke filling his irises. His knuckles were white as they gripped the dagger so tightly she thought it might break in two, his chest heaving up and down with ragged, furious breaths.

Erik met Commander Gray's violent glare and shrugged. "We needed a change of scenery, boss."

Commander Gray shoved him aside, pointing his dagger at Erik's heart. "I'll deal with you later," he told Erik, his voice holding a promise that, had Lea not been so scared of the storm, would have caused her to run away from him. Commander Gray turned to look at her for the first time, his eyes widening in fury as he took in her appearance, cursing under his breath. He was at her side in an instant, grabbing her face and turning it to see where the blood had come from.

"It's not mine," she whispered, gesturing to the body of the fenrir several feet away. His hands fell to her waist where her dress had torn, and she sucked in her breath as his fingers found the cut just below her hip bone. Her heart pounded in her chest at his proximity, his electric touch pushing away the pain in her hip and filling her with something...different.

He looked back up at her, eyes full of wrath as he felt the blood running down her leg.

"Well... most of it isn't mine."

Relief flashed across his face so quickly she nearly missed it before he roughly grabbed her arm and pulled her back toward the house, her feet tripping over rocks as she tried to keep up.

"Could you not just fucking *listen*?!" he screamed.

She had seen him angry several times before, but never like this, and she felt truly afraid of him for the first time.

Lea tried to pull away from him, his anger too intense to be so close to. "Could you lower your voice like ten octaves? And let go of my arm. You're hurting me," she whimpered.

His hold immediately loosened, but his anger remained. "I've given you food. I've kept your friends safe. I didn't kill that boyfriend of yours on the spot when he used the magic he's been hiding from us for years. I told you I'd help him at the trial... You are acting like a selfish little girl. Can't you see I'm fucking protecting you?"

Lea's mouth dropped open in disbelief at what she was hearing. Did he really think she should be grateful that he was having her watched like a criminal, locked away and helpless? "You call keeping me prisoner as the man I love is sent away, maybe killed, protecting me? I was with your friend. We were safe."

His eyes flashed, and he whipped her around to face him.

"The man you love?" He laughed—actually laughed at her, but there was no humor in the cruel sound. "From what I saw in the tent, you had no clue he cared about you two days ago. No passion, no... basic communication. If you think that's *love*, then I don't think anyone has ever shown you what love really is. Why would they? You act like a spoiled, self-centered child, never listening to what you're told." He let her go as they reached the porch steps.

She froze, avoiding looking up at him. *Was he right?* Tears began streaming from her eyes as she thought about his words; Her father, who hardly came home anymore, who couldn't be bothered to stay sober on the occasions he was home. Her mother, gone, unable to love her anymore. Thomas, who had never told her how he felt. She thought of her empty house, her days spent in the garden, alone. She had always felt on the outside of things... but she realized she hadn't felt truly loved in a long time, and how dare he remind her of it.

She kept her eyes turned down and her voice soft. "And I can't imagine anyone could love you with a heart so cruel, so how could you possibly know what being loved feels like?" She turned and walked inside, slamming the bedroom door behind her and curling up on Thomas's bed, letting her tears fall until there were none left.

Her body was exhausted, and her heart was shattering. She tried to sleep as the hours passed, but her mind wouldn't calm enough to allow her to rest. Giving up, she stood and went to wash, deciding that maybe a cup of tea could help soothe her. Chilled from wearing her wet clothes for so long, she draped them over the washbasin and dressed in a soft shirt of Thomas's before going to build a fire in the living room.

She walked to the fireplace, knowing exactly where they kept the wood and matches from the years she had spent sitting around this fire with

Thomas and his family. As she was stacking the wood, a rough hand landed on hers, warming her cold hand almost immediately and sending a jolt running up her arm, telling her exactly who was touching her. Lea looked up angrily, but her heart ached in her chest like a traitor at the sadness she saw etched in the lines of his face. He didn't deserve her sympathy. The situation they were in was one created entirely by him and his misguided sense of duty.

"Allow me. Please."

"I know how to start a fire, you know." She bristled at his offer, still so very angry.

The Commander kept his hand on hers, silently waiting for her to relent.

She wanted to shove him off, fight him, tell him she didn't need his help, but she was just so tired. Without a word, she stood and walked to the chair closest to the fireplace, grabbing a blanket and tucking her feet under her as she sat. She could still be angry at him from over here, while he built the fire she so desperately wanted for warmth.

"I owe you an apology." he started, continuing to build the fire.

Lea stilled, her mouth opening in surprise. *Did the troll actually know how to apologize?* Or maybe... Did he realize that keeping her locked away wasn't protecting her? She felt hope bloom in her chest.

"I am deeply sorry for how I reacted; the things I said earlier. I left to deal with some... business, and when I returned, you were gone. The table was overturned and glass was everywhere... I panicked. I promised your friend I would keep you here and safe, and I don't make promises lightly—never ones I can't keep. My temper got the best of me, even more so when I saw you wet and covered in blood, wearing Erik's uniform. I just... I'm sorry." He scraped together two pieces of flint he pulled from his pocket, small sparks bursting into larger flames as they spread through the logs. The Commander stood slowly before turning around and walking toward her chair to kneel down in front of her. "I didn't mean what I said. If you say you love the boy..." He cleared his throat.

"Thomas." His voice sounded strained as he said the name. "Then I believe you, and I'm sorry that I have to keep you from him."

Returning to the fireplace, the Commander finished stacking the wood in silence. Did she believe him? He clearly still wasn't planning on letting her go, but she had to admit this confession was catching her off guard. If he believed she loved Thomas, he had to let her go. *Maybe I can convince him.*

"My mother died a couple of years ago. My father... Well, he never recovered. I've been all but alone since then. My friends, especially Thomas... they're it for me. They're all I have." Lea felt tears pricking her eyes and turned her face away from Commander Gray, not wanting him to see her pain. He shifted in front of her, reaching out and gently pulling her face back toward him, the intensity in his eyes making her want to cry even more.

"Thomas is the only one who has watched out for me, protected me. He held me when my mom died and didn't leave my side for weeks, stayed with me even after his own father died. He was almost fired from his job. A job he needs to keep his family fed and housed and warm. Thomas risked that to stay with me when I couldn't handle facing a morning alone. He made me eat when I was wasting away to nothing; made me laugh when I thought my world was going to end."

The Commander looked away, the flames flickering against his face reminding her of how handsome he had looked on Fire Night. It had only been a few days ago, but now, everything seemed to have changed.

"He sounds like a good man, then," the Commander said quietly.

"I've been too caught up in my grief over losing my mother to realize how he really felt, just grateful that he was here. But he *was* here, loving me the whole time, and he demanded nothing in return for it. And now, because of me, he's sitting in a tiny tent waiting for a trial that might lead to him never seeing his family again, maybe worse." Her voice cracked on the final word, the tears she had been holding back finally falling over her dark lashes and trailing down her cheeks.

"It's not your fault, you have to know that—" he started.

"That is not what you told me yesterday." She stopped and looked at him pointedly. She took a deep breath and continued. "You say I've never been loved, but what else can you call that? You act like it's a feeling everyone should know, but you're keeping him prisoner, taking away my chance to know what it feels like. "

"I have to, Lea." He swallowed, looking up at her.

"Don't call me that. That name is for my friends. For people I trust."

He sat back as if he had been struck, his eyes widening before he nodded. "I have to, Azalea."

"So you keep saying. But you're also keeping me prisoner. The little magic-less flower—a human—nothing to you at all." She wiped her eyes quickly, not wanting to cry in front of him. "I'm nothing to you, and still, you're ignoring your other duties just to keep me here, away from Thomas, and you won't give me a reason." She finally met his eye. "You say you don't hate me, Commander Gray, but you're the only reason that I am locked in this house, the only person taking away any chance I may have to know what love is supposed to feel like."

Lea had no more words to change his mind, so she stood, turning back toward her bedroom. She left the Commander alone, kneeling before an empty chair and staring into the fire.

CHAPTER II

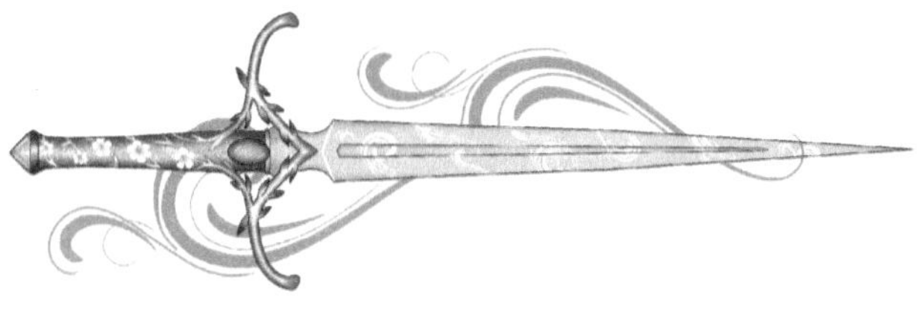

Lea had laid awake most of the night, unable to sleep with the Commander's words burning in her mind. He thought no one loved her... had basically told her she was unloveable. That was fine. He would be leaving in a few days, and hopefully, she would never have to see him again. It wasn't that she cared what the Commander thought of her that kept her awake, tossing and turning. It was the fact that she wondered if his words were true.

She finally fell asleep as the beginnings of light peeked through her curtains and woke several hours later after the sun had already passed halfway through the sky. Tomorrow was the trial. There was nothing she could do today other than wait, so she buried herself deeper under the duvet. She was about to drift back off to sleep when she heard voices from the living room. Deciding to investigate, she walked out and saw Janelle standing in the doorway, arguing with Erik. Janelle held a book in her hand, and Lea was worried she was about to hit him over the head with it as she wildly waved it around while she argued. Concluding that assaulting Erik wouldn't help their cause, she stepped forward to intervene.

"Janelle!" She walked to the door and grabbed the arm that held the book, giving her a hug. "I'm so glad you're here," she whispered into Janelle's ear, taking her hand and squeezing it.

Erik turned toward her with a sheepish look on his face. "Lea, you're awake. I wanted to apologize... I should have known better than to take you out of the house when Gray was already so on edge."

"You don't need to apologize. I needed to get out, and the Commander's bad behavior is no one's fault but his own." She smiled at him, a small olive branch. "So he's not here then?"

"He's not inside this house, if that's what you're asking. And I'm not sure your friend should be either..." He looked between Janelle and Lea, unsure.

"I just brought her a book, you idiot. I'm sure she's bored since you and that giant oaf are keeping her stuck inside with nothing to do. Strip search me if you don't believe me." She opened her arms and stepped forward with a shimmy.

"Gods above," Erik said, stepping aside, a blush creeping up his neck. "Not necessary. Come on in. Lea, please, behave. I'm on ice so thin with the Commander that I'm not sure it can take another crack. Got it?"

"Sir, yes, sir." She saluted him, winking and pulling Janelle into Thomas's room.

"Women..." Erik said under his breath. "I'm watching the both of you!" he shouted from the hallway.

Lea pulled Janelle in for another hug, holding onto her for far longer than she normally would.

"What happened, Lea?" Janelle pushed Lea off her gently and held her at arm's length so she could look at her. "I've been worried, spill."

"I'm fine." The words tumbled from her mouth. "Erik and I went for a walk, and I fell, and then—*whoosh!*—the fenrir's head was gone, and the Commander's magic is terrifying. Actually, *he's* terrifying, and apparently, no one loves me, and I can't think about this anymore." She rubbed at the ache in her forehead. "You brought me a book. Tell me this means you have information and you're not just trying to help me pass the time with..." She turned the green book over in her hands, "The Importance of Nettle Plants in the Use of Garden Pest Control."

"Lea." Janelle grabbed the book from her. "I don't even know where to begin to unpack that. I have information. It's not a lot, but it's something."

"I'll take anything," Lea said eagerly.

"Apparently, Prince Alaric will arrive tonight. They have a tent so big set up for him in the camp that I wonder what he could possibly use all that space for. It has a day magic flag on top, and guards have been walking through the market asking girls if they would like to help provide "royal entertainment" this evening." She cringed. "The town hall has been set up, and there are royal banners everywhere. They'll have the trial there, I think. It's full of chairs, so I don't think it's a private trial; I think I'll be able to watch... to help you. Please, Lea, tell me your plan."

She was saved from answering and admitting that she didn't have a solid plan yet by the sound of the front door opening and closing.

"At least you're here... and the cabin is intact..." the Commander grumbled to Erik.

Without a word, Lea and Janelle scurried to the door, pressing their ears against the rough-grained wood.

"Look, Gray, I know you're still pissed at me about yesterday, but... You've seen her. You can't keep her cooped up inside, out of the sun. She needs it. This isn't good for her."

"And letting her get injured and then almost eaten by a fenrir was good for her?" Gray spat back.

Janelle's eyes darted to Lea's, opening in shock as she mouthed, "Again?" Lea just shook her head, pointing back toward the door and the conversation floating through it.

"I'm insulted that you don't think I can handle one fenrir. I'm your second in command. I could take on five fenrir without using a drop of magic."

"It doesn't matter, Erik," he whispered harshly. "You may be second in command, but it is *my* command you are under. We can't let him find her. You know this!" A fist slammed against the table downstairs, rattling the dishes sitting on top of it. "It will put this entire village at risk. No one is aware of her suffering more than I am, but if that suffering is what it takes to keep her from being sent to trial right alongside that boy, to live and allow countless others to live, then that is a risk I am willing to take."

Janelle and Lea raced back to the bed when they heard his voice coming closer, sitting and opening the book just in time.

The Commander swung open the door, taking in the two girls who appeared to be demurely reading side by side on the bed.

"No knock?" Janelle asked.

"House rules," the Commander said gruffly, shifting his eyes to Lea. He strode forward and plucked the book from her hands. "Pest problem?" he said, looking back at Janelle and handing the book to her.

"Yes, actually. We have been plagued by one very large pest lately." Janelle looked him dead in the eye. Lea cracked a small smile, loving her friend even more at that moment.

"If you don't mind, I need to speak with Lea alone." Gray stared back, unflinching.

"Seems like you've had plenty of chances to speak to her alone, seeing as you've had her locked up for the past several days."

"And in one more day, I will be gone, and she will be free. Please, allow me to walk you out." He looked at her expectantly.

Janelle was about to reply, something filled with cursing that would likely anger the Commander and make life harder for Lea, when Lea reached out and placed her hand on Janelle's arm, silencing her.

"It's okay. I'll see you tomorrow."

Janelle looked at her and stood, walking ahead of the Commander and escorting herself out, not allowing him time to follow.

The Commander turned to her and held out his hand, and she flinched away slightly in surprise. They locked eyes as the moment hung between them. "If you're up for some fresh air, I'd like to escort you on a walk."

She turned her options over in her mind, deciding that playing nice might allow her more freedom over the next twenty-four hours, giving her the privacy she needed to help Thomas. She allowed him to help her stand and, uncomfortable with the tingles running up her arm, gently pulled her hand away as they walked through the hallway.

"You're dismissed, Erik," Gray told him, opening the front door and walking out before waiting to see if he would actually leave.

Lea followed behind him, instantly comforted by the fresh air. Standing to the side, the Commander gave her a few moments in silence to enjoy being in the sunshine before beginning to walk toward the well. Lea followed, and he slowed his pace so that they were walking side by side.

"I'd like to apologize again for my behavior yesterday. The way I spoke to you..." his voice trailed off. "It's been a long time since I've lost control of my anger, or my magic, like that." They continued on in silence under the large oaks in the sun-dappled shade. "You're right that I am keeping you away from Thomas, but it's not for the reason you think. There is a lot at stake here, Azalea. I don't think you understand the potentially catastrophic danger this whole situation has put you in... has put your entire village in." She thought of the mysterious "he" she had overheard the Commander and Erik talking about, and how they couldn't let him find her. *They weren't talking about me,* she thought, correcting herself. *I'm no one but a girl from a small town whose friend has magic.*

"I still don't see how one human with magic can cause—"she deepened her voice—"catastrophic danger for the entire village."

"It's not something I am at liberty to discuss with you. But it is still true. This could cause a chain reaction that the kingdom is not prepared for."

Lea let out an exasperated breath. If he couldn't, or wouldn't, tell her anything, then why keep apologizing? "It doesn't appear that anything I say could cause you to change your mind. So, if I may, what is the point of this conversation?"

"The point is that this is the situation we are in. I will not let you leave, and Thomas must stand trial. I know you don't see it, but this is for the good of the kingdom. I'm sorry it has to be this way, but that doesn't change that this *is* the way it has to be."

Tears collected in the back of her eyes, and Lea tried to pull ahead of him for a sliver of privacy.

"Azalea, wait." He reached out and grabbed her arm, his magic sending shockwaves from wrist to shoulder.

She turned to face him, looking down at the hand sending a cooling warmth down her arm. How was it possible his touch did both?

"This doesn't change anything, but maybe it will give you some answers." He reached into his pocket and pulled out a wrinkled envelope. The parchment was extravagant, a beautiful cream with a dark blue wax seal holding it closed. The Commander gently placed it in her hands with a sad smile and turned, walking into the shade of a large oak and settling beneath it.

Lea stared at the letter in her hand, running her fingers over the dotted grains of the paper. She took a few steps forward, expecting the Commander to tell her to stop, but he remained relaxed against the tree, his attention on the sky above rather than her. *Did he already know what the letter contained?* She continued walking until she reached the well, still within the Commander's sight but far enough away to allow her some space to breathe. She sat down and leaned back against the cool, rough stone of the well. Looking at the slightly crumpled parchment in her hand, she traced the seal showing the crest of the royal family. Taking a deep breath, she broke the wax crest in two and gently tore open the envelope.

She was pulling out the letter when something fell from the envelope into the grass. Reaching down, she picked up the tiny metal object. It was a piece of steel, formed to look like a moonflower, just like the birthmark that was hidden on the inside of her arm. The petals themselves were gently curved around a small round cut of rose quartz, the petals crafted to look like they were blowing in the wind. Lea gasped, immediately recognizing the piece of pink stone. It had once sat in a ring her mother wore on her right hand, one she had not seen in years. She closed her fingers around the charm and held it tightly in her fist, then opened the letter.

Lea,

I was awoken this morning by the Commander holding out a pen and parchment and telling me to "write to her." I don't know what led him to allow me this gift, maybe it is a last wish for a potentially dying man, but I am grateful all the same for the chance to tell you the things I should have said a very long time ago.

I think I have loved you since we were ten years old. You found me skipping rocks at the lake one day in the summer. Do you remember? You tried to skip one, and it sank right down to the bottom. You were so angry, and you tried again and again, but your rocks just wouldn't skip. Three days later you came to get me, dragging me down to the lake and challenging me to a competition. You skipped your rock six more times than I did that day, and I will never forget the look of triumph on your face as my rock dropped below the surface before yours did.

Back then, I was too young to know what I was feeling, but as we got older, that feeling only grew, and by the time I knew what it was, I was afraid to tell you. Who wouldn't be? You're the most beautiful girl in the village, but you're also the kindest, the funniest. I never felt worthy, and it never felt like the right time to tell you.

We both know it's unlikely I'll get to remain here, existing as I did before. I pray they will allow me to live and that maybe someday we will meet again and I can tell you these words to your face rather than through parchment, but for now, I am grateful that I'll meet my sentencing with you knowing how I feel.

I love you, Azalea Delphinium Astrantia. You have made my life worth living. Please, stay with my family. I asked my brothers long ago to take care of you if something should happen to me. I knew I could not hide my magic forever. They are your family, too, Lea, and thinking of you alone in your cottage causes me more worry than this trial I am facing.

Your mother gave me a ring of hers several years ago. She told me it might help me to "allow what's in my heart to give me courage." I didn't realize it then, but I think she always meant for you to have it and for the crystal to help me find the bravery to tell you I loved you. I've held onto it, a constant weight in my pocket. I used the steel from my dagger to form it inside a moonflower. Infused in the flower is my magic, and while I'm not sure how you could use the moonflower as a weapon, it gives me some peace to think of you carrying a piece of me with you.

Do not be a hero, Lea... Do not try to save me. Live your life, and find happiness. Should I be facing the executioner's sword tomorrow, that is my dying wish.

I will love you whether here on earth or through the veil, and should that be where I am going, I promise I will give your mother all your love.

I love you. I'm sorry. I love you.

Thomas.

Lea sat there by the well on the hard ground until the sun sank below the horizon, barely noticing as the air cooled around her and the crickets began their evening symphony. She read the letter again and again, her eyes so full of tears they distorted the words. She wiped them on her sleeves until her skin was raw, her nose red, and her head aching.

She pulled the necklace from beneath her shirt, adding Thomas's charm onto the chain and leaning back against the well, tears still streaming from her eyes.

As the ripple of magic marking sundown passed through her, she felt a hand on her shoulder accompanied by that familiar jolt of energy that marked the Commander's touch. He looked down at her, the sorrow in his eyes an expression she had not seen on his face before. He wiped a tear away with his thumb, his lips curved down in a frown and his touch gentle. Too exhausted to stand, to walk, she allowed him to pick her up from the ground and cradle her against his chest. She realized how cold she had been as his warmth seeped through his jacket, and she let him pull her closer, shielding her from the chilly breeze. Lea told herself it was only because she needed warmth that she allowed his arms to hold her so close, refusing to admit that she enjoyed feeling his protective embrace. They didn't speak as he carried her home, Lea clutching the charm like it was the most valuable thing she'd ever owned—and maybe it was. Proof that she was loved, proof she had belonged to someone. She had to save him, had to find a way to convince the Commander to let him go or let her go to him. She couldn't live in a world without Thomas, one where he could be sent away or killed. A sob burst from her throat at the thought. He couldn't die.

The Commander laid her in her bed, and she noticed the windows had been opened, just a bit, allowing fresh air to circulate through the small room.

He laid a blanket atop her, brushing another tear from her eye as he cupped her cheek. "I know you don't believe me, but I wish it didn't have to be this way," he said, as close to an apology as he could offer, before he left her alone to grieve what she could never have.

CHAPTER 12

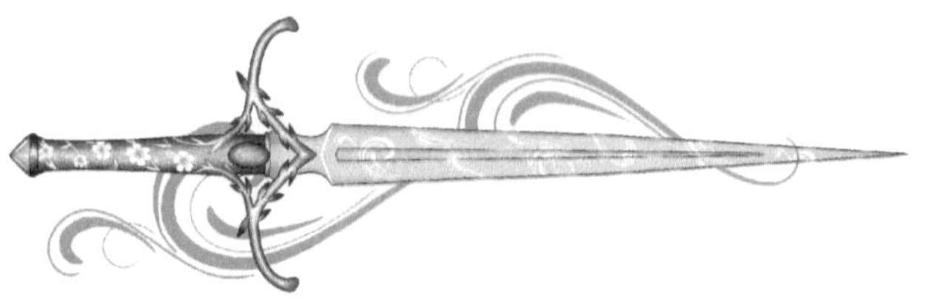

L ea awoke with the ripple of morning magic. Too anxious about the trial to risk sleeping any later, she rose from the bed and set in motion her plan for saving her friend, knowing that Thomas would never forgive her for what she planned to do today. She thought about Gray's words, that he would try to help Thomas... But it wasn't enough. She couldn't trust anyone but herself to fix the mess she'd made. Walking to the dresser, she grabbed her mother's wooden box from the bottom drawer, then pulled out the letter and the different colored vials inside.

She carried the three bottles over to the open window and set them side by side. "I need some magic, Mom," she said under her breath as she crouched down to look between the vials. Blue, green, and black... with no clues to what they held.

"The wind will guide me..." she said, feeling absolutely ridiculous as she repeated the words from her mother's letter. She continued to stare at the bottles of magic in front of her, waiting for some sort of sign. When nothing happened, she began to fear that she would have to guess which jar of magic might help her through the day. This had to work. It was her only plan, the only thing she had come up with over the last few days that could possibly help her.

Lea had looked at the vials several times over the last year, wondering what magic could be held inside. She'd wanted to open them one by one, smelling the contents to see what might happen—wondering if one of them could magically ease the pain she still felt from the loss of her mom—but she knew that she might need the magic inside one day and didn't want to waste a single drop on an impossible task. She turned away, walking back toward the box to see if there was something else that could help her, some sort of clue as to what the vials held... *Magic* was all her mother's note had said. *Really helpful, mom.* As she was walking back toward the bed, she heard a *clink* behind her. A glass vial had somehow dropped gently to the wooden floor without breaking and rolled toward her feet.

The vial was blue, the color so solid she wasn't able to see through the glass to the contents inside. Picking it up from the floor, she felt the breeze through the curtains brush against her hand as if lifting it toward her face. She uncorked the bottle and tentatively took a sip. *Dandeli on... Rose hips...?* Lea tried to think of the different flavors to help her identify the potion. Still unsure, she tipped the bottle and downed the remaining contents, tasting a strong ginger flavor. *Magicae Praesidium,* she thought as she felt magic begin to spread through her body—a warm tingling sensation. She had made this potion with her mother before, even drank it several times, though never with magic. *Where did Mom find magic?*

Without containing magic, it was a calming draft for sleep, but once infused with power of either the day or night, it temporarily protected whoever drank it from all effects of the supernatural. *Perfect.* At least Gray couldn't incapacitate her with his powers again if he did find her. She could fight him. She would, for Thomas.

The rest of her plan fell into place as she walked back to the box and placed the empty vial back inside, unable to part with it even though it no longer had a use. She placed her mother's letter, along with Thomas's, back into the box and hid them again in the satchel in the bottom drawer with shaking hands. Her mouth ran dry as she realized it was time. Steeling herself against her nerves, she left the room in search of the Commander.

She found him sitting alone at the kitchen table, determination evident in the stiffness of his posture. He didn't say a word as she sat down in front of him and met his eyes.

"When is the trial?" she asked, skipping all pleasantries as she scooted in her chair.

"Three hours," he said tersely.

She nodded. "Will you be staying here?"

He stared at her, clearly aware that she was fishing for information, but he continued, surprising her. "I'm required at the trial. Erik will be staying. I just wanted to tell you goodbye." He waited for a response, then stood when he was met with silence. Nodding at her with a small, tight-lipped smile, he turned to leave. Her heart squeezed in her chest at the sadness on his face, and her stomach ached for her to say something... to not let this be the last interaction they would have. *You don't care about him*, she reminded herself. *You're sad that Thomas is in danger, nothing more...*

"Just let him go. Please..." she finally begged, standing and stepping toward him. He froze in the doorway.

"If it were up to me, you would all be able to continue on with your lives here, hidden away in the mountains like nothing had ever happened... You'd never have seen me again after the Fire Celebration. But this is out of both of our hands now."

Lea pretended to feel defeated, slumping down in her chair and placing her head in her hands. She needed the Commander to think she believed that saving Thomas was a lost cause.

"Thank you for giving me the note," she told him. She went to the living room, curling up in the corner of the couch, and peeked up at him through her lashes, desperate to see if he was falling for her lies.

Letting out a sigh, he took a step forward, studying her. "If only I believed you, Lea," he said sadly, coming to stand in front of her, his broad form filling every inch of her vision. "I'm not foolish enough to think you won't try to pull some ridiculous stunt to save your friend. I told you before that I keep my promises, and I promised him that I would keep you here, safe." He raised his hands from his sides, which were now glowing with a strange dark gray-blue light. Lea scrambled backward as he began to step toward her.

"What are you doing?" she cried, standing up and trying unsuccessfully to run around him toward the bedroom.

"This won't hurt you, but it will make you sleep, no different from the other night when I found you in the tent. I promise this will be over soon, Azalea..."

"Please!" She screamed as she tried to back up, the backs of her knees bumping against the couch. He gently grabbed her forearms and the light began to spread around her body, but besides the ripple of electricity she always felt with his touch, she felt... nothing.

The vial! She had forgotten about the potion! His magic wouldn't work on her. Thinking quickly, she gasped as she let her eyes roll back into her skull, trying to remember how his magic had caused her to feel before she went unconscious days before. She allowed her head to slump down against her chest and collapsed toward the floor. The Commander caught her easily, before she could add to her ever-growing list of injuries, and gently lowered her down on the couch, his hands remaining on her arms.

Several seconds went by as she tried to keep her breathing slow and steady. She felt herself cradled against a strong chest as she was lifted into the air once again. She let her head roll backward and allowed her limbs to relax and swing with the cadence of the Commander's steps. His strong hands pressed firmly against her skin, sending ripples tingling through her body, and she wondered why she could still feel this part of his magic with the potion running through her veins. Gently laying her down on the bed, he covered her with a blanket and placed a pillow beneath her head. She struggled to keep her face still and her breathing steady as what felt like several silent minutes passed.

A hand brushed against her cheek, small shocks following the trail the Commander's fingers took as he tucked a strand of hair behind her ear.

"Stay strong, Little Flower," he said quietly, thumb gently moving across her jaw. She felt his warm breath across her face as he leaned down toward her. *What was he doing?* Lea struggled to keep her eyes shut as he trailed his fingers through her hair, pushing it back once again from her face. She felt him lean forward, his face so close to hers that she was scared if she moved even an inch, her face would touch his. *Was he going to kiss her?*

"And stay hidden," he whispered, before pulling his hand away and taking a step back. She felt the loss of his touch somewhere deep in her chest—felt his warmth leave her as he turned away and walked out the door.

She opened her eyes to look at the clock, not daring to move another muscle. *What if he comes back?* She couldn't risk it. Three hours, he had said. It was half-past twelve, and if she guessed correctly how long their conversation and his... incapacitating her had taken, she would guess the trial would begin at 3:00. She remained lying still, closing her eyes again when she heard the door open. Loud footsteps sounded nearby as someone moved past her toward the window. The curtains were pulled all the way back, and she tried not to wince at the unexpected brightness of the sun against her eyelids. Lea heard the window open the rest of the way and immediately smelled sweet jasmine, carried on the wind from the vine along the fence of her garden.

"I tried to tell him, flowers need the sun or they won't survive," Erik said to himself. She felt the blanket tuck more securely around her, then heard him walk away and shut the door behind him.

Lea opened her eyes and kept them on the clock, watching the minutes tick by, but Erik did not return. When twenty minutes were remaining until the trial, she stood, quickly tiptoeing to the dresser. She hurriedly removed the purple vial and opened it, placing a dab of the gel from inside on the back of her hand. Within seconds, the area she had touched had turned a dull brown. Just as she had hoped it would.

Years ago, she had made this lotion for a girl suffering from acne. While it hadn't cleared her blemishes, it did lead to brown spots over the entirety of her chin and nose. Lea squeezed it into her hands and quickly rubbed it through her hair from roots to ends. Taking a brush from Thomas's dresser, she combed the concoction through her hair, evening out the product. She let it rest for just a minute, then hurried quietly to the washroom and rinsed it out before turning toward the mirror.

Perfect, she thought, seeing that her golden locks had turned an ashy brown. Lea was surprised looking at her reflection, how sallow her skin was, how dark the bags looked beneath her eyes. Quickly plaiting her now darker hair, she changed into the clothes Janelle had brought her. She began to pack her satchel with the wooden box and a small throwing knife she had found in one of Thomas's drawers the day before, her heart racing with adrenaline as she listened for any sign of Erik coming to check on her. She removed her necklace, now decorated with the moonflower charm, and placed it within the zippered pocket of the satchel, knowing that too many people would recognize it if it were to slip out of her shirt. Lea just needed to get inside the meeting hall unidentified, and she hoped her disguise would allow her to do so. After that, they wouldn't be able to stop her from doing what she needed to do.

Without looking back, she slipped out the window, thanking Erik silently for opening it enough for her to pass through soundlessly, and hurried toward the meeting house where her fate would be determined. Her legs shook with each step as she thought about what she was about to do, about the fact that this might be the last time she walked toward the center of the village—a death march. She didn't care; she would do anything to save her best friend.

By the time she arrived at the meeting hall, a large stone building with a metal door and two tall sets of windows on the front, the trial was well underway. She peeked through a window but was unable to see past the throng of people inside, the room so full of men and women that her view of the front where Thomas would be sitting was completely blocked.

Shit.

She'd be walking in blind. Was the Commander in there? And if he was, where was he?

She took a deep breath and opened the door to the hall, slipping inside quietly. She kept her eyes downcast as she walked along the wall, shielding herself behind the bystanders watching the spectacle.

The Commander was here. The same electricity she had been feeling at his touch for days seemed to pull her feet toward the front, electricity buzzing along her skin. Fighting against the pull, she forced her feet to stop moving and paused to listen to the trial.

"I never wanted to hide from the Crown," Thomas was saying, his voice calm. "I just didn't know how else to take care of my family with my father gone... You can understand that, right?"

Lea walked along the side of the hot room, finding a place where she could make out the trial proceedings. Her heart squeezed when she saw Thomas seated at the front with his hands tied in front of him with a thick cut of rope. He looked exhausted, his eyes void of the usual spark that was always dancing in them. Lea's eyes focused on his wrists, red and inflamed where the rope bound him. *Those bastards!* Fury filled her chest.

Taking a deep breath, she turned her focus to Thomas and who surrounded him. His family was sitting to the right of him, thankfully unrestrained. Worry creased his mother's face, but Lea was relieved to see Nora sitting safely beside her, holding her hand. It was clear that Thomas's family was not on trial today, and for that, she was grateful.

Behind where Thomas sat, a tall man with blond hair and overly embellished clothing lounged in the magistrate's chair. His posture was slightly slumped, sitting with one ankle crossed over his knee and his arms across his chest. *Prince Alaric*, she realized. Though she had heard descriptions of him, along with the rest of the royal family, she was surprised by how young he looked. She had expected the man who would soon be ruling their kingdom to look like... well... a king. The prince had smooth skin, as if his hands had never wielded a sword. His trousers seemed more appropriate for a nice carriage ride than a three-day trek on a horse. While he didn't seem evil like she had expected the heir of the Black King to be, he had a sense of danger about him, something she couldn't quite place her finger on. Something in his posture, in the way his large hand wrapped around the arm of the chair, squeezing it so hard his knuckles were white.

Prince Alaric's eyes never left Thomas, watching him with keen attention, listening intently and asking the occasional question.

Finally, she took in the Commander. She had felt him, knew where he stood without her eyes ever seeing his form. He stood to the right of the prince, his hand on his sword, his feet apart as if ready for battle. He, unlike the prince, was not looking toward Thomas, but rather was scanning the crowd before him like a mountain lion looking for its prey.

He knows... Lea's hands began to shake. *How is that possible?*

The energy radiating from him was intense, as if daring anyone seated in the meeting hall to challenge him, willing them into submission with the fierceness in his eyes and the set of his jaw. Looking at him, she understood why he commanded the entirety of the Royal Army. He was terrifyingly fierce, and it was obvious that he was a man who was not to be challenged without consequence. Lea watched as the villagers avoided his darting gaze, how they shifted in their seats when they felt him look their way.

Janelle sat in the front row along with Danielle and Solomon, head swiveling side to side, obviously wondering where Lea was. Lea knew her friends would not be happy with what she was about to do, but she pushed the thought aside as she snuck further toward the front.

The prince sat up straighter, pausing before beginning to speak in a calm tone.

"It seems obvious to me that you've broken the law, and while it is admirable that you'd want to save your family, the law is clear. You've carried magic you should have reported. Magic that is the property of the Crown, that you've hidden and used for selfish purposes and financial gain."

"It wasn't like that. Who else could feed my brothers and sisters? My mother...?"

"Stop." Alaric's voice was quiet but firm. "Your intentions do not matter. You've admitted to hiding your magic, admitted to weakening the kingdom by staying hidden rather than serving the king. I find you guilty." The prince's tone wasn't angry, but he had a look of determination on his face that said he would not be changing his mind.

Lea tried to breathe through the butterflies racing from her stomach up her throat, choking her. Squeezing her fingers into fists, her fingernails cutting into the palm of her hands, she began to push her way more quickly through the crowd that had been hiding her from view...

"Your Majesty!" she shouted out, her throat burning at the words. She felt the whole crowd turn to her, adrenaline rushing through her body as she neared the front of the room. "Thomas is lying." She took one last step forward so that she was now in clear view of the prince.

She watched as Thomas's eyes opened in surprise, despair immediately clouding his features. A pair of furious green eyes swung toward her as the Commander stepped forward. Prince Alaric turned to face her, and suddenly, the room felt significantly warmer. He narrowed his eyes at her, looking less than pleased with the interruption.

"He isn't the one who was using magic. It was me," she stated firmly.

Lea met Thomas's eyes, and she heard the crowd gasp around her as they strained to see who had just admitted to treason in front of the

Crown Prince of Desia. Worry and terror flashed across Thomas's face as he turned to the prince. "No!" he screamed, his calm demeanor from moments before cracking. "She's lying. She doesn't have magic! She's lying to protect me!"

The Commander stepped forward as his shadows grew around him, looking at her with a wave of anger so fierce she took an involuntary step back. The meeting hall erupted in a cacophony of raised voices. Some screamed that it couldn't be true, yelling about the bad potions she had made for them over the years, and that surely if she had magic she could have avoided such disasters. Others yelled that Thomas was innocent, that he would never deceive the Crown unless to save her. The voices grew louder, causing her ears to ring. Janelle was trying to push her way toward Lea, but Lea looked at her and shook her head, silently pleading with her to sit back down. The damage had been done.

Prince Alaric stood and held up his ring-adorned hand. "*Silence.*" The word was full of anger, yet he did not need to yell. The floorboards under their feet vibrated and the walls shuddered, the room suddenly insufferably hot. The voices within the hall quieted, tapering off into complete silence after just a few moments. "Step forward," he said, looking straight at Lea.

Thomas looked as though he might throw up, while the Commander stood frozen mid-stride, hand still on his sword, his furious eyes darting between her and the prince.

"You are telling me that this man, who confessed to every single one of his charges, is a liar?" Prince Alaric slowly walked toward Lea. "You expect me to believe that you are the one responsible for all the weapons crafted with magic that allows them to strike down our fiercest enemies?" As the prince spoke, she felt the heat of the room subside, just a bit.

"Yes. He loves me, and he wants to keep me safe, so he's taking the blame." She met Thomas's eyes as he dropped to his knees.

"And am I not to believe that you are trying to save him because you love him as well? Is there a reason you waited until the verdict had been determined before coming forward and confessing?" Alaric asked.

Lea's eyes darted toward the Commander, who gave her the smallest shake of the head. She wasn't sure why he didn't want Alaric to know that he had been holding her prisoner, but at that moment, some strange pull deep inside her told her to trust him.

"I was scared. I didn't want to be killed or taken away from the only home I'd ever known. This isn't about who is taking the blame for me. I realized I couldn't let anyone, no matter who it was, pay the price for my choices."

The prince turned, facing Thomas. "And what do you have to say about this?" he asked.

"She's lying, trying to protect me." He reached toward her with his bound hands, desperation coloring his movements. "We've been friends since we were children. She has no one here and thinks she is doing something noble by giving me the chance to stay with my family. She holds no more magic than a dragonfly on the hill." Thomas met her stare, his eyes sad. "She's an ordinary girl, trying to create some excitement in her lonely existence," he said, turning away.

Lea knew he didn't mean what he'd said. She could feel the weight of his letter in the satchel hanging from her shoulder; even still, the truth his words carried was a knife in her chest.

The Commander stepped toward Thomas, his eyes black with fury and shadows radiating from his fingers.

"That's not true!" she cried. "It was my magic that made the dagger glow. Thomas was too far away, protecting his sister. He couldn't have done what I did, even if he says that he could. He's not that powerful." She looked outside, seeing the sun still high in the sky. "Ask him to show you. I promise he won't be able to do it," she added, knowing how much his magic weakened during the day.

"And she won't be able to show you a damn thing because she *doesn't. Have. Magic!*" Thomas shouted, slamming his hands on the floor in front of him.

"ENOUGH!" the prince roared, his patience finally failing. To be honest, Lea was surprised he was even listening to their fighting rather than killing them on the spot, based on his family's reputation. He looked between them, holding one hand out toward Thomas and one toward Lea. "One of you is lying. Shall we find out who it is?" The prince's hands began to glow a vibrant orange and shot out a blast of fire toward each of them. Thomas quickly shielded himself with what little magic he had available during the day, arms covering his face as he leaned back against the heat.

"No!" She heard someone scream, the room darkening as clouds passed in front of the sun and blocked out the light. It would have plunged them into complete darkness had the flames coming from the prince's hands not been so vibrant. Lea stood tall, looking the prince in the eye as the fire engulfed her, the heat causing her eyes to fill with tears. She tried to keep her panic down, reminding herself that the potion she had drank earlier would protect her. *I'm safe,* she repeated over and over. She smelled the tips of her hair singeing from the inferno, and when she took a breath, the air around her was so warm that breathing it in seemed to burn her lungs from the inside. The heat became so intense she was unable to maintain eye contact with the prince, and she closed her eyes against the pain of the fire.

"Well," he said, pulling his flames back into himself and brushing off his hands as if he had just touched something dusty. "It looks like we have two traitors in this village." He looked at the Commander. "Arrest them," he ordered, turning his back on the crowd and walking back to his chair.

Arrest *them*. Not her, but *them*. "No!" Lea cried. She had failed. She hadn't saved anyone. Her arms were wrenched behind her back, and she was forced to her knees while Thomas was thrown to the ground in front of her. She tried to reach out to him, but it only caused her wrists to throb with pain.

As she struggled against the guards holding her back, she met the Commander's eyes. He looked at her with a combination of anger and confusion, his eyes wide as he clearly thought through his next move. She grimaced in pain as the guard squeezed her wrists tighter. When she opened her eyes again, she saw the Commander furiously striding toward her, pushing the other guards aside and taking their place, restraining her far more gently. The now familiar cool of his magic soothed away the pain in her wrists, which had been throbbing moments before.

The meeting hall roared, men and women rising to push their way toward them as if trying to shield them from the prince's verdict. As she looked around, she saw fury in the faces of the other villagers, the neighbors she had grown up alongside.

The Commander walked her forward and passed her to Erik, who apparently had arrived sometime during the chaos, a loaded look passing between them as the Commander stepped toward the prince. "Prince Alaric, may I speak with you? I have some additional information you may find helpful." The prince looked at the crowd, growing angrier and more unruly by the second as they shouted, arms raised in foul gestures.

"Control them!" he shouted toward the soldiers lining the walls before turning to walk through the back door. The Commander followed behind him, not bothering to spare her a glance as he passed.

The soldiers walked through the crowds, their presence alone causing the spectators to quiet, though the undercurrent of hatred for the Crown still felt thick in the air. Lea tried to make eye contact with Thomas, but he avoided her gaze, his jaw clenched in anger. After several long minutes, Prince Alaric and the Commander returned. The prince sat back, staring at her intently before moving his gaze back to Thomas.

"I do not appreciate lying in my court, and it appears that you both have been lying to the Crown for a very long time. The punishment for this is death." The crowd's energy rose again, voices growing stronger as they shouted out in protest. Prince Alaric held out his hands. "However, the Commander here made a point I had not considered." He looked at Thomas. "Your weapons are strong and efficient, and I imagine you have not yet used your full power to forge them as you were trying to avoid detection. We can't afford to lose that talent, however justified your death may be." Lea noticed Thomas's mother visibly relax.

"And you," he turned to Lea. "The Commander says he's seen you perform healing magic that rivals what our best palace healers can perform."

She turned toward the Commander, meeting his eyes. "But—"

"But nothing," the Commander said, coming to stand in front of her, facing the prince. "I saw her heal her own wounds, severe injuries that disappeared in a single night. I didn't realize at the time that it was magic that had healed her so quickly. I was distracted by the prisoner and his family, but there is no other explanation. With the... tensions rising to the south, and more soldiers returning injured, we could use another talented healer in Auropera."

The Commander stood stone-still as he waited for the prince's response. As she looked at the tension in his shoulders, his ever so slightly shaking hands, she realized it was this, or death. He had just allowed her to see the sun rise another day, so she remained silent as she waited for Prince Alaric to make his final decision.

The prince just nodded at the Commander before turning to the assembly. "Let it be told to all those who pass through Bearswillow; the Crown was merciful to the traitors who dwell here. You are both sentenced to a lifetime of servitude to the Nestruir family, however the king sees fit." He turned to Lea and Thomas, a wicked grin crossing his face. "Welcome to the Court of Suns and Stars."

CHAPTER 13

The Commander gently took Lea's elbow and led her out the back door as the crowd behind her started to protest again. She strained her neck to search for Thomas but could not see him through the throng of people rushing to the front of the hall. The Commander turned and pulled her away from the path she had expected him to follow, leading her toward the army camp rather than back to Thomas's house.

"Why did you—" she began.

"Not. Now," he said sharply, tugging her forward more quickly. "Not a single word, or I swear to you, Azalea, I will strangle you myself." She looked up at him to find lines of both worry and anger creasing his forehead. She decided not to push him, allowing him to pull her along as she tried to keep up with his long strides. Entering the camp, a guard allowed them through with a salute to the Commander. It looked different during the daytime, with more guards walking about the tents, some loading up horses and others sharpening their weapons. They continued along to the center of camp, curious soldiers' stares following them as the Commander dragged her behind him. He suddenly turned toward a larger tent set off alone, unlike the tents in quads that filled the rest of the camp, and led her directly to it, opening the tent flaps and gesturing for her to enter first. Tentatively, she took a step forward, stopping just inside the entrance. *What was waiting in the tent?* She felt a zap in her backside and jumped, the Commander's magic pushing her forward into the large space.

The tent was far larger than the one that Thomas had been kept in and looked significantly more comfortable. A large pallet of furs and blankets sat in one corner, large enough for her to spread her arms and legs out wide and still not touch any of the corners. A writing desk sat along the opposite wall, along with a trunk with a padlock on the front. She felt the Commander's presence as he came up behind her, invisible hands grabbing around her hips and waist and turning her around.

He stood before her with his arms crossed in front of him, anger seething from every pore on his body. "How the *hell* did you do that?" He stepped forward, shoving a finger toward her. "What the *fuck* just happened back there, Azalea!? You just ruined your life—you almost *lost* your life. Do you realize that? And for *what*?" he screamed at her, his eyes furious.

"I don't know what you're talking about," she replied, staring right back at him.

"You know *exactly* what I'm talking about." His shadows snaked forward, pushing her backward until the backs of her knees knocked against his trunk. "How did you get engulfed in the Crown Prince's flames, possibly the most potent day magic ever seen, when the sun was at its highest point in the sky, and live? How are you not covered in burns? How are you even here to begin with? You should be asleep until morning, at *least*, with as much magic as I used to knock you out."

She continued staring into his eyes, clamping her mouth shut tightly, refusing to answer his questions. Her remaining two vials of magic were in the satchel hanging from her shoulder, just inches away from where he stood, and she was unwilling to give him any information that could lead to him finding them.

"I thought you were going to die, Azalea. *Fuck*! I almost watched you burn alive." He pulled his sword and sheath from his belt and threw them, crashing the weapons into the writing desk and toppling its contents onto the hard ground. "*Why* are you even here? I told you in no uncertain terms to STAY PUT!"

"Why am I here?" She screamed back at him, furious at the fact that he felt so strongly he could control her life. "Because I don't let people I *love* suffer! I've seen *enough* suffering! I have no one, *Commander!* It's just me." She stepped toward him and held her arms out wide. "Do you see anyone else out here fighting to keep me here? You yourself pointed out that I'm a self-centered brat who's too difficult to love." She tried to breathe evenly, her anger filling her with heat. "Thomas has a family that loves him, that *needs* him. No one needs me. It's better that I'm the one who ends up dead rather than someone people depend on, someone who so many people love." Lea was nearing hysterics, the reality of what she had just done crashing down on her.

The Commander stepped toward her slowly and bent down, so close that his enraged eyes were even with hers, his hot breath warming her cheeks.

"*No one*," he grabbed her chin roughly between his strong fingers, "is better off with you dead. Do you understand me?" he growled, a low threat wrapping around her middle and squeezing tight. "If I ever hear you say that again, you will not like how I will respond." He stared at her for several long moments for emphasis before pushing back.

The Commander placed a hand on his face, running it across his scruffy jaw and through his long brown hair in frustration. "I was going to help him, Lea. I told you that! I'd planned to convince the prince to bring him back to work in the castle. He would have spent the rest of his days making weapons for the Royal Army, able to use his magic out in the open. He could have made a life there. And you could have stayed here, safe. Now the prince is enraged by your whole circus act, and I'm not sure he'll be afforded the same freedoms I could have gotten him before.

And more importantly, I'm not even sure I can keep *you* safe from him now."

Lea noticed she was shaking and crossed her arms around herself, trying to hold her pieces together.

"Why would I believe you'd help him? You've done nothing but try to destroy him from the moment you saw his magic."

The Commander looked down at her trembling hands and exhaled slowly. Gently, he gently pushed her backward so that she sat down on his trunk. He took a knee in front of her, their faces at the same level in this position, a dark look crossing his already dangerous face.

"I am not a good man, Azalea. I have killed more men and Fae than you could imagine. I have magic so dark running through my blood that you would never be able to look at me again if you saw the destruction I have caused. I will kill without thought, for the people I care about, and to protect this kingdom."

He reached out toward her, then drew his hand back, standing up. Deciding to sit down beside her on the chest, he lowered his voice to almost a whisper. "Thomas isn't the only one with magic in this village, Lea. There are others, innocent people who only use their magic for good, to help their friends and neighbors. I wanted the prince to see only one man with magic, an outlier who somehow escaped detection, not a town full of magic that needs a witch hunt to smoke out those breaking the law. I wanted a quick trial that would allow the prince to leave immediately after so that he could forget about Bearswillow and go back to whatever he does to pass his time at the palace. I am not a good man, but that doesn't mean that I enjoy watching the Crown burn villages of innocents to the ground, trying to flesh out the magic within."

Her mind raced—*more magic?* Who could possibly hold magic besides Thomas, but... hadn't they hidden Thomas' magic from the rest of the village? Had she really just put the rest of Bearswillow in danger by trying to save him? The Commander moved to place a hand on her knee as if sensing her anxiety, but she flinched away. He couldn't be the one to calm her right now. As she scooted backward on the chest, pressure erupted behind her breastbone... was she having a panic attack?

"I didn't realize. I..." She pressed the heels of her hands into her eyes, trying to stop the dizziness and pain she felt spreading through her entire body.

"I need to go speak to the prince; try to convince him we should leave right away and stave off any notion that he should investigate this further." He stood and turned toward the door. "You should heal yourself. You made a mistake, albeit a huge, potentially catastrophic one, but it doesn't mean that you should allow yourself to suffer. I'll send Erik to guard you in the meantime." With that, he turned and left the tent, taking his pulsing shadows with him.

"Heal myself?" she questioned aloud, her vision becoming spotty through the pain. He knew that what he'd said wasn't true. He'd been the one to heal her when her injuries had been so severe. Why taunt her when she was already at rock bottom? No, below rock bottom—what was below rock bottom? Did she smash her head into rock bottom when she fell there? The pain became even more intense in her chest, and she closed her eyes. She tried to stand, but instead fell to the floor on her hands and knees as the pain seared throughout her body. A scream erupted from her throat as the tent flaps flew open and heavy footsteps returned.

"Lea, what's wrong?" Erik said, rushing to her side and lifting her up to carry her toward the pallet. She shook her head, barely able to speak.

"My chest... it hurts." Her voice was softer than usual and sounded far away to her own ears. The darkness continued to spread across her vision, and she could hear Erik speaking to her as she let that darkness spread throughout her body, swallowing her whole.

CHAPTER 14

"**W**hy didn't she heal herself? And why can't I heal her?" She heard a voice ask through the fog as she began to wake, her vision still fuzzy around the edges.

"I don't know what to think, Gray. None of it makes sense. I think if she could have healed herself, she would have. You didn't see her. The pain seemed like it was going to kill her... I was almost relieved when she passed out and stopped screaming."

She recognized the voice belonging to Erik. *I was screaming?* she thought, trying to clear her vision.

"Do you think Thomas is strong enough to have healed her? He wasn't alone with her for more than three minutes... I didn't think he had that much power." It was the Commander, she realized, wondering how she hadn't recognized his deep rumbling timber as soon as she'd heard it.

She groaned, trying to sit up. Her chest still throbbed, but she was grateful that the pain had faded, now more of a dull ache. She felt two pairs of hands on her in an instant, and she arched into the warmth involuntarily, the pain easing further.

"Hey, Little Flower," the Commander said, helping her to sit. She tried to get her eyes to focus as she rubbed her sore sternum.

"Did it work? Did you convince the prince to leave?" she croaked, looking at him hopefully.

"Yes," he replied, sitting back so he could look at her. "Though Erik should have come to get me as soon as you fainted…" He looked at Erik pointedly.

"You know we have to get out of here, Gray." He shrugged. "We can't risk staying in this village even for another day. You trust me as your second, and I made a judgment call. She was fine." Erik gave her a small smile, patting her hand. The Commander glared at Erik before turning back to Lea.

"How did you convince him?" Lea interjected.

Erik and Gray looked at each other, a silent conversation happening between them. "There are… tensions in some human villages in the kingdom. They are angry with the Crown for their policies against magic. I told him we couldn't afford another uprising at the moment and reminded him that Bearswillow was our most important outpost when traveling South; that we needed it and its people to replenish supplies. He saw reason," the Commander finished, leaving no room for questions.

"Thank the gods he did," Erik muttered as he looked away.

"We're leaving at dawn," the Commander continued. "Prince Alaric doesn't like to travel when his magic is weakened. You have about two hours to rest before we leave." He smoothed her hair behind her ear. "Azalea, what happened… Why didn't you heal yourself?"

Did she hit her head when she blacked out? Was the Commander actually being *nice* to her? "I don't understand why you keep saying that. You're the one who healed me after the fenrir attack. I felt you restart my heart. I don't have magic, *Commander*. You know that… If I could have healed myself, I promise I would have stopped it. I've never felt pain like that before." The Commander and Erik shared another look.

"First—" the Commander paused, letting loose a breath that caused his shoulders to relax slightly—"will you please call me Gray? Second, I didn't heal you, Lea. I restarted your heart, but there was no time to do more before the fenrir attacked me. When I got back to the cottage and cleaned your wounds, they were already scabbing over and closing up on their own."

"Wait…" She moved back slightly, looking up at the Commander. "*You* were the one that bathed me?" Heat flooded her cheeks as images flashed through her mind. Her clothes had been changed, bandages applied… how was it possible that this man had seen her so intimately and she didn't even remember it?

He had the decency to look embarrassed, if only slightly, as he shuffled from foot to foot. "I worried the bites would get infected. I've dressed many wounds before. And yours is far from the first female body I've looked upon, Azalea. If it makes you feel better, Nora was there helping me and made sure you stayed as modest as possible."

Lea groaned, placing her head in her hands. "But you saw…"

He looked at her, a hint of a smile on his face. "I saw nothing of importance, Azalea. Please, don't worry."

She sagged in relief. "So, we leave in two hours, then?" she asked, ready to change the subject.

"Yes, I went to your house and got you this." He gestured to a small trunk.

Walking over, she opened it and saw what had to be half of her wardrobe—trousers and tunics, boots and undergarments, and, to her surprise, a few trinkets from around her house. A hairbrush of her mothers, a bouquet of dried flowers she'd kept on her windowsill to ward off evil, and a book of fairy tales that her father used to read to her each night. She felt tears collecting in the back of her eyes and stood, closing the trunk.

"I'd like to wash before we leave if that's okay," she said, not looking toward Erik or the Commander, hoping they wouldn't hear the way her voice was shaking.

"Of course." They stood as one. Erik took his leave as the Commander moved the buckets of water, causing some to slosh out onto the ground.

"What are you doing?" she asked as he grabbed a washcloth.

"Helping you bathe, of course. I enjoyed it so much the last time..."

She gasped, blushing and turning to shove him backward. A mischievous half-smile grew as he took in her embarrassment. Was he... *joking*? Was this man even capable of joking? "I'd like you to leave, *Commander*," she said, feeling a strange flip in her stomach when she looked at his smiling face. When he wasn't scowling... her heart began to beat in an abnormal rhythm, a cadence unfamiliar to her that caused her to suck in a sharp breath. Why was she thinking of him like that? *He's your warden... nothing more.*

He walked to her, placing the washcloth in her hand, and Lea jumped at how potent the electricity of his touch felt at that moment. She could feel the rush from her hand straight to her toes, a tingling that made her feel awake... *aflame.*

"I will leave, but only if you will agree to call me Gray," he said as he raised his brows, interrupting her racing thoughts. "We'll be spending a lot of time together over the coming days."

"I would like a moment alone please, *Gray*," she conceded, her voice quiet, tired.

Gray nodded and turned to leave, a tiny smile on his face and triumph in his eyes.

Lea studied him, her eyes raking across his face, which suddenly looked far less stern. *Was he really that happy she called him by a different name?*

"I'll come to get you when it's time to go. Dress for warm weather, we will ride through the day and rest after sunset. I'll have your trunk brought along so you can have warmer clothes for the evening..."

She thanked him, turning away to find some soap to wash with.

"And Lea," he said, standing in the doorway, "don't plait your hair. I think I will enjoy watching the wind through it as we ride." With that, he left.

Lea felt her cheeks warm as her heart stuttered in her chest. She walked to the front of the tent and tied it shut to make sure she had complete privacy. Was he teasing her? He had saved her, saved Thomas... *But he was still the enemy.* Lea's eyes flicked toward the door, the pain behind her breastbone worsening the smallest amount as she thought the words. *Wasn't he?*

CHAPTER 15

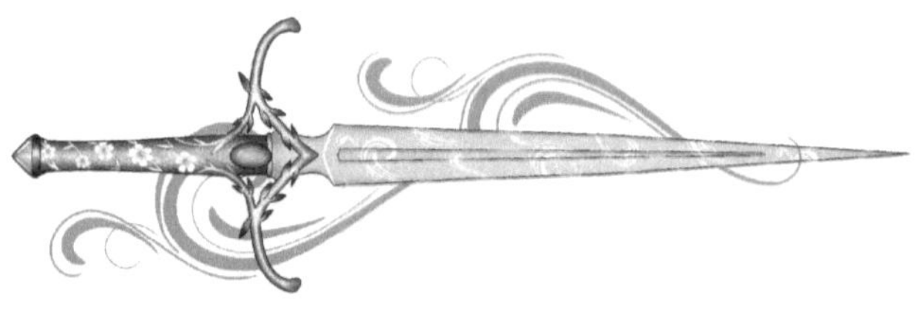

Lea finished dressing, choosing a simple pair of trousers and a tunic with black boots and defiantly plaiting her hair in a simple braid down her back. Retrieving her necklace from her satchel, she clasped it around her neck, hiding it below her shirt. She wrapped the satchel in a heavy coat in the trunk and placed it at the bottom, praying that no one would go through it and her letters and last two vials of magic would remain safe and undiscovered.

As she stepped outside the tent, she couldn't help but smile when she saw the beautiful beginnings of pink light creeping over the horizon. She looked to the Commander... Gray, and noticed him staring at her hair. He met her eyes and shook his head slightly, the challenge in his expression causing goosebumps to rise on her arms. Turning to say something to Erik, he broke away from the group and strode toward her.

"It's time to go. Do you have everything you need? We likely won't stop for several hours."

"I do," she said nervously. "Will there be a carriage for myself and Thomas?" She looked around for him, knowing it was unlikely they would get to travel together, but wishing all the same.

Commander Gray placed a hand on his belt and cocked his head to the side. "Oh, no. I took care of that. I told the prince I was afraid you might run, that you might attempt to free yourself and Thomas again. So, I've been assigned as your personal guard, Little Flower. You'll be riding with me." His eyes filled with mischief, and a wide smile crossed his face as he gestured for her to walk toward the horses.

Her jaw dropped, "I can't... I..." she sputtered. Three days on a horse with this man? A man who she couldn't tell if he hated her or tolerated her or... "I can manage. I'll ride next to you, I promise. You can tie my horse to yours." She panicked at the thought of being so close to him for minutes, let alone days.

Commander Gray scoffed. "Yes, trusting you has worked out so well in the past. Oh no," his gravelly voice caused Lea's pulse to quicken. "I think I'd prefer you close by for this journey. Come." He turned and walked toward the horses gathered at the other side of the camp, and she had to jog to keep up with his long strides.

"I thought you had no need to order me around, *Commander.*" He glanced over at her without breaking his stride.

"On this trip, you are under my command. The forest is dangerous, and it's my job to get you to Auropera safely. I am your Commander, and you are at my mercy. Do you understand?"

"No, I don't, you arrogant asshole!" She ran to him and poked him in the shoulder angrily. "I will not heel at your side whenever you tell me to. If that's a problem, then I suggest you assign me to another guard."

He paused briefly. "You'll stay with me. I enjoy a challenge. Now, *come.*" He resumed walking, pulling her forward as he stormed ahead. Lea dug her heels into the ground and refused to take a single step. Commander Gray slowed and sighed heavily. "That is not the typical reaction I get when I say those words to a woman."

Lea's jaw dropped, a vile sensation filling her gut, and Commander Gray laughed, rubbing a hand through his thick scruff.

"Fine. Lea, would you walk your beautiful little ass over here, pretty please with sugar on top?" His tone was sarcastic, but wait... *Did he just call me beautiful? Only moments after speaking about his past... experiences?* Surely it was part of his wry humor. Lea ignored both of his comments and followed him several paces behind as he walked to a large black horse ahead of her, the only one that appeared big enough to carry Commander Gray's weight. Without asking permission, he scooped her up from behind her knees and practically tossed her into the saddle. Placing his foot in the stirrup, he jumped up behind her, his thick thighs settling around the outside of hers.

Commander Gray grabbed the reins and Lea's back warmed as he shifted closer behind her, wrapping both arms around her sides as he reached forward to pat the horse's neck. Lea's fingernails dug into the leather of the saddle in front of her as familiar tingles ran through her forearms and her heart raced at his closeness. She was angry with him, wasn't she? He was taking her from her home—as a prisoner no less! So why was her body reacting this way every time he was near her?

Commander Gray clicked his tongue and the horse trotted forward, moving toward the front of the group of riders. "Nervous are we?" his deep voice rumbled in her ear.

Lea shoved her elbow into his gut, wincing as her bone bounced against his hard stomach. "I have nothing to be nervous about," she replied curtly, "other than making sure you don't kill us riding on this mammoth of a horse."

She felt Commander Gray stiffen behind her as Prince Alaric appeared several horses ahead. Shrinking backward against his muscular chest, she studied the prince as she tried to remain hidden from his view. He sat atop a beautiful horse the color of honey with an ivory-white blonde mane and tail moving slightly in the breeze. He didn't look wicked, but something about him still caused her blood to run cold as soldiers continued to gather around.

They all stood still, watching from their horses as the sun continued its ascent into the sky. The horses began pawing their feet at the ground, a sense of anticipation spreading among them. As the rumble of magic spread and the bottom of the sun crested the horizon, she felt Commander Gray lean toward her, his breath warm on her cheek against the cool of the morning. Chill bumps rose along her arms as her stomach flipped, his stubble brushing against the back of her neck. "Better hold on Little Flower. I ride hard," Commander Gray spoke directly into her ear, sending a shiver down her spine and heat directly to her core.

One of his hands left the reins as he wrapped his arm around Lea's front, pulling her more firmly against him with his palm spread across her stomach. As he kicked his heels to urge the horse forward, a canter growing quickly to a gallop, she felt Gray pull away the band holding her hair back, her plait unraveling as the wind whipped through it.

He didn't say a word, but she could feel Commander Gray's triumph, practically see his grin, as he continued to hold her tightly against him. The horse increased his speed, running so fast that she was forced to hold onto Commander Gray's forearms to steady herself, and she felt him shift behind her as her wrists encircled his arms. What was he doing? Was he flirting with her? She was a human... his prisoner. She'd fought him nearly every minute of the last several days. No, it *couldn't* be flirting.

As they rode across the hills, her blonde hair flying behind her and the wind on her face, she thought back to the feeling she'd had days ago as she walked through the market, arm in arm with Thomas. She had felt like something was coming, had been aware that things were about to change. This wasn't anywhere in the realm of what she had been expecting to happen, but as they raced toward the sunrise, toward the place she would forever call home from this point forward, she couldn't help but feel that maybe, somewhere along this journey, she would get her chance at *more.*

Gray had been serious when he'd said they would not be stopping for several hours. Based on the sun's position in the sky, Lea assumed it had been at least five hours since they had last stopped, a quick break with just enough time to water the horses and relieve themselves. The pace they maintained made it too difficult to hold a conversation, but Gray had asked her several times if she was okay or if she needed anything as they raced across the mountainous path.

The mountains became rolling hills the further they galloped from Bearswillow, a rhythmic cadence that caused Lea to struggle to remain alert. Her eyes grew heavy, the exhaustion from the last several days taking its toll. Gray's arm remained around her waist, pinning her to his front while the other hand held the reins, though he and the horse seemed so familiar with each other that he didn't need to give much direction.

Lea's head nodded as she leaned back against Commander Gray, and she felt a laugh rumble in his chest.

"Rest, Little Flower. I've got you," he said. She wanted to argue, wanted to resist the kindness he had been showing her. After all, Lea didn't need the pity of the man who held her captive, who still kept her from speaking with Thomas, but she didn't have the energy to fight. She allowed her head to rest back against his shoulder, and her eyes drifted shut.

She awoke as the horse slowed, sitting up straighter and gently pushing against Gray's arm holding her tightly to him. She stretched her neck to look up at the sky, watching as the sun dropped below the horizon. Ahead of them, several tents were set up, and it seemed that some soldiers had ridden ahead to get camp ready for the prince.

"I'm sorry I fell asleep," Lea told him, arching her back as she tried to wake her muscles.

"It was the most peaceful time we've ever spent together," he deadpanned, "Though I didn't realize when I told you to rest that you would drool on me." He said, wiping at his sleeve.

"I see Commander asshole can't stay away for too long," she said, attempting to sound angry but finding that, at that moment, she didn't feel that way. She leaned to the side, swinging her leg over the saddle and jumping down off the horse before Gray could stop her.

"*Shit.*" She grimaced, underestimating how much a jump from such a height would hurt. She reached down to rub her shins, testing out the movement of her ankles. Gray jumped down with ease, giving her a once over as he led his horse over to a trough of water that was currently being filled by a very young soldier. Lea walked toward the gigantic horse and patted his mane.

The beast turned his head to look at her, and after a pause, whinnied and swung his head to rest upon her shoulder, almost as if hugging her. Lea reached up and wrapped her arms around his neck, nuzzling her face into his dark mane.

"How does someone so sour get a horse so sweet? He bribes you with sugar, doesn't he?" Lea asked the horse as he nibbled at her shoulder. Gray glared at her while unpacking the bags hanging from the saddle.

"Of course he likes her," the Commander said under his breath.

"Yes, of course, he likes me," she parroted, scratching the horse on his nose, causing him to nibble at her sleeve. "You seem to be the only person who doesn't, you know."

"I feel so much more for you than just dislike, Little Flower," he said under his breath. "And I'd be careful if I were you. The last person who tried to pet him almost lost a finger." The horse snorted. "That's right, that bastard *did* lose a finger, didn't he, boy?" Gray glanced at the horse over his shoulder.

"I don't believe you bit off a man's finger for a second," Lea told the horse.

"You're right. The man raised a hand to him *after* he tried to bite him... so *I* took it. It's the last thing that hand ever did." The horse whinnied as if thanking him. Gray continued speaking as if cutting off a man's hand was a usual part of his routine.

"His name is Obsidian. He's my favorite horse in the royal stables." The Commander pulled an apple out of the saddlebag and reached forward to give it to him. "And I bribe him with apples, not sugar." Obsidian happily took the apple from his hand and ate it in a single bite, nose flaring as he pawed his feet.

"No more, Obsidian. You've been running too hard. You'll get sick," Gray said to him. The horse huffed, but turned back to the water.

Lea looked around, searching for Thomas among the royal soldiers meandering around camp. Some were carrying bundles from their horses, while others were already sitting around the many fires. Her intent in examining her surroundings was not lost on Gray.

"You won't find him here. A second caravan left a few hours before us to travel ahead of the prince. The boy left before first light with them and will likely reach the palace at least half a day before we do. But don't worry, I'm sure the love-struck human will be waiting for you when we arrive."

She tried to keep her head up, to not let him know that the only thing that had gotten her through the ride today was the hope that she would get to see Thomas this evening when they stopped. Gray grabbed her arm, gently turning her and grabbing her chin. He forced her eyes to meet his, her mouth running dry at the intensity of the contact. "It's for the best, Azalea. If the prince suspects you care for each other more than he already does, he'll find ways to use that against you both."

"He was perfectly reasonable at the trial, Gray. Except for trying to burn us to a crisp... I guess." Lea shrugged. "But he listened to you easily enough when you offered this solution…" Gray stopped dead in his tracks and leaned closer to her, speaking in a coarse whisper.

"Do *not* mistake his calm public demeanor for his true character."

He turned and walked into the maze of tents, straight past the largest tent which was flying the Royal Crest and had a day magic flag atop it, the prince's tent. As they continued toward a group of tents in the back right corner of the camp, Lea noticed that a few others had flags as well. Some flew the symbol of the day, while other flags were adorned with the symbol of night magic, though most tents were bare—a reminder of the scarcity of magic.

Gray walked straight through the flaps of his tent and Lea paused outside, wondering where she was supposed to go. Several soldiers had gathered around the fire nearby, roasting some sort of small animal. Their faces were ruddy as if they had broken into the ale several miles ago while riding their horses. She scanned the rest of the area and noticed Erik unloading a light brown spotted horse a few tents away. As she walked toward him, she was quickly flipped over a broad shoulder. Suddenly upside down, she again found Erik as his head swung toward her, and a booming laugh escaped him as he watched Commander Gray carry her over his shoulder into his tent. "Goodnight, sunshine!" Erik called after her.

Gray set her down once inside and leveled her with a look. "Do you not understand what personal guard means?" he growled. "You are to stay with me. While we ride, while you sleep, while you eat. You'll not be out of my sight again until we are within the palace walls." Lea looked around, the tent closing in on her. It was not yet dark outside, allowing her to see how small the space was for her to share with such a massive man.

"While I sleep?" Lea squeaked as her stomach flipped and her heart shuddered. *In this tiny tent? It's much too intimate,* she thought, despite the fact that the ache behind her breastbone eased the slightest bit at the words.

Seeing her panic, he spoke again. "I've stayed with you for the past several days, Lea. This is no different."

"No different?" She spread her arms out, gesturing to the tent. "There's no door between us here, Gray, and only one bed... I can't."

"I'm going to stop you right there, Little Flower," he said, unbuckling his sword from around his waist. "I haven't slept since the night we fought the fenrir. I have stayed with you, alone, in a house for the past four days and have been a perfect gentleman. I even saw you naked and still, even though I've had to fight against every impulse to do otherwise, I haven't touched you. Have I?"

"Wait, I thought you said you didn't see anything—"

"You have fought me at every single turn, and I have left you unharmed," Gray cut her off. "You may sleep in the bed, in my arms, or on the ground if you like, but one way or another, we *will* sleep."

"You really haven't slept in four days?" she asked, feeling an odd stab of sympathy for the Fae. Gray shook his head, unbuttoning his jacket.

"There were things that needed to be taken care of. And I couldn't trust you... obviously."

He did look exhausted. Dark circles shadowed underneath his eyes and she could see the tension pulling his shoulders up toward his ears. She remembered how tired he had looked after she'd awoken from sneaking into Thomas's tent, and that had been days ago. She glanced at the bed, then back at Gray, considering his words. "But... You sleep with your shirt off," she said.

"So I do. And my trousers as well, if you must know. I'm happy to sleep in less if it would make you happy," he said, sliding his jacket down his arms as Lea's stomach rumbled. He paused, turning to look at her with apologetic eyes.

"You slept through our rations earlier as we were riding. I didn't want to wake you when you were so tired. I know the past few days have been... *difficult* for you." He threaded his arms back through the jacket and walked toward her. "Come on, let's get some dinner for you. We can rest after."

"It's okay," she said, placing her hand on his arm. "Honestly, my empty stomach is the least of your worries right now. You look exhausted."

"I'll be fine for another hour. Let's go."

"I'll just grab something to eat, and I'll come back here, I promise. You can get Erik to guard me while I eat, but you need to sleep, Gray."

He looked at her, appearing to gauge if her words were sincere. Apparently, he decided they were not as he grabbed her hand with a *zing* and pulled her forward. "I need something in my stomach as well; we have another long day of riding ahead of us tomorrow."

"You still don't trust me." She interrupted him, pulling away her hand.

"And you still don't trust me," he said, eyes turning toward the pallet. "Besides, the only man I trust in this camp is Erik. You remember the soldier you bumped into at the market? Being on the road... it does something to a man. I'd like to think I can trust all the soldiers under my command, but as we have seen before, that is not the case." He opened the tent flap.

Nausea filled Lea's stomach at the memory of the oily man's hands running across her body. He was right. But surely that was an exception. She couldn't imagine many of his soldiers acting out against his orders. Not when they were so clearly terrified of him.

"You don't trust the prince, then?"

Gray stopped dead in his tracks, allowing the flap to close again. He turned back to her, his face so serious it surprised her. "With you, I especially do not trust the prince. It would serve you to remember that, Azalea. The sun's brightness calls to flowers like you, but it can play tricks on the mind, a mirage that fools you into thinking you are safe. You'll stay away from *him*, most of all. Do not go near him, both here on the road and within the palace walls. Do you understand?" Gray had reached forward while talking, grabbing her face in his hands, fingers threading into the hair at the base of her head.

Lea's face reddened, shocks buzzing through her limbs at the intensity of his touch. His eyes were earnest, and frown lines creased his face. He was worried... but why?

"If you only listen to me on one thing, because the gods know you haven't listened to a damn thing I've asked of you yet, let it be this; stay away from him, Azalea. Please."

She stared at the lines on his face, momentarily stunned by the combination of his desperate words and the energy coursing from his hands, still sending tingles to the tips of her hair. It surprised her how vulnerable he appeared as he pleaded with his eyes for her to just promise him this one thing. "Okay," she said, watching to see if his shoulders would relax. "On *only* this one thing, I will listen to you."

He nodded at her and released her face, satisfied with her answer as relief replaced the worry on his face. He took her hand again, and they walked out the front of the tent. Gray led her to the fire, letting go of her just before those sitting around it looked up at him.

"Commander," a young boy said, jumping up to stand.

"Sit, Matthew," Gray said. "Please." He returned to the log he was sitting on, giving Gray a wary smile. Erik stood, then walked toward Lea and handed her a stick holding the meat from some sort of small animal. Gray walked to the fire to grab his portion as Erik led her to a log closer to the flames, providing warmth that she hadn't realized she was missing.

"I hope today wasn't too hard for you," Erik said. "Though, I'd imagine you'd take riding a hundred days through the blistering heat over a single day stuck inside a cottage." She opened her mouth to respond but stopped when the last of the sun disappeared below the horizon, shimmering magic bending the branches of the trees as it raced across the kingdom. Gray sat down and took a slow, deep breath. When he looked back up, Lea noticed the bags under his eyes had receded and his green irises were brighter than they had been twenty minutes before.

"He's been running himself ragged for months," Erik said, leaning closer. "But I don't think he's slept in days. I told him he can't sustain this, he needs his strength to—" He stopped abruptly, then sighed. "I'm glad the night has come and his magic can revive him a bit, but I'll be glad once we're back home where he can truly rest." Erik didn't look at her as he continued eating. Lea noticed Commander Gray watching her every so often, making sure she was okay or that she hadn't tried to run; she wasn't sure. Mostly, he allowed her to sit with Erik, taking in the warmth of the fire and admiring the stars above her head. She noticed that, while those sitting within this circle of the fire were at ease around Commander Gray, the other soldiers within the camp avoided him completely, often turning to walk the long way around him, their eyes widening in surprise and fear when they noticed him sitting at the fire. *At least it's not just me that finds him intimidating,* Lea thought.

She finished her dinner in a haze as she watched Commander Gray, noticing the fatigue in his movements, and nudged Erik with her shoulder. "I think it's time for your Commander to sleep," she said in his ear. "Goodnight Erik," she told him, rising and walking into the tent without looking to make sure Gray was behind her. She didn't need to ask his permission to return to the tent, or anywhere for that matter, yet she knew he would follow her immediately. It was only a moment before the tent flaps opened again, and she felt his presence behind her.

She didn't trust Gray. He hadn't earned that from her yet. He had held her prisoner, kept her away from Thomas and her other friends, held Thomas's family captive, and made her feel unloved and unwanted. But he had also made her feel valuable at times, protected her, and lied to the Crown Prince to save her life; the prince that he was sworn to serve. He'd made sure she was clothed and had items of comfort from home for her journey. She wasn't sure which way the scale tipped, the balance between his duties as the Commander, and the kindness he had shown her, teetering somewhere near the middle. He seemed to want to protect her, and to be honest, he had done so on several occasions. He needed rest, and that was something that she could allow him.

Lea removed her shoes and walked to the pallet, sliding under the covers fully clothed and wiggling all the way to the back wall, as close to the canvas of the tent as she could get.

She didn't say a word, didn't feel like she owed him any, while she laid still and closed her eyes, waiting for sleep to come. After several minutes, she heard Commander Gray place his jacket over the back of the chair by his writing desk and then the clunk of one boot, followed by another as he threw them to the floor. The pelts shifted beneath her as Gray climbed into the bed next to her. She could feel the heat of his body immediately, the pull in her chest urging her closer as the cold air from the seam in the tent seeped in through a small crack. She shifted closer to Gray, just a few inches, searching for that warmth.

They laid there in silence, her heart beating furiously in her chest. She'd never even slept in the same bed with Thomas, the boy that she was closest to in the world. Suddenly, she felt hyperaware aware of every inch of her body. How could she feel the man next to her, even though there were inches of space between them? She felt when he shifted, felt every breath he took in and out. Lea began to shiver, unsure if it was from his closeness or to escape the chill seeping through the tent wall. Suddenly, she felt strong arms surrounding her, and before she could protest, he pulled her toward him and flipped them over so that his back was now against the tent wall. The difference in warmth was instant.

"Goodnight, Little Flower," Gray said, reaching over her and tucking the blanket firmly around her front, sealing off any cool air from sliding under the covers, then scooting away, giving her the space he knew she wanted. Or, that she had *thought* she wanted.

"Goodnight, Gray," Lea said, unsure why, at this moment, sleeping with the enemy, she felt so very safe.

CHAPTER 16

When Lea awoke she was sweating, the end of a nightmare fading away into wisps in the air. Her breaths were ragged and heavy as she struggled to remember what she had been running from in her dreams. Remembering a hot, bright light that burned her arms as she tried to push it away, she looked down at her forearms. Her arms still stung from where they'd been burned in her dream, yet her skin remained unmarked. She felt a bead of sweat trickle down her back. Pushing the covers off, she fanned herself, taking deep breaths to calm her racing heart. What had she been dreaming? Had it been the prince trying to burn her alive? No. That didn't feel right. But the heat. She had actually felt its sting until something had woken her. Some noise... She racked her brain. No. A voice.

As her pulse slowed, she scanned the still-dark tent, but the only thing she saw was Gray sleeping soundly next to her, lying on his back with one arm resting above his head. She closed her eyes. *It had seemed so real.* Straining her ears, she tried to listen for whatever had pulled her from her deep sleep, but all she could hear was the rustle of branches in the wind and the music of crickets. She laid back down, deciding it had been a trick of the mind.

"*Follow...*" She heard the voice again, a whisper so soft she wondered if she was creating it in her mind. Follow... who? Where? She laid there waiting. "*Follow, daughter of the sun and the stars... Follow...*" The voice was closer this time, unmistakable and beckoning to her from just outside the tent.

She stood silently, creeping forward into the night, toward the voice. It sounded familiar to her, but she couldn't place why. *"Follow..."* Something overtook her as her body obeyed the command, pulling aside the tent flaps like a puppet on a string. As she stepped outside the tent, she noticed the embers of a dying fire and so many stars, unlike anything she had ever seen before. There were thousands of them—tiny bright white pinpoints in the sky. She stood there in awe, her heart fluttering in her chest, eyes tipped up and the wind whipping her hair around her face.

"*Follow the darkness. His time is coming. Follow...*"

The wind suddenly stopped, and the voice faded away. She shivered, suddenly so cold, realizing that her feet were bare and she wore only a tunic and pants, no layers that could provide her warmth. What—or who—had that been? It wasn't a voice she recognized, but the pull she felt—it called to her in a way she couldn't explain. *Follow the darkness,* the voice had said. Lea tipped her head back up to the dark sky.

A voice cleared behind her, and Lea jumped. She turned around and stumbled backward, nearly falling when she saw Gray standing in front of the tent, watching her. *Shit,* she cursed silently.

"I didn't—I wasn't leaving. I promise, I just—"

"I know," he said, "I heard." He held his hand out to her with genuine concern.

"You did?" she asked, her voice shaking. Gray simply nodded and continued holding out his hand. She stepped forward and placed her small hand in his much larger one, feeling that jolt of electricity she had become so familiar with. He held her gaze before scanning the night outside their tent, his eyes deathly serious, before leading her back inside.

"What did it mean, Gray?" She didn't know why, but she felt scared, uncertain of where the universe was trying to pull her. Tears filled her eyes, and she felt angry at herself for how many times she had cried over the past several days.

What was happening to her life? She had been ripped away from her home, unable to even tell her father where she was. It was unlikely she would ever see her friends again. Thomas wouldn't even look at her after the trial, and she wasn't sure if he would ever forgive her after what she had done. Now the stars themselves were trying to pull her somewhere, tell her something, and it all just felt so... *big... more...*

Gray tilted her face toward his and wiped his thumbs underneath her eyes, brushing away her tears. His usual stern expression had been replaced by a softness that filled her with warmth. *How can he look so terrifying and yet kind at the same time?* "You don't have to follow anyone anywhere you don't want to go," he said firmly, his deep voice wrapping around her so tightly it caused her breaths to become shallow.

She held his gaze, feeling her heart trying to let go of the anger it held toward him. She took a step away. *Prisoner.* The word bounced around in her mind, settling in her chest as the ache that had been present for days grew stronger.

"Besides the palace?" she asked quietly as she turned her eyes down, her meaning clear. His eyes grew serious, sad.

"Besides the palace," he confirmed.

"I'll do what I can to make it a happy place for you, Lea. I promise you." She just nodded, overwhelmed and unsure of what else to say.

Gray climbed back under the blanket covering the pallet, moving to the far side by the tent wall. He pulled back the covers for her. "Rest, Azalea. I'll keep the nightmares away tonight."

She wasn't sure what made her trust him, maybe it was the sincerity she had seen on his face just moments before, but she decided that just for tonight, she would. She crawled into the bed and scooted close enough to feel his warmth, allowing it to soothe the chaos inside her while remaining far enough away to avoid touching him. Gray shifted beside her as she laid on her back, staring up at the ceiling. She felt him grab her hand, and then a shock, immediately followed by a cool sensation in her palm. Her limbs became heavier and the tension in her body released.

Lea closed her fingers around his as she laid there, grateful for the contact—for something to ground her back to reality. She was safe, and knew with complete certainty that for some reason, Gray would protect her from anything that threatened to change that. She allowed her eyes to close as they laid there in comfortable silence, her fingers wrapped around his. Just for tonight, she would let go of her anger. She could go back to fighting him tomorrow.

She was surprised when she awoke hours later in the exact same position, well-rested and ready for the dawn, the ache in her chest far less noticeable. Gray kept a tight hold on her hand when she attempted to sit up, pulling her back down and turning her to face him. His long brown hair was messy from sleeping and the tension on his face had all but disappeared, the circles under his eyes only a memory.

"Good morning, Little Flower."

Her heart began to race. Why did he keep calling her that?

"We'll be out with the army soon, where everyone loyal to the king is always within earshot. I wanted to make sure you were okay before we left the privacy of this tent."

"I am," she replied with a nod, and really, she was. Her worries from the previous night were still there, lingering under the surface, but she felt safe knowing that she would be with Gray for the rest of the journey... That he would keep her safe from the whispers and the woods.

He tightened his grip around her hand, pulling her attention away from her own thoughts. "Don't trust anyone with what happened last night, Lea. Do not speak of the whispers. If you need to talk to someone, if I'm not who you want to confide in, then you can speak with Erik. He's the only other soldier you can trust."

Lea nodded, but her mind was racing. *What would happen if others found out about the whispers? What is he not telling me?*

"Let's go face the dawn." He stood with a sigh, pulling her to stand before letting go of her hand. He went to retrieve her shoes and jacket, handing them to her. "Erik is outside by the fire. You may go sit with him, if you'd like, while I dress. Make sure you eat breakfast. We likely won't stop until sunset nears."

She gave him a nod, the smallest smile on her lips. "I'd like that. Thank you." She turned and walked from the tent, seeing Erik right where Gray said he would be.

"Well, good morning Sunshine!" Erik's voice boomed, a grin on his face. The soldiers around him groaned, shooting him looks that told her they felt he was far too chipper for such an early hour.

"Morning, Erik. May I?" She gestured to the seat on the log next to him. He patted it and reached forward, grabbing a tin saucer and a kettle from the fire. He poured her a cup of tea and scooted closer to her. "You look rested. It suits you," Erik told her, and a blush flushed her cheeks.

"You look... like you need to shave," she replied, smiling into her cup. Erik's laugh reverberated through the camp.

"That I do, Sunshine, that I do," he said, clapping his hand down on her knee several times.

Lea smiled and bumped her shoulder against Erik's. It felt nice to have a friend, to be around someone who wasn't actively grumpy for at least twenty-three hours of the day. Another soldier passed along a bowl of porridge with nuts and fruit, and she realized how hungry she was. She finished her whole bowl by the time Gray walked out of the tent, and she couldn't help but think that he had stayed inside to allow her some freedom, or at least the appearance of freedom. He looked between her and Erik before going to get his own breakfast, settling down diagonally from her next to a soldier who appeared to be nearing his forties, several years older than most of the men in the Royal Army. They bent their heads together in an intense conversation, Gray glancing over at her every few minutes.

As the sun rose higher in the sky, soldiers around her stood and walked toward their horses, packing up the rest of their bags and climbing atop their saddles. Erik helped her to stand and walked her over to Gray, who led her toward Obsidian.

The horse whinnied when he saw Gray approaching, kicking his feet in excitement when he walked closer. "Good morning," Gray said, patting Obsidian's neck affectionately before turning to Lea. "After you."

She looked up at the giant horse, then back at Gray, and noticed him holding his hands cupped before her. She placed one foot in his hand and grabbed the horse's mane. With a deep breath, she pushed her heel down with as much strength as she could gather and was surprised when she felt herself plop successfully on the saddle. Gray used the stirrup and climbed up quickly, settling in behind her as he had the day before. "Want to try?" he asked in her ear, handing her the reins.

She attempted to look back at him to see if he was serious, but his proximity to her didn't give her room to turn her head. She grinned, taking the reins from him.

"I have one condition," he said.

She groaned, attempting to hand the reins back to him. "Of course you do. Let me guess... you now own my soul and I can never step more than three feet away from you."

"I was going to say, don't fall asleep this time." He closed her fingers around the reins. "Though owning your soul does sound—" She cut his words off with an elbow to the ribs.

The horses stood together as they had done the morning before, waiting for the sun to crest over the hills. As magic spread through her body, she clicked her heels into Obsidian's side and took off, racing toward the sunrise as she felt Gray's hands pulling her hair free once again, her golden strands tangling in the wind. A traitor of a smile crossed Lea's face at the freedom she felt. She was anything but free, but for today, she could pretend.

Lea held the reins for hours as they passed endless trees along a well-trodden dirt path through the forest, Gray holding her around the waist while she steered Obsidian. The day passed far more quickly when she held the reins, but she eventually had to pass them over when her biceps began to throb. Warm from the exertion of riding and the heat of the day, she shrugged off her jacket and rolled up her sleeves to let the sun kiss her skin.

She placed her arms on top of Grays, her hands circling his forearms. Lea knew it was a bad idea as his electricity traveled through her fingers, but her hours in the sun had filled her with energy, with confidence. She felt bold as she touched him, a smile widening across her face as she relaxed against Gray and enjoyed the sun.

"Freedom looks good on you," he said into her ear.

Lea laughed under her breath. "Says my jailer..." she replied.

"I'm not your jailer, Little Flower," Gray rumbled as he leaned forward, his warm breath against her neck causing her stomach to clench. "I'm your liberator."

CHAPTER 17

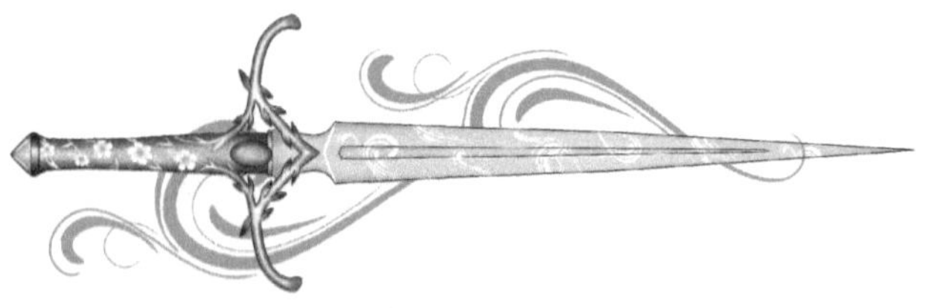

Gray helped her off Obsidian and walked with her toward this evening's camp. Lea, despite currently being a prisoner and technically, property of the Crown, felt alive. Her face was wind-chapped, and the bridge of her nose felt the tiniest bit sunburned. Her hair was tangled from hours in the wind, and her legs were sore from holding herself on Obsidian. It was as if her time on the horse had awoken something inside her that had been lying dormant, and whatever it was, she wanted more of it.

The evening passed uneventfully. Gray left her with Erik as he walked amongst his soldiers, checking in with different groups who sat around separate fires. She and Erik traded stories with each other, though most of Erik's tales sounded embellished if she was being honest. Throughout the night, Gray left her alone, free to spend her time with whomever she pleased as long as Erik was with her, but she felt his eyes on her the entire evening, warming her blood even more than the fire she sat beside.

Lea remained by the fire and watched as, one by one, the soldiers near her rose and said goodnight, retiring to their tents. Before too long, there were only a few men who remained. She thought about how her life had changed in the past few days. Would she ever find a cure for the Lonely

Death now? Without her garden, she couldn't imagine they would allow her to work on such things when the Lonely Death stayed far away from the royal family. In fact, she'd heard rumors that all of Auropera was protected from it by the king's power. And the voices... A shiver ran through her at the thought. Would they find her again tonight?

Gray came to sit beside her, settling so close she could feel his warmth through her shoulder. His electricity pulled her closer toward him, her arm barely brushing against his with a zap.

"I know what you're doing." His gravelly voice rumbled through her. Lea continued to stare at the fire, avoiding his gaze. "If the whispers followed you here, Azalea, I promise I will keep them from you tonight, but you can't avoid them by staying awake forever." He stood, holding out his hand. "Come on. I have a surprise for you."

She looked up at him, fire dancing in his eyes. Was this a trick? A ploy to get her to trust him more? To let her guard down? Furrowing her brows, she allowed him to help her rise, her hand remaining firmly in his as they walked into the tent together. Gray guided her toward the back corner of the tent, where a large basin held steaming water. "I thought you might like to wash, so I had my men warm some water on the fire."

Her muscles ached as she looked at the water, longing to feel the relief the warmth would bring. *He did this for me? Why?*

"You won't be washing me..." She crossed her arms across her chest and took a step back.

"Shame," he teased, his fingers brushing against hers as he handed her a washcloth. "I have some correspondence I need to attend to. I'll allow you some privacy to bathe." He turned away.

He's actually going to leave me alone? Lea was shocked that Gray appeared to be beginning to trust her, but her relief ended when he stopped walking once he reached his writing desk. Gray pulled out the chair and sat down, facing toward the front of the tent and away from the basin next to her.

"I don't think we have the same definition of privacy." Lea made a point of stepping away from the bath loudly, her feet stomping to prove a point. He didn't turn around.

"It's late, Azalea. I don't want to leave you alone with the sun no longer in the sky. I promised you I'd protect you and that I'd be here if the whispers came. Just pretend I'm not here," he told her like it was the obvious solution. "You can trust me."

She looked at the back of his head, bent over his writing desk. *Pretend the extremely attractive giant Fae male isn't here as I strip naked? Yeah... okay.*

Lea walked back toward the bath, running her hand through the water and creating small ripples and sounds as if she had just stepped into it.

"As much as I'd like to join you... I said I wouldn't look, Lea. Bathe, please, so we can rest." His head didn't move an inch as he continued writing.

Plunging her hand deeper into the bathtub, she flung water toward the back of Gray's neck with a wicked smile. Gray stopped writing, going deadly still.

"This is your one chance, Little Flower. Get me wet again, and I'll have to return the favor."

Her mouth dropped open as she froze. Surely he just meant he would drown her in the bathtub? Yes, that was it. She was convinced. Lea grabbed the bar of soap sitting on the trunk and placed it on top of the towel and clothing Gray had left for her on the floor by the basin, then undressed quickly and stepped inside the warm water. She kept her eyes on Gray, noticing his writing pause briefly at the sound of the ripples before he continued with a deep breath.

Sinking down deeper, her shoulders fell under the water as she rested her head back onto the porcelain. Lea took a deep breath to release the tension in her muscles, then let out a sigh as her soreness eased. Gray's shoulders stiffened as the sound escaped her lips, his hand pausing above the parchment again as he shifted in his seat before continuing on.

Lea watched the back of Gray's head as he continued to work, watching the shadows dancing from his hands through the steam rising around her. She tried to make some sort of plan—a way to not just survive at the castle, but to find joy—but her mind was consumed by thoughts of the beautiful Fae only feet away from her, at the fact that she was naked for the second time in front of him. Even if she had been wounded and unconscious the first time. Could she trust him? Or maybe, even get him to help her find her way in this new life she was being thrust into?

As the water cooled, she finally turned away from him to reach for the soap. Days worth of dirt seemed to fall off of her as she washed the grime from her face and moved on to rubbing the bar into her shoulders. Lost in enjoying the feeling of finally being clean, a quiet moan escaped her lips as she massaged her stiff neck muscles.

"You're testing me, Little Flower." Gray's rumbling voice was deep and quiet, with an edge to it she hadn't heard before.

"Testing you...?" she said with a dry mouth as she slowly looked back toward him through wet eyelashes. Gray had put down his pen, his hands now braced on the edge of the table in front of him. His knuckles were white with the force of his grip, and the shadows bursting from his hands had spread, trailing down the sides of the table and floating along the floor—toward her. They puddled around the base of the bathtub, pulsing along with the tension in the room. Lea's breaths became heavy as heat flooded her core.

Gray squeezed the desk tighter. It was as if he could sense her arousal, the wood groaning under the strength of his powerful hands.

"The water must be cool by now." His rough, gravel-filled words made Lea squirm.

"You're right, very cold," she sputtered, even more acutely aware of the fact that she was soaped up and naked so close to this man who, she had to admit, did strange things to her body. "Let me just wash my hair. "

"I swear to you, Azalea, you have less than a minute until I can't promise you I will stay in this chair. And if I see you, I can promise you that sleeping is not what you'll find yourself doing tonight," he growled, each rumbling syllable traveling across her skin. She could see every line of the muscles running down his back and arms, his shoulders rising and falling with ragged breaths as he tried to call back his shadows. Not sleeping... Was he planning on punishing her for not listening? *Or did he mean...* Lea paused, her face turning beet red as the realization crashed over her. A shiver ran down her spine, and she mentally kicked herself for considering his words as she quickly dunked her head in the now cold water and washed her hair with the bar, reaching for the towel as she stood and stepped out of the water. Even standing in the cool air, Lea felt herself growing warm at his threat. *Stop it*, she chided herself. *He is still your prison guard, your warden. Nothing more.*

Gray held his breath as water sloshed onto the floor, a crack forming beneath his fist where his grip strengthened on the table at the confirmation that she was now standing, undressed, just behind him. Letting go and scooting his chair back, he ran his hands down his face before placing his palms flat against the desk and standing, forearms straining as he leaned forward over the now-cracked wood.

He grabbed his correspondence, pushing it into a pile and tucking it into the desk with deliberately controlled movements. He flexed his fingers, opening and closing his hands, and she felt a whisper of touch against her skin, just on the outside of her hip. She gasped, quickly reaching for the clothing at her feet as Gray began to take off his jacket, still facing away from her. Picking it up, Lea found only an enormous dark gray shirt. She paused, but as Gray began to unbutton his sleeves, she decided that she would be less vulnerable under the blankets, even if only in a shirt, than standing before him in a towel. Pulling the shirt over her head as quickly as she could, Lea climbed beneath the covers.

Gray continued to undress, taking off his boots. He finally turned toward Lea at the sound of her climbing into the bed.

His eyes met hers as he lifted his shirt, pulling it over his head and tossing it to the floor. They held a fire in them, a hunger. He was staring at her with such intensity, Lea wondered what he was searching for inside her, what question he was looking for the answer to. It couldn't be that he simply wanted her... could it?

Wearing only his trousers, which hung loosely around his hips, he walked to the pallet and crawled onto the side closest to the wall, sitting propped up against several pillows.

The silence was loud, but not as loud as her heart pounding in her chest.

"Do you have a comb?" she asked, both worried that her hair would tangle beyond repair and also trying to break the tension of the moment—this palpable connection that was always trying to pull them together.

Lea was very aware that, between them, they wore only two articles of clothing. The thought made her clench her thighs together as she became hyper-sensitive of every sensation within her body. She could feel the rough shirt scraping against her nipples, a stark contrast to the soft bedding that wrapped around her legs.

"No, I didn't think... here." He grabbed her under her arms and pulled her in front of him as if she were made of air, pulling her to sit between his spread legs. She could feel the hard length of him against her hip as he leaned back against the tent wall. He was affecting her in a way that she didn't understand, and it was clear from the way he had to shift behind her, that she was affecting him, too. Lea couldn't breathe, not when she had no clue what he was planning to do.

To her surprise, he did none of the things she had begun to imagine in her mind. He did not lean forward to kiss her neck or rub his hands up and down her arms. Rather, he began to untangle her hair, his fingers combing through the knots as he gently massaged her scalp.

She struggled to keep her breathing even, savoring every touch against her scalp and trying to relax as he steadily worked at her tangles.

"Why are you being so kind, Gray? Why, all of a sudden, do you care?" Lea didn't know how else to ask the questions that had been worrying her mind since they had left Bearswillow... The questions that grew and multiplied as they spent more time together and he showed another side of himself that was... more gentle somehow. He continued to untangle her knots in silence, taking his time as he let his fingers trail through every inch of her long hair.

After he finished, he let his arms settle around Lea's waist and pulled her gently against him. She allowed the back of her head to rest against Gray's chest, his warmth seeping through the thin shirt separating them.

"I've lived a long time, Azalea. I've seen a lot of death, much of it at my own hand. You know my magic is dark. You've witnessed it. That darkness has consumed me for as long as I can remember. But what I haven't seen much of, is *life... light.* The palace, the royals living within it—they steal away the light and the good and starve you of everything you need to thrive, leaving a shell that just... survives." Gray took several deep breaths, Lea's body rising and falling with his chest. His voice softened as he began to speak again. "You remind me of the light I used to carry, Little Flower. It's not *sudden* that I care at all, I just... I wanted to keep you away from that place..." He broke off. "I won't let them take that light from you, Azalea."

They continued to lie together, Gray's arms wrapped around her front, her head resting against his chest. They didn't speak for a long time, Gray's fingers running absently along her forearm to the sounds of croaking frogs and dancing crickets, the wind softly carrying their chorus across the camp. Gray lowered them down slowly and turned her toward him to lie against his chest. His breath was warm against her cheek and her heart raced, thumping furiously in an unfamiliar rhythm. Lea knew she should pull away, wasn't sure what this was that was happening between them, but she was unable to, enjoying this new closeness that was forming between them.

She thought of how he had saved her the night the fenrir attacked, then had taken her home and cleaned her wounds. Thought of how he had kept her from going out alone with the fenrir still nearby, how he had kept her locked up to prevent her from ending up precisely where she was. She disagreed with what he had done, but she saw that maybe he truly had been trying to protect her the whole time.

"You don't hate me?" she said after a while. "We can be friends, then?"

"No, Little Flower." He laughed under his breath. "Friendship is not what I want from you. Never, not for a single moment, has it been what I've wanted." As he said the words, he looked down at her. His green eyes met hers as he gave her a look that was anything but friendly. Her breaths became shallow, and her heart pumped impossibly faster. What were these feelings she was having? Ones that didn't make sense in her mind even though her body seemed to constantly fight to be closer to him, her skin singing with each electric zap.

Gray slowly moved his hand from her waist where it rested and dragged it lower, over her hip and down her thigh to where his shirt hung. His touch was confident, but questioning, as if sensing her hesitation. His eyes stared straight into hers, asking for permission. Lea allowed her body to overtake her mind as she closed her eyes and gave in, arching into his touch when she felt his palm move against her skin.

She felt his stare burning into her face as he drew small circles on her thigh with his fingers, slowly tracing upwards. When he reached where his shirt laid against her leg, he pushed his hand underneath and flattened his hand over her thigh, slowly dragging it back upward. "You're even softer than you felt in my dream last night."

The air left her lungs at his words, leaving her speechless. She felt him trace along the outside of her leg, a tingle spreading beneath her skin as he moved higher, now rubbing over the outside of her hip, thumb tracing along her hipbone as it rose. He didn't stray from the straight line up the side of her leg, but she could feel his touch in every inch of her body as his hand reached her waist.

She was bare beneath the shirt. His fingers resumed the small circles that he had been drawing on her leg, and Lea arched toward him, pressing her breasts against his chest. Her body was not her own, her movement out of her control. Gray groaned as his fingers pressed into her lower back, pulling her even closer. He ran his hand back down her leg, slowly, before he pulled it across him, her knee hooking around his hip. She could feel his impressive length pressing against her, and she rolled her hips involuntarily, shocked at her own boldness. She'd never done more than kiss a man, and none of those kisses had felt anything like this. A rough growl left his throat as she rocked into him once more.

His hand found her hip, pulling her harder against him. Lea moaned as Gray slid one hand beneath her shirt and slowly raised it to rest against the side of her ribs, just underneath her breast.

He dipped his head toward her neck. "When I saw you at the market, you were walking along with your eyes in the sky instead of the world around you, and you just looked so beautiful, so vibrant. My magic called me to you." He sent a small zap through his fingers, now running back and forth across her ribs. "I hadn't seen someone look so bright in a long time, and I knew right then that I had to keep everything dark in this world away from you."

"Were you following me? That day the soldier..."

His hand rose higher, and Lea's breath hitched. "I've followed you many times. From the moment I saw you, I needed to protect you. I thought it was just my role as the Commander calling me to protect something good, but then I saw that soldier put his hands on you, and I felt... not jealous, but something darker... possessive... Something that made me want to kill that guard where he stood." His lips began to gently caress her neck, making her body hum. She reached up and threaded her fingers through his hair as she rolled her hips again, the feeling unlike anything she had ever experienced before. His lips traced along her collarbone, not quite kissing, causing shivers to run through her body.

"You have good self-control then," she said breathlessly.

Gray's breath was ragged as his lips found her jaw. "I killed him that night, after the fenrir attack. I would have done it that second, but I didn't want you to have to see it. No one touches you and lives, Little Flower."

His words raced through her mind, but she was unable to process them with his touch starving her brain of oxygen. He continued to drag his lips across her jaw, just under her ear.

"And then you danced that night. Twirled like the brightest comet racing through the sky under the stars that rule my magic, and I couldn't look away. I was so angry that I couldn't come to you. Couldn't take you out into the woods and do wicked things to you under the moon." She groaned. "And I realized that it wasn't just my role as Commander in the army that made me want to protect you, it was something that I needed to do, unlike any need I've ever had before. I'm sorry I've kept you prisoner." He brushed his lips against hers, and she tilted her chin up, seeking more. "I'm sorry I've made your life so difficult." He pushed his hand higher, thumb tracing the curve of the bottom of her breast as he brushed her lips with his again. "And I thought I would be sorry that you are here, after trying to keep you away for so long. But I told you, Azalea, I'm not a good man, and I find myself very," *brush*, "selfishly," *brush*, "not sorry."

Lea arched toward him at the exact moment he brought his face down, and his lips found hers as if he'd wanted nothing more than to taste them for years. His other hand came to the back of her head, pulling her toward him as the hand that had been teasing her skin raised to graze against her nipple. Lea moaned, and her lips parted. Gray slid his tongue into her mouth, claiming her as their kiss grew deeper. Gray growled as she rolled her hips against him again, and he lowered his hand down to her backside and squeezed.

"Still think we're *friends*, Azalea?" he said against her lips, the rumble going straight to her belly.

"Friends can kiss," she whispered back, unsure why she was afraid to admit what was happening between them.

He pressed his hips into her, and she gasped at how hard he felt against her stomach, only separated by the thin trousers he wore. "My cock doesn't get this hard for my friends, *Little Flower*."

She moaned as his mouth claimed hers again, this need inside her pulling her closer to him. "*Fuck*," he cursed as she continued rocking herself against him, chasing toward... *something*.

"Have you been with a man before, Azalea?" he asked her, and she shook her head as he continued to palm her breast with a wicked look in his eye. "How is that possible?" He breathed out the words. "Do you want me to stop?" he asked.

Lea thought about his question. She knew that if she said yes, he would listen. He would stop what he was doing, stop making her feel this way, and they would continue on as they had before. But that wasn't what she wanted.

"Please, don't," she panted. He pushed her down so that she was lying on her back and crawled over her, devouring her mouth as she writhed beneath him.

"So polite tonight. Where were these manners when I met you? Or in any of the moments since?" he said as his lips dipped to the hollow of her throat. The hand squeezing her breast lowered, slowly moving down to her belly button, then between her legs. She parted for him, her body instinctively reacting to his touch.

She lifted her hips toward his hand as he slid a finger through her wet folds. "Fuck Lea, so ready for me." He lifted his head to look into her eyes as he plunged one finger inside her, then stilled. Lea arched against him, her head pushing back into the pillow behind her as he moved his finger in and out.

"More, Gray, I need more." She could barely speak, riding his finger as her hand gripped the bed beneath her.

"Anything for you, Little Flower. I'll do anything." He pulled away his hand, and she felt like the loss might kill her.

"Gray, please..."

He lifted her, quickly pulling her shirt over her head in one swift motion. She watched as his eyes took in her exposed skin, traveling from her breasts down to where his hand returned. He pushed two fingers inside her. "Fuck. You're so beautiful."

Bending over her, he took her right nipple into his mouth, sucking hard as his fingers thrust in and out. Lea's hands found the back of his head as something built inside her. Her breathing became ragged as pressure built within her, foreign but all-encompassing. It filled every inch of her body as he continued to move. "Gray, what's happening? Please, I need more. Oh gods, Gray." Her words became nonsensical, her body writhing as Gray switched his attention to her other breast. He bit down on her nipple at the same time his fingers curved inside her, and Lea felt the pressure inside her burst. Gray captured her mouth with his as her moans became louder, outside of her control. She screamed his name, but he caught it with his tongue as she felt wave after wave of pleasure unlike anything she had ever felt before pulsing through her. His fingers rode her through her climax, and as he removed them, she could feel his warmth in every inch of her skin. Her breathing began to slow as he turned her so that he was spooning her from behind, his erection pressing into her back.

"Fuck being your friend, Lea," he told her gruffly as he kissed the back of her head.

Lea's mind raced, coming down from what they had just done together. She thought of Thomas, the man who loved her, then thought of the man now holding her who had made her feel a passion she'd never even thought of with Thomas. She wasn't sure if she should feel guilt, or just allow herself this small piece of happiness.

As if sensing her thoughts, Gray brushed Lea's hair back from her eyes. "It's okay, Little Flower. Let's just rest now. There's time for overthinking another day." He tucked the covers more firmly around them and pulled her closer. *He's right,* she thought. All her worries could wait until tomorrow. "Goodnight, Gray," she whispered, falling asleep in his arms.

The wind did not come for her that night. She woke sometime later to find Gray gone; the blankets tucked around her firmly to keep out the chill. She lay awake for what felt like hours until the pink light from the beginning of the sunrise peeked through the tent, but Gray did not return.

CHAPTER 18

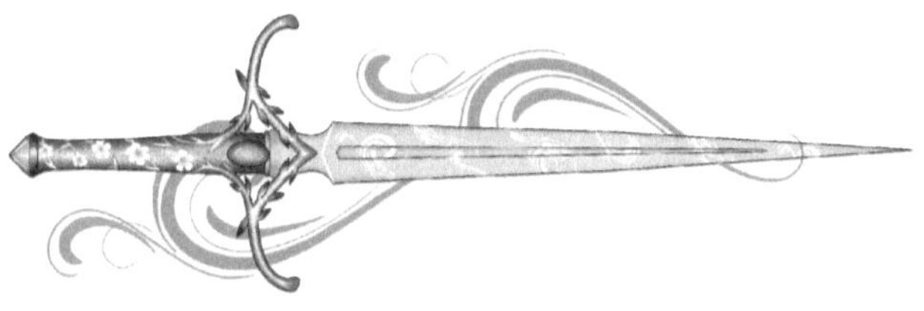

Lea climbed out of bed and dressed, knowing that they would leave before too long and that she would need to be ready. She dressed quickly and walked outside the tent to find Erik sitting by the fire, waiting for her.

"Sunshine! How did you sleep?"

Lea lowered her eyes as heat flushed her face. *He doesn't know anything. He's just asking you how you slept,* she reminded herself. "I slept well, Erik. Thank you. Have you seen Gray this morning?" she asked.

"Gray had some, uh, loose ends to tie up. He should be back shortly, but he asked me to get you fed and bring you to the horses. He'll meet us there." Erik handed her a bowl with thick oatmeal, the same breakfast as yesterday.

"Erik?" she said, stirring her food around in the bowl. He turned to look at her. "Is living in the castle as bad as Gray makes it sound?" She realized she was nervous and that the closer they got to Auropera, the harder the butterflies in her stomach flapped their wings.

Erik took the bowl from her hands and stood, holding out a hand to her. She took it, and they began to walk toward the horses and away from listening ears. "The palace is a beautiful place. Magic courses through every piece of iron and stone holding it together. But it is also a very dangerous place. You'd do well to listen to whatever Gray has told you and just keep your head down. There are…" He paused, thinking of what to say. "There's a restlessness throughout the kingdom right now, Lea; you can feel it in the palace walls. Follow Gray's lead, and you'll be fine. I'll be there to help you, too." He nudged her.

"Will I be able to see Thomas once we're there?" She was glad Erik was there to answer her question because asking Gray after last night felt… unkind, messy.

Erik stopped and turned to her, hesitating as a sort of sadness crossed his face. "If that is what you wish." He touched her arm with a polite smile, then turned back toward the horses. As they approached, she saw Gray brushing Obsidian, speaking to him in words she couldn't hear. Erik cleared his throat as they approached, and Gray turned to him.

"Thanks for bringing her. We'll see you tonight," Gray told him. At his dismissal, Erik nodded and walked toward his own horse.

Lea stood there, clasping and unclasping her hands, avoiding Gray's gaze.

"I made you come once, and now you can't look at me?"

Her eyes jumped up to his. "Quiet!" she somehow shouted and whispered at the same time. His eyes held humor as he approached her.

"I'm sorry I wasn't there when you woke up this morning. I had—"

"Loose ends to tie up," she said, cutting him off. "Erik told me."

He stepped toward her, fingering the braid in her hair. He pulled the tie away, causing it to once again fall loosely around her shoulders. "The brown is fading… I'm glad. It didn't look like you." He reached up to tuck a strand behind her ear.

"Commander." A voice behind them caused Gray to pause as the air shifted around them.

Gray's demeanor changed immediately as he reached forward and picked at a strand of her hair. "Damn bug," he said, swatting at her face before turning. "Prince Alaric. How can I help you?" He bowed his head as he asked, his voice calm as he took a subtle step in front of Lea, partially blocking her from the prince's view.

The prince looked between them, one eyebrow raised. "I'd like to speak with you in private."

Gray turned to her. "Go to Erik and wait for me. You do not take a step away from him, or I will tie your hands together and make you run behind the horse for the rest of the journey." Lea stared at him, hesitating. "Now!" he yelled, causing her to jump. She turned toward Erik and ran to him, her pride bruised. She rubbed at the ache in her chest as she came up behind Erik and tapped him on the shoulder.

"I've been banished. And Gray is back to being an asshole," she told him quietly. Erik turned and looked at Gray, now speaking with the prince. Concern colored his face. "It's not what you think. Come on, help me pack up the horse. I need you to look like I'm telling you what to do. Look down at your feet. I'm going to yell at you now, okay?"

She was becoming more confused by the minute, but Erik hadn't given her any reasons to doubt him so far.

"Okay." She went to pick up a bag when a voice boomed behind her. "What did I tell you?! Get the fucking bag!" he shouted. "Now!"

She jumped, hurrying to grab the bag and bring it over to Erik. "I'm sorry..." he whispered. "Did I say you could look at me?" he shouted again, shoving her aside while apologizing with his eyes.

After another few minutes of terse yelling, whispered apologies from Erik, and rushed packing, Gray joined them. "It's time to leave." He said nothing else as he turned and walked away.

Lea scrambled to keep up with him. "Gray, what was that about? Why are you all yelling at me and pretending you all hate me suddenly?"

"Get on the horse, Azalea," was all he said. He hoisted her up, then followed behind her, sitting so that there were several inches of distance between them. She tried to turn back to look at him, to ask him why he had suddenly turned so cold, but he leaned forward, speaking into her ear.

"Eyes ahead, Azalea. Today, I am the Commander of the Royal Army, and *you* are my prisoner." Lea didn't respond. She didn't have to try to look like a prisoner, because despite what had happened last night, she remembered that she *was* his prisoner. His behavior after the prince's visit reminded her that she did not belong here—with him, or in his world.

They rode through the day, and her body ached. She had not realized as they'd galloped across the landscape with almost a foot of space between them how much his support against her back had helped her in the days before. Lea could feel Gray's frustration and anger bridging the distance between them and spent most of the trip worried about his sudden change in demeanor. She understood she was his prisoner, and that in public, at least, he was doing his duty to bring her to the castle. But why all the anger? Did Gray regret last night? He didn't say a word to her as they continued racing toward the castle, and when they stopped for the evening, he simply helped her down from his horse and walked her over to Erik.

"Watch her," he barked, jabbing a finger in her direction. They stared at each other for several seconds, another one of their silent conversations.

"Gray, please–" Lea's voice shook a bit as she spoke, confusion coloring her words as she searched for what to say.

He turned on his heel and stormed away, not even sparing her a look.

Lea's eyes pricked with tears as she tried to remain calm, remembering that even though Gray had told her he was infatuated with her, she was still his prisoner. She'd known that, seen it time and time again. He would still deliver her to the palace that he worried would steal her soul. His words meant nothing when his actions showed her the truth; she was nothing but property of the Crown. She wasn't sure how she had somehow forgotten those facts.

Her thoughts drifted toward Thomas, who was likely nearing the palace or would be there first thing in the morning. Guilt flooded her, feeling like she had betrayed him for a man who had barely looked at her today. Lea walked with Erik toward the fire but realized that she wasn't hungry.

"Erik, I think I just want to sleep. Do you think you can stand guard outside my tent?" His eyes glanced toward the clouds gathering above their heads, then darted to the woods that Gray had disappeared into. Erik nodded and walked with her to Gray's tent, entering first to make sure that it was safe before allowing her to follow.

"Call out if you need anything," Erik told her before walking out the door.

She dragged her feet over to the pallet, sitting down on the side and placing her head in her hands. The tent seemed smaller suddenly, colder, and she shivered as she pulled a nearby fur around her shoulders. *How had life gotten so hard so quickly?* She walked over to the wooden trunk and pulled her mother's box from the bottom, taking out Thomas's letter and bringing it back to the bed. She read his words again, letting them soothe away the pain she felt from Gray's behavior toward her today.

This was a man who loved her, who would never share a night like she had with Gray, only to ignore her the next day. She laid down and read the words over and over until she fell asleep, holding the pages in her hands.

She opened her eyes to find Gray pulling the covers over her. She sat up, groggy, fumbling around for the letter that had been in her hands before she fell asleep.

"Don't worry, it's back in the box with your mother's things," Gray said tersely, pulling his jacket back on, though she hadn't heard him take it off to begin with. It felt odd, knowing that he'd been in the tent for some time without her knowledge.

"I'm going for a walk," Gray told her, words clipped. He walked toward the front of the tent. "Erik is outside," he spat before storming back through the tent flaps without looking her in the eye.

Lea sat there, stunned. Had he read her letter? Was he actually angry with *her*? He had no right to feel anything toward her at all, let alone anger. She was the only one who deserved to be angry, with him treating her like one of the royal courtesans and then reading her private letter! She wrapped the blanket tighter around her shoulders and stormed outside to where Erik sat, looking for Gray but unable to find him in the dark. Erik looked up at her, standing immediately. "What's wrong, Sunshine?" He reached toward the blade on his hip and looked behind her, scanning the tent.

She folded in on herself as she wrapped her arms tighter around her chest. "Nothing."

Erik lowered one eyebrow and turned to sit by the fire. "Now, I'm big and dumb, but I'm not stupid. You look darker than a rain cloud, Sunshine. What happened?"

"I'm fine," Lea sighed, "but Gray woke me and then stormed out of the tent like I had done something to him. He's treating me like I have the Lonely Death all of a sudden."

Erik motioned her closer to the fire, and she walked to him, sitting down by his side. He placed his arm around her and she leaned into him, grateful for the friendly contact.

"Gray is... complicated, Sunshine. He's too noble for his own good, even though he thinks he carries only darkness inside him. He's stubborn to a fault. You did nothing wrong. This whole situation, it's just... hard on him."

"Hard on *him*? What's *hard* is leaving the only home you've ever known without even getting to say goodbye. What's *hard* is traveling the country with an abnormally large Fae with two completely different personalities that change with the wind! *That* is hard! Why would having me here be hard on him?" Lea placed her head in her hands, exhausted. "I'm not that bad of a roommate, Erik, I swear! I pick up my own socks, and I never steal the covers." Erik patted her hand with a chuckle.

At least he appreciates my attempt at humor, she thought bitterly.

"Just let it pass. I'm sure he'll be back to fighting with you soon enough, and you'll wish for a quiet moment alone with me." She smacked him on the arm but scooted closer to him, happy to have some company other than her racing thoughts. They remained seated around the fire for what felt like hours, not speaking, staring at the flames before them.

Gray eventually walked back into the camp, stopping when his eyes found Lea seated next to Erik. He nodded to Erik, then turned toward Lea.

"We still have a few hours until sunrise, if you'd like to rest. We'll arrive at the palace tomorrow, and I'd prefer you to not be exhausted when we get there. You'll need to be alert and ready."

"Ready for..."

"Anything, Azalea. Ready for anything." He continued to stand there, waiting for an answer.

"Give me something here, Gray. What dangers am I going to face that seem to have you so worried that you can't even look at me?" Her voice cracked, the words sounding far more vulnerable than she had intended.

He raised his head, looking her directly in the eye. "Please. Let's just rest. There is time for answers another day." His face looked like stone, and she noticed shadows bruising under his eyes.

"Okay," she conceded, her shoulders slumping in a mixture of exhaustion and defeat. "I'll rest." She pushed up from the log to stand and patted Erik on the shoulder before leaning down and speaking into his ear. "Thank you."

She followed Gray into the tent and watched as he undressed, leaving his shirt on this time. *Is he honestly ignoring me?* Irritation flitted across her features. He had been cruel, and she had hated him only days before. But now, he was acting as if she was the one who had done something wrong, and Lea found that it bothered her.

"I'm not sure what I did, but... I'm sorry. I can tell you're upset with me." Lea wasn't sure what she was apologizing for, but she wasn't sure how else to fix what was going on with him.

Gray didn't respond, making a point to avoid her eyes.

"I don't know why I even care if you are," she confessed quietly.

He continued to get ready for bed with his back toward her. "I'm not angry with you, Azalea. Let's just go to sleep."

"I just... I don't understand. Was it the other night? Because—"

"The other night was nothing but a mistake," he said, cutting her off. "Something that I should never have let happen." He finally looked at her, his expression closer to pity than she wanted to admit, and her heart sank, a dull ache blooming in her chest.

Of course, he regretted the other night. Their kiss, their... Dammit! Lea cursed herself. She was foolish to think that a Fae, let alone the Commander of the Royal Army, could ever possibly be interested in her. Hadn't he said it himself? *Spoiled. Unloveable.* Tears filled her eyes as she sank down onto the bed.

"Okay, you don't have to say anything else, then."

"Azalea, I warned you; I'm not a good man, but I'm trying to be with you, right now. After tomorrow you can forget all about me. I want you to forget all about me... make a new life in Auropera with someone who *is* good. Someone who can love you like you deserve to be loved. Someone who is already waiting for you. I'm just not capable of that; fate has different plans for me."

Fate? Did he expect her to believe that it was fate that was causing him to toss her aside now that he got what he wanted from her? No. This was all an excuse to get rid of any feelings she might have for him before they got to the palace. "Please, please, just stop talking. I'm fine, just... stop." Her voice came out choked, and her eyes burned with tears she refused to shed as the pain in her chest grew breathtakingly painful. She'd known this man for five days, he owed her nothing. It wasn't as if she had loved him, or even liked him all that much for that matter, but the rejection still stung. It was just another hurt to add to her list.

She could feel Gray staring at her, swore that she could feel his need to reach out and comfort her, but he did as she had asked. He climbed into bed, facing her back, as they both laid awake in silence.

CHAPTER 19

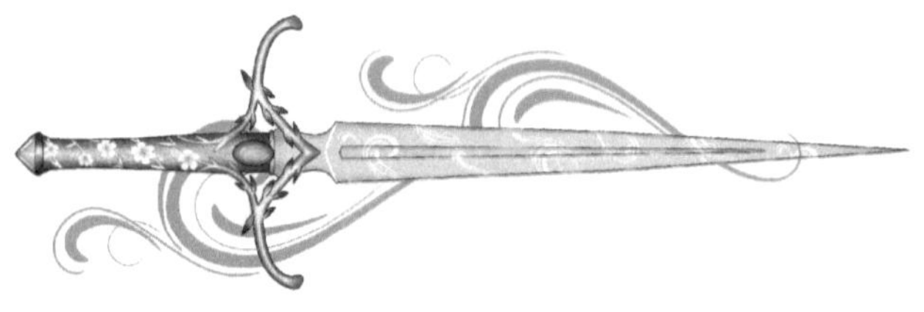

Lea had a feeling neither of them slept after that. She kept her eyes closed but could feel Gray's restless energy behind her, along with the burn in her chest that was telling her to roll over and talk to him, make things right. As the sun rose above the horizon, Gray wordlessly stood and dressed, pausing with a lingering look before silently leaving her behind in the tent.

Only then did Lea let the tears fall from her tired eyes, alone in the bed. Just for a few moments, before rising and squaring her shoulders as she began getting ready to face her last day with Commander Gray.

She braided her hair once again, and after dressing, went outside and found Erik. She walked over and sat by him as he wordlessly made her a bowl of oatmeal for breakfast. He handed it to her, then patted her hand and sat back. She ate in silence, trying unsuccessfully to keep her eyes from scanning the camp for Gray, but finding only smaller, unremarkable soldiers who blended into one another as they ate their breakfast and chatted quietly with one another.

Once the soldiers around her rose, beginning the musicless dance they performed each morning as the sunrise approached, Erik helped her up and walked her over to where Gray stood next to Obsidian. Lea walked to the horse, patting his mane and scratching his nose.

"You still like me, right, boy? I don't know what you like about that owner of yours... You should buck him off into the mud, I think." The horse whinnied as if laughing at the same time Erik leaned over to say something to Gray, his concerned eyes flicking over to her before walking away. Gray bowed his head and took a deep breath before tightening the strap on the horse. He turned toward her, hands fisted at his sides.

"This will all be over soon," he said as he reached out to her to help her onto Obsidian, but she walked past him, not wanting to accept his help. She somehow got her foot into the stirrup and, grabbing Obsidian's mane, pulled herself up onto the giant horse, her biceps screaming in protest as she used all her strength to haul her small body into the saddle. Lea was confident that it had not looked graceful, but she had done it on her own, and that was enough.

She scooted forward into the saddle and waited for Gray to hop up behind her. He did so wordlessly and remained several inches away from her as he had the day before. He effortlessly guided Obsidian into the line of soldiers waiting for the magic of dawn to pass through them, their signal to resume their gallop toward the palace.

The silence between them felt like another person, something tangible that couldn't be ignored.

"I know you don't understand, Azalea. But you're going to find happiness. We'll be at the castle by midday, and then I'll leave you be. You'll be my prisoner no longer."

Lea let the words brush past her ears, refusing to let them into her body. She ignored him, feeling confident that even if he kept his word and stayed away once they were within the palace walls, she would never forget how alive he had made her feel as he'd touched her, and how unwanted he had made her feel the very next morning. Magic rushed through them then, and the horses began to run. The breeze on her face calmed her, her hands in Obsidian's mane and her hair remaining tightly inside her braid.

The closer they got to Auropera, the more nervous she became. What would happen once she was there? What would happen once they realized she was not a healer, that she was nothing more than an ordinary human? And was it her imagination, or did Gray seem more restless today? He gripped the reins tighter and sat more upright, head swiveling side to side as he searched for something... or someone? She could feel the tension rolling off of him and into her, and if it didn't stop, she thought her heart might explode in her chest. His emotions were drowning her, radiating off of his skin and dancing across hers along with the electric current his touch caused, and it wasn't helping calm her nerves in the slightest.

Suddenly, the horses turned to the left as one, as if they had trod this path a hundred times and knew the way home on their own. As they descended a hill, she saw a massive stone wall at least a hundred feet tall towering in the distance, a large sandstone castle peeking out from the top of it. Around them, farmland stretched in every direction, with small cottages, cattle, and fields of vegetables dotting the landscape. Her hands itched to dig into those fields, feel the roots of the vegetables and hear the buzz of the bees. She felt her fingers warming at the thought.

As the farmland turned into cobblestone roads, the homes began to multiply and cluster closer together.

"The houses are so close to one another." Lea broke the silence. "How does the Lonely Death not spread?"

Commander Gray stiffened. "There is no Lonely Death here, Azalea. You're safe from that, at least."

As the clop of hooves sounded throughout the street, Lea noticed doors and windows opening. Men and women, all fae, were walking outside to watch the cavalcade pass. Some waved while others peeked from behind their curtains. The women were beautiful, wearing flowy dresses in earth tones with flowers woven into their hair or around their necks and wrists as jewelry. Their beauty was soft, directly contrasting the fierce and sharp features of the men mixed among them. Many bowed at the waist as they watched them pass, a few nodding to Gray behind her when they rose.

As they continued cantering through the streets, Lea observed the homes, noticing that on many of the doors were beautiful jewel-toned designs painted around the handles and across the top and bottom of their entryways. On their thresholds between the grass of their gardens and their front doors were dozens of flower petals scattered in a line while numerous herbs hung above windows. She was looking at one particularly beautiful door painted a vibrant purple with black, white, and rose pink designs when Obsidian suddenly stopped, causing her to lurch forward. Gray grabbed her before she could tumble off the horse, and pulled her upright, holding her for just a second too long against his hard chest before scooting backward in the saddle again.

"We're here, Little Flower," he said in her ear, almost sadly, pulling her braid gently to lift her head up toward the gates in front of them. His touch did not last long, but she felt its loss acutely as she took in the enormous wooden portcullis that waited before them. There were six guards, three on each side, that stood in front of them, waiting to open the door. The horses behind them parted as a honey-blonde horse with a snow-white mane trotted up the middle, coming to a stop directly beside them. Prince Alaric turned to look at them with a blonde eyebrow raised, his posture erect. A smirk widened across his face as he took in the tension and distance between them. He moved closer as the excessively large door rose, providing her first glimpse into the palace grounds. Hints of grass and a few flowers peeked out from the other side entrance, but that was all she could see between the soldiers now filing past them. The prince leaned over, placing a hand on Commander Gray's shoulder, then turned to look at Lea.

"Beautiful, isn't it, human? I'm sure the Commander here has all sorts of plans for you within these walls." His voice was taunting. "After all, the golden child has not graced our doorstep in quite some time. Interesting that he plans to stay here now, don't you think?" He turned toward Gray, squeezing his shoulder tighter.

"Welcome home, *brother*," he said, before releasing his arm and kicking his horses' sides.

"*Brother...*" Lea froze, the presence sitting behind her suddenly feeling so much darker—more terrifying. She could feel the shadows trying to escape his body in the bright midday sun, the rage rolling off of him making her dizzy. She repeated the word again, louder, testing the feel of it in her mouth. The last several days ran through her head... The army's fear of him, the magic he'd shown when Erik had taken her from the cottage that day, wilder than anything she'd ever witnessed... His promise that his word held weight with the royal family. *How did I miss this?*

"Yes, Little Flower." His voice sent shivers down her spine, suddenly sounding deeper, more powerful as he leaned his head down to speak in her ear. A sharp current of electricity ran from where his breath touched her neck down her arms. "Within those walls, I am not Commander Gray..." he said, every rumble from his throat calling the clouds to close in on the sun. "I am Evander Nestruir, youngest son to the King of Desia, and the Prince of the Night."

CHAPTER 20

The Commander—*was he still the Commander if he was also a prince?*—clicked his tongue and Obsidian once again began trotting forward toward the doors of the palace, leaving her and the stranger sitting behind her to follow Alaric under the ancient stone archway, toward the complete and utter unknown.

Brother. The word echoed around in her mind, complete nonsense. *Brother.* Brother to the Crown Prince. The youngest son of the Black King. The man she had spent the last five days with, *the Night Prince.* Her breaths became shallow as she tried to remain upright on the horse, scrambling forward as if increasing the space between them might cause her urge to vomit to lessen.

"Stay calm, Little Flower. You need to breathe," Gray told her. No. Not Gray. He was Evander. His voice was suddenly darker, more powerful... or was it just her imagination?

"I need to get off, I need—" she began to hyperventilate, bracing herself forward on the horse as her breaths wheezed in and out of her lungs. She tried to focus on the warmth of Obsidian's neck under her hands, how smooth his hair was between her fingers. Ahead of her, Prince Alaric was looking back at them, watching with an arrogant smirk as she struggled to breathe before turning back and spurring his horse to go faster toward the front of the castle.

"Breathe slowly; you are safe. I am still Gray. Still the same man you've been with for the last five days. Breathe, Lea."

The same man? How could he say that, when in reality, he was the youngest son of the Black King? No, she didn't know the man behind her at all. Unable to speak, Lea closed her eyes and tried to focus on slowing her heart rate enough to not faint or fall off the horse. Evander reached around her and dipped his hand below the neckline of her shirt, and Lea immediately jumped away, swatting at his hand in a panic.

"Calm down," he told her gruffly, pulling the necklace from underneath her shirt and bringing her other hand up to hold it. He placed the jasper charm between her thumb and the base of her first finger, and she rubbed them without a thought. It was as if the stone was calling to her.

She breathed in slowly through her nose and out through her mouth while focusing on the cool stone in her hand. She felt Evander place his palm on her shoulder, felt him breathing in cadence with her as her pulse slowed. His energy pushed into her chest and surrounded her lungs, forcing them to open wider and contract back more slowly. *He's just Gray, just Gray*, she thought with each breath, knowing in her soul that it wasn't true but choosing to believe it anyway.

She kept her eyes closed and her breaths steady until she felt the horse stop and Evander remove his hand from her shoulder while sliding off behind her. A moment later, a hand reached out to her. She allowed that hand to help her down, realizing that there was no jolt of electricity at the touch. She opened her eyes to find that it wasn't Evander, but Erik, who stood before her, an apologetic look across his usually cheerful face as he turned her toward the entrance to the palace and started walking her toward it.

She watched Gray's—No, *Evander's* back as he disappeared through the large stone archway covered in ivy, shadows curling along his hands in the middle of the day. It looked like he was sucking the light out of the air around him as he stormed away, fury rolling off his broad shoulders. *Evander, the Night Prince.* She was in shock, like she couldn't feel her feet that were somehow moving forward underneath her.

"Come on, Sunshine. The hard part is almost over." He led her toward the entrance; giant, ornate iron structures set into two large wooden doors. The doors parted before them as they walked forward, and Erik continued to guide her inside.

"You knew," she said quietly, stating the fact rather than asking it as a question. She knew Erik was loyal to Evander, but she felt hurt that he had not warned her.

"I know you're upset, but we can't discuss this now. You'll be going to meet the prince and king for them to decide your placement within the castle. It will be the last part of your sentencing. I need you to listen to me, Sunshine. This is the most important conversation you will have for the rest of your life. The Black King is not a kind man, but he will not see you as important enough to make you suffer under his hand. He will likely dismiss you quickly and forget you ever graced his office. The prince's behavior will be determined by yours. Act passive, respectful—do not challenge him. You do not want him to focus on you, Lea."

Lea tried to keep up with all that he was telling her, but she couldn't help but feel a sense of foreboding as he walked her through the winding hallways. "Do not mention Thomas, and do not mention Gray. Remember, you were our prisoner on this journey and nothing more." He stopped before a large wooden door, at least eight feet tall with an X etched into the stone arch surrounding it. He turned to look at her, nodding as if sending her strength, then knocked on the door in front of him.

Rather quickly, a soldier opened the door and greeted Erik, allowing them entrance. She looked around to see a large room with floor-to-ceiling bookcases with very few books lining their shelves, surrounding an enormous wooden table. It had six wooden chairs, all focused around the side farthest from the door, a map spread out in between them.

"His Majesty and the Crown Prince will be along shortly. Please, make yourselves comfortable." The soldier closed the door behind him as he left the room. Lea stepped forward to sit in the closest chair, but Erik shot his arm forward, stopping her. He placed his hands in front of him and stepped backward to move out of the way of the entrance. Lea remained beside him with her eyes downcast, taking deep, slow breaths and trying not to vomit all over the ornate tile floor.

The door opened and Erik immediately dropped to one knee, pulling Lea down so that her kneecaps crashed into the floor. She winced at the bite of pain that ran up her legs. She bowed her head and listened as she heard the click of several pairs of boots along the tile. "Erik, you may rise." She felt Erik stand beside her and heard him take a step forward.

"Your Majesties. I have the prisoner, Azalea Astrantia, before you, charged with hiding knowledge of magic from the Crown. We found she has healing abilities she may be unaware of, and that she could be of benefit to the palace healers." He stepped back to stand next to her once again.

"You may stand, Azalea." A deep voice slithered to her ears. His voice sounded wrong, like it did not quite belong to the man before her, but rather, several men whose voices spoke in unison. She rose on shaky legs and stepped forward, lifting her head only high enough to see the Fae who would be determining her fate.

Sitting at the head of the table was a green-eyed, heavyset Fae with dull black hair, ruddy cheeks, and a thick, graying beard. He leaned forward, placing his fingers beneath his chin. Rings adorned each finger, and the crest across his chest told her that he had night magic. "Your Majesty," she curtsied, recognizing him, although barely, from the portraits that hung throughout the kingdom of their strong and mighty ruler, though in the portraits he had looked far stronger and far mightier. Beside him, Prince Alaric sat with the same smirk on his deceptively handsome face. He almost looked kind as he smiled at her, but something hid beneath his eyes that made her wary. She curtsied toward him as well, deeply.

"Prince Alaric, thank you for ensuring my safe journey here. I am grateful for your kindness and forgiveness."

Prince Alaric stood. "I trust your trip was comfortable," he said, walking toward her.

"More than I deserved." She kept her eyes downcast as he walked in a circle around her.

"My brother told me you are a healer. What are your abilities, specifically?"

"I think the Commander may have been mistaken. My mother was gifted in healing, but I've caused more harm than good while tending to the sick. If I healed myself, then I was not aware that I held that ability." The door opened and then slammed behind her. She flinched, her stomach dropping as the room darkened, just a bit.

"Ah, my son. Welcome." The king stood as another man entered. She saw him through her periphery, but she had known who it was before she had set her eyes on him, felt that electrical pulse that Evander sent through her whenever he was close by. She yearned to look at him fully, search his face for what he may be feeling, to see what information she could discover within his sharp, dark features.

"Father. Alaric." He walked toward them, shaking his father's hand and nodding toward his brother.

"It has been months, Evander. Does the army need your guidance so much that you are unable to visit home? Visit your mother?" The king asked him, his strange voice echoing through the chamber as he spoke to Evander like he had forgotten that she was there.

"The unrest in the south was more difficult to control than I had anticipated. It has been dealt with, and I plan on remaining here for the time being." Lea felt his eyes on her as she kept her head down. She felt a caress against her arm, an invisible hand gently touching her, comforting her... A calmness flooded through her that allowed her shoulders to fall slightly. She felt her eyes being pulled in Evander's direction, but she refused to give in, keeping her eyes focused on the king.

"Welcome back, brother. I did not get to spend as much time on the road with you as I would have hoped. You seemed rather preoccupied, what with the prisoner and all. And speaking of said prisoner..." He gestured toward Lea. "We were just discussing the human's punishment." His words were friendly, but the look he sent Evander was taunting. "The human said you lied, that she does not hold any magic and that she would do more harm than good in the infirmary."

Lea's stomach sank at his words. She couldn't stay locked up inside every day. She'd go insane.

Evander turned toward her, somehow urging her to look at him with the intensity of his stare. "Is that what you said?"

She gave in to the feeling of his eyes on her and looked toward him, then the prince, unsure how to answer. "I don't think you lied, Gr...Your Majesty. I just... I don't know how I healed so quickly."

Alaric sighed as if he expected this answer. "If she holds no magic, then I see no value in her working here. She should be made an example of. It's been too long since we've had a public hanging, don't you think, Evander?"

Her breaths became shallow, and pain spread up her neck as if a noose was already tightening around it. "Please, I can try to learn to heal or serve in whatever way Your Majesties see fit. I'm good at growing plants that can be used in medicines and potions," she was rambling and realized that descending into hysterics wouldn't help her convince them to let her live. Slamming her mouth shut, she tried to stop the flow of words that were trying to escape through her teeth.

"It would be foolish to harm her," Evander said. "We already discussed the unrest in the south. The people of Bearswillow love Azalea. I can almost guarantee that there will be an uprising in the village if they find out that we've harmed her."

"And since when do we allow humans to determine our punishments?" Alaric responded angrily, looking pointedly toward Evander.

"And since when do you let the actions of one insignificant human anger you to the point of risking an entire outpost?" Evander retorted.

"She will be executed, as an example." Small flames emerged from Alaric's balled hands, the same bright orange she had seen during the trial.

"Enough," said the king wearily. "Evander is right. Frankly, Alaric, I do not understand why you insisted I be here for this sentencing when I have judges perfectly capable of coming to the same conclusion I have. Bearswillow is an important outpost. We can not risk losing its goodwill. She will remain here. I'm sure we need a servant somewhere within the palace." Prince Alaric turned toward his father.

"So once again, you side with your youngest rather than the heir who will rule this kingdom someday in your stead?"

"It is simply strategy, Alaric. There will be times in your rule that you must use your judgment, overlook some indiscretions for the larger picture." The king looked at her and she was surprised that, rather than looking angry, he just looked tired.

"Will you pledge loyalty to the Crown and serve your position to the best of your abilities?"

Her jaw dropped, and she nodded quickly, unable to form words in her shock.

"Then it is decided," the king said, beginning to stand.

"If you let Evander decide her punishment, then I must insist that the human be his responsibility. I do not wish to see the traitor throughout the halls of the Palace."

Alaric looked directly toward her. "You will work as a maid in Evander's quarters. You will not interact with the royal family or guards in any capacity other than for work. Should I find out that you are breaking this rule, or I find that you are not performing your job to the best of your abilities, I swear I will have you executed. You do not get second chances within these walls. Do you understand?"

The room darkened around them, several of the candles extinguishing at once.

"You expect me to babysit her? I don't have the time for this sort of distraction!" Evander slammed his palms down on the table in front of him so hard that the wood groaned beneath his hands. "I am the Commander of the Royal Army of Desia, the first line of defense to protect this kingdom. I do not have time to supervise the actions of a foolish human, especially one so unfamiliar with our world."

"Then you should have thought more thoroughly before you insisted she had magic and brought her to the Palace," responded the King. "Besides, she is just a maid. You will hardly notice her, if you notice her there at all. We are done here. Erik, show Lea to the servant's quarters and find Elise; inform her of the human's new assignment." He rose and left the room without another word. Lea stood still next to Erik, unsure what the right course of action was.

Evander walked toward Alaric slowly, the candles he passed extinguishing one by one as he walked by, shadows rising up the walls. He walked so close to his brother that his shoulder pressed into Alaric's as he leaned forward to speak into his ear. "You will regret this, *brother. That is what I swear to you.*"

Without a glance in her direction, he turned and stormed out, slamming the door behind him so hard that she felt the reverberations in her feet.

"Get her out of here," Alaric spat. Erik grabbed her arm and quickly began pulling her from the room before the prince spoke again.

"Wait. Human." She stopped, unable to move, the chill of his tone freezing her to the spot. "Nightmares usually come in the dark, when our eyes are closed and we are unsuspecting, unknowing of the threats floating around us. I want you to remember that *I* am of the day. Even when your eyes are wide open, when you're aware of everything around you and the light is illuminating all you can touch, you *still* will not see me coming."

Erik resumed walking and pulled her out the door, closing it firmly behind them. She felt tears pricking the back of her eyes and struggled to keep her breath even as the prince's words rang in her ears. They had only left the room seconds after Evander, but he was nowhere to be seen, every torch within the hallway around them extinguished. Erik stood next to her in the near-black corridor for a moment, allowing her to collect herself before he pulled her to the right and down the staircase. Once they were three flights down, he stopped and turned her to face him.

"I tried, Erik. I kept my head down... Why does he want to punish me?" She was beginning to hyperventilate.

"It's not you he wants to punish." Erik pulled her to him into a fierce hug. "Evander will protect you, sunshine. I *will* protect you. Okay?" He didn't allow her to answer as he walked down one more flight and pushed open a smaller door. "Elise, dear," he called out into the large kitchen. "I have someone for you to meet."

CHAPTER 21

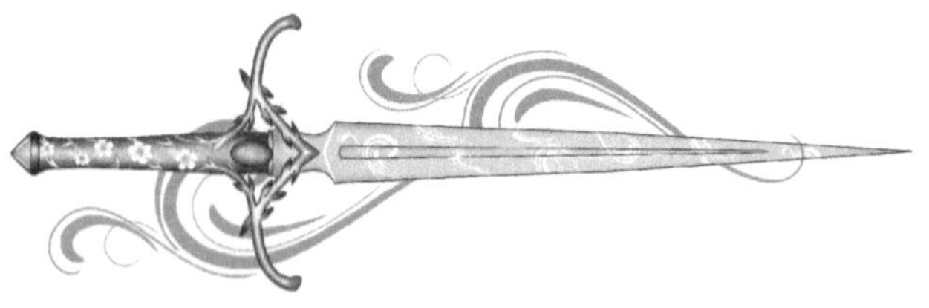

Erik placed his hand on Lea's shoulder and gave her a small push forward into the kitchen toward the Fae woman before her. She was tiny, barely reaching four feet tall, with milky-white skin and graying hair pulled into a high bun with wisps escaping all over. Lea was taken aback by her beauty. She had rosy cheeks, and even at her older age, the only sign of the many years she had lived was the set of laugh lines bracketing her heart-shaped lips. A white uniform swallowed her tiny body with an apron around her waist and a spoon tucked behind her ear. She turned and gave them a broad smile, walking forward briskly and slapping Erik on the arm with the towel in her hand.

"I know for a fact you have been home for at least forty-five minutes, Erik Arthur Andersen, and you wait this long to grace my door? She continued to scold him as she walked to the counter and picked up a silver plate holding what was quite possibly the largest sandwich Lea had ever seen. She walked back toward him and thrust it in his hands, turning around and walking back to the counter immediately. How had she not worn a path through the stone floor with her feet? This woman seemed like she never stopped moving.

"And now you get soggy bread for it. Evander came right away, in a piss poor mood he was, though. Barely even finished his sandwich. Hardly said a word." She pulled out butter and what appeared to be several thick cuts of bacon. "I told him there was no room for his sour mood in my kitchen. It would spoil all the food in here." She assembled a sandwich and walked over to Lea, holding the plate out toward her. Lea gave Erik a questioning look—was this for her?—before raising her arms and taking it from her, muttering a quiet thank you.

Elise stopped moving for the first time since they had entered the kitchen. "Alright then, who is this delicate little thing?"

Erik polished off the rest of his sandwich and licked his fingers. "This here is the reason for Evander's sour mood. Her name is Lea, and she has been assigned as a maid to his wing of the castle. Direct orders from Alaric. Which is why I did not come straight here to give my favorite girl a hug." He set his plate on the counter and lifted the tiny woman into a fierce bear hug, spinning in a circle as she swatted at him affectionately to put her down.

Lea took a bite of her sandwich and actually moaned, realizing how little she had eaten over the past week. "I'm hurt, Erik Arthur," she teased through a mouthful of food. "I thought I was your favorite woman."

"Elise here might as well have raised us, Sunshine. You'll have to be okay with a close second." He winked, then turned back to the short woman.

"She'll need a room assignment and a *lot* of guidance, Elise. Alaric seems to have taken a special interest in her, if you know what I mean." He turned to Lea with a grim look on his face, and she paused her chewing to brace herself for what he would say next. "Are you going to finish that?" he asked her.

"Leave the poor girl alone to eat. She looks as if she's never had a full meal." She pushed Erik backward. "We'll just have to make her blend in. I'll get her a uniform and a bath drawn. She won't be able to clean a thing with all this dirt on her skin. I'll room her with Emma, I think.

No singles at the moment, I'm afraid, dear." Elise rambled on, and Lea wondered how her jaw didn't get tired with words constantly falling out of her mouth.

"Thank you, anywhere is fine," Lea said, then quietly added under her breath, "As long as Emma's not another unknown Prince of Desia."

"She's not!" Elise singsonged over her shoulder.

Lea's eyes darted up in surprise that she'd heard her.

"I am a mother, dearie, and a Fae, after all. You'll have to speak more quietly than that if you don't want me to hear it!" Elise continued bustling around the large kitchen, grabbing supplies from different cabinets. "Finish that sandwich, girl. If Alaric is watching you, then you will have to work twice as hard as the other maids. He's always liked playing with pretty things, hasn't he, Erik?"

Lea turned toward Erik.

"Elise has been here for hundreds of years. She chased us around this very kitchen when we were all boys. You can trust her."

Lea swallowed the last bite of the sandwich with a gulp, surprised at Elise's age. Hundreds of years? How long did the Fae live? Erik took her plate along with his, walking to the sink to wash them.

"He's a good boy, always cleans up after himself," Elise told her, grabbing her arm as she steered her out of the kitchen. "I'm a man, Elise!" he shouted after them. She scoffed. "Men never need to shout that they are men... but boys... anyway, he is still a good one."

As they continued walking, Elise pulled her closer so she could speak into her ear. "There are servant passages I will show you soon, no time for it today, but I tell you this because you should remember, you can not speak freely within these walls. There are very few places within the castle where secrets actually remain secrets. You'd be surprised at the places people can hide here, and with Alaric taking a special interest in you, you'd be wise to be very mindful of what you say and where you say it." She patted her arm. "Emma is a good girl. The prince has never shown interest in her, so do not put her at unnecessary risk by talking with her outside of your dorm if you can help it, but it's safe to do so in your room. There aren't hidden passages within the servant's quarters, so there are fewer opportunities for eavesdropping. They're mostly there for us to remain unseen as we travel within the palace. Here's our first one." They turned and walked into a small alcove Lea had almost missed, then turned a corner. Elise pushed a very narrow door open, and a dark tunnel opened up before them.

"How am I going to remember where to go?" she asked Elise, worried about the prince keeping his promise of executing her if he thought she wasn't doing her job. "What if I get lost and I'm late for work and then he chops off my head?" Lea's stomach dropped. *I can't do this...*

"You'll only need to memorize a few since you will be spending all your working time in Evander's quarters. Try to remain unseen there as well if you can; Evander is a very private man, and he will not enjoy having someone in his space. Normally, we only deep clean when he is away traveling, and do a light tidy when we see he has left his room for the day." They continued to walk down the stone passageway and then turned to take a right that led to a stairwell until they evened out into another hallway lit by torches. No art or tapestries hung on the walls, and she shivered at the cold draft she felt floating down the hallway. They walked to the seventh door on the right and stopped. Elise swiftly knocked.

"Emma dear, it's me." Lea smiled at Elise's motherly tone. The door opened to reveal a small girl standing in the doorway. She was very petite, with light brown skin and brown, curly hair pulled into a loose braid that fell over her shoulder. Her dark brown eyes reminded Lea of black coffee and were full of kindness. She stepped forward and gave Lea a hug. Lea stiffened in surprise, and Emma immediately let go of her, stepping back and beginning to rub the fabric of her skirt between her fingers. "Oh... I'm sorry. I've been told not everyone likes to be touched. You just look so worried." Emma turned her attention to Elise. "Hi, Mom."

Elise is Emma's mom? And she's trusting me to live with her?

Emma hugged Elise in a tight embrace. "Do you have a stray for me, then?" Lea bristled at her words, but then warmed when she turned to look at her new roommate smiling at her.

"She was brought by the Royal Army today. Poor dear hasn't the slightest clue how to be a maid. Let's go inside, shall we?" Emma stepped back and allowed them into the room. The walls were stone like the hallway outside, and two beds sat in the middle, one decorated with a pretty blue quilt that appeared handmade. Little ribbons and charms hung from the bedposts, and a jar of crystals sat on a small table next to the bed. She noticed sketches scattered on the floor to the left of the bed, and she itched to look at what type of things her new roommate liked to draw.

"The prince has taken an interest in her, and she seems dear to Erik. He asked me to help her, and so I am asking you to do the same."

"I'll try not to be too much of a bother." Lea stepped forward. "I'll stay out of your way."

"You could never be a bother. I get lonely in here, actually. I have a hard time turning my brain off after a long day around people, so it will be nice having someone to speak with at night." Emma spoke quietly and appeared genuinely caring. For the first time since stepping into the palace, Lea felt a small sense of relief.

"I'll leave you to acquaint yourselves with each other. Emma, I'm going to draw her a bath. It'll be the first thing you need to learn as a maid, but for tonight, I think you've learned enough." Elise gave her a knowing look. "Dear, can you grab the girl a towel and maybe a change of clothes from Leslie down the hall? They seem about the same size." Elise looked her up and down. "Yes, I think that will do. Bring her to the bathing chamber in about ten minutes. Her things will need to be brought up to the room, so I will need to track that down as well."

Elise left the room, and Lea could hear her continue to speak to herself as she walked down the hallway back toward the staircase they had come from.

"Here, let me help you get ready. You look exhausted. Lea, was it?"

Lea nodded and gave her a small smile as Emma led her over to a wooden chair in front of a mirror, a makeshift vanity. She sat down, her mouth opening in surprise when she looked at her reflection. Dirt caked almost every inch of her skin, and she had lost weight since before the trip. Her eyes were sunken into her tan skin, and her cheeks and lips were chapped from the sun and wind atop the horse. She was grateful that her hair was braided because it was frizzy around her face and matted at the back near the nape of her neck. Emma took the band from her braid, and Lea flashed back to that first day she'd ridden on the horse with Evander. "*Freedom looks good on you*," he had said. *Bullshit*—she'd been a foolish girl to believe him. Emma began to untangle her hair and then went and got some oil from a chest in her room.

The oil smelled heavenly as she pulled the dropper out—rosemary and orange. "This might help with the tangles, but I think you're in for a battle in the bathtub, I'm afraid." She laughed.

Lea thanked her as she left the room to get her a change of clothes. She walked to the window, hoping to see the sun beginning its descent in the sky; *sunset would be in less than an hour*, she guessed. *What would night in the castle be like?* She already missed the sound of the wind outside her window from home, and tears began to prick her eyes.

"It might not be home," Emma said quietly as she ran her hand over the sketchbook next to her, "but there are good people here, Lea. I know you're sad right now, but it *is* possible to be happy here." Emma walked up and placed a hand on her arm. "Maybe we can go to the commons later. You can meet some people. Mom makes us good meals and we play games at night, sometimes go for walks outside when we're certain the royals won't need us again for the evening."

"You mean I don't have to stay in this room when I'm not working?" She felt a fraction more air fill her lungs. "I can have some freedom?"

"Of course, Lea. You'll also get paid for your work here, and we like to go into the village on our days off. If you're able to keep your head down and remain undetected, it's not a terrible life we live here." She offered a reassuring smile. "Come on. Your bath should be ready now."

Emma walked her down the hallway toward the end of the hall, calling out names as she passed doors to tell her who lived within them. She tried to remember, but they all blurred together as they passed room after room. As they neared the end of the hallway, there was one large door to the left and one to the right.

"Our bathing chambers are shared, but the girls use this one here." She gestured to the right. Lea pushed open the door and saw a chamber about twice the size of the bedroom she would share with Emma. It had six wash basins and three large bathtubs inside. There was a fireplace warming the space, as well as a small window that ran horizontally in the middle of the wall to let in more light, but also allow privacy to those inside. The tub in the middle was filled with warm water, soapy bubbles floating on the surface. Lea inhaled deeply, and the smell of jasmine sent a pang of homesickness shooting through her heart.

"Does the window open, Emma?" Lea asked, longing to smell some sort of fresh air.

"No, but the one in our room does. I'll crack it for when you return." She smiled and walked to the tub, placing the change of clothes, a towel, and a washcloth on the floor near it. "You have no responsibilities tonight, so no rush. I'll find you some bedding, and we can go through your duties when you get back. Take your time, Lea. Everyone should be in the commons right now, so no one will bother you at this time of day. Come back whenever you're ready." Emma offered her an encouraging smile as she softly pulled the door closed, leaving her alone in the room.

Lea wasn't expecting the sob that erupted from her throat the moment the door closed behind Emma. They wracked her body as she crumbled to the floor, finally letting go of all the emotions she'd been carrying. The ache in her chest grew as she cried for her mother, the pain especially acute after seeing the love Elise had for Emma. She cried for Thomas and his family, that they had to be apart, and the stress she knew they were feeling about how they would survive without him. She cried for her village, because how could she possibly work on finding the cure to the Lonely Death as a maid hundreds of miles away? And finally, Lea cried for herself—for the crack in her heart from the Commander's rejection and lies, for the danger she was now in with not only one, but two Princes of Desia entangling themselves into her life.

CHAPTER 22

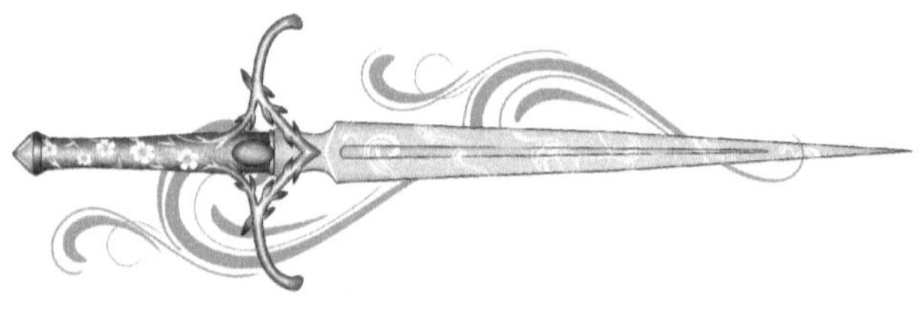

Lea cried until her pain had eased enough to stand again without her legs shaking and found that she was grateful for the unexpected release of emotions. Feeling a bit lighter, she undressed and tried to list all the things she was grateful for in her mind. Stripping bare, she placed her necklace atop her clean pile of clothes, still in her line of sight. She felt more naked without it than without her clothing.

She stepped inside the bathtub and sighed, letting the warm water wash away the chaos of the last twenty-four hours. Even at home, she often just washed in cold water from the well, the effort far too much to heat several buckets full over the fire. She sank into the white clawfoot bathtub. There were small fissures in several places in the porcelain, and she guessed they were old tubs from guest rooms within the palace that were replaced as their beauty cracked.

She grabbed the washcloth and bar of soap, lathering up and taking her time washing the dirt from her body. A lovely-smelling shampoo had been left for her, and she washed her hair twice, grateful for the oil Emma had put in it when the tangles came out in her fingers as she gently ran them through her hair.

"Looks like you didn't need my help on the road after all, Little Flower," a deep voice echoed from the entrance, bouncing through the chamber. Lea jumped, splashing water onto the stone floor. A dark figure stood in the doorway, his silhouette matching that of the rugged Fae she had spent the last week with. He took a step forward out of the darkness, and Lea's heart nearly stopped at the changes she saw in the Fae before her. His face seemed darker, harsher in a way. His strong jaw was accentuated by the silver epaulets now donning his shoulders. He seemed larger, more threatening somehow, though under his harsh exterior, his eyes were soft... wary.

"Evander!" She tried to slump deeper under the water, but was unable to fully submerge her body and legs at the same time. "Get out! You can't be in here!" Trying to move the bubbles to cover herself, Lea let out a string of curses as they popped in front of her.

Evander gave her a wicked grin before his stare locked on her red nose and swollen eyes. His demeanor changed immediately, all signs of playfulness gone as he quickly strode forward, coming to stand next to the bath. "What happened?" his voice was low and held a promise of pain for whoever had caused her sadness.

"I'm fine. It's been an overwhelming week, in case you hadn't noticed," she bit back while scooting lower into the bath. If she hadn't been so sure that Evander's heart was stone cold, she would have wondered if the expression she saw cross his face was guilt. "Can you get out?" she hissed while trying to cover herself more fully with her arms.

"I've seen your body far more intimately than this, Azalea," he said, voice deep and throaty. His eyes remained on her face, though she could somehow feel his attention on every inch of her exposed skin as his hands reached toward her ever so slightly before flexing his fingers and placing them in his pockets.

"I talked with Erik. I needed to make sure you were okay after..." he trailed off, gesturing toward the door.

"After this insignificant human was assigned to your chambers? Or after your brother threatened my life at least three times in a single meeting? Don't worry, I'll stay hidden, Gray, or should I call you *Evander*?" Her words held more venom than she'd intended, but she was too drained from his back and forth, the pain in her chest too nagging and severe for her to bother to correct her tone. She thought she saw hurt in his eyes, but it didn't seem possible that her curt words would be able to break through the armor he had worn around himself since after the night they'd kissed.

"I'm still Gray," he told her quietly. He took a single step closer, his serious expression darkening. "That is who I prefer to be, who I am outside of this place. But yes. Here, I am Evander."

"Any other lies I should be aware of? Like when you said you'd protect me, and now your *brother* seems determined to chop off my head? You lied, Evander. About everything." She sat up slightly in her anger, and Evander's gaze slipped down to her breasts. He took a slow inhale, looking back into her eyes as he let the breath out, a rumble coming from his chest. His hands fisted at his side, darkness pooling around them. Azalea's mind flashed back to the night she'd bathed in the tent, so similar to what was happening now, but so very different. Her body reacted to the memory, heat blooming within her as she recalled the feeling of his touch along her skin, dancing along her legs. She shook her head, lowering her eyebrows in a glare as if trying to prove to him, and herself, that this was not something she could move past.

"You're angry with me. That's for the best." His words were firm, but his voice was sad. Softer than normal, and against her better wishes, Lea yearned to soothe the pain that tinged his face.

Neither of them moved, Evander's deep breaths perfectly matching the rhythm of her own.

"I told you I'm not a good man, Little Flower. You've now met my father, my brother—seen where I come from, who I belong to." He looked down, and his eyes found her necklace lying on top of her clean clothes. He stared at it for several moments and she knew he was taking in the moonflower charm and the magic within it. Stepping away, he crossed the room to look out the window.

"The boy... he is here. Safe. The prince is allowing him to work with our blacksmiths. You may see him whenever you wish." Pain laced his words.

Lea knew he hated Thomas and blamed him for her being here, which was now his own personal problem to deal with. As he spoke, the rumble of magic marking sunset passed through the room. The second the rumble ended, the darkness surrounding Evander grew, encasing his entire being. It looked like smoke but somehow solid at the same time, wispy but so thick it was almost opaque. The fireplace went out as if doused by water, and steam rose from the embers within. The darkness that had outlined him and surrounded his hands reached out toward her, floating through the air as if they were going to wrap around her and hold her prisoner once again. The energy she felt from Evander, that tug within her chest, pulled her toward those shadows, and she lifted a dripping hand toward them, suddenly needing to know how they would feel against her skin.

Evander took an immediate step back, his calm composure slipping with the setting sun. His brow creased, and his jaw clenched as he fought to contain his magic. "I brought your trunk to your room. You should have everything you need. You'll let Elise know if there's anything else." He turned to walk away, taking slow steps. The darkness radiating from him floated in the air, reluctant to leave. The fringes of his shadows became more slender as they stretched and reached toward her, fighting against his retreat, before returning to their master's side. He stopped when he reached the door and placed his hand on the latch, but did not open it as his shoulders rose up and down with controlled, deep breaths. Lea watched a wisp of black smoke float back toward her, the shadows hesitant, as if asking permission before touching her, beginning just below her breasts and slowly sliding upwards.

Lea froze, both fascinated and terrified of the darkness that was calling to something inside her. What was happening? Did the shadows have a mind of their own? Or was Evander controlling their every twist and curl? She felt an electric current, a tingle that traveled across her skin and caused her to arch against the sensation. The darkness ran up her body and across her breast before crossing back toward her sternum and climbing up her throat, pushing her head back to rest against the rim of the tub and forcing her to look at Evander.

"Not everything was a lie, Azalea." With those words, spoken so softly she almost wondered if they had been said at all, Evander left the room, taking his shadows with him.

Lea was left in the dark, unable to see her surroundings or the answers to the questions running through her mind. What was Evander—the name felt odd within her thoughts—trying to do? How could he hate her one moment, insult her and push her away, then make her feel such heat in the next? *And what's wrong with me that I allow him to do it?* Lea sighed and stood, reaching around for her towel and clothes in the darkness.

After dressing, she slipped her necklace back underneath her shirt. Lea walked back to the room, grateful that she remembered which one it was. When she entered, Emma startled her as she ran forward to grab her shoulders and shake her slightly.

"Lea. *Evander* was here. *Prince Evander. The Prince of Desia.*" Lea paused, unsure what to share with her new friend. "You know...the very scary and terrifyingly attractive Fae Prince of the Night known for ripping off heads and kicking small puppies." Lea couldn't tell if Emma was thrilled or terrified as she stood there bouncing on the balls of her feet, hands flapping at her sides. "He brought your trunk. The prince *himself* brought your trunk."

"Trust me, I know he was here, Emma," Lea said, deciding to trust her. She needed an ally, and based on Erik's love for Elise, she had a strong feeling that Emma could be trusted. "You can blame him for the cold, pitch-black bathing chamber."

Emma's jaw dropped so low Lea that could see the pearly white teeth in the back of her mouth. "He came into the bathing chamber!? While you were..." She gestured up and down her body as she blushed, eyes wide.

"Completely naked. Yes, he did." Lea turned and walked over to a hamper and placed her dirty clothes inside. "And, from what I've seen, he only rips off fenrir heads. It's excessive if you ask me." She paused, thinking of Obsidian. "But he actually seems to enjoy animals." She mentally kicked herself at her response. *Why are you defending him?*

"Fenrir? What are you talking about? Prince Evander only leaves his room to attend meetings and swindle food from my mother. I've hardly seen him even take dinner with his own family. I don't think you're understanding... He doesn't care about us. Any of us. But he was here, in this room. And he seemed so conflicted, Lea. Like he's hurting. What happened?"

"Emma, I just spent three days on a horse with him. You said he brought my trunk. It's not a big deal."

"It is literally the biggest deal. Gods, are you really that clueless?" she asked, rocking back and forth.

"I really wish people would stop calling me that," Lea mumbled under her breath.

"Look, I don't know what's going on with you two, but you need to be careful. My mother adores him, and usually, I trust her judgment completely, but there's something dark about him, Lea. He's hiding something. I can *feel* it. Just... be careful, okay?" Emma was genuinely concerned, and despite the fact that Lea had met her only an hour earlier, that worried her. She seemed like the kind of person that could read someone's intentions, see under their exterior and down to their souls somehow.

"He hates me, Emma. I'm sure he just came up here to ensure that there was no joy to be found anywhere around me. There's nothing to worry about other than if I can get his floors clean enough for His Majesty's royal feet. So, how does one... maid?" She smiled with an overly sweet grin, making a point that the discussion was over. "Do I wash his undergarments with soap made of gold or silver?"

"Oh, Lea," Emma sighed. "You can change the subject all you'd like, but a man like that wouldn't allow you two steps into this castle with your head attached to your neck if he hated you." Emma went to sit on her bed and stared at her. She sighed. "You just use lye soap. Only use a little, or it will blister your hands."

They spent what felt like hours discussing her duties as Evander's maid. What supplies to use, what times were best for laundry and such when he was most likely to be in his chambers, and what hours of the day his rooms would most likely be empty for her to enter and clean. In addition to tending to Evander's wing of the Palace, she would help serve meals with Emma in the evenings. Emma told her where the closets were that would hold cleaning materials, fresh linens, and the like.

After Emma had explained what had to be every last detail about being a maid, most of which she forgot in her nervousness, Lea was even more exhausted than after a day atop Obsidian. Emma, noticing her fatigue, turned off the light and climbed into bed, and Lea followed her lead. They didn't talk for a long time, listening to the sounds of the night outside drift in through the open window, very different from those at home. She could hear the trot of hooves on the packed ground pulling wagons around the side of the castle, the chatter of soldiers as they patrolled the grounds—Lea missed the croaking of frogs and the rustling of the wind through the trees.

"Lea? I'm glad you're here," Emma said before turning toward the wall to fall asleep. Tears once again stung the back of her eyes, and she was unable to answer, but Lea somehow knew Emma didn't expect her to.

So much had changed, and none of it was within her control. For the first time, as she listened to the whistling breeze, she hoped the whispers might come and tell her what to do, to give her some direction. But all she could hear as she closed her eyes was the violent rumble of familiar thunder in the distance.

CHAPTER 23

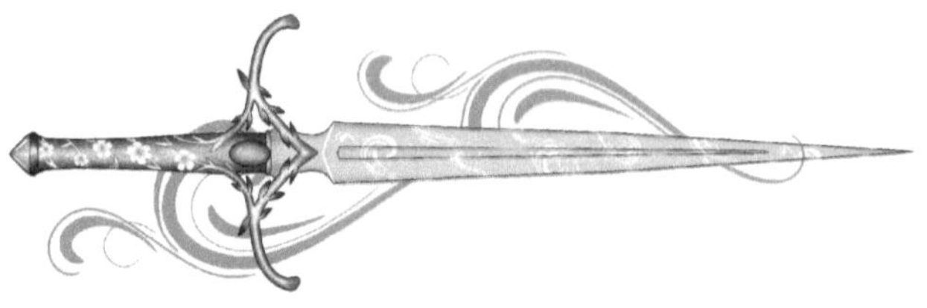

Lea woke with the morning magic to find Emma already dressed and bathed, her brown hair plaited into a simple braid down her back. She gave her a small smile.

"Good morning, Lea. Are you ready for your first day?" She stood from the vanity and walked to the small closet. "Mom brought your uniform this morning." She handed over a bundle of clothing before stepping back and placing her hands on her hips.

"Head down, do your job, and come back here before supper to serve the royal family's meal with me."

"Sir, yes sir," she saluted Emma with a smile. Emma turned to walk toward the door, then paused, and Lea wondered what she had forgotten.

"Oh, and Lea?" She turned. "When I open this door, you will see that there is a very handsome man standing outside it waiting for you. Tonight, you must tell me all your secrets." She winked at her, then opened the door to show Thomas leaning against the opposite wall, wringing his hands and shifting side to side. His clothes were clean, nicer than the ones he wore back in Bearswillow, and Lea was pleased to see that his skin looked less sallow than it had at the trial, his cheekbones less prominent. He stood up immediately when the door opened, allowing

Emma to leave before crossing into the room and pulling her into a tight embrace.

"Lea, I've been so worried about you." His words were muffled as he spoke into her hair. She wrapped her arms around him and pressed her face into his chest, the familiarity of his embrace pulling sobs from her throat. "I hate that you're here, Lea, but I'm so glad to see you." He pushed her back to arm's length, looking her up and down.

"You're okay, right? Are you? Why are you crying, Lea? Did he hurt you?"

Lea laughed through the sobs. "I just, I didn't realize how much I needed to see you. You're alive. Thomas. We're here, we're safe."

Thomas pulled her back toward him and onto the bed, laying back and allowing her to curl into his side. His hands remained on her body, running through her hair and down her arms as if he needed to prove to himself that she wasn't a figment of his imagination.

"I thought you'd be angry with me. You wouldn't even look at me at the trial," she said softly, still trying to control the sobs that were threatening to erupt in her relief at seeing him.

"I *was* angry with you. I was so furious I couldn't see straight, couldn't speak. For two days, I was shaking with the need to get the anger out of me after that damn trial. I thought it might swallow me whole. But, I told you in that letter," he tipped her head up toward him, looking at her with a love so clear in his eyes she hated herself for missing it before. "I love you. With every breath, I love you. And because of you, I'm alive, and with every breath I get to take, I will love you. You gave us a chance at a life together, Lea. I'm selfish for being happy that you're with me right now, I know that, but if anything good has come out of this, it's that I was finally brave enough to tell you how I feel. You finally know." He stared at her, his face now so close to hers she could feel his breath across her cheek.

"We can have a life together, Lea." And with those whispered words, he kissed her, softly, less desperately than he had in the tent. It felt slow and unhurried, as if they would have their entire lives to explore each other's lips. Lea hesitated for only the briefest of seconds, remembering the fire that had burned within her at Evander's touch. She quickly pushed those thoughts from her mind and returned the kiss, reaching for the hand now cupping her face and twining her fingers with his. He continued to kiss her for only a few more moments before a knock sounded at the door.

They jumped apart as the door opened. Elise immediately walking inside, already talking.

"I thought you might want a bit of breakfast and that maybe I could help you with your uniform before I show you Prince Evander's quarters. I was sure I'd see you out with Emma by now..." She trailed off as her eyes took in the scene before her: Lea's tear-streaked face and swollen eyes and lips, Thomas's ragged breaths and mussed hair.

"I see then..." She didn't seem angry, but rather, confused as her eyes continued to bounce between them. "I'll advise you to not let either prince see you like this... for both of your safeties." Thomas stood and gave Lea a quick kiss on the head before walking toward the door.

"I need to get to the workshop, anyway. Can't be late my first week on the job." He looked back at her once more, a shy smile crossing his face. "I'll find you later," he said, with a lingering look before turning and walking away.

Elise walked to the door and shut it quietly, then pulled Lea to the chair to help her brush her hair and braid it in the style most of the servants wore. The silence between them was suffocating as Elise stood and silently handed her the uniform. So... she *could* stop talking then. Was there a rule she'd broken about kissing boys in her room or something?

Lea stripped and began donning the outfit, a floor-length petticoat and skirt over a long-sleeved, canvas material shirt with a corset Elise tied for her that pushed her breasts up toward her chin. Every article of clothing down to her apron and undergarments was a pristine white, and she wondered how she was to keep it all clean as she was... well... cleaning.

"Elise, I feel like I need to tell you that you didn't find me kissing some random boy on my first day here. I've known Thomas my whole life. He's the entire reason that I am at the palace in the first place."

"It's not my business how you spend your time, dear. I only hope you think through what you're doing. Evander isn't leaving again with the Royal Army… This is the first time he has planned to stay in this castle for more than a few days in years. I have a feeling that has something to do with you. Just be careful. He is a good man, despite what he thinks of himself, but his temper is renowned for a reason, and even the most stubborn hearts can be broken, Lea. Now, come."

Without allowing Lea to reply, she began walking from the room and down the corridor, turning left at a different alcove than the one she had come through the previous evening and continuing down a similar staircase. As they twisted and turned through different doors and hallways, Lea felt wholly confident that she would never find her way back to her rooms ever again.

After what felt like several minutes of walking through a maze, they entered the main hallway. Tapestries with fraying edges lined the halls to one side and large floor-to-ceiling windows spanned the other. She followed Elise until they turned and went under a large archway that led down another set of steps. When the steps ended, she stepped out into one final hallway, a dead end with four doors to each side and a large door at the very end of the hallway. Energy pulsed from the room. She felt a pull from deep inside her stomach, that familiar electricity that passed through her each time Evander was around. *He's in that room*, she thought with a shiver.

Lea tore her eyes from the door to look around the hallway and saw paintings hanging on nearly every inch of the stone walls. Different scenes of night sat within the frames: constellations, phases of the moon, and sunsets. She turned in a circle, taking in each piece and the way they all seemed to sing to her.

"These two rooms on each side are guest quarters for when Prince Evander is entertaining. The door to the end of the hallway is the master suite, which has his bedchamber, washroom, sitting room, and a large study. The door to the right is another entrance to his study, which is to remain locked at all times. The door to the left is the princess's quarters—bedroom, bathing chamber, sitting room, and closet, should Evander ever take a wife." Lea felt a flash of jealousy at the word, a warmth in her cheeks and the back of her neck as she remembered the night they'd spent together. *Stop being silly. He's not Gray. Not the same man you thought he was that night.*

Elise continued to speak quickly as she ticked off the things Lea needed to know–what to dust and which floors to scrub, that the linens should be changed daily in each bedroom even if the room was vacant. Lea tried to listen to her words but was unable to take them in as she looked back at the large door at the end of the corridor, the energy from inside growing stronger.

"That should be it then," Elise interrupted her thoughts. "If I were you, I would start at these rooms at the end here. Evander is likely still sleeping or taking his coffee on the balcony at this hour. Come find me should you need anything." She turned and walked away, speaking to herself about the next task on her list, which appeared to be finding Erik to tell him to stop sneaking butter rolls.

Lea turned, walking to the nearest door, hoping to look inside and take inventory of what she would need, only to find it locked. She walked across the hall, testing the knob of the door opposite the one she had just tried. It remained firmly closed. She went through each door one by one. She could not enter any of the rooms, and no one had mentioned that she would need a key. She pointedly avoided the door at the end of the hall that was still calling for her to enter.

Unable to access any of the rooms and unwilling to begin with Evander's personal chambers, she decided to start by mopping the floor of the hallway. Walking to the cleaning closet outside of Evander's hallway, Lea grabbed a mop and bucket, along with some soap. *Shit*, she'd need water, of course... but where could she find some?

Lea turned and noticed a man walking down the hallway outside the door.

"Excuse me!" she called out to him, stepping back into the hallway. The man turned to face her, his eyebrows raising as he took in her long, blonde hair. "Can I help you..."

"Lea," she answered, giving him her biggest smile. "I know you're probably busy, but can you show me where I can get some water? Or just tell me, if you don't have time?"

He walked toward her, offering her his hand. "I'm Joshua. Let me grab the water for you. You're far too beautiful to be lugging a bucket of water all the way from the spigot."

"I really don't mind doing it," she replied, not used to this kind of attention from men.

"Nonsense. Where should I bring it when I'm done?" he asked kindly. Deciding not to fight him, she told him to bring it to Prince Evander's wing, then returned to his hallway with arms full of soaps, towels, and brushes. She laid the supplies out on the floor as she waited for the water.

Walking over to the largest painting, she became engrossed in a picture of a night sky with stars shining above a range of mountains that reminded her of home. The mountains were smoother, not quite so jagged and sharp, but she still closed her eyes and pretended she was looking at the pointed cliffs that surrounded her village. She thought of the sound of the birds chirping, the trickle of the water in the stream from the melting snow and ice atop its peaks.

A door slammed. "And here I was worried you'd work yourself to the bone to avoid execution..." the voice trailed off. Suddenly, suffocating energy filled the hall and Lea's head snapped up to see Evander locking his door. Her face warmed immediately, and she cursed her body at its reaction to seeing him. He looked... gorgeous. Terrifying and *Royal*.

Dammit, heart, he's an asshole! She cursed to herself before taking a deep breath and opening her mouth to speak.

"Um. I'm just waiting for some water. The doors are all locked, and I didn't have a key, so..." She felt more uncomfortable in his presence in the light of day, unable to hide her emotions in darkness. He took in her appearance, his eyes darkening. She stepped back, unsure what she had done to anger him so quickly as he approached her.

"You've been crying again," his voice held none of the teasing it had only moments before. He reached up and touched the skin beneath her eyes. *Zap.* His electricity caused her heart to kick into a faster rhythm, and he let his hand drop to her arm. *Zap.* His eyes went tight as he searched her face. "Lea, who—"

"Well, this certainly isn't the kind of hard work I implied when I assigned you to my brother's rooms. I didn't assign her as your personal whore, Evander."

Evander and Lea both looked up to see Alaric leaning against the stone entryway. Evander's eyes flicked back to her briefly before walking forward unhurriedly.

"You'll not disrespect my staff that way, Alaric. Why are you in my quarters, anyway? I believe your balls had not yet descended the last time you entered these slums." His tone seemed unbothered, but the tension rolling off him showed both Lea and Alaric that the Crown Prince's words had done as he'd intended.

Alaric gestured behind him, and Lea saw Joshua step forward, buckets in hand.

"I found Joshua here outside fetching water. Odd, since his duties include maintaining the Royal stables... He told me a pretty blonde girl needed his help, and he'd offered it." Joshua set down the bucket and looked at her, sending her an apology with his eyes that he could not say aloud.

The prince looked between Lea and Evander. "I think a lesson is in order." He strode toward her, hands igniting with fire. "That you are a servant." He said the word as if there were nothing more vile. "A human." She stood corrected. "That you cannot bat your eyes and ask others to perform the duties that I have assigned *you*!" The heat radiating off his hands caused her to break out in a sweat, her blood warming to near boiling in her veins. She took an involuntary step back, but before Alaric could make another move toward her, Evander stepped in front of her, pushing her behind him.

"Interesting, brother." Alaric took another step forward, raising his burning hands toward them both.

"Douse your flames, *brother*," he spat the word back at him. "She is mine to punish—my responsibility, as you decided yesterday. You'll not lay a single finger on what is mine, or tonight, as you sleep, I will burn you from the inside out. All I need is the smallest gap... A keyhole, a crack in the wood." Evander seemed to grow taller before her eyes. "You've seen me do it before," he taunted, shadows dancing along his fisted knuckles. "Or do you not remember?"

The silence stretched on between them as if they were both sharing a memory that was better left forgotten. Alaric turned and flicked his wrist. Lea flinched as Evander stepped forward, only to see that Alaric had directed his magic toward Joshua, the arm closest to them now engulfed in flames. He screamed, shaking his arm as if he could flick the fire away, but it only caused it to spread further up his sleeve. Lea smelled burning flesh and closed her eyes against the sight of him screaming in pain, her throat filling with bile as she tried to block out the horror in front of her. Joshua plunged his arm into the bucket of water, the flames dying off but the pain remaining, clear as day on his face. He pulled his arm back from the water, and burns encircled his arm from his hands to just above his elbow, charred black skin with areas of white showing, likely the bones of his fingers.

Alaric looked at Lea. "Next time, you perform your own duties. Anyone I find assisting you will meet a worse fate than this." He looked at Evander. "Your move, *brother*," Alaric said as if they were simply playing a game of chess, before turning on his heel without waiting for a reply and leaving the corridor, the clicking of his heels echoing as he climbed the staircase.

Lea ran around Evander, who still stood in front of her. She kneeled in the spilled water from the bucket next to Joshua, who now half lay on the floor, his arm hugged to his body as he writhed in pain, screaming in an agony that reminded her of the cries of those suffering from the Lonely Death.

"I'm so, so sorry. I didn't know. I would have never allowed you to help me if I'd known." She touched Joshua's injured arm, her hands still warm from the prince's heat. She wanted to help him and tried to think of what her mother had done to the burns she had treated in their village. If she knew where the herbs were, she could try to make a poultice... or maybe something that could help him sleep through the pain. The burning grew in her fingers, the same burning that she had felt in the presence of the prince's magic, and she noticed a breeze through her hair, though... *there are no windows open*, she thought in the back of her mind. She felt a warmth growing in her chest and allowed it to spread down her arms, keeping her eyes closed. The wind picked up, lifting her other hand and placing it right atop Joshua's burned flesh. The heat faded from her hands as quickly as it had started. She opened her eyes, realizing that the screaming had stopped. She looked toward him and noticed Evander now standing above them, a look of astonishment on his face.

He pulled her up by the arm so fast it caused her head to snap backward. He grabbed the back of her neck, steadying her, before speaking urgently. "I need you to tell me honestly, Azalea. Did you know you had magic?" She pushed him away.

"I've told you, I don't have magic, Evander. I don't know what—" he turned her toward the burned man behind them.

"Look at his arm, and tell me the truth. Did you know?" She paused and looked down at Joshua's arm, the one that had been nothing but charred skin and bone moments before.

Lea felt her jaw drop as she took in the puckered pink skin, now a constellation of scars that appeared to have been healing for weeks. "What the fuck?" she whispered as she bent closer to get a better look at the now-healed skin.

"So, I guess I can trust you didn't know then," he replied sarcastically, walking to Joshua and pulling him up. "Does the prince know which are your quarters?"

Joshua shook his head no, still unable to speak.

"Return there, now, and quickly. I will tell the weapons master of your injury, that you will need at least a fortnight off of work. You will need to avoid Alaric at all costs, and should he ask why you are not scarred, you tell him I healed you. I will take those consequences." Joshua nodded. "Yes, Your Majesty." He turned to Lea. "Thank you, daughter of the sun," he said sincerely.

Daughter of the sun?

"Joshua—" Evander stopped him and strode forward, towering above him as he looked into his eyes. "Azalea was not present when this burn occurred. You do not know her. You have never laid eyes on her before." He took another step toward him, so close their shoes nearly touched at the toes. "There are three people present in this room. I am confident that both Azalea and I will take this secret beyond the veil. If I hear a single whisper of Azalea and her magic, there will be no doubt in my mind who it came from, and nowhere in this kingdom or beyond that you will be able to hide from my shadows." Evander grew more imposing as his darkness spread around him. "I will find you, and I will create a nightmare that invades your mind and terrorizes your thoughts. My shadows will burrow so deeply into your soul that you will pray for a swift death. I will find your friends, I will find your family. Do not make that mistake."

"I swear, please. I won't tell a soul." Joshua was stuttering, unable to look Evander in the eyes.

"Then go," he said. "Be well." Evander turned without waiting for him to leave, locking eyes with Lea before stepping forward and grabbing her once again behind her neck. "You're coming with me."

CHAPTER 24

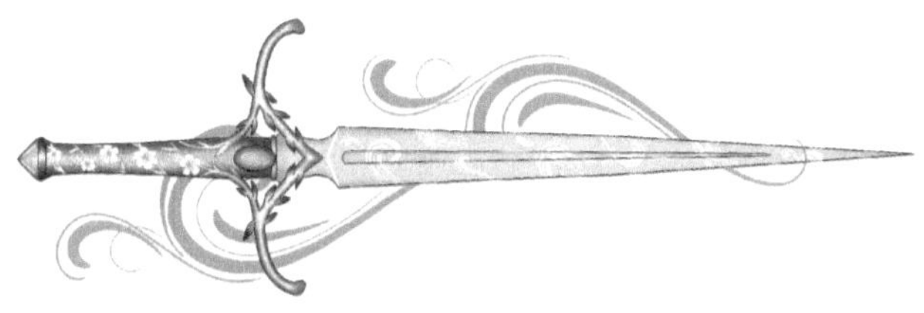

Evander pulled her toward the end of the hall where his bedroom loomed in front of them. Her feet remained rooted to the floor as he unlocked and pushed open the door to his bedchamber. "We don't have time for this, Azalea. Please," he told her urgently.

She didn't want to go, didn't want to be in a room alone with him. But what the hell had just happened? What had she done? Evander waited patiently until her feet started moving, an acknowledgment that she would go with him, before pulling her the rest of the way inside.

She entered the chambers, first noticing the enormous four-poster bed that took up the left side of the room. It was a deep walnut color, the brown so dark it was almost black, with thick, gray and cream blankets and pillows. She felt as if she and her four friends could all fit inside and have room to roll around without touching. The bed sat on a plush carpet that matched the cream of the bedding. It was surprisingly homey and bright, for someone who spoke of his "darkness" in every other conversation.

Two large nightstands sat on either side of the bed with stacks of books on top, and Lea couldn't wait to sneak over and see what the Night Prince enjoyed as reading material. Across the room was a comfortable sitting area in front of a wide fireplace. Two large leather chairs sat on each side of a dark sofa, a square table between each piece of furniture. Papers were scattered across the table, and a few had fallen to the floor haphazardly. It surprised Lea that the Night Prince would be so messy with his correspondence.

"You really didn't know you had magic then?" He turned to her.

"You've asked me that at least, what..." she counted on her fingers, "four times already? If I had known, I would have told you by now. I was certain you'd healed me after the fenrir attack. My mother was the healer, not me. I've never had magic, Gray."

He paused at the use of his name, but quickly recovered. "How old are you, Azalea?" he continued.

"Twenty-three. Why in the world would that matter?"

"Twenty-three is very late for magic to show itself. Usually, you'd have seen something by the age of fourteen, fifteen at the latest. Erik told me he thought you held magic of the day, said you needed the sun on your skin the same way that he did, but I doubted him. We'd never seen you perform anything resembling magic. I thought maybe Nora or Thomas had used their powers to start your healing before I got there after the attack..." He turned to her, his expression so deadly it caused her to shrink into herself to try to escape it.

"You can't tell a soul, Azalea. Alaric will kill you if he finds out. The king will sanction it, and there will be nothing I can do to stop them." His words were frenzied, as if he was racking his brain for some other solution.

"Why would he care? It'd prove him right, wouldn't it? That I had magic all along?"

"It would prove him a fool! That a human with magic was able to trick him and work her way into the palace, during a time when there are many who would like to infiltrate the castle and land exactly where you are. Pride will be Alaric's downfall, but it will also be yours if he finds out."

Lea felt as if she couldn't stand any longer, her legs trembling beneath her like they would give out at any moment. She stumbled over and sat on the bed before she fell, placing her head in her hands and breathing deeply.

"I couldn't even control it! It just happened! I didn't do it on purpose..." She heard Evander turn. As she raised her head, she saw the flicker of the candles surrounding the room.

"Healing will call to you. You may have more gifts, but this will be the strongest for now. If anyone so much as sniffles around you—gets a papercut—you leave their presence immediately. That feeling you felt before you healed him. Do you remember it?"

She nodded. "My fingers grew warm, like they were burning from the inside."

"If you feel it again, you will find me right away. Use any excuse, but we can't allow Alaric to find out. Do you understand the gravity of this situation? Your public execution could be the match that ignites a wildfire, spreading rebellion through the kingdom before we are ready for it. Do you understand me?"

She didn't really, but nodded anyway. *Don't tell anyone*; that part she understood. "Yes," she said firmly. He might be okay with her death, but she could tell from his urgency that his army was not prepared for a rebellion.

"I need to find Erik. He might be able to help us figure out what's happening and why your gifts have been so delayed. You're dismissed for the day. Return straight to your room. You'll be safe from Alaric there. He wouldn't risk being seen in the servant's quarters. I will handle him if he comes down here again."

He looked back to the window, dismissing her. She walked to the door, unsure if she should mention to him that she didn't know the way back to her room. She stood in the doorway, trying to think of what to say when he spoke again.

"You don't know the way," he said, a statement rather than a question, and she wondered if he could read her mind.

He turned and lifted his hand, creating a small collection of black mist about the size of her first and releasing it into the air. It floated in front of her like a breath that escapes in the winter. "Follow it back to your room; it will show you the way. Pay attention this time. I can't afford to let much of my power go during the day with Alaric on a rampage."

Before she could thank him, the bubble of darkness floated out the door. She scurried behind it as it led her back through the winding corridors and doorways that all looked the same until it disappeared through her door. She opened the door to find the darkness was gone, though she thought it might happen to pop back up next time she was changing her clothes.

She stared at her hands, hands that were tanned from the sun but held no flames, no burns. She gripped the necklace around her throat, rubbing the jade between her fingers and silently asking her mother once again to send her the wind that she'd promised would guide her.

CHAPTER 25

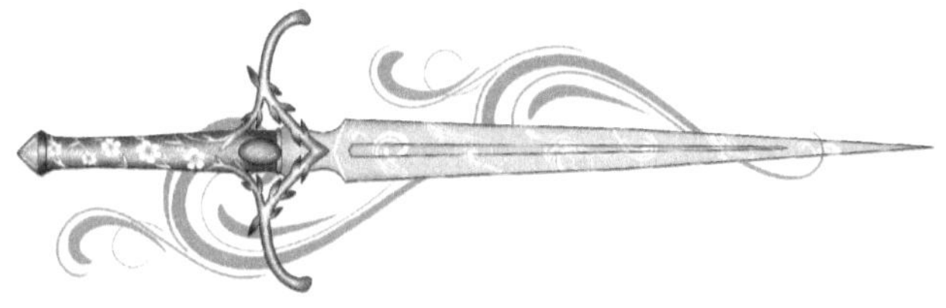

Lea had several hours to herself to examine the events of the day before Emma returned to the room, ready to collect her for dinner service. Emma helped her plait her hair in an elaborate braid matching her own, apparently the uniform for women when in formal settings such as dinner for the royal family. As they walked through the halls, she tried to catalog each turn, adding to the map in her mind of the secret halls that spread throughout the castle.

"Do not look them in the eye and follow my lead. We are to remain against the wall unless called for, or a course is being served." When they entered the kitchen, Elise was standing by the large wood-fired stove, flour coating her face. Before her, the counter was filled with a feast fit for... well... a king. Four other servants waited along with her, and Emma pulled her over to join them.

"Everyone, this is Lea. She has no idea what she's doing, so cover for her." She heard a mumble of "got it" and "sure" before Elise started thrusting plates in their hands. Bowls of fruit and platters piled high with butter rolls, salad, and a large vat of vegetable soup. Lea was handed a tower of rolls and prayed to the gods that they wouldn't topple as she entered the giant hall.

A long polished table sat in the middle, with at least forty chairs surrounding it. The chairs were plush, with red cushions that matched the elaborate tall curtains hanging around the many windows. There were ornate black ties adorned with different variations of golden suns and silver moons around the middle of the curtains, allowing the light to enter. There were four fireplaces, one on each wall, so big she thought she could walk inside one and stand up straight without her head even coming close to touching the top. She must have slowed as she took in the beautiful room, because the servant behind her stepped on the back of her shoe, causing her to stumble.

Lea was somehow able to recover without dropping a single roll. She let loose a breath of short-lived relief at the same moment she looked up to find Prince Alaric's eyes on her, the exact same green as his brothers, but somehow they held far more venom inside them. She quickly turned her eyes down toward the floor and followed Emma to the table, placing her platter where she pointed.

After they had put down their designated plates, they walked to the wall across from the windows and stood against it, eyes downcast. Lea looked up through her eyelashes and saw the king sitting at the head of the table. The queen sat to his left, far more beautiful than the stories told her to be, with chestnut hair almost down to her waist and the same piercing green eyes as her sons. Alaric sat to the King's right, and Lea could sense by the raised hair on her arms that he was acutely aware of her every move. Next to Alaric sat an older man dressed in all black with the symbol of day magic, a golden sun with long curving rays, across his chest. Herald, the king had called him. He had cropped blond hair and a stern expression, looking vaguely familiar in a way she could not place. The seat beside the queen had a place setting ready—at least nine different forks, spoons, and knives around the beautiful black and silver plate—but the chair in front of it remained empty. Evander's seat, surely, but where was he?

As the king began to eat, the others following his lead, Lea's mind drifted to Evander. She wondered if he'd been able to find Erik, and when she'd be able to speak to him about it next. Lost in her thoughts, Emma tapped Lea's wrist and indicated that she should follow her to clear the plates on the table. They carried them into the kitchen to exchange them for what must be the main course; roasts and dressed birds—chickens, she thought, though they were far bigger than the ones she had made for her family at home. The platters also held roasted vegetables, and Lea's mouth watered as she smelled the spices. She carried her plate in and sat it before Herald and turned to walk away. She was stopped by a hand on her elbow, squeezing so tightly she winced as she was forced to turn back to the table while the rest of the servants continued on without her to resume their places along the back wall.

She turned and met Alaric's eyes. "Serve me, human." He let go of her elbow and scooted back his chair enough that she had to stand in front of him to fill his plate. Her eyes flicked to Emma's, who nodded once and quickly returned her eyes to the floor. Lea walked forward slowly and reached for the roast in front of Alaric. The king kept on with his conversation with Herald as if nothing was amiss, though she could feel the queen's eyes on her as she cut a large portion of roast and placed it in front of Alaric. She turned to walk back when he stopped her again, this time grabbing her waist and pinching just above her hip, so hard she was sure she would have a bruise when she undressed tonight. "Did I dismiss you? Cut it up." She glanced around, looking for some clue as to what was happening, before turning back to the prince's plate and cutting his roast into bite-sized pieces with shaking hands as he leaned forward to speak to her.

"Afraid when your protector isn't here?" His words were quiet but vicious. "He won't be with you every second, human. If I were you, I would always be looking over my shoulder. You never know what's lurking around the corner. So many places to hide within these palace walls." Lea felt him trail his hands up the back of her legs, slowly and cruelly, before sitting up and leaning back in his chair, suddenly pulling her down onto his lap as she cut the last piece and set the knife down. "Feed it to me."

Her face heated with shame as she reached forward, unsure which fork to use. She picked one up at random and stabbed a piece of meat, lifting her hand to place it in front of his mouth. Alaric just sat there, staring at her, until she pushed it between his teeth. He did not speak another word to her throughout dinner as she gave him bite after bite of roast and fed him wine from his goblet when he pointed to it.

"Too lazy to feed yourself, son?" the king asked, and Lea felt Alaric stiffen behind her, hope blooming in her chest that the king would make his son leave her alone.

"The girl was slacking on her work today, Father. I've decided to keep an eye on her, give her extra duties as I see fit, including serving me so I can ensure she is earning her room here. Can't have the servants dallying around with free time, can we?" he replied coolly. The king stared right through him, his eyebrows lowering.

"Just don't let this... little game you're playing interrupt your duties," King Nestruir finally replied, clearly not believing Alaric's reasons for his interest in her. Lea deflated, her stomach twisting into knots. The king didn't care what Alaric did, so long as it didn't interfere with his work as the Crown Prince. How could this family be so cruel?

As dinner ended, Alaric stood without warning, dumping her onto the floor. He looked down at her. "Over your shoulder, *Little Flower*," he said the words mockingly as he turned and walked out the door. The blood in her veins turned to ice, and she began to tremble. How did he know Evander called her that? She was certain Evander had been more careful using his nickname for her... This had never been about her. She was simply a pawn in Alaric's war against his brother, and the thought terrified her.

The other servants walked toward the table to clear the dishes, so she stood from the floor as quickly as she could. Lea grabbed the nearest plates and practically sprinted into the kitchen, the china rattling in her shaking hands. She placed the dishes on the counter and leaned her hands next to them, bracing herself with her arms to allow her to take in deeper breaths, trying to calm her racing heart.

"What happened, dearie?" Elise walked up to her and began rubbing her back. "It couldn't have been that bad?" Emma came through the doorway and ran to Lea, placing her dishes on top of the others.

"Lea, are you okay? That was awful! What did he say to you?"

"I'm fine." She took another deep breath. "I'm fine," she said again, more to herself this time than to Emma and Elise. "Except Alaric is going to kill me." She cringed, turning toward Elise and grabbing her hands. "Can you take me off dinner service? I'll do anything, Elise."

"No, Dearie, I'm afraid not," she said with sad eyes. "Alaric requested you personally. If you're not present, he will punish you, of that I am certain."

Emma grabbed Lea's arm, pulling her away from her mother.

"We'll figure something out. I'm sure there's a way to get you off dinner service," Emma told her confidently, though the way she rubbed her arm in comfort told Lea that she didn't really believe the words she was saying. Lea went through the rest of the evening in a fog, trying to think of how she could appease Alaric, how she could escape this precarious situation she had fallen into. She wanted to see Thomas, brainstorm with him for a solution, but realized she knew so little of the layout of the castle. Was his room even in the same wing?

Lea sat on her bed as the sun set, watching as it disappeared inch by inch below the horizon and hoping that Thomas would come to her room before he began work for the evening. The room darkened as she waited, her hip throbbing where Alaric's fingers had pinched at her flesh, but the magic hour passed, and the darkness grew, and no one knocked on her door.

CHAPTER 26

Lea walked herself to Evander's quarters the next morning, grateful that she remembered the way. As soon as she entered the hallway, she felt the pulsing from the door at the end calling to her. Was it just her subconscious itching to look deeper inside the private quarters of the Prince of the Night? To get a glimpse of who he was behind closed doors? Or was it just *who* was in the room that was calling to her? The energy tried to move her feet toward it, to convince her to enter. Instead, she turned, starting with the first room on her left.

She'd made sure to get a key from Elise this morning and spent the next several hours cleaning the guest rooms and changing all the linen, walking back and forth to the storage closet at least seven times. She worked until her back ached and her fingers were sore, trying to find any task that could be done to buy her more time to stay in the guest rooms of the wing. Each time she entered the hallway, she looked toward Evander's door to see if he had left, but the electricity still thrummed through it, calling to her, pulling her. She found her toes turning toward the door as she dusted the paintings after she'd finished the guest rooms.

"Stop!" she whispered to the door before rubbing her hand over her face in embarrassment. She stubbornly turned her feet to face the door that exited the hallway, before moving on to wiping the window sills and airing out the curtains. She looked around at quite possibly the cleanest hallway she had ever walked through. The moment she'd been avoiding was here. She had nothing left to clean but the room that begged her to enter, no more ways she could stall.

Lea took a deep, steadying breath and walked toward Evander's room, coming to a stop at the outside of his door. She stood there for several moments, trying to muster the nerve to rap her knuckles against the door. She felt a gust of wind against her back, lifting her arm and lightly brushing her knuckles against the rough, dark wood in front of her. *What the fuck? Where did that wind come from?*

"Not cool, whoever you are!" she whispered to the air around her. She turned to look behind her when the door suddenly swung open in front of her, an agitated Evander filling the doorway.

His muscular body was so large she couldn't see into the room behind him as his chest rose and fell with angry, ragged breaths. His green eyes were bright against the dark chestnut of his long hair. Lea didn't normally like long hair on men, preferring shorter and cleaner cuts, but on Evander, it looked so rugged. So... confident and manly.

"Do you plan on standing there all day, or were you ever going to knock?" he asked irritably. She lowered her hand that now hovered just above his chest where she had been about to knock. The look in his eyes told her there was nothing more unwanted than her presence at this moment, yet the pull remained, trying to force her closer to him.

"I'm sorry. I've cleaned the other rooms, I wasn't sure..."

"It's fine; just come in," he sighed, his irritation lessening as he stepped aside and rubbed the back of his neck. "Next time, just knock, Azalea. I can't handle feeling you just standing outside my door." *He could feel it, too?*

Lea ran to grab her supplies, stumbling over her feet in her nervousness, and walked into Evander's bedchamber. She glanced at his desk, on which a quill and uncapped ink sat next to a haphazard stack of parchment. What had he been working on?

Continuing to move through the room, Lea felt his eyes on her as he watched her every movement, a buzzing that made her skin feel extra sensitive. She felt the way her shirt sleeves brushed against her arms, her hair tickling across her collarbone as she took inventory of what might need to be done. She was aware of every movement as she dusted around the room, starting with the large dresser. Was she walking weirdly? Why had she never paid attention to the way she walked before?

"I spoke with Erik," Evander said, breaking the uncomfortable silence and walking to his sitting area across the room. He bent forward to shuffle through a stack of papers on the table. "After gloating that he was right, he agreed that we need to be very careful. He offered to teach you how to control your day magic, but he'll need to find a safe place to practice, somewhere no one will be able to discover you. Your magic will be easier to control at night, so you'll train then. He'll find you when it's time." Lea continued to clean, her heart warming a bit at Erik's offer to help her.

"Thank you for speaking with him."

"I'm the one who brought you into this lion's den. It's not like I can let you get killed because of me, can I?" he said sardonically, his tone verging on sarcastic. His answers were short, and she knew he wanted the conversation to end by the gruff tone of his voice.

"I'm sorry I'm such an inconvenience to you," she said angrily under her breath, knowing that she was being childish but unable to help herself at that moment. It wasn't as if she had asked to be in the castle at all, let alone to be his personal servant. She would rather not be here as well.

He stood suddenly and tossed down the papers he had been looking at.

"Inconvenience is an understatement." He walked to a different stack of parchment, shuffling through it. "I can't begin to tell you how much

I regret not locking every door and window of that damned cottage from the outside. You shouldn't be here." He kept his head down as he searched through the piles for whatever he was looking for.

"If you had just let Thomas go, I wouldn't be here! If you'd let me help him escape the camp, I might be halfway to Calir right now... So if you can find a mirror large enough, I suggest you look into it and think about the fact that it is actually *your* fault that I am here!" She walked toward him, her finger pointing in his direction.

He leaned forward with his hands on the back of a chair as he turned to look directly into her eyes, the lights in the room flickering around them. "I did everything, *everything* I could to make sure you would *NOT* end up here!" he yelled at her, so loud she felt as if the walls might shift and tumble around them with the force of his voice. He took a step forward and grabbed her chin in between his fingers, forcing her to look up at him. "You don't get to rewrite history and take your own accountability out of what has happened. I warned you, several times in fact, to stay in that house. I kept you safe. I told you I would take care of everything. You ignored it all, showed up to that fucking trial where there was nothing I could do without putting you in danger with Alaric."

"I needed to save Thomas!" she screamed back at him, poking him in the chest.

"I don't fucking care that Thomas is here! I never cared what happened to him! Do you not get it? I would have beheaded him myself if I had thought that it would keep you safely back in that gods' forsaken village of yours!" he roared, his chest heaving in anger as he pulled her face closer. "I'd do it now if it would allow me to send you home."

She met his eyes to see that they were filled with shadows, so black she almost couldn't distinguish the green pupil inside from the black surrounding it. Tears filled her eyes, her throat closing around words she wasn't able to say. Evander took a deep breath and let go of her jaw, taking a small step back.

"I don't want you here any more than you want to be here, Lea." Each word was punctuated as he said it, as if he wanted to ensure that she soaked in every painful syllable. Lea lowered her head and turned away from him, not wanting to look at his angry face any longer.

"I'm sorry I'm here. I don't know how to change that. You can request that I be assigned elsewhere," she said quietly, trying not to give him the satisfaction of showing the hurt in her voice.

"A sure way to get you executed," he replied as if she had recommended he let her try to poison the King's wine. He threw down the papers in his hand, clearly angry that he could not find what he was looking for. He braced his hands again on the back of a chair and took several slow, steady breaths before turning and walking into his study, leaving her standing alone in his room, unsure of what to do.

Lea hoped this was his way of letting her finish her work and leave quickly. She walked toward the bed in order to strip it, hoping that she could complete the task before he returned and be on her way to grab clean bedding, giving her a few moments alone to collect her thoughts.

She pulled back the covers and began to take off the sheets, removing the pillowcases and throwing them all into a pile on the floor, before crawling on top of the large bed to reach the far corner of the fitted sheet below it. The room grew darker, just a bit, and she looked up to see Evander standing statue still in the doorway to his study, a book in his hand, his eyes locked on her.

"Did I invite you into my bed?" His words were deadly quiet, fury etched in every syllable as he squeezed a book between his large fingers, the leather of the binding groaning in protest.

Shadows danced around his hands as his nostrils flared with each heavy breath. He stalked toward her as she scrambled off the bed quickly. She felt a wave of embarrassment at the suggestion, followed by her cheeks warming at the memory of his body against hers in the tent. His eyes flashed as if he could sense her thoughts as he continued to stalk toward her. Was she aroused at his fury that she'd touched his bed? *There's something seriously wrong with me*, she thought as she continued to back up until she hit the wall behind her.

Evander's steps continued until his chest pressed up against hers, pinning her to the wall as he grabbed her arms and held them above her head. She could feel him hard against her stomach, and she arched into him involuntarily, confused by her body's reaction to this man who clearly hated her. He leaned down to speak into her ear, his breaths ragged and hot against the side of her face. Lea wasn't sure if he was about to devour her or burn her alive.

"You're not to touch my bed again unless you are beneath me and I am between your legs." His voice was barely above a whisper, but she could feel the rumble pass down her throat and straight into her core. "Are you ready for that, Little Flower? To have the Night Prince inside you, fucking you until you won't even remember another man's name? Because that is the *only* thing that happens when a woman is on my bed." She didn't answer, couldn't answer with the feel of his abdomen against her chest, overwhelming her senses.

She felt the buzz of electricity through his fingers around her wrists as his darkness ran down her pinned arms, across her back, and around her neck. Her eyes locked on his lips. *Is that what I want?* Her breaths were ragged as images of him crawling over her filled her mind, and a growl ripped from his throat as his eyes met hers hungrily. He pushed away from her suddenly, backing toward the door.

"I can't do this, Azalea. I don't want you here." He snarled, a low rumble that she felt in her belly, her heart racing. He opened the door and, with the trance broken, she quickly walked out, the ache in her chest growing so intense she winced at the pain. Evander braced his arms on either side of the large doorway, as if blocking her from entering again. She watched his chest rising and falling with each breath as he stared at her standing in the hallway. Tears gathered in her eyes, and as she met his gaze, she saw a flash of pain in them, so brief she wondered if she had imagined it.

"I'm sorry," she said through her tears, unsure what to say or what she could do. Evander took a deep breath, and she noticed some of the green return to his eyes. "Just go. You're dismissed for the day," he said quietly. She recognized a little of Gray in the man called Evander standing in front of her. He seemed so much angrier than the man she'd met weeks before, so much more closed off. She ran quickly back to her room to prepare for dinner service, wondering what a human girl from a small mountain town could have possibly done to gain the hatred of not one, but two Princes of Desia.

CHAPTER 27

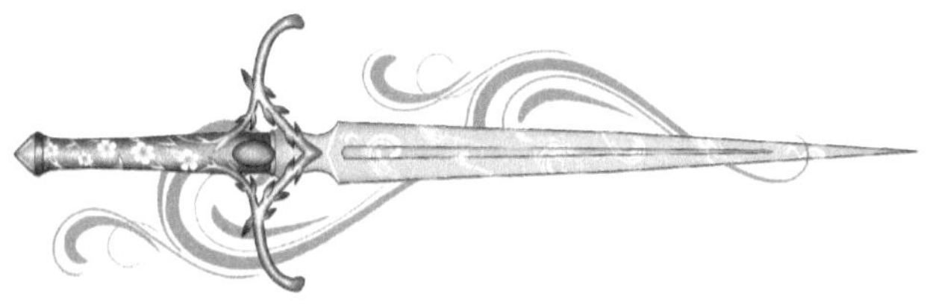

Dinner that night proceeded much the same as the previous evening, Alaric humiliating her by forcing her to personally feed him, rubbing his hands along her back and arms throughout dinner as if she were a pet of his to train, pinching and squeezing and burning her skin when she wasn't fast enough or graceful enough. Bile burned the back of her throat, and embarrassment heated her skin with every touch.

Lea felt dirty after those dinners, after those hours of trying to hold her composure as he jabbed at her with his words, trying to get a reaction out of her that would allow him to punish her. Every night after dinner, she went immediately to the bathing chamber and scrubbed Alaric's scent off of her, the reminder of his hands on her like oil touching her skin.

She did not see Evander the next day as she cleaned his quarters, nor the day after that. Each time she entered his room, she felt her heart race as she stripped the bed, performing the task as quickly as possible as she tried not to think about his threat... *or was it a promise?*

She fell into a rhythm; clean, serve, bathe. Evander disappeared, Alaric taunted, and Thomas stayed away. After the fifth day, Emma entered the room as Lea brushed her hair.

"You can't stay in this room forever, Lea. Come, meet the others," Emma said when she finished. She patted Lea's shoulder and turned to walk away, leaving the door wide open behind her.

With little choice other than to follow, Lea walked behind Emma down the corridor until they entered a large room with an old wooden table and chairs, a chess table, a dartboard, and several ratty chairs and couches occupied by other servants. She recognized many of the faces from serving dinner with her at night, but didn't know any of their names. Guilt crashed over her as she realized that she was so worried before every dinner—so preoccupied during and so disgusted after—that she had not bothered to learn them. She gave them a small smile, apologizing for not introducing herself sooner.

"Yeah, well, I would be preoccupied if the prince made me feed him by hand as well," said a girl with curly blonde hair. "I'm Charlotte." She told her as she shook Lea's hand firmly with a smile. Charlotte introduced her to the rest of the group in the chamber, pointing to Jeremy and Andrew, who were playing darts. They were both tall with kind eyes, and they reminded her of Thomas's brothers with their competitive spirits.

Emma pulled Lea over to a seat at the table where the girls were gathered. A redhead named Brianna gave her a friendly smile and a small wave, while the other, Claire, just looked her up and down, causing Lea to smooth down her hair self-consciously.

"So Lea," Claire finally spoke, leaning toward her. "Who did you have to blow to get your assignment?" She tilted her head. "Personal servant to both of the princes. Surely you performed some favors to get there." She spoke with a smile as if it was only a joke, but an undercurrent of jealousy filled her words.

Lea rolled her eyes, leaning back in her chair. "I'll gladly let you have them both; should I mention it to Evander?" Lea replied, staring her down.

"Calling him by his first name? I don't believe the *Night Prince* would be happy to hear a servant discussing him so casually," she replied.

"And I don't think *Evander* would take kindly to another servant accusing him of requiring sexual favors," Lea retorted angrily, raising her voice just a bit before Emma interjected.

"Don't speak of things you don't know, Claire. Lea has been nothing short of wonderful, and you've seen what Prince Alaric does to her during dinners. If you'd like to take her place, then I suggest you offer yourself up at the next meal." Emma grabbed a deck of cards and began to deal them out, reaching out to touch Lea's hand as she dealt to her first.

"Oh, I'm only joking, Emma. I'm sure Lea wants nothing to do with the princes... either of them." Claire said the words pointedly and put on a fake smile. Lea cataloged her reaction, knowing that Claire fell firmly in the camp of people who could not be trusted.

"Who cares about the princes? They're so boring," Charlotte said. "Alaric is cruel and shallow, and we hardly ever see Evander. Where does he spend all his time, Lea? Does he stay in his rooms? Does he... have company?" She wiggled her eyebrows, fishing for gossip.

"He's hardly there. I've only seen him twice since I got here, to be honest. He's always in his quarters. I hardly know him any better than I know any of you." She thought back to this afternoon and how she had not recognized the man standing in the doorway.

"Except for the night he came to the bathing chambers..." Emma faded off, her eyes widening in panic as the words rolled off her tongue.

Thomas took that exact moment to walk into the room. "And who was it that decided to visit you in a bathing chamber, Lea?" Lea looked up and met his eyes as he gave her a broad smile and came to kiss her cheek, but tension bracketed his eyes. "I'd say, as your boyfriend, I should go pay a visit to whoever thinks he has the right to disrespect you that way." Emma's eyes grew wider as Lea turned to her. "*Sorry*," she mouthed as her cheeks turned red.

"It was Evander. He was just bringing me my trunk the first night I was here. I was covered by bubbles. It's fine. Nothing to see here, everybody."

The table went silent. "Evander visited you in the bath..." Thomas said the words quietly, but each word was laced with anger. "That bastard saw you naked?"

"So, shouldn't you be leaving to have that talk with him?" Claire jabbed, knowing that the chances of him confronting the Night Prince were nonexistent. She turned to Brianna, "Seriously, is this girl screwing everybody?"

Lea stood, a tight smile across her face. "As pleasant as this evening has been, I'm going to go to bed." She turned and stormed from the room, her footfalls heavy as her anger propelled her forward. Walking to her room, she yanked open the door before entering and slammed it behind her in fury. *What was that girl's problem? Did she think I actually wanted this kind of attention from the princes?*

It wasn't a full minute before the door opened and Thomas entered.

"What was Prince Evander doing visiting you in the bath, Lea?" Thomas said accusingly, hurt filling his eyes.

"Why do you care? You haven't visited me, so someone may as well have! And since when am I your girlfriend without the courtesy of a conversation, Thomas?" she replied back. "I am tired of everyone else choosing everything for me. Where I will work, how I spend my time, who I date, who visits me while I'm in the gods' damned bath. Do you think I invited him there?"

"I'm not sure how else a man comes to be in a private room while a woman bathes."

"Oh, please. Please tell me how I'm supposed to keep the Night Prince from doing whatever the hell he wants. Enlighten me!" She threw her arms out, waiting for an answer.

Evander was avoiding her, and Alaric was tormenting her. She hadn't seen Thomas in nearly a week. A week that had been straight from hell, if she was being honest. He did not have the right to judge her for anything that was happening to her.

Thomas sighed and walked over to sit on Emma's bed, giving her the space she needed, and she relaxed slightly, turning to sit on her own bed. She crossed her legs under her and grabbed a pillow, hugging it to her chest.

"Where have you been, Thomas? It's been days since I saw you last."

"I'm sorry. You're right, I have no right to question you. I knew that bastard Prince wanted you the first time I saw him with you... but I know you'd never hurt me like that."

The words stung as she thought back to her night with Evander on their journey here. No, she would never intentionally hurt Thomas, but it would hurt him to know what had happened all the same.

"As for why I haven't visited... I've been so busy, Lea. The king wants me to make more weapons than I can keep up with, so most nights I work until sunrise to make my quota while you're asleep. I've wanted to come to see you, I swear." He looked at his watch. "Look, Lea, I don't have much time before I have to leave, and I don't want to spend it fighting. Please, forgive me?" He gave her a boyish grin, so familiar to her that it made her muscles relax and her anger melt away like ice on a summer day.

"If you promise to take your head out of your ass, then yes. You're forgiven."

Thomas hopped up and walked to her, pulling her to him as he laid down against her pillows. He cupped her face and kissed her, his lips whisper soft across her own. Lea hesitated for a moment. *Is this what I want with him?* The image of Evander's stern face flicked before her eyes. "I really am sorry, Lea. I thought of another man touching you, and I... I couldn't take it. I know you better than that. I know that *you're* better than that."

Lea bristled at the words, but he was right, wasn't he? Evander was the son of the Black King, a member of the royal family she had grown up hating.

He kissed her again, more deeply, and Lea tried to let herself melt against him despite the nagging feeling that something wasn't right, ignoring the guilt she felt. She relished feeling his hands roam her body, hands that did not pinch her or make her feel like she was covered in mud. A touch she would not have to wash off when he left.

"I'd love to stay here all night kissing you, Lea, but I have a meeting of sorts I must attend before work."

"Can I come to visit you? I'm not having the easiest time here, Thomas."

"Of course you can, any time. I'm on the opposite side of the castle, above the infirmary. It's near the door that goes to the horse stables, on the top floor." He kissed her softly again.

"But I really need to tell you something today. Now. It's why I made sure I could get here before work, so you could know before you met too many people and made alliances you might regret." He continued to run his hands through her hair. "There are things happening here, hidden behind the corridors and deep in the dungeons. People who aren't happy with the King, who want change. Promise me that you'll be careful what you say and who you talk to within these walls. I wish I had time to tell you more. I'd planned on it before... Anyway, I'm going to be late. I have to go."

Lea didn't know what to say. "You're leaving, just like that? What are you talking about, Thomas? You can't drop a bomb on me like that and then just run out the door!" Lea was many things, but patient was not one of them. Thomas knew this. He looked at his watch again, clearly torn.

"I really have to go, Lea. I don't have time. I'll come find you tomorrow." He leaned to kiss her again. "I love you, girlfriend." He gave her a wide smile as he strode from the room.

"I haven't agreed to that, Thomas!" She ran to the door and called after him. "Thomas!" He just gave her a wink before turning out of sight.

CHAPTER 28

Lea slept fitfully and was relieved when she went to Evander's wing and found that she did not feel the magnetic pull coming from behind the door at the end of the hallway. Seeing an opportunity to avoid awkwardness and an argument, she walked quickly to the large wooden door and knocked, entering when she did not hear a reply. She hoped she could finish his rooms before he returned and avoid continuing whatever the hell that was that had happened days before. Quickly moving to finish the task that had caused the deterioration of their ability to be in the same room together, she began to take the blankets off the bed.

Removing the second pillow from the bed, Lea noticed a folded letter tucked beneath it. She picked it up hesitantly, staring at her name scrawled across the front with a heavy hand.

Little Flower,

I'm sorry for my actions, my anger, and despite what I said, I am not sorry that you are here.

Gray.

Lea flipped the page over and over, looking for more, some sort of explanation for the words she'd read four times already. The back of the paper remained blank, and the questions inside her mind only grew. *What did he mean? All week he's wanted nothing more than to get rid of me, and now...?*

She ran a frustrated hand through her hair before she placed the note inside her apron with a huff and continued to clean, quickly walking to each corner of the bed to change the bedding and linens, avoiding climbing across it, before tidying up the space. She avoided Evander's study, unsure if he would want her to enter, and left before he had the chance to return. Her thoughts continued to twist, and she knew she wasn't ready to face Evander for another conversation so soon after reading his note, at least until she could decide what it meant.

She continued to walk toward the closet where the laundry was kept for washing, considering Evander's words, when she noticed Thomas standing at the end of the hall, one that she had never seen him in before. He had not yet noticed her as he looked toward the doorway in front of him, checking his watch before walking quickly to it and knocking twice, then twice more after a pause. The door swung open, and she caught a glimpse of a very tall man, or maybe a Fae, standing in the doorway. She was struck by his hair, black as the night itself. Thomas nodded to him, quickly holding his hand to his heart with his thumb tucked into his palm before stepping past the door and allowing it to close.

The whole encounter had been fast, less than a minute, but in that time she had witnessed an urgency in Thomas's movements that she had never seen in the relaxed boy she had grown up with. She considered following him and knocking on the door. After all, Thomas had never kept a secret from her before, but she decided against it, knowing she couldn't give the prince any excuse to believe that she was not performing her duties. She placed the laundry basket filled with clean linens, wincing at the pressure against one of the bruises left by the prince's cruel fingers.

She'd taken care to not try to heal herself of the bruises and burns that dotted her arms and legs like stars in the night sky, not that she knew how anyway, worried that the prince might pull up her sleeves to find them free of the evidence of his sadism.

Deciding Thomas's strange meeting was none of her business, she scrubbed floors and dusted curtains, missing her garden back home and the feel of the sun and wind on her skin. Would she ever smell fresh air again? She allowed herself to spend the afternoon lost in daydreams of home, returning to her room just in time for dinner service.

The prince was particularly cruel during dinner that night, far more demanding, pinching her leg under the table so hard he broke skin when she had torn his roll open to butter rather than cut it in two. She felt his anger and wrath in every touch, each time he squeezed her thigh so hard she was certain she would bruise, each time he burned small circles in her skin the size of his fingertips. Lea wondered what had caused his mood to be more foul than usual and tried her best not to anger him as she fed him bite after bite.

She walked out of the kitchen that night after dinner, choosing not to stay behind to help with the cleaning. Emma's eyes told her to go as Elise walked toward her, silently handing her a small bag of healing bath salts and nodding toward the door. Lea soaked for what felt like hours, the sting of her wounds mixing with the warmth of the water and fading to a dull ache of soreness as she stared at the fire.

Lea heard a knock and looked to see Emma enter the bathing chamber, walking to the fire to warm another bucket of water. Emma wordlessly added the hot water to Lea's bath before turning to leave, the kindness of the gesture causing Lea to break. She began to sob, letting her tears mix with the salted water of the bath until she was bone tired. She stood and dressed, quickly braiding her hair as she walked back into her room and climbed into bed. Lea noticed the window had been cracked open, another kindness from Emma, and listened to the sounds of the wind as she tried to fall asleep.

Her exhaustion didn't mean that she was allowed the rest that she so desperately needed. Lea awoke to a knock at the door, so quiet she wondered if she had imagined it. She laid as still as she could, barely breathing as she waited for another knock. Was it Thomas coming to see her? Or had Evander been wrong, and Alaric waited outside her door, ready to continue the pain he had caused her at dinner tonight?

Instead of another knock, the door opened slowly. Lea scrambled back in bed, her heart beating furiously as she looked for something she could use as a weapon. She reached blindly at her nightstand, grabbing the hairbrush she had laid there earlier in the day, and holding it out in front of her.

A dark form entered her room, the black of the night blocking out the features of a burly man. She swung the hairbrush through the air as a small spark emerged from the shadowy form's hands, illuminating a pair of dark eyes in the flickering light.

CHAPTER 29

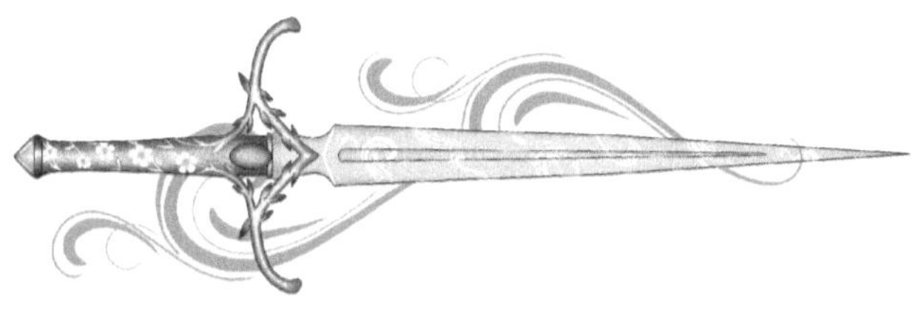

"Gods dammit, Erik! You frightened me." She hissed at him in a whisper, trying not to wake Emma. Erik's head swung to her choice of weapon and his eyes filled with humor, crinkling around the corners. He pressed a finger to his lips as he pointed toward her boots. She obeyed his silent instructions, quickly pulling pants on underneath her night dress and lacing up her shoes. Without a word, they walked out of the room and into the dark corridor.

"Quiet as you can, sunshine. We need to move fast while the guards are changing shifts. If we get caught, it won't be good for either of us," he whispered. Erik walked forward, steps surprisingly quiet for such a large man. She followed behind him as he walked into the servant's corridors, leading her further down into the depths of the castle.

Lea tried to take in her surroundings, but could only see a few feet in front of her as the light from Erik's torch illuminated the cold stone walls. Every so often he stopped, holding up a hand to listen, occasionally turning around and choosing a different route. She felt a chill in the air and rubbed her arms, wishing she had taken the time to put something warmer on top of her thin dress. The cold bit further into her with each staircase they descended, and Lea began to feel a bit trapped, as if the rock above her head could crash down at any moment and crush them in this underground tunnel system.

Erik walked them to a dead end with a wide metal door and several locks along the side. Pulling a bronze key ring from his pocket, Erik unlocked them one by one and pushed open the door. If Erik hadn't been such a jovial man, she might have worried that he was leading her to her death down in the dungeons.

Flicking his hands, the room illuminated, at least twenty torches instantly lighting as one, the room beginning to warm more quickly than a normal fire could heat it. She stepped inside and heard the door close behind her, the locks clicking one by one as he secured them from the inside.

"So, were you going to brush my hair to death? Make it so soft and shiny that the beauty of it killed me?" Erik's voice boomed through the space as he laughed, pulling his hair over his shoulder and batting his eyes.

"At least you'd look presentable. It looks like you rolled right out of bed to come kidnap me in the night," she teased him, but in reality, it looked like he hadn't slept in days.

She looked around the room, a cavernous stone space with no furniture and a huge black mat in the middle. There were several buckets of water along the far wall, as well as a pile of straw and several piles of sticks.

"That I did." His face turned serious. "Gray told me about what happened with Prince Alaric. We need to figure out what your abilities are and how you can control them."

"He said that you had told him you thought I had day magic. How did you know?"

"It was the way you walked into the sun as if part of your soul returned to you when you stepped into the light. Our magic ties us to that energy. Have you ever felt like you needed the sun to live, that the days when the clouds covered it, you felt tired? Weak?"

She thought back to the days in her garden, finding refuge in the sun at every opportunity after her mother died. She nodded. "I thought I just needed to be in the garden. I didn't think it had much to do with the sun."

"You'll need the light and fresh air even more now that your powers are beginning to manifest. It won't be good for you to go too long without the sun recharging you." She thought about how tired she had been since entering the castle, realizing that she hadn't stepped foot into the daylight since she'd arrived.

"Be careful who is around you when you go outside for now. Your powers will get stronger when there are no walls between you and the sun in the sky. You'll be more likely to slip up. Don't go out with anyone who you're not sure you can trust. If Alaric finds out you have magic…" He paused and rubbed his hand through his hair, "Well. Let's just say it will be hard to protect you."

"I'm not sure he could treat me much worse, honestly," she replied, turning to sit on the mat. Erik grabbed her elbow gently before she could step away.

"Has something else happened, Sunshine? I've only heard about him following you to Gray's rooms. Has he shown more interest in you?" His eyes exposed his worry, as if Alaric's interest in her would be the worst news she could tell him.

She rolled up her sleeve to show him the back of her arm, dotted with small bruises and burns from Alaric's fingers pinching and singeing her flesh. Erik pulled her sleeve up higher, touching the red burns and deep purple bruises.

"Alaric did this?" His voice was quiet but held a venom in it that made her want to pull away. She nodded. "When?"

"Every night, at dinner. He forces me to sit in his lap, makes me feed him, pinches me if he's displeased with anything I do, shoots fire into my skin if I so much as look in the wrong direction." Her words were quiet, filled with shame, despite the fact that she knew it wasn't her fault that the prince was targeting her.

"And no one has stepped in? Not a single person has tried to help you!?" Fury radiated off the usually happy, laughing Fae before her as a scowl crossed his usually smiling mouth. It looked so out of place on him, Lea almost laughed.

"What are they supposed to do, Erik? He's the Crown Prince. It's me, or it'll be someone else. You heard what he did to Joshua for helping me."

Erik placed his hands on her arm, and she felt a warmth push into her, the soreness easing a bit. "This will never happen again, I can assure you of that." He moved to her other arm. "I don't have enough magic to fully heal you at night, but this should help with the soreness at least." He took a deep breath. "Lea." The intensity in his voice caused her to look up at him. "I would not allow Gray to see these bruises. Nothing good will come of it. Do you understand?"

Lea thought back to Evander's reaction when Alaric had stepped toward her in the hallway, ready to incinerate her in front of him. She wasn't sure why he cared so much about what Alaric did to her, likely his sense of responsibility for allowing her to be brought here. She was the ever-present thorn in his side that he now felt a duty to protect, but it did seem like he didn't want physical harm to come to her, even if the motivation to keep her safe was because of his duty.

"I understand. And I agree. Thank you, Erik." She placed her hand on his arm and gave him a small smile, breaking the tension in the room.

"Alright, then! Let's get into this. What do you know about magic? Day magic, specifically."

"I know it gets stronger with the sun and that it tends toward fire and heat."

"But what do you know of its history, of how it came to be this way?"

She'd never considered there to be a reason for the day and night magic. It just *was*. "Hasn't it always been like this?"

"No, Sunshine." He turned and walked to the wall, sitting and leaning back against it. Lea followed and sat in front of him, crossing her legs as she faced him.

"Lesson number one, never sit with your back to the door. Know every entrance, every exit, every window, every place big enough that someone could hide. He reached forward and lifted her as if she were as light as a daisy and turned her so that she sat beside him against the wall.

"Now, that's better. Back to the story. Thousands of years ago, Fae were created by the gods to protect humans. They were larger, stronger, harder to kill, and every one of them held magic that was just as strong under the midday sun as it was under a full moon. They lived in Auropera, back when the land was fertile and fruitful enough to sustain their every need, given as a reward for protecting the humans from the evil that roamed Desia."

Lea leaned her back against the wall, getting comfortable. "Behind the veil, the *Fe Fiada*, until it fell, right? I never learned that the Fae were created to protect humans, though. I thought we both just... existed." Lea told him, trying to think back to her history lessons as a child.

"That's because history is rewritten by those with power, Sunshine. We were created to be your protectors, able to go through the *Fe Fiada* and roam among the humans as the first line of defense against the demons that hunted them."

"I thought those were just bedtime stories our mothers told us at night to make us behave."

"No. They were real—are still real. That's part of what the Royal Army does. We fight those demons, keep them so far away from you humans that you doubt their existence. We've driven them west, and have been lucky enough to keep them there for almost a century."

A shiver ran through Lea as she thought of the monsters that her mother had told her of, ones that ate bones and drank blood, that sucked your very being from your body as you withered into nothing. Erik continued, not noticing her discomfort.

"At first, the Fae did protect the humans. But power corrupts even those with the best intentions, and soon, their greed changed them. They used humans as slaves, acting as false gods on earth. Humans toiled in the fields, harvesting until they died from exhaustion, even though Auropera provided them everything that they needed to survive. The humans went hungry while the Fae feasted."

"It doesn't sound all that different than it is now, Erik." Lea said quietly, thinking of the food and labor those in her village were forced to give to the Fae living in the capital."

"I know it seems that way, and you're not wrong. But it was even worse before. So much so that the gods noticed, and it angered them. They fractured the Fae's power in two, half to be ruled by the goddess of the moon, and half to be ruled by the god of the sun. They thought it would prevent anyone Fae from holding too much power, bringing them closer back to their original purpose."

"And how did that work out for them?" she joked.

Erik smiled and said, "Not well. It caused division among the Fae, those with night magic warring with those with magic of the day, humans trapped in the middle. They fought for hundreds of years, the world full of fire and shadows. The gods were angry with the Fae, so ungrateful for the power that they had been given, but the humans needed help, no longer protected and even harmed by those who had been created to protect them."

"Did they send down fire and brimstone to teach them a lesson?" she asked him, not sure how this history lesson could help her learn to control her own magic.

"No, they shot down the stars themselves, crashing them into the Fe Fiada in a fiery apocalypse, opening the wall between the two worlds for all to pass through. Auropera no longer belonged to them. And along with the stars they sent down their descendent, gave her the chance to change the world. Queen Emmeline, have you heard of her?"

She shook her head. "I've never heard any of this."

"They gave her both magic of the day and night, magic stronger than had ever been seen. Emmeline burned the world, Sunshine, killed every Fae with hate in their heart, all who were unwilling to work together to create unity. She brought back the balance. She was loved, the most beautiful and powerful ruler this kingdom had ever seen, and there was finally peace for the first time in hundreds of years."

"She only killed the Fae with hate in their heart?" she asked. "So there were Fae who sided with the humans?"

"Yes, more than you think. Just as there are Fae now who wish for a better life for humans. Many Fae were mated to humans, a bond chosen by the god and goddess themselves, a love so intense it would join the life forces of the two mated. Once sealed, one could not live without the other. Their children were blessed with magic. Those Fae fought alongside their human mates in the war, trying to save both of their lives. Other Fae had simply befriended humans, saw them as more than slaves and lesser beings, and fought to help give them a better life."

"Mates? Like... soulmates? I've never heard of someone actually finding theirs," she pondered aloud.

"That is because there hasn't been a pair of true mates in well over a hundred years," he told her seriously, his voice low and brows pulling inward. "It is a gift from the gods, who it appears haven't found anyone worthy of such a gift in a very long time."

"What about Queen Emmaline? Did she have a mate?" Lea asked.

"She did, a love unlike any seen before. But his heart stopped beating with her last breath, together in death as they were in life."

"What happened to her? How did she die? Shouldn't she have lived for hundreds of years like you all do?" she asked as she tried to picture the queen in her mind.

"King Nestruir happened, Lea. He was best friends with the queen's mate, and with the help of a witch and some very dark magic, he killed her in cold blood under the cover of night." He paused, allowing the words to sink in. "You've heard that magic began to fade around the time the king took the throne?" Lea nodded, unsure where Erik was going with this line of thinking.

"Why did it fade?" she asked.

"No one knows for sure. Some say it's a punishment from the gods for killing their descendant, the only Fae capable of keeping peace. There's really no way to know, but what we do know is that now, a Fae to be born with magic is rare, and for a human to have magic... it is even rarer."

"Evander said that there were more humans in my village with magic, so it can't be that rare."

"Gray and I..." He paused as if wondering how much he should disclose to her. "We've known about your village for a long time. Known about the magic within it. There are no other towns and cities we've come across that hold magic in the numbers yours does. We don't know why, but we've tried to keep you all protected for years."

"I don't understand. You work for the king. Why would you help us hide from him?"

"There's a lot you don't understand, Sunshine. A lot that it is not my place to tell you."

She rolled her eyes and bumped her shoulder into his.

"What was the point of this history lesson, then, if you can't even tell me what it means?"

"The point is that you need to understand where your power comes from, why it runs through your veins, and what it is capable of. Your magic is from the goddess of the moon. It is a gift, and misusing it brings consequences."

She considered this as they sat in silence, the quiet stretching between them comfortable.

"I just don't understand. Where did my magic come from?"

"One of your parents would have had to have been magical, Lea. At least one of them."

"That's impossible. My mother could heal, but only with the magic the earth provided. The plants she grew and the herbs she mixed." She scoffed at his words, but deep down she knew, had maybe always known, that her mother's abilities had been *different*.

Hurt filled her belly as the realization crashed over her. Adelaide had to have known that her healing was more than just a gift for mixing tinctures and salves, and yet her parents hadn't told her that her mother had been gifted by the gods. She'd known that Lea was magical. Her letter had practically admitted it. Lea's eyes stung at the betrayal that she hadn't trusted her with that knowledge before she died.

"Sunshine." Erik's voice was gentle. "It doesn't help tomorrow's healing to pull open yesterday's wounds. I'm sure they had their reasons. You might not know, but I saw them with you. Your parents loved you more than life itself. Now." He stood up and brushed his hands on his pants, "The sun will rise in about two hours. We only have a little time to practice before we need to sneak you back into your room."

Lea stood, following him toward the piles of straw. He picked up a piece and focused on it, starting a flame at the top and watching as it burned down to his fingers. "Focus on the warmth inside of you, in your chest. It's a part of you like a muscle you can flex. Try to push it to where you want it to go." He handed her a piece of straw.

"I thought I could heal. That was my power." She dropped her hand by her side, trying to think of any other times that she had done anything resembling magic.

"Healing is your gift. A special ability you can perform, among a few others. But all those with day magic can summon fire. Just as all with magic of the night can summon the dark, though the strength of that power varies. Just try it."

Lifting the straw between her thumb and index finger, Lea held it in front of her about a foot away from her face. She took a deep breath and closed her eyes for a moment, searching for that heat that she had felt in her chest and fingers when she'd healed Joshua, but she felt nothing. She tried to imagine the warmth there, taking her other hand and placing it on her sternum, rubbing as if she could wake the magic from its rest deep within her. Opening one eye, she peeked through her eyelids to see her piece of straw very much not on fire. She turned to Erik, dropping her arms to her side. "It's not going to work. I feel nothing, Erik."

Erik walked to her and placed a firm hand on her shoulder. "You need to relax. Your magic is only manifesting. For now, it usually reveals itself during times of extreme emotion."

"I am extremely annoyed that I am out of bed in the middle of the night and failing at magic class. Does that count?" she retorted, sagging backward into Erik, surprised at how easy their friendship felt after knowing each other for such a short time.

"You need to think about something that will bring on strong feelings. When I was learning to master my magic, I mostly thought about the kitchens running out of butter rolls. But anything will work: anger, fear... lust."

"Gray." The word burst from her mouth before she had a chance to think about it. "Shit. I'm talking about the anger part. Just–pretend I didn't say that out loud, Erik, or I swear I'll have enough embarrassment inside me to set that tangled hair of yours on fire." Erik didn't say a word, but she could feel his assessing stare on the back of her neck. Was it anger or fear that had brought his name to her lips? Her mind drifted to their night in the tent, the feelings of his hands running against her skin, the teasingly slow circles around her breast. If she was being honest with herself, she knew exactly which emotion had prompted thoughts of him.

She jumped back as heat pricked her fingers, dropping the straw that was smoking as flames crawled up the long dry stalk. Erik slapped her on the shoulder with her victory, throwing her forward a step as he picked up a small handful of straw and threw it on top of the burning piece.

"Good. Now, put it out."

"Can't we just celebrate a win, Erik? Where's my "Congratulations, Sunshine! You're so amazing!" He held his hands out toward the fire, indicating that there would be no celebrations unless she could douse the flames. She huffed out a breath as she took a step forward, thinking about how she could call the flames back to her. She thought about how Evander's magic bent to his will, how the shadows moved where his body told them to. Lea thought of the night in the bathing chamber, when his shadows had called to her, touched her...

The flames grew stronger in the small straw pile as a larger one simultaneously burst into flames, heat flashing toward her and ash floating up toward the tall ceiling. She turned to Erik to see surprise etched along his features before he stepped forward and threw a bucket of water on both fires.

"You're sure you've never felt your magic before, Sunshine? That was far more than I'd expect you to be able to do without the sun high in the sky, especially since you've been stuck inside for so long." His words weren't accusing, but rather, he appeared confused.

"I really wish everyone would stop asking me that, Erik. I promise, swear on the gods, on my life, on my mother's grave, that I had no idea. Is that enough?"

"I believe you, Lea. I didn't mean for it to sound otherwise," he said gently. "But it is surprising that you can produce flames as tall as me on your second attempt. You need to be careful, don't go out in the sun without myself or Gray. We can cover for you if something like this happens and we're with you, but without us, we'll be fighting against Alaric and his executioner. Who, by the way, I hear is now performing his beheadings with a sword made by your friend, Thomas."

"You know, it's nice that you care if I live or die, Erik," she nudged him with her shoulder.

"I do enjoy having you around, Sunshine. But it's not just for my benefit that I want you alive. I don't want to see the way the world would burn if you were to die."

"I'm one girl. The world would be just fine." She didn't mean to sound self-deprecating, but her time on earth so far had taught her to be realistic. People die, bad things often happen to the best people, and fairness was not a word that the gods knew the meaning of.

"The world, maybe, until the darkness swallows it whole in retribution," Erik told her, turning before she could answer. "Come on, sunrise will be soon. We need to get you back. You'll have a long day today on so little sleep without recharging in the sun. You need to push through it, Lea. I have a feeling Alaric's attention will only grow."

She followed behind him as they walked back to her room, the trek up the stairs far more difficult than their descent down to the training room. Erik was correct. She did feel tired, drained in a way that she had never quite felt before. She felt as if she had been carrying bricks up and down these stairs for hours, her feet so heavy she could barely lift them enough to take a step.

Erik brought her to her door, nodding before telling her that he would be seeing her tonight.

"Tonight?" she asked. "Are we training again so soon?" How was she going to keep up if she worked all day and trained all night with no sleep?

"Dinner," he replied, almost sternly, as he touched the back of her arm where he had healed her in the dungeons. "I promised you that will never happen again." He nodded to her before turning away. Lea smiled at her friend's back, feeling grateful to be adding one more person into the very small circle of people she knew cared for her, cared about what happened to her.

She turned to her door and pushed it open, confused to find a mattress on the floor between Emma and her own bed, a petite girl with light purple hair, dyed with the berries from Lea's garden back home, sitting on top of it.

CHAPTER 30

"**J**anelle!" Lea screamed, suddenly wide awake. Lea was not a hugger by nature. She didn't mind the occasional affection of those she loved, but had never been one to hug with greetings or farewells. But seeing her friend, she had never wanted to embrace someone more. She ran and launched herself at Janelle, both of them grabbing onto each other as if they thought that they would never see the other again.

"I missed you so much," Lea said into her ear. Janelle pulled back, squeezing her arms gently before rearing back and punching her in the chest.

"What the fuck were you thinking? You *promised*. You promised you would let me help. I told you, you're not the only person who loves Thomas, and he's not the only person who loves you."

Guilt immediately ate at her as she realized that once again, someone she loved was here in Auropera rather than back in the comfort of their own home.

"I didn't want to ruin your life, too; you weren't the one who got Thomas in this situation. I'm sorry, Janelle. How are you even here?"

"How do you think I'm here, Lea?" Janelle said, anger and hurt filling her voice. "I work here now, volunteered to serve the Crown. I told you that if you were going to do something stupid, I was going to do something stupid right along with you." Emma walked into the room, hair wet from bathing, and looked between Janelle and Lea.

"Oh, you're back. Mom brought her a few hours ago. She's been assigned to the kitchens. Says that she told her she'd be staying with you or she'd oversalt every meal she helped Mom make for the rest of her life. But, I like living with you and she's my mom, so she obviously wasn't going to kick me out of my own room, and there are no open rooms at the moment, so here we are! The three of us, roomies!" Emma sounded sincerely happy, and Lea loved her for the fact that she saw this as an opportunity for another friend and not a slight to her own friendship with Lea.

Lea turned back to Janelle. "I'm sorry, I really am." She didn't know what else to say. She *was* sorry, and she realized that she needed to listen to her own complaints and stop making decisions for other people.

"Then that's that. When do we start?" Janelle stood and went over to the uniform that Emma had grabbed for her.

"That's it? I'm forgiven?"

Janelle leveled her with a look, one that she had missed since leaving home. "If you ask me anything else like that, I swear, we will no longer be friends." She parroted the words that she had told her back at Thomas's cottage. "You're my best friend, Lea. You'll always be forgiven."

Lea noticed that Janelle's eyes were wet, her voice a bit choked, and she paused. Janelle did not cry. Lea had never once in all their years of friendship seen tears running down her face. She felt a pang of loyalty, wondering how such a terrible day had reminded her that she had so many people in her corner: Erik, Emma, and Janelle. She hoped this was an omen that the tides were changing.

She let Janelle wipe her eyes without looking her way, knowing she wouldn't want anyone's attention during a moment of what she would consider weakness. They all finished dressing as the ripple of magic passed through the room, marking the start of their day.

With a new energy buzzing through her, and hope that she had not felt since entering the castle walls, she left to face her day, turning toward her friends and blowing them each a kiss.

"Have a good day, dears!" She smiled and turned back to walk out the door, smacking directly into the large body that was filling her doorway.

"Fuck!" She grabbed at her nose that had bashed into an extremely hard chest, tears filling her eyes from the pain as Janelle ran up behind her.

"Is that oaf seriously still bothering you?" Janelle asked, walking forward and pushing him backward out of the doorway. "Don't you think you've done enough, *Commander*?"

Emma cleared her throat, curtsying low. "Prince Evander," she said, her eyes downcast.

Janelle froze, staring between Emma and Evander, who was giving her an arrogant smirk. Evander looked around Janelle to Emma, who was just behind her.

"Emma, call me Evander please," he turned back to Janelle. "And you. I'm aware of what I've done to lead us all here. But, thank you for reminding me. How is your pest problem, by the way?"

Janelle looked to Lea, clearly in shock. "You didn't think to tell me he was the *Night Prince*?" she hissed, grabbing her apron and walking to the door.

"Excuse me," she said to Evander, before slipping behind him and scurrying down the hallway. Evander turned his attention back to Lea, grabbing her face in his hands, and pressing against her nose gently with his thumbs. Lea winced, and his eyes darkened. "It's not broken. Why the hell did you storm through the door? I didn't expect you to come running out of here like your room was on fire." He let go of her face, stepping back.

"And I didn't expect your pecs to be harder than a brick wall, but here we are." She prodded her nose again. "Why *are* you here, Evander? I'm not late."

"I talked to Erik. He said you need some air." He looked over her shoulder at Emma. "Emma," he nodded, "have a nice day." Evander grabbed Lea's elbow and led her toward the stairs. "Erik was worried about you and thought you needed to recharge. You haven't felt the sun in almost two weeks. Come." He slid his hand down her forearm to grab her hand, and his familiar energy pulsed through her skin. Shooting Emma an apologetic look, she allowed him to lead her through the tunnels, the promise of feeling the sun too tempting to ignore. They continued along, winding and turning until they were inside a familiar corridor.

"We're at your rooms... Did you need to grab something before we went outside?" She shuffled her feet as she stood there, trying to hide the disappointment that she wasn't already feeling the sun's warmth on her face.

"I think I found a solution to your problem." Evander gave her a gentle smile before leading her down the hallway toward his quarters. He turned to the left when they reached the end, rather than entering his chambers. Unlocking the door, he walked inside, pulling her behind him into the room meant for Evander's princess. The room was bare aside from a sprinkling of furniture: an empty bed, dresser, armoire, and two nightstands. Attached to the room was a sitting area, with a pink couch and two chairs surrounding a fireplace. Evander walked her quickly through the room, walking to the windows lining the back wall that she realized were doors opening to a large balcony.

He pushed open the doors and stepped aside, motioning for her to move forward. Lea looked out to see the room overlooking a garden below, filled with topiaries and rose bushes, fountains and blooms in every color. She took a deep inhale, holding the fragrant fresh air in her lungs and feeling instantly refreshed. She let out the breath as her fingers reached forward, wanting to tend to those beautiful flowers in front of her. She took a step, then another, stepping into the bright sun that was shining onto the balcony.

She tilted her head back and took the deepest breath she could; the light burning her eyes through her eyelids as she felt a million pinpricks washing over her skin. She stood there, minutes passing as she felt the warmth fill her body, closing up the empty parts inside her. "Thank you, Gray," Lea whispered, still facing the sun.

"Flowers need the sun to survive. I'm sorry I didn't realize sooner. Come here whenever you like. This space is yours." Evander lifted a hand to her face, rubbing her cheeks where the sun had begun to flush them red. "Makes me almost want to leave the darkness," he said, before turning and leaving her alone on the balcony. She felt the constant ache in her chest ease a bit, allowing her ribcage to expand further with each deep breath. What did he mean, leave the darkness? Lea thought of the shadows that burst forth from his body, the violent storms he could call around him with the flick of his fingers. He couldn't leave the darkness. He *was* the darkness.

Moving to the bench at the edge of the balcony, she laid on her back, looking up at the sky as she watched small, bright-colored birds fly by and fluffy clouds that reminded her of freshly picked cotton balls floating above her head. She felt the sun reviving her, felt her muscles growing stronger and her lungs opening wider. She closed her eyes and breathed deeply, settling into sleep in the middle of the day.

Lea awoke hours later feeling refreshed and recharged, her skin pink from baking in the sun's rays. She walked back inside and into the hallway, contemplating if she should knock on Evander's door to thank him, or leave him to his afternoon in peace. She was saved from making the decision by his door opening.

"Just standing there again? You really do seem to have a personal vendetta against knocking," he said with a smirk.

"House rules," she teased, smiling at him shyly, testing out this new-found friendliness that seemed to have settled between them.

"Alaric is in meetings with Father for the rest of the afternoon. You're safe to go back to your dorm; rest, enjoy some time with your friends."

He nodded to her before returning to his room, closing the door behind him. She felt his absence like she felt the absence of the sun outside, and despite every rational thought, she hoped that maybe the next time she spent time on the balcony, he would enjoy the light with her.

CHAPTER 31

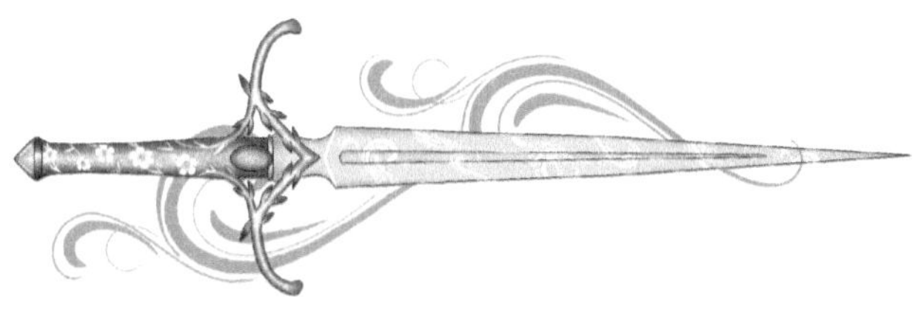

Lea did rest, bathing and braiding her long hair as she waited for Emma to finish her work for the day. She'd almost forgotten that she was allowed free time and was excited to explore the city of Auropera a bit, and even more excited that she would not have to spend dinner being taunted and burned by the prince.

Emma returned to their room, informing Lea that Janelle was being trained by her mother and had not been in the palace long enough for the evening off. Lea's heart fell; she had really been looking forward to some time with her friend. The ache was soothed a bit when Emma told her that Claire had tomorrow evening off and wouldn't be accompanying them tonight. *Good*, she thought. She didn't trust her and was glad she could now relax without watching her back all night.

They made their way out of the castle and meandered slowly toward town, enjoying the brisk evening as they walked on the cobblestones leading out of the castle grounds. Dragonflies circled her head, and she laughed as one landed on her wrist. Despite the fact that it wasn't home, Auropera was beautiful, the castle grounds spotted with fountains and greenery. Emma's heels clicked on the ground as she wrapped her arm around Lea's. Lea smiled, happy to see Emma enjoying herself. She worked so hard. There was no one more deserving of a night to relax than her.

"Are you ready to spill your secrets yet?" Emma prodded, bumping her shoulder against Lea's.

"I don't really have any secrets to spill," Lea replied, wondering what she was talking about. Was it her magic? Did she suspect there was something she was hiding?

"And I'm supposed to believe that there is no secret to having two handsome men falling for you?"

"Evander isn't—" Emma waved her hand through the air.

"Okay then, if you're not ready to admit that... Thomas, then. He's certainly enamored with you."

"Thomas is a great guy, I've known him my entire life." They heard bounding footsteps on the road behind them, and Emma turned to look at who might be causing the noise.

"Speak of the devil," Emma said right as Thomas wrapped his arms around her from behind and spun her around. Lea squealed as she tried to swat him away.

"Thomas! What are you doing here? Emma said you had tomorrow night off."

"Well, now I have tonight off. I couldn't let my girl go exploring town without me, could I?" He gave her a wide grin.

"I told you I haven't agreed to that—" She paused, exhaling and allowing a small smile to creep across her face. "You know what? Not tonight. We're having fun tonight. No arguing about what we are, no professions of love... Got it?" She pointed her finger at Thomas playfully.

"I swear it." He put his hand over his heart and she exhaled in relief. "My love," he ended the sentence, jumping back in anticipation of her hand swinging out to hit his shoulder.

"Thomas!" Lea lunged at him and he darted around her, bumping into Emma and causing her to stumble.

"So sorry, Emma," Thomas apologized with a laugh. "My girl here is playing hard to get..."

"Enough! Emma?" Lea turned to her and spoke sweetly, "Any boys caught your eye?" Emma blushed as they stepped onto a larger road, very close to the center of town now.

"No, no. Too busy working, I guess. Anyway, this is it."

Lea stopped and turned in a circle, taking in the center of Auropera. She'd never seen a city like it. Well, she hadn't seen any cities at all, but she'd never even imagined a city like this one. It was somehow filled with nature. Thick green grass thatched the rooftops, and some of the buildings themselves seemed to have erupted from the stone in the ground. Tall, vibrant green trees stood in the middle of roads, and pockets of flowers sprouted haphazardly from the cobblestones, butterflies flitting between the bright-colored blooms. Beautiful people, mostly Fae with a few human servants and soldiers mixed in, walked from building to building, almost floating as they bought bread from the squat building with white smoke rising from grass-covered chimneys. Others chatted on chairs and benches formed from large vines and mushrooms outside various shops. It was a city built by the gods, built by a magic so beautiful it nearly brought tears to Lea's eyes.

Emma grabbed her hand and pulled her toward the tavern across the street, a tilted building with the back half merging with the sloped hill behind it. Fascinated, Lea followed without argument, tiptoeing around the flowers haphazardly growing in their path that she couldn't bear to step on.

Thomas pushed open the door in front of them and Lea was met with upbeat music; *a guitar and a fiddle*, she thought. She looked around and was instantly taken aback by the sheer number of Fae inside. Men and women gathered around tables, some playing cards, while others sat in small groups sipping ale and wine, laughing amongst themselves. Not a single one looked up when they walked in, not surprised or bothered at all to see humans entering what was technically their space.

She followed Emma and Thomas to a long wooden table with benches for seating nearby and recognized Brianna sitting there, brown hair loose around her shoulders today and a tattoo peeking out just below her right collarbone. She sat with another girl she didn't recognize with shoulder-length black hair, a fair complexion, and a welcoming expression.

"Leslie, this is Lea," Emma introduced them.

"Oh! Thank you for letting me borrow those clothes," Lea told her earnestly.

"No problem. I've been the new girl here. I know what it feels like." Lea gave her a smile, which Leslie returned.

"Who wants a drink?" Thomas asked, counting the hands that rose into the air before standing and walking to the large bar against the wall. The bar was a vine, thick tendrils of strong wood interwoven with itself, twisting and curling to create the extensive structure holding all the alcohol.

"Is everything here this beautiful?" Lea asked Emma.

"Auropera grew from the land itself before the Fae angered the gods," she whispered back. "All the old structures are like this, built from the earth and crafted by the gods themselves."

Thomas returned with the drinks, a glass of cherry wine for Lea and Emma and ale for the rest of them, and they settled back into easy conversation. Thomas remained close to her, his arm around her shoulders or his hand playing with her hair, and she settled into the familiarity of his touch. She'd spent so many evenings with him like this around the fire. There was no need to overthink it now.

They were speaking about how Leslie had met her boyfriend, Daniel, when Thomas suddenly froze next to her. Lea followed his eyes to a dark corner of the tavern where an imposing man sat flanked by several others. No, there was no way he was a man. He was too large and looked too powerful. He had to be Fae. Lea couldn't make out much of his appearance in the shadows he sat in until he stood, making eye contact with Thomas and tilting his head toward the empty seat in front of him.

The nearby torch illuminated him and Lea suddenly recognized the man Thomas had met with behind closed doors days before.

His black hair was pushed out of his eyes, revealing a clean-shaven face that highlighted his deep brown skin and intense dark eyes. He had tattoos curling up both of his arms, elements of nature, it looked like. She made out what looked like wind-blown trees, and a fire overtaking a field. One was particularly striking, a sun being covered by the moon, a total eclipse, with the sun's light glowing around the outline of the full moon. *How did his tattoo seem to glow like that?*

Thomas bent over toward her, kissing her hair.

"I have to go. You'll be safe walking home with Emma?" he asked her.

"Can't you stay, Thomas? This is the first time we've spent any time together since I got here." She didn't mean to sound whiny, but it was true. She missed her friend.

"I know. But I told you, things are happening that I haven't been able to explain to you yet. I want to be part of something bigger. If I want to do that, then that is the one man I can't say no to." He stood to leave, nodding seriously at the intimidating man standing at the table, waiting for Thomas to comply.

Lea grabbed his arm.

"Are you sure this is a good idea?" she asked nervously, eyes darting back to the enormous tattooed Fae. "He seems dangerous, Thomas."

"Not dangerous... powerful." He looked at her with determination before turning and walking over to the ominous man's table. She saw Thomas tuck his thumb and place his hand over his heart before sitting down at the table, leaning forward to join the discussion. Their faces were serious, grave, and Lea felt a sense of danger wash across her as she wondered what Thomas was getting himself into.

CHAPTER 32

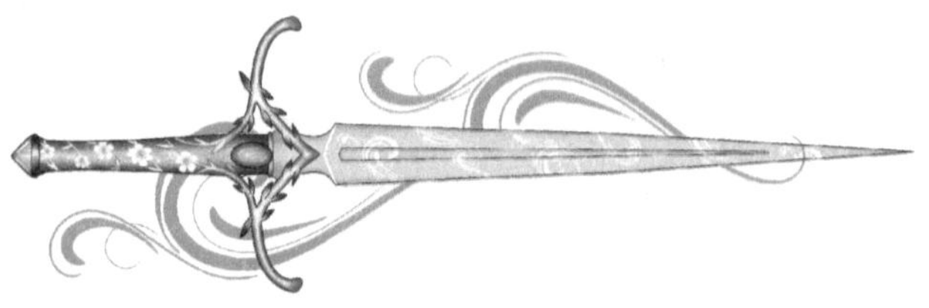

Lea could feel the bile burning the back of her throat as she prepared to walk into dinner service for Alaric the next evening. Emma rubbed her arm gently in solidarity, and she was grateful for her time in the sun this morning that had renewed her spirit enough to face what was about to happen.

"I heard Erik tell you he would be here. I believe him, Lea. He doesn't seem like the type to lie." Lea nodded. Emma was right, after all, she trusted Erik that tonight she would be safe.

She followed behind Emma as they walked into the hall, her heart stopping as she saw the table exactly as it had been each night previous. The King, Queen, and Crown Prince sat along with Herald, an empty place was set next to the queen, and Erik was nowhere in sight.

She walked toward the table with reluctant steps to place down her tray when the giant doors at the front of the hall opened and Evander strode in, meeting her eyes and giving her a slow nod as he walked to his seat. Lea felt the knots in her stomach untangle, a wave of dizziness passing over her as she realized that tonight, she might be safe from Alaric's punishing fingers that were suddenly digging furiously into the arms of his chair. Lea didn't need to look at Alaric's face to see the fury she could feel radiating from his body. Erik followed a moment later, settling down next to Evander, and Lea almost cried in relief. They were here. She was going to be okay. Emma placed her overflowing bowl of fruit on the table and scurried to the kitchen, presumably to get Erik a plate of his own.

"Surprised to see you here, son." The king reached for his fork at the same time his voice slithered across the table. "Finally ready to join the family?"

"Yes, Evander. I must say I find your timing absolutely perfect," Alaric said as he snapped his fingers above his head, his way of letting Lea know he wanted her to serve him. She walked forward and placed her tray down before him with shaky hands, then filled his plate with the various foods laid out on the long, ornate table.

"I was told I've been missing some important...conversations that are occurring at dinner. I am the Commander of the Royal Army, after all. It's my duty to protect the people of this kingdom." He met her eyes again, a silent promise, an acknowledgment that he was going to protect her. "If business is being discussed, I should be here. Azalea, would you mind filling my plate as well?" She let loose a breath and turned to walk around the table to him, grateful to put some space between herself and Alaric, when he roughly grabbed her arm and pulled her down into his lap.

Lea winced as his fingers crushed around her forearm, an unblemished patch of tan, freckled skin that would now have a hand-shaped bruise on it tomorrow.

"Did I dismiss you from serving me?" Alaric crushed her leg within his fist under the table and she winced, reaching forward to cut up the roast in front of him.

She felt Evander's eyes snap up, and she avoided his gaze, praying for this torture to end quickly. Evander placed his napkin on the table as thunder began to roll in the distance, leaning forward and placing his chin atop two fingers.

"Has Azalea been reassigned as *your* personal servant, Alaric? Or is there something I'm missing here?" Evander's voice held a threat, a guarantee of retribution for Alaric's behavior. The room went silent, and she felt the temperature drop in front of her as heat simultaneously radiated from her back.

"She is your personal servant, *as well* as being assigned dinner duties. I will use our servants as I see fit and do not require your permission, little brother." Alaric gestured for his wine, and Lea reached for it, shame coloring her face.

Dark shadows slithered across the table, wrapping around her wrist and holding it there, causing her arm to stop mid-air. They wrapped around her injured arm, her pain slowly ebbing away as they caressed the red, bruising skin. The shadows took the goblet from her hand, returning it to the table as Evander stood slowly, his movements reminding Lea of a cougar slowly stalking its prey.

"Let me make myself clear, *big brother.* The human is *mine.*" Evander's last word wrapped around her like a vice, the intensity in his declaration making each head at the table turn toward her. She looked down at the shadows that were crawling up her arm, finding every injured spot and soothing them.

"MINE!" Evander roared, the silverware rattling on the table as his anger crashed through the room. "*Mine* to punish. *Mine* to command. *Mine* to torture or reward. *Mine* to do with as I please. In case you don't remember from our childhood, I do not share what is *mine.*" Evander's shadows slipped across the table like dark fog, surrounding her as they spiraled up Alaric's arms and around his torso. "Get your hands off of her. I promise you will not like what happens if I have to tell you again."

Alaric remained silent, squeezing her tighter for just a moment before leaning forward to speak in her ear. "Over your shoulder, human," he reminded her tauntingly. He shoved her away from him as if she had the Lonely Death, and she stood, taking a quick step back.

"Azalea, over here, please." Evander's words were commanding, but his tone was gentle. Lea walked around the table and Evander inched his chair back enough to allow her to sit on his lap. He gave her a nod, and she positioned herself on his knee, leaning forward to fill his plate as he placed his large hand on her leg, giving her a gentle, reassuring squeeze.

Lea felt the blush creeping up her cheeks and tried to tame it, embarrassed that she was moved from one prince's lap to another in front of her friends and the rest of the royal family. She knew what Evander was doing. He was both marking her as his in front of everyone, as well as sending a message to Alaric, and she was grateful.

"So, Alaric, are you ready for the hunt this weekend?" Erik said through a mouth full of potatoes as he cut into another bite with his fork. "I think with our new weapons, we will bag enough to feed the kingdom for the year!" His boisterous voice broke the tension in the room as he gestured to the sword at his hip.

"They are quite remarkable; we're lucky Evander recommended that boy come to work here. It'd be a shame to have left such a talent rotting in the ground," the king said, answering him.

Lea winced at the callous discussion of the loss of human life. He was supposed to be their ruler, protecting them as well as the Fae. Did life really mean so little to him? The conversation around them turned to weapons and the upcoming hunt, and Lea relaxed a bit as the attention in the room turned away from her.

"You're here. At dinner, with your brother and Father," Lea whispered, taking special care to make sure her voice was only loud enough for Evander to hear her.

Evander rubbed his thumb on her thigh, as if he could feel the sting of the pain that still lingered from Alaric's anger.

"You needed me," he whispered. "You should have told me this was happening."

She felt cool energy push into her skin. Not cold, but the refreshing cool of stepping into the stream on a hot day. He shifted under her, then leaned forward to speak in her ear, sending shivers down her spine. "I'd have been here every night if I'd known, Little Flower. You're safe now." He patted her thigh once more before leaning back into his chair.

Evander lifted his wine to his lips as she remained on his lap, protected from everything but Alaric's piercing stare. His rage was palpable—she felt it with every breath she took. She kept her eyes downcast, Evander's hand possessively remaining on her thigh, his thumb sweeping in small, comforting circles that sent tingles into her toes. She could feel Alaric's glare on her, calculating, planning.

Evander shifted her body so that she was turned in toward him rather than facing the table, leaning over to speak to her quietly as if he could sense her discomfort from Alaric's stare.

"Did you enjoy the sun today? You look beautiful with the color back in your cheeks." Her cheeks colored further at the compliment.

"I did. I feel better than I have in weeks." She offered him a genuine smile. "Thank you. Did you mean what you said? I can go there anytime?"

"Of course. Day or night, the space is yours." He squeezed her leg gently. "Now, everyone is watching. We need to show Alaric that you are *mine*, that I will not allow him or anyone else to harm you." He said the word with such intensity, she couldn't help but feel like in that moment she *was* his, and she wasn't sure what it meant about her that her thighs instinctively squeezed together at the comment. She nodded at him and picked up his fork, stabbing a roasted carrot and lifting it toward his mouth. Evander met her eyes as she pushed it between his lips, and she sucked in a breath as he bit down on the fork, his teeth scraping the metal as she slowly pulled it from his mouth. Why was feeding him so sensual, so different from feeding his brother? She squirmed in his lap as he licked his lips, suddenly aware of every hard inch of his body pressing against hers.

Lea continued to feed him bite after bite as his hand moved higher on her leg, his other arm pulling her closer to him. She could feel her neck flushing as her breaths grew more shallow, her stomach swirling every time his fingers swept higher. She was in the middle of feeding him another bite, Evander giving her a wicked, sideways smile, when the doors to the hall opened. Lea looked up to see Thomas enter, followed by Emma, who looked at her with apologetic eyes, her fingers wringing repetitively.

"Ah yes, Thomas, thank you for coming. And thank you, *Emma*, for going to fetch him for me." Alaric said Emma's name in a way that worried Lea, as if proving he knew exactly who she was and her relationship with Lea... as if proving that he didn't have to hurt *her* to cause her pain. When had he called for Thomas? Had she really been so distracted feeding Evander that she hadn't heard when he'd called Emma over to him? This had to be Alaric's revenge for Evander embarrassing him in front of his father.

Thomas walked forward, his posture guarded and movements stiff. His eyes flicked to her as he neared and she stiffened, feeling like she had just been caught kissing a boy in the closet.

Lea felt Evander sit taller behind her, pulling her the smallest bit closer, his touch suddenly possessive. Thomas bowed deeply to the king as he moved his eyes back to the rest of the table. "Your Highnesses."

"So, this is the blacksmith whose weapons are the talk of the palace. Tell me, why hide your abilities for so long? Here, you could be famous, wealthy. You could be known all over the kingdom for the weapons you craft to strengthen our army." The king spoke as if genuinely curious as to why someone would not want to hand themselves over to be taken away from their family and friends to serve him.

Thomas's eyes flicked to Lea briefly. "I apologize, my king. I didn't realize that my weapons were so badly needed. I had people back home whom I loved, very deeply. Who I couldn't imagine hurting by leaving behind and moving on to... different things. Different people. I beg your forgiveness." His words were clear. He was hurt by what he saw. The news of Evander visiting her in the bath, and now her sitting on his lap with a flush in her cheeks and his hand on her thigh. She shifted forward, pleading with Thomas with her eyes to look at her, to show him it meant nothing, that it was just another part of this game of survival she was playing every day. But... was it? Even as she thought the words, she felt the pain behind her sternum grow in intensity, urging her to take back her thoughts and admit that maybe, even if she didn't want to have these feelings, they were more than *nothing*.

"Continue to make weapons of this quality, and all is forgiven. Come, boy. I have a special project I'd like to discuss with you. He gestured to the queen's seat next to them, and she silently stood, pushing back her chair and nodding at her husband before leaving the room. Thomas walked to the chair and sat, his face reddening as he pulled at his collar in discomfort. She glanced forward to see Alaric with a wry smile on his face, leaning back and staring at them as if playing a game of chess, planning his next move. He'd done this on purpose, the next step in his plan to completely destroy her and get revenge for his brother humiliating him.

The king leaned forward as he began to talk to Thomas about a sword and shield he wanted him to make as Evander spoke into her ear. "He will understand, I'm sure. He'd want you protected from my brother as well." She turned to meet his eyes, furrowing her brow. "I know you're not actually mine, Little Flower, but sometimes it's nice to imagine for a moment, isn't it?" Lea's heart skipped at his confession, and confusion bubbled in her belly. He didn't want her here. He'd said it again and again. But his words felt like more than his duty to protect her. They felt... heavy. He gestured for her to rise. "You're dismissed. Goodnight, Azalea."

Lea stood and walked from the room, grateful for the dismissal and wanting some space to sort through what Evander had just said—what Thomas had said.

She needed to speak to Thomas, to clear up any confusion about what they were. If he loved her, he was doing a poor job of showing it. He'd come to see her only twice in the weeks she had been here and those moments had been brief. Then he'd left her last night to follow the command of the powerful Fae in the dark corner. She loved Thomas, too, but was it the same kind of love he had for her? She thought of the comfort she felt when he held her, the familiarity of his touch that soothed and calmed her. But, shouldn't there be more? There should be heat. Passion. Not once had her body reacted to Thomas the way it did when Evander so much as looked at her.

She returned to her room, praying that Thomas wouldn't come to talk to her about what he had seen, or what he thought was going on between them. She couldn't speak to him tonight, didn't know her own feelings well enough to talk to the boy who loved her, who was hurt by her actions.

When Thomas knocked on her door that evening, Emma answered as Lea sat purposefully out of sight on her bed.

"She wasn't feeling well after dinner, Thomas. She's fast asleep. Do you want me to wake her?" she asked, her voice so kind.

"No, Emma." Lea watched Thomas reach out and touched Emma's arm. "It's okay, let her rest. She'll be speaking with me soon enough."

CHAPTER 33

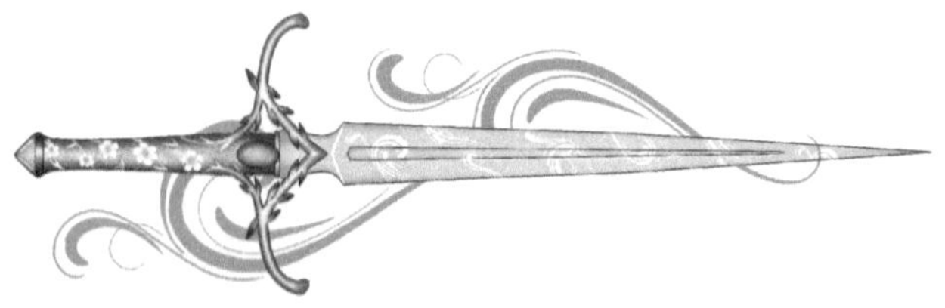

Lea reported to her morning duties to find Evander absent from his chambers, so she spent a few minutes in the sun before returning to her daily work. She had stripped the beds in the guest rooms, though she still didn't understand why since Evander had no guests, and was carrying the bedding toward the laundry when she saw Thomas stroll through a door ahead of her, three swords in his arms as he walked back toward the blacksmith. He paused and stared at her for a moment before rushing toward her and touching her elbow.

"We need to talk," he said urgently, looking down at her. Lea nodded, nerves filling her stomach as she tilted her head toward the supply room that held the laundry bins. She moved forward as Thomas followed behind her, wishing she could put off this conversation for another day. Lea entered the room to place the sheets among the other dirty linens before turning to him.

"What is going on between you and Evander?" Thomas asked quietly, accusation tingeing his words.

"You have no right to be angry with me. You've come to see me twice since I've been here, and in the meantime, I've been tormented by Alaric every night, humiliated and assaulted. If Evander hadn't stepped in, I'd be far more marked with bruises than I am now."

"The prince hurt you? Why didn't you tell me?" He stepped toward her, but Lea held her hand out in front of her, stopping him.

"When would I have told you, Thomas? Exactly how would I have told you when I haven't seen you, spent barely any time with you in the past few weeks beyond a couple of kisses and cryptic warnings? Let's be honest. The only reason you're here now is because you're jealous, seeing me sitting with Evander—who was protecting me from Alaric, by the way."

Thomas looked down at the floor. "That's not fair, Lea. You know I love you. I've made that clear, but there are things happening here, things I can do to help, to be part of something bigger, to help change this place."

"Yes, things you haven't bothered to explain to me. Even as you stood in my room warning me to be careful. "

"You don't understand. I'm doing it *for* you, Lea, for our life together. Can't you just trust that? Know that I'd rather be wherever you are?"

"I want to believe you. You have no idea how much I want to, but I just can't make myself. If you wanted to be where I am, Thomas, you would be." Her voice was barely a whisper, but her resolve was strong. She had too much self-respect to let him convince her that his absence was for her own good.

Thomas walked toward her and grabbed her face in his hands, pleading with his eyes.

"I need you to understand, Lea. I love you." He pressed a soft kiss against her lips, and Lea pulled back, but only an inch. "Please. There's a way we can make Desia better, there's—" The door slammed against the wall as it opened behind him, and Lea's heart dropped into her stomach when she saw who was standing in the doorway.

"Wasn't there something I said I would do if I found you weren't working to the best of your capabilities?" Alaric leaned against the door frame, pretending to think. "Oh, yes. Execution." He turned. "And you," he leveled a glare at Thomas. "You should be making weapons, exhausting your magic to serve this kingdom. You'd think that as a charged criminal, you'd be on better behavior, wouldn't you?"

Thomas took a step back, dropping his head as his hands began to shake. "I apologize, Your Majesty."

Lea dropped into a curtsey, fear filling every pore as she dipped her eyes down and apologized. She didn't want to die here, in a laundry closet. "As do I, Prince Alaric."

Alaric walked to her and grabbed her arm roughly around her biceps.

"No, you're not. But you will be." He threw her down onto the stone floor with so much force she gasped as the air was knocked out of her lungs. She grabbed the side of her head, a knot already forming where it had smashed into the ground.

Thomas took a step forward, reaching out to her, but Alaric turned and blasted flames toward him.

"You will not help her. This is your punishment. Intervene, and I will incinerate you. And I promise you will not have enough magic to protect either of you this time." He turned back to Lea.

"You lied to me, human." He sauntered back toward her, fire dancing in his hand. "You tricked your way into the castle, pretended to have magic to worm your way into our midst. I have no doubt you're working with the rebellion."

Rebellion? "I'm not! I don't know anything about a rebellion!" she cried through the pain in her head. Was this what Thomas had meant about changing the kingdom for the better?

Alaric stopped before her, leaning down and bringing his flaming hand to her cheek, pain searing her soft flesh as his finger burned a line across her face. She screamed as pain radiated from the burn. "I do love to hear you scream." He brought his leg forward, kicking her directly in the stomach, once again pushing the air from her lungs. She doubled over in agony, trying to protect herself from the next kick she knew was coming.

She turned her head to search for Thomas, who stood against the wall. His face was turned away from her, unable to look at what Alaric was doing. Why wasn't he helping her? Saying anything at all? She pleaded with her eyes for him to glance in her direction, but he refused, tears filling his eyes.

"You make my brother think he can challenge me, all to protect a *worthless. Magicless. Human.*" He delivered a kick with each word as if to emphasize its meaning. Lea called out to Thomas, begging him to help her as pain wracked her body, but he turned his head further away from her as tears spilled over his lashes.

"I told you that you would regret coming here." He kicked her in the cheek. Blood erupted from behind her teeth and dripped onto the stone floor from her mouth.

"I told you to always be looking over your shoulder." He kicked her in the ribs, and the air rushed from her lungs as the *crunch* of bone echoed through the room. The pain grew so severe, she couldn't move, couldn't think. She felt her fingers and toes go numb, a coldness creeping up her limbs.

"I told you to serve me, and instead, you listened to Evander. Instead of listening to your Crown Prince, who will one day rule this kingdom and all who live inside it, you listen to his weak younger brother, who will be nothing but forgotten." He kicked her in the teeth, and she rocked onto her elbows and knees, gagging as blood dripped down her throat.

Lea struggled to breathe as each inhale sent fire through her ribcage, unable to expand enough to fill her lungs with oxygen. Stars danced in her vision as she coughed more blood onto the floor, holding her stomach and praying for relief.

"Let this be your warning. I will be the one to end you." Alaric crouched before her, careful to avoid the splatters of blood dribbling from her mouth. He grabbed her by the hair, jerking her head to force her to meet his venom-filled eyes. "I will be the face you see before the final death comes for you."

Lea thought that moment might be now—her journey beyond the veil. She couldn't imagine healing these injuries, could hardly breathe through the pain. She tried to focus on his face, but his features blurred as the room spun around her. He released her hair and reached forward, pushing her hair out of her eyes and smearing blood from her cheek across her face and into her hairline.

"But I will very much enjoy breaking you first." He stood and delivered one final kick to her back, her vertebrae snapping as her legs went completely numb, before turning and walking to Thomas, speaking low enough that Lea couldn't understand his words. Thomas's eyes widened in fear, his hands clenching at his sides as his face turned white as snow.

"I'll be back for you, human," Alaric said to Lea as he walked out the door and closed it behind him.

Thomas ran to her, grabbing her in his arms and pulling her to his chest.

"Fuck, Lea. I'm so sorry." He placed his hands on her, healing energy pushing against her body but repelling off of it. Lea felt as if she wore a shield, as if she was surrounded by a barrier that couldn't be broken. "FUCK!" he screamed. "Why isn't it working?"

Lea's vision blurred as he picked her up, her left eye closing as the swelling grew and obstructed her view. Her head pounded, and waves of nausea crashed through her. She tried to speak and realized her jaw was broken, that she was unable to open her mouth enough for words to pass through. She could feel her heart slowing, blood filling her lungs as breathing became more difficult.

"You'll be okay, Lea. We'll get our revenge against Alaric, against this whole fucking family!" Thomas shouted, his voice shaking as he hurried her through the corridors to her room. "When we're through, they'll be reduced to rubble and bones, the whole fucking lot of them."

She moaned, the halls around her spinning so fast she was forced to close her other eye. Thomas kicked open her door and walked to her bed, laying her down gently upon it. He pushed the hair from her face and pressed a kiss to her forehead. Lea felt his lips trembling as he spoke into her hair. "I'm so sorry, Lea. I'm sorry I couldn't protect you. I love you." He kissed her head again. "I love you. I'm going to get help." He turned and sprinted out the door.

Lea tried to roll herself to her side, to curl her knees into her chest, but she was unable to move as she prayed for the pain to stop. Each inhale felt like breathing in glass shards as she struggled to take shallow breaths, the pain throbbing through her entire body. She closed her eyes as the room spun once again and prayed for the gods to help her, kill her, do whatever it took to take the pain away.

"Find the Darkness." She heard the wind through her open window, unsure if the voices were hallucinations from her head injury, or the wind speaking to her again. *"Follow—"* The whisper disappeared as thunder rattled the windows.

The room grew darker as the sun moved behind large gray clouds, and she thanked the gods for the darkness, a blessed reprieve from the light that had been worsening the pain behind her eyes. Tears fell against her pillow, wetting the cloth beneath her head and mixing with the blood still running from the cuts along her lips and face. It had only been minutes since Thomas had left her when she heard the door to her room open, but the agony was too severe to allow her to look at who had entered.

Lea groaned as she felt a cool cloth against her forehead, and she opened her eyes to see Elise standing over her, gently washing the blood from her face. A wave of pain ran through her when she turned her head, and she bent over the bed, vomiting into the bucket of water Elise must have brought.

"Breathe, dearie. I've called on a healer. You're going to be okay." More tears filled Lea's eyes as she felt Elise's motherly attention, knowing that she at least had this woman to help care for her.

"It hurts, Elise," she stuttered weakly, searching for a position that would ease the stabbing pain in her stomach and the searing pain in her ribs, the throbbing pain in her head.

"I can't believe that bastard did this," she heard Thomas say from across the room. "I should have stopped him... Why couldn't I heal her, Elise?"

Elise held her hand up. "And what could you have done against Alaric?" The wind blew harder outside and the rumble of thunder grew closer. *A storm is coming*, Lea thought absently.

Lea flinched when she heard a boom of thunder that shook the walls as the door slammed open, the wood splintering from the force of it hitting the stone wall. Evander stepped through, eyes black, his hands fisted in anger and fury etched into the lines of his face. Darkness surrounded every inch of him, small tendrils of black immediately filling the room, searching for her.

"Where is she?!" he roared. Lightning crashed just outside, illuminating the room and revealing the bloody, broken woman he was searching for.

CHAPTER 34

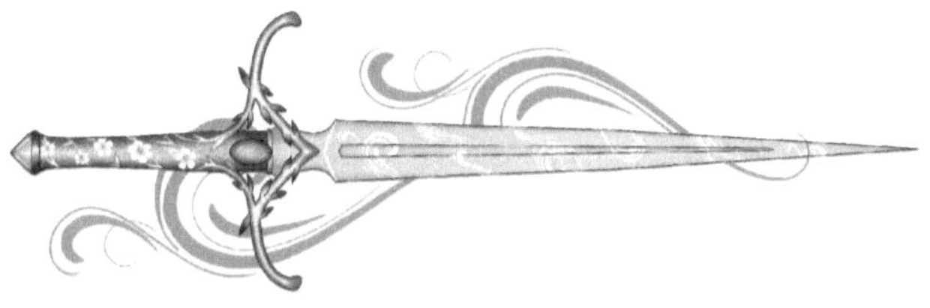

Elise stepped aside and Evander's eyes latched onto Lea, widening with rage as he looked at her broken body. His green irises were so black she wasn't sure they'd ever been green to begin with, his shadows reacting as they pulsed around him.

Evander stepped to her side in two strides, placing a hand on her cheek and pressing his forehead against hers. "Who did this to you?" he growled, the fury in his voice so potent she thought it might plunge the entire world into an eternal night. He wiped away the blood from under her eye as his hands trailed her face, his fingers tracing along her broken jaw—he froze, his eyes darkening as he realized her injuries were so severe that she couldn't speak.

He placed his hand along her cheek and jaw, his fingers brushing against her swollen eye so gently Lea wondered through her pain if he himself had suffered through injuries like this before. She sighed as she felt his cool magic pushing into her cheek, the pain in her eye fading enough to open it a bit. She felt the bones of her jaw begin to knit back together, the agony fading enough for her to swallow again. A tear fell from her eye at the relief she felt, both from the fading pain and from the fact that Evander was here. She was going to live. He wouldn't let it be otherwise.

"You're okay," Evander said as if reassuring himself as he pushed his magic deeper into her bruised skin. "I felt your pain and thought..." He closed his eyes against whatever thought had just crossed his mind. "It doesn't matter, because you're going to be okay." His hands moved to her chest, her ribs, her stomach, his full attention on sending his healing energy into every broken part of her. She felt her bones healing in her jaw, her back—sensation returning to her legs. Tears of relief filled her eyes as she wiggled her toes. *I can move again,* she thought, not caring about the pain that was radiating down her legs as the numbness subsided. Evander finally stopped moving, placing his hands softly on either side of her face and tracing her cheek with his thumb.

"I can't take it all away, Little Flower. Not until night... But, does it hurt a little less?" She answered with a nod, the stinging in her jaw making it difficult to form words. He breathed a sigh of relief and pressed a kiss to her forehead before abruptly standing and stalking toward Thomas, palms out toward him. "Who the *fuck* hurt her!?" He shoved Thomas backward into the wall. "Was it you?" He grabbed Thomas around the throat before he could respond, choosing to use his own hands rather than his shadows, and pinning him against the wall so that his feet dangled at least a foot above the ground. Lea watched the tension in Evander's jaw as veins bulged in his arms; the embodiment of rage.

Thomas shook his head, trying to speak but unable to get words out as Evander's hand around his throat cut off all his oxygen. Thomas's fingers clawed against his hand as shadows seeped from Evander's fingers, traveling across Thomas's body and pinning his arms by his side.

"It wasn't Thomas!" Lea croaked through her pain as she pushed the covers away and tried weakly to stand. The room spun, and she fell toward the ground, bracing for an impact that never came. Instead, she landed against a hard chest that smelled like the wind that carries in a rainstorm. She opened her eyes and relaxed as she saw Evander on his knees, holding her firmly against his chest.

"I need to know who hurt you, Little Flower. I need to know whose heart will take its last beat in my blood-covered hands after I rip it out of their chest," he whispered into her hair, his voice shaking as she started to sob. Lea didn't understand what was happening, how Evander was here, taking care of her, but it didn't matter. He was here now, and it made her feel safe, protected enough to allow her to drop her guard and give in to the fear. She had been sure that she was going to die, sure that the pain was so severe she would feel it even after her death.

"It is exactly who you think it was, Evander," Elise replied softly. "Thomas saw it happen and came to get me to help as soon as they could escape your brother." Evander froze, the room darkening further as shadows crept toward Thomas's feet. Evander stood still as stone for several seconds, the only movement his deep breaths that caused his chest to rise and fall. He reminded her of a snake poised to strike, of the deep breath one takes before firing an arrow. He placed Lea gently on the bed, slowly pushing her hair behind her ear as he placed his forehead to hers once again. His eyes were tender and furious at the same time as he backed away, turning back toward Thomas, his hands fisting as his shadows grew impossibly larger.

"You. Were. Fucking. *There*!?" His fury grew with every word, the boom of his voice rattling the stone floor. "You fucking coward!" Evander stormed toward him again and slammed his fist into Thomas's nose. She heard him cry out and the sound of bones crunching as Thomas fell toward the floor with his hands across his face, blood immediately trickling between his fingers.

"You're a bastard, just like your brother!" Thomas screamed as he knelt over, trying to stop the bleeding.

"I'm at least a bastard who would never, *never* let someone touch the woman I love. Look at her!" He grabbed Thomas by his hair, lifting his head with a jerk and forcing his eyes to meet Lea's. Thomas's face crumpled as he looked at her injuries, defeat and shame evident even through the blood coating his nose and mouth.

"I'm so sorry, Lea. You know I couldn't help you."

Evander's fury grew, his shadows shooting forward to grab Thomas. "You are weak, just like your excuses. You have known this woman your entire life; claimed to love her! She risked her own life more than once to save your pathetic excuse of one. You should have died before letting him lay a finger on her! *You* should be the one bloody and broken in that bed!" He threw Thomas back to the ground, his knees cracking against the stone floor before he rolled and crashed back into the wall. "You failed her. And you don't fucking deserve her." Evander leveled him with a look, the thunder outside growing closer, then turned back to the bed.

Evander gathered Lea in his arms gently, sweeping the hair from her face with a shaking hand while avoiding all the places the pain still throbbed through her body.

"Elise." Evander's voice was quiet when he spoke to her, never taking his eyes off of Lea. "Please bring all of Azalea's items to my quarters. She'll be staying in the room next to mine from now on."

"Of course, Evander, I think that's for the best. I'll have a healer sent to you immediately," she replied, speaking to him with a motherly tone, just as she had to Lea.

"Don't bother. I will be able to heal her more quickly," he replied, raising his eyes from Lea's face to look at Elise. He held her gaze for a moment, an unspoken conversation occurring between them before he nodded his head. Elise's expression morphed to one of surprise, a small smile crossing her lips.

Why was Elise smiling? Was she seeing things from the head injury? Lea shook away the thought. "I want to stay here, with Janelle and Emma, Evander. You can't just kidnap and keep me prisoner again," Lea croaked through her pain. Evander lifted her chin and leaned down toward her, his eyes fierce as they met hers.

"Azalea. You are in no condition to argue, so you will listen to me, for once. I will keep you chained to my side if that's what it takes to keep you safe. Do not doubt that I will kill every threat in this castle, steal you away in the night and live among the monsters to protect you. I broke my promise to you before and let you get hurt. That is not a mistake I will ever make again." His words were pained, and he held her stare for a long moment before turning and walking toward the door. He stopped when he reached Thomas, looking him up and down with disgust.

"I want to be clear that the only reason you are alive right now is because I know it would break her heart to see me kill you. You should be ashamed of your cowardice, of the fact that you let a woman be beaten in front of you... A woman you claim to love." Evander's shadows once again reached out and wrapped around Thomas's throat. Taking another step toward him, he lowered his voice.

"The next time you don't protect her, you die by my hand, and I will enjoy watching the life leave your eyes as I remind you of all the ways you've let her down." He paused, looking at Lea. "And I won't care who's watching." He released the shadows that were choking Thomas and pulled Lea more tightly against his chest, cradling her like an injured bird, before carrying her from the room. Lea heard rain beating against the windows as the thunder boomed closer. She heard the torches lining the hall extinguishing as they passed, their crackling heat smothered by Evander's rage—rage unlike she'd ever felt before rolling off of him. Servants parted as he carried her through the halls, averting their eyes as they scattered.

"I'm okay, I think. You can put me down, Evander. I'm in too much pain to run away." Lea placed a hand against his chest, and he sucked in a breath.

"You'll be in my arms for far longer than it takes to get to my chambers, Little Flower. I need to feel your heart beating." He pulled her closer, his breath warming her cheek as he tried to calm his breathing. "Just let me do this. Don't fight me; just for tonight." He paused and looked down at her, the exhaustion in his eyes and lines of worry across his face surprising her. "Please," he whispered. Lea felt his magic trying to escape through his skin, could feel his distress, the ferocity of his rage. She nodded at him, a sudden need overwhelming her senses to allow him this minor concession, and he exhaled before continuing to walk down the hallways that led to his rooms.

Lea placed her head against Evander's chest, suddenly exhausted.

"Rest, Azalea. You're safe now," he soothed as his shoulders tensed and his eyes darkened. "You're the only thing in this fucking world that's safe tonight."

Lea allowed her eyes to close as the rhythmic cadence of his steps lulled her into sleep, her pain finally fading as she let the darkness claim her.

CHAPTER 35

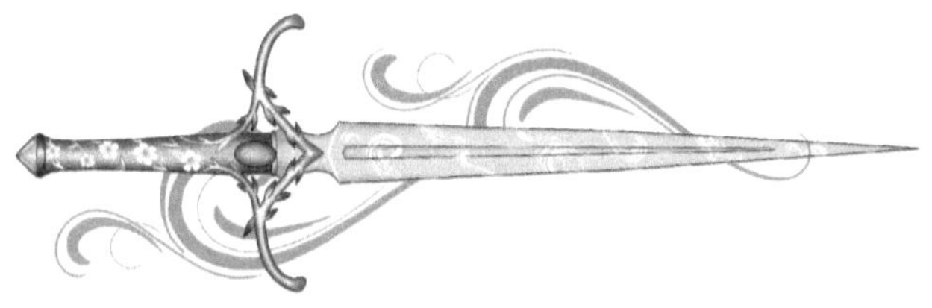

The crashing of thunder and lightning woke Lea some time later, and she peeled open her eyes to see clouds passing by the twinkling stars of the night sky through the windows. Blinking several times–*it doesn't hurt anymore*–she shifted onto her side and stared out at the rain pelting against the windows, a steady patter as fat drops hit and raced down the glass. A large bolt of dark silver lightning lit up the sky, and Lea jumped as the room illuminated, revealing a furious Fae sitting only inches from her bed.

"It's me, Little Flower. Just me," he said, reaching out to smooth her hair away from her eyes. Lea winced, anticipating pain as he caressed her jaw, but relaxed when all she felt was the familiar buzzing sensation that she still didn't understand, the one that always accompanied Evander's touch. A hum left her lips at the pleasant sensation.

"How long have I been sleeping?" she asked, slowly rising to a sitting position and finding that all that remained of her pain was a dull ache in her stomach where Alaric had repeatedly kicked her. Lea prodded her lips and jaw to find them only slightly swollen. Her ribcage expanded as she filled her lungs with air. It was the first deep breath she'd taken since that initial kick that had cracked her bones. She sat up straighter, her vision following the shadows that were radiating out from Evander, floating across her bed like a protective layer.

"You healed me?" she asked, despite the fact that she already knew the answer.

He nodded. "You slept about nine hours."

"How did you heal me so quickly? The pain, it was so..."

"I know. I felt it. I could feel your agony, but I didn't know where you were. I ran to my chambers, but you weren't there... Looked on the balcony in your room, and I could feel that you'd been there earlier, but not for hours at least." He reached out and held her hand.

"You could feel my pain? How?" She almost whispered the words, not quite understanding what he was saying. She had never felt his pain before, or anyone's, for that matter. His eyes softened as he ever so softly touched her still-swollen lip.

"It doesn't matter how. I'm sorry it took me so long to find you."

"You were there in minutes, Evander." Minutes that felt like hours... days even. But he didn't need to know that. She reached out, needing to comfort him. She watched the lines of tension across his face ease a little with her touch, and he squeezed her hand in his, the grip around her fingers so strong she wondered if he was trying to keep her from slipping back into the darkness.

"Minutes in which I could feel your suffering!" His pain was palpable as he brought her hand to his face, kissing her knuckles one by one.

Lea opened her mouth to ask how he could feel her once again as his eyes turned black, the room growing darker along with them.

"I almost brought this castle to the ground, Azalea. The pain you were feeling, I nearly... If you hadn't been inside it, I would have reduced this cursed place to rubble, along with everyone in it." His voice was rough, ragged.

Lea stared at him, unsure how to respond to his confession. They were quiet for several moments as the storm raged outside.

"Where's Alaric?" Lea broke the silence, wincing as she said his name. She wondered how she would avoid him, how she was going to continue to live in a place where someone so clearly wanted her to suffer at his hands before she took her last breath... at those same hands.

"He will pay for this, but the fact that he was the one who hurt you... It makes things complicated. If anyone else had laid a finger on you, *anyone*, I would already be bathing in their blood as I ripped them apart piece by piece, reveling in their screams as my shadows suffocated them. But killing Alaric... It's not something I can do."

Lea's mouth ran dry. "Why? You said you've killed more men than I can imagine. Why not him? Is it because he's your brother?"

"It is. But not for the reason you think. I made a bargain long ago—a spell—or maybe it's a curse." Evander's voice lowered as shadows flickered in his eyes.

"I don't understand... you asked for a spell that doesn't allow you to kill Alaric?" Lea tilted her head to the side in confusion. Why would he wish for such a thing? What could have caused him to protect such an evil soul?

Evander seemed lost in thought for a moment, his eyes glazing over as if a memory was playing in his mind. "I paid a heavy price long ago for a spell that would keep my family safe. Because of it, no one in my family can kill another from the royal bloodline. I cannot kill Alaric any more than he can kill me."

"But why? Why would you agree to that?" Lea questioned.

"It doesn't matter now. The bargain was a mistake. It didn't protect the ones I loved in the end. But there are other reasons I can't kill him tonight, despite my need to end him. Alaric's death puts the kingdom at risk right now. We're not ready for his death, no matter how much I need to feel my shadows burrow into his veins, to feel the life seep out of him slowly. But I promise you, Azalea, I will feel the last beat Alaric's heart takes as I rip it out of his chest. I will stake his head on my sword and ride it through every village in this kingdom. I'll show everyone what happens when they hurt you."

"Do you really care, Evander? Past your duty to protect the people of this kingdom? Past your responsibility to keep me safe after saving me at the market and everything else that has happened since? You don't want me around until something threatens to hurt me and then you promise world-ending suffering to whoever caused that pain. You've told me, several times actually, that you don't want me here, but then you take it back. You tell me you can feel me... that it hurts you to feel my pain. Is it me you want? Or just your need to protect me from your brother?"

He dropped to his knees in front of her, and the sight of the Prince of the Night kneeling at her bed made the small pit of anger she still felt from his constant rejection soften. His head was even with hers as she sat on the bed, and she was struck by how handsome his face was. The anger was still there, but underneath it was the softness she had seen so rarely. He cupped her cheeks with his hands, his fingers threading into her hair, and she could feel the tingle all the way to her toes from his gentle touch.

"Of course I fucking want you." He shook her face in his hands, the tiniest bit, as if he was trying to wake her up. "I have never once, from the moment I saw you, not wanted you, Azalea." He brought his face closer, his breath mingling with hers in a dance that seemed to pull the oxygen from her lungs.

"All I do is want you. Every night as I lie in bed, I dream of you and remember running my hands along your skin. I hear echoes in my mind of when you moaned my name, the noises you made as you came on my fingers. I want you each day as I feel you hovering just outside my door, and all I want is to go to you, take off that stupid uniform you're forced to wear, and taste your lips." Her breaths became shallow and quick as she looked at his handsome face, still so angry, but also *yearning*...

"You all but threw me out of your room the last time I was in here. Told me what would happen if you saw me on your bed again... Is that what this is about? You want my body? Another name to add to the list of the "female forms" you so kindly told me you have looked upon?" she whispered, trying to reconcile the words he had said days ago and the words he was saying now.

"Your form is the only one that makes me feel this way. But it's not just your body. It's every single part of you, Azalea. I couldn't bear to see you on my bed and not take you as mine. In every way possible... in every sense of that word. I've tried to control myself around you, and aside from a few moments of weakness... I think I've succeeded. But seeing your ass up in the air while you leaned over my bed, the bed I've dreamed of you under me on more times than you can fathom? It took every ounce of self-control I had not to rip the clothes from your body and take you right there, that second, and claim you as mine forever. Damn the consequences."

"Oh," she said breathily, and he smiled at her. An actual smile. One that filled his face and brought a rare glimmer to his eyes that were usually filled with anger and shadows. She saw a dimple appear on his cheek, and she turned into a puddle at the beauty of seeing this man look happy, even if just for a moment.

"Yes, oh. Always so good with words, Little Flower."

"You want me... Just me," she whispered, almost to herself. Was she in a dream? No, this was something she hadn't let herself dream at all. Something she had wanted, but never let herself truly admit.

"Repeating what I say again, are we?"

"I don't understand, Evander. If you wanted me, then why didn't you tell me? You've done nothing but push me away. After we kissed that night in the tent, I thought things had changed with us, but it only seemed to make you hate me." He brushed a thumb against her lips, and a shiver ran straight down her spine.

"I told you back at camp. I'm not a good man. I'm not good for you. It's dangerous to be with me. Alaric saw me with you that day, and he could tell that I cared more about you than I would for a prisoner I was bringing to the king. He allows me authority as the Commander of the

Royal Army because it puts me below him, and pretends to be reasonable when in front of his subjects, but it's all an act. He will never miss an opportunity to hurt me. I was worried if he knew how I felt about you... I didn't want this to happen." He touched her injuries, one by one, heat following his touch as anticipation burned inside her. "I didn't want him to hurt you."

"You seem more powerful than Alaric. You could have protected me from him." He winced at her words, as if taking all the blame for her injuries.

"I'll go to the veil hating every fiber of my being, knowing that this is my fault," he whispered his apology. Lea leaned toward him, reaching out to touch his face and trying to get him to bring his eyes back to hers.

"I didn't mean it was your fault this happened. You know that," she said gently.

"It wasn't just about Alaric, Azalea. I came back that night after riding with you all day, hours when I so desperately wanted to touch you, but I wasn't willing to risk it. I spent the whole ride racking my brain and searching my soul for what the right thing to do with you was. And then I found you asleep on my bed, tears streaking your cheeks, and a love letter from another man cradled in your arms."

"Did you..." she wasn't sure why she was asking. She'd known he'd read it the night she'd woken up to see him dressing again, leaving a trail of anger and frustration behind him as he'd stormed out of the tent.

"Read it? I did. Every word is seared into my memory. I couldn't forget it if I tried. Thomas seemed good, sincere. He said he loved you, and I wanted that for you—a safe life, where you were loved and far away from all the things that could hurt you."

Lea bit her lip, pausing before allowing the words she was thinking to leave her mouth. "Like you?" she asked.

He nodded sadly. "Me, my brother, my father—all the danger that would come with me loving you. Away from everything that's happening here, that has already been set in motion."

"You had no right to read my letter, Evander. And no right to make that decision for me." She tried to keep the hurt from her voice, knowing that he was experiencing enough pain without telling him it wounded her that he'd taken that choice away from her.

"Please, please call me Gray. I can't stand to hear that name come from your beautiful mouth. He's not who I want to be for you, Lea. He's who I must be in front of my family, the kingdom. But with you... I don't want to be that man."

Lea looked at the sincerity on his face, watching the vulnerability behind the tough and jagged exterior of the man in front of her grow.

"Okay, Gray. If you promise to tell me how you came to have that name," she conceded with a small smile, and she watched Gray's shoulders sag in relief at her small act of forgiveness.

"All in time, Little Flower. It's a promise." He nodded at her seriously. "I know I had no right to read your letter, Azalea, but... I just wanted to keep you safe. That's all I've ever wanted for you. I wanted to keep my father away from your village, keep you away from the trial, then away from this place. And I failed at all those things. But then you were there, in my arms, like I'd wanted for so long. I'd waited for you, watched you, and now, after all this time, despite my best efforts, you would be coming home with me. There was nothing I could do about that anymore, so I thought maybe I could have you. Maybe you could actually be mine. I'm a selfish man, but you just had so much good inside you... I needed to know if he would be better for you."

She blinked away tears, understanding the way he had treated her, the push and pull she'd felt with him from the very beginning.

"And you decided he would be..." she replied softly.

He nodded solemnly.

"And he just wasted the only selfless thing I've ever done, the biggest gift I have ever given to anyone." Gray leaned down and kissed her fingers one by one, and she closed her eyes at the sweet feeling of his soft lips touching her skin. "He lost his only chance. Because if he's not what's best for you, then I *promise* you, I will be."

She stared at him, her heart bursting at the words she hadn't realized she wanted to hear from him so badly. He waited for her answer, a predator waiting to pounce, her breathing ragged as her hands itched to reach out and touch him. He wanted her. Not gone, but here, with him. He wanted her permission, her acceptance of his confession. And so she nodded, giving it to him.

Gray took a deep breath as lightning flashed again, lighting up the room as he launched himself forward, lips crashing down on hers as he covered her with his body. Lea's breath hitched as she felt his hard length against her thigh, impossibly thick for having only just touched her a moment ago. He took her mouth opening in surprise as an invitation and thrust his tongue inside, licking and sucking as if feasting on her could make him whole again. He rocked his hips into hers while her hands found his hair, her legs wrapping around his waist.

"You're mine," he growled against her mouth, his words of ownership slipping between her lips and into her lungs, settling next to her heart. "You need to understand. I was selfless once, but if you give yourself to me, Lea, you will never escape me. I will own you, body, heart, and soul."

Lea moaned as his hand found her breast, kneading her soft flesh as she arched into his touch. She couldn't think, too drunk on the feel of his lips to form a sentence as his body called to hers, and she responded. A tether deep inside her reached toward him, her magic tangling with his, and Lea knew the choice was already made for her. She nodded, speechless from the sensation of belonging to someone else so completely, as he reached his hand beneath her shirt.

"I need to hear you say it, Little Flower," he said roughly, fingers finding her nipple, swirling and teasing as his other arm braced above her head to keep his weight off her still-healing body.

"I'm yours. I'm yours, Gray." She looked into his eyes as she said the words, suddenly unafraid of the vulnerability of baring her soul to him before baring her body to him. The connection that had tethered them together all of these weeks pulled taut between them as his magic settled deep inside her chest.

"Fucking right you are, Lea," he growled as he ripped open her dress and pulled down her bra, her breasts springing free, his mouth immediately finding a nipple and swirling his tongue around it. "Mine," he growled again, with each kiss that he pressed along her breast and up to her jaw, then back to her mouth. His kisses were wild, uninhibited as he tasted what he wanted, but he was careful to avoid where her injuries lingered.

Her hands found the buttons of his shirt, her fingers trembling so hard she couldn't grasp them. Gray rose to kneel over her, grabbing the shirt from behind his head and pulling it off, throwing it to the ground. His eyes raked over her body as he hovered above her, his breaths ragged. He leaned back toward her, ready to claim her as his, but Lea held her hand up and pressed it against his chest, stopping him. Her eyes were caught on the tattoo over his left pec, the black lines she had seen from far away and forced herself to ignore. She propped up on her elbows and examined the image. *Was that..?*

Gray paused, his forearms straining as he hovered over her for a moment before rocking back on his heels as she came to sit in front of him. She lifted a finger to trace the lines that laid over where his heart thumped in his chest.

"My mountains?" she looked up at him questioningly, then back at the tattoo. It was the rugged mountains that circled her village, the ones she had looked at every day of her life, surrounding a field where a single wildflower rose from the ground. She looked up at him through her eyelashes, a blush coloring her cheeks.

"Is that..."

"Yes, Little Flower," he pressed her forward, laying her back as he crawled up her body, kissing and nipping her skin as he moved up toward her mouth.

"I've spent a lot of time in those mountains, watching your village and making sure you were safe. You haven't known it, but you've always been mine."

Gray found her lips again as she moaned his name, pushing her panties down and her legs apart. Starting at her knee, he trailed his fingers up her legs toward the apex of her thighs, dragging one finger slowly between her folds. She writhed under him, her hands grabbing at his shoulders as she held on tightly to him, trying to ground herself as the exquisite sensation of his touch filled her body.

"Fuck," he groaned, "always so ready for me." He slowly pushed a finger inside, then another, before returning his mouth to her breast. She felt her legs shaking as his fingers began to pump in and out of her, her body turning molten as she let her hips rock along with his movements. Lea grabbed the back of his head and pulled his mouth back down to her breast, giving in to the need that was filling every inch of her. She cried out his name as he bit down on her nipple, just enough to cause a small sting of pain that he soothed away with his tongue moments later.

"Say it again," he growled, curving his fingers inside her as she screamed out his name.

"Gray!"

He pumped his fingers harder, one hand between her thighs while the other grabbed the back of her head. His lips found her mouth again, devouring her. "You're mine, Lea," he said again, adding a third finger, stretching her at the same time he bit down on her neck. Lea exploded, strangled moans leaving her mouth as wave after wave of her release coursed through her body. He continued to push his fingers in and out, wringing every bit of pleasure from her body, goosebumps covering her from head to toe.

Gray forced her eyes to meet his as he pulled his fingers from inside her, unbuttoning his trousers and pushing them down before kneeling over her again. He grabbed himself in his wet hand, covered with the proof of her pleasure, and stroked his impossibly large length up and down as he stared into her eyes. She watched as a bead of cum dripped from the tip of his shaft, mixing with hers as he continued to stroke himself.

"I've dreamed of feeling your cum coating my cock every night since I first touched you. You can't begin to imagine all the ways I've imagined fucking you."

"There are that many ways?" she asked before she could stop the words from leaving her mouth, then cursed herself for showing her inexperience.

"So many ways, Little Flower. But not tonight. Tonight, I need you under me, where I can look into your eyes and see that you feel the need I have for you. I need you to know that you are everything I've ever hoped for, a gift I never deserved, but wanted more than life itself." His eyes were full of unspoken words, his desperation clear as he leaned over her. "I need you to know I pushed you away because I wanted to give you everything you deserve. I promise you, I *will* be everything you need." He leaned over her as she felt the tip of him find her entrance.

"Everything?" she asked shyly, feeling herself grow wet again as heat gathered in her core.

He smiled, a sight so rare and so beautiful it stole her breath away, before he leaned over and took her lips against his again.

"Everything," he whispered. "This might hurt, Little Flower, but I promise you, that is not what you will remember from tonight." He pressed himself into her slowly, a rumble leaving his chest when she winced, grabbing the sheets in her hands as pain seared through her. He paused, kissing along her neck and allowing her time to adjust.

"Breathe, my flower. It's only the feeling of me marking myself inside you, stretching you so that you fit only me." Her core clenched at his words, the pain easing as she listened to him claim her with his words at the same time he claimed her with his body. "And gods, do you fit me," he groaned as he moved deeper and deeper, pausing when he reached the end of her.

Lea moaned, her hips rocking against him as he seated himself fully inside, against the intensity of feeling him stretching her. She gripped his arms as she attempted to take all he had to offer, his mouth finding her nipples again as he let himself fill her.

"Everything, Lea," he whispered, looking back into her eyes for a moment before finding her mouth again, his hips beginning to move. He pushed fully inside of her, every thick, silky inch of him gliding in and out as he spoke her name like a prayer. Lea met his rhythm as his speed built, the pain fading away as pure pleasure filled every inch of her body, leaving no room for anything else as his mouth moved between her lips and her breasts.

"Mine, Lea. You've always been mine, will always be mine." He thrust his hips deeper, and she groaned his name, running her hands along his corded, powerful arms, his back muscles firm as she pressed her nails into them, anchoring herself to him. They moved together as the pressure built inside her once again, his eyes locking onto hers. It was an intimacy so intense, she wasn't sure she'd ever recover from it, from the way he looked at her as if she was the one who put the stars in the sky.

"Gray, it's so..."

"Fucking perfect, beautiful. Come for me, Azalea. I need to feel you come undone on my cock." He thrust deeper, never taking his eyes off of hers. "I've never needed anything more."

Lea believed him, his words so impassioned it sent her over the edge, and she felt herself pulse around him. Gray thrust himself deeper once more, groaning and calling out her name before heat filled her and he stilled, dropping his forehead onto hers and kissing her so sweetly she wondered if he'd really spoken such dirty words moments before.

He pulled himself from her and stood, walking to the bathing chamber to fetch a washcloth. He returned, then wet it in the glass of water next to her bed and moved to clean her. She blushed and reached for the cloth, closing her legs.

Gray grabbed her hands, stopping her as he pinned her with a stare. "You will never feel shame around me, Azalea. I told you that you're mine. That means mine to fuck—" he said gruffly before leaning down to press a kiss to her forehead—" and mine to take care of." He gently opened her legs again and cleaned her before walking back into the bathroom. She pulled the covers over herself, suddenly feeling more naked than she had when he was inside her.

Gray returned from the bathroom, climbing into the bed and pulling her close against his chest so that she was facing him. He breathed deeply as his fingers traced around her arm, her ribs, her breasts—that familiar electricity following everywhere he touched.

"I can feel your magic," she said. "Every time you touch me, sometimes even when you don't." She placed her hand across his chest on his tattoo and felt the tingle spread through every place her skin touched his.

"My magic calls to you, calls me to you. No one else can feel it," he said, sending a jolt through his fingers as he circled her nipple.

She jumped back in surprise, but his powerful arms held her firmly to him.

"I still don't understand. How did you heal me so quickly? How did you know I was hurt?"

He laid in silence for a few moments, continuing to draw his map of lines along her skin.

"That's a conversation for another night, Little Flower. You need rest. You're still healing." He turned her around and wrapped his body around hers, her head resting on his arm, his other wrapped over her naked body.

Lea wanted to argue, to demand answers, but fatigue overwhelmed her as her head hit the pillow.

"You'll tell me tomorrow," she said with a yawn. Gray laughed against her hair.

"Goodnight, My Flower," he said, and she let herself relax, listening to the rain against the windows as the thunder faded away, wrapped in the warmth of the man who had claimed her as his.

CHAPTER 36

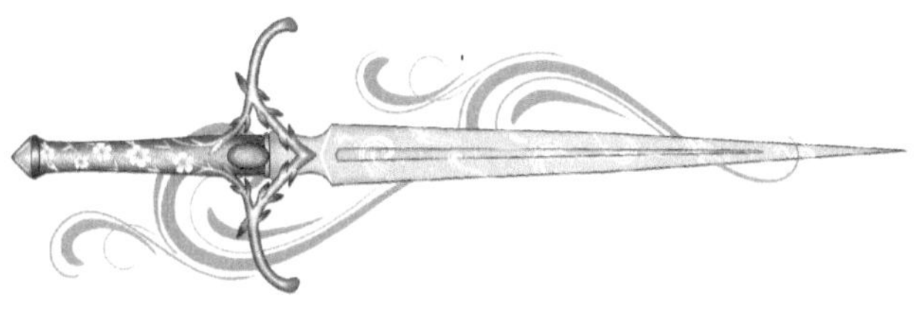

Lea awoke to an empty bed, disappointment filling her as she rolled over to the dip in the mattress still warm beside her and a note next to her pillow. She looked out the window to see that the sun was nearly halfway through the sky, and she jumped up, realizing she was very late for work. She quickly opened the note as she stood, pulling the blanket around her and walking into the room next to Gray's, hoping that Elise had brought her a clean uniform.

Little Flower,

I had an important meeting that couldn't be missed this morning. If the fate of the kingdom did not depend on my attendance, I would have stayed wrapped around you. I wanted to wake you, like the selfish man I am, taste you again and have you come on my mouth as you woke, but you need to rest. Erik is watching Alaric so that you will be safe. I will find you when I'm done.

Yours,

Gray

Lea blushed reading his words, a flush blooming on her cheeks at the reminder that he was far from done with her. Was the tension in the south getting worse? The meeting must have been important for him to leave his bed with her naked beside him.

Lea walked into her new room to see that it had completely changed since the day before when she'd been out on the balcony. Instead of bare bones and empty furniture, she saw a beautiful four-poster bed with carvings of flowers and vines climbing the wooden posts. The mattress was covered by a light blue blanket, so similar to the color of the dress she had worn on Fire Night. There was a small sitting area inside, the couches and chairs covered in a moss-green fabric. Bookcases filled with books she didn't recognize lined the back wall, and a vanity with every color and shape of bottle sitting atop it sat beside her bed. Light curtains draped the large doors that opened to the patio, blowing in the gentle breeze, and she realized that the doors had been left open to allow in the fresh air.

The wide balcony surprised her even more. Potted plants were every-where, in different sizes and shapes and in various shades of green. She ran her fingers over the flat waxy leaves of a fiddle leaf fig before turning to take in the rest of the space. There was a bed hanging from ropes attached to the ceiling, swaying as it hung a foot above the ground, just slightly, when the wind picked up. It had the plushest pillows she'd ever seen, and she dreamed of grabbing one of those books and curling up in the sun, swinging in the breeze. To her right, there was another sitting area, two chairs, and a small table that held a tray. She walked toward it to see colorful fruit and buttered sweet rolls on top of it, as well as a cup and tea kettle. She picked up the kettle and was about to pour herself some tea when she noticed another note tucked into the handle.

I gave you a cup made of tin rather than the china you deserve, but your history with glasses made me nervous for your safety. Don't forget to eat, and drink your tea.

Gray

Lea smiled to herself, seeing that once again, he cared about her hydration more than was rational. Grabbing a piece of fruit, she brought her tea inside, walking to her armoire and pulling out her uniform for the day. Eating and dressing quickly, she hurried to the supply closet to grab her supplies. Most of the next hour was spent cleaning the guest quarters, and Lea was in the middle of scrubbing the floor of the first room when she heard the door open. She looked over her shoulder to find Gray standing speechless in front of her.

"What are you doing?" he questioned, brows furrowed.

"Forming my escape plan. Care to help me?" She rolled her eyes as she turned back to her work, scrubbing the already clean floor. He walked over and knelt in front of her, grabbing her hand and taking the brush from it. She sighed in irritation as she sat back to look at him.

"Gods, I'm not actually trying to escape, Gray. But I have work that I need to get done. Can I have it back... Please?"

"What part of last night, of you being *mine*, made you think I'd allow you to remain as my maid?"

"I have to, Gray. I'm sure Alaric will check up on me. I won't give him another excuse to lay a hand on my body again."

Anger caused his shoulders to rise and his eyes to flash black.

"First of all, I'm insulted that you could think for a second I'd ever let someone lay another finger on you. Second, I met with my father this morning, and he agreed that your talents are wasted on laundry and," he gestured toward the bucket on the ground, "scrubbing floors. Janelle will tend to our rooms now. I thought you might like to still see her."

She reached out and touched his arm tenderly, pausing before speaking for dramatic effect. "She's going to eat you alive."

He laughed. "I can take her ire if her aim is to protect you. Now come on." He grabbed Lea's hand and pulled her to stand before leading her through the halls and out into the open air, walking away from the main gate and around the side of the castle. Servants turned away as they passed, clearly afraid of Gray's presence.

"Will they tell Prince Alaric where I am?" she asked, worry etched in her voice.

Gray squeezed her hand. "They know too well what will happen should they betray my trust. Even if they did, Erik will alert me if Alaric comes to find you. I told you, I won't let him hurt you again."

The small aches that still remained from the night before vanished as Lea breathed in the fresh air, and she realized that the ache in her chest that had been present since the trial was gone. She allowed her lungs to expand further, breathing in the sweet smell of grass as her feet trampled the long stalks.

They meandered further from the main walls and through a copse of trees she didn't recognize. They were the tallest trees she'd ever seen, the trunks large at the bottom and then tapering into nothing as they reached the top. The leaves on the sharply angled branches were white, tipped in a deep, blood red.

Gray looked at her and gave her a tiny smirk, brushing his pinky against hers as they continued walking, and pulling her focus from the trees around them. Electricity sparked between their hands, and she had to pull hers away at the intensity of it, lifting her hand to push her hair behind her ears.

The forest opened before them to a wide-open field with rows upon rows of mounded dirt, enough space to plant a thousand bushes of vegetables or plots of herbs, with different plants popping up in groups. To her far left, she saw different vegetables: tomatoes, peppers, onions, garlic, as well as what appeared to be hundreds of potatoes. Her fingers tingled as she looked upon the plants, noting yellowing leaves on the tomatoes that required pruning and spacing of the peppers that needed to be corrected.

"Your new assignment," Gray said, placing his hand on her lower back and steering her to the right. Dozens of raised beds sat in the sun: peppermint and camomile, turmeric and basil.

"Healing herbs?" she replied, looking up at him with a beaming smile. She wanted to pinch herself. Would she really get to spend her days out here? Could she continue to work with her moonflowers, and give the kingdom a chance to beat the Lonely Death from here at the Castle?

"I know you don't think you have strong healing magic, but you healed yourself after the fenrir attack. Lea, I watched your skin knit back together as I bathed you and dressed your wounds. I had initially thought Thomas had started the process for you, but I know now that he doesn't have the power to do so. You were the only one who could have healed Joshua. I'm not capable of healing him like that. There is no other explanation." He turned to her and led her closer to the plants that were singing her name, the wind stirring behind her as if pushing her toward them.

Lea immediately walked toward the basil and pinched off the top sets of leaves, hoping to encourage them to grow larger and bushier. She pushed her hands into the dirt to pull out some mint, leaving more room for air to circulate around the fragrant leaves. Sighing in contentment, she kicked her shoes off and let her toes press into the grass below her.

"I've never seen anyone glow in the sun the way you do." Gray crouched down next to her. "It's what called me to you. You were shining so brightly when I first saw you that my eyes were burned by your light."

Lea smiled shyly, despite the fact that they'd shared far more intimacy the night before than a silly compliment. "Do you say that to everyone with sun magic? Don't we all glow in the sun?" She looked up at him beneath her lashes before pressing her hands back into the dirt. "And I thought you said back then that I was only a human, not worth seeing the outside of my mountains?" she teased, no malice in her tone. His eyes darkened as he looked at her, sending a tendril of shadows toward her to her chin, lifting her eyes toward his.

"It never mattered that you were just a human, but you're right. I hoped you'd never see outside of your mountains. I'd hoped you'd have stayed ignorant to everything outside of those jagged rocks." He pulled his shadows back. "If I'd been successful at keeping you safe, you'd still be there."

Lea looked up at him, sensing that he was falling back into the blame he felt for her being here. She walked toward him and placed her hands on his biceps.

"You can't control the fates, Gray. Danger can find you whether in the place you call home or on the adventure you've always longed for." She lifted her hands to his face and pressed a kiss against his mouth, pulling back to see dirt streaked across his cheeks. She doubled over in laughter at seeing his strong jaw and cheekbones covered with the soil from her hands. Gray lifted his hand to his face, pulling it away and looking at his fingers.

"This isn't exactly what I was thinking when I wanted you to do dirty things to me," he teased, reaching toward her and grabbing her around the waist. He pulled her into his arms, and Lea laughed harder.

"It's exactly the kind of thing I've wanted to do since I met you." She rubbed her hand across his face again, this time from his hairline to his chin, hardly able to breathe from laughing so hard.

He kissed her, the dirt on his lips spreading along hers.

"I don't hear that sound enough, Little Flower," he pressed a kiss to her cheek, rubbing his dirty face against hers as he set her down.

"I have another meeting, but I will see you after dinner this evening. You can take yours with your friends upstairs or in your rooms. I'll need to eat with my family—stay close so I can watch Alaric. You can come here whenever you like." He grabbed her hand and pulled her over to the raised bed containing turmeric, standing behind her as he pressed his hands on top of hers into the dirt.

"Feel free to get filthy. I'll enjoy bathing you again tonight." He grabbed a handful of soil in each fist and dragged them up her arms, jumping backward as she grabbed a handful of her own and threw it toward him. He laughed as he turned around, hands in the air as if surrendering.

"I'll make sure to roll around in your sheets before bathing *myself*," she retorted, turning toward him.

"Terrible argument. You're welcome in my sheets anytime you please," he told her as he disappeared into the tree line.

As she turned back to the gardens, her eyes found a small cart holding various tools. Shears and small trowels hung from hooks, while different seeds and a watering can sat on the top. Alone in the garden of her dreams, she began her work, pruning here and there, moving some of the plants. Lea realized just how much she'd missed this, needed this, and was suddenly angry that Alaric had forced her to remain locked inside, even when he'd been told of her skills. She felt useful out here in the gardens as the tension she didn't even realize she'd been holding released from her shoulders as she dug and watered. She worked for hours, sweat beading along her brow in the full sun, as she wandered over to the tomatoes, unable to help herself from peeling off the yellowing leaves at the bottom of the plants.

"Lea." She jumped as her name was whispered against her face. She turned around, seeing no one as the wind picked up around her.

"Follow the darkness. Beware the light."

The voice was so soft it didn't sound real. What did it mean, and who was it that kept sending this message to her in the wind? Was the darkness Gray? It seemed like the obvious choice. The voice had only appeared once he'd come to Bearswillow. Or was it more literal? She was drawn to the stars, the night sky... Maybe it was warning her to stay away from Alaric and his day magic. Or maybe it was dangerous for her to be out here alone in the light of day. Lea suddenly felt exposed as she looked around the large open area with nowhere to hide. She picked up her things and walked back to the castle, breathing a sigh of relief when its stone walls came into view. She never thought she'd be happy to be returning to her prison, but she couldn't help but feel safer as she walked inside and returned to her rooms.

Lea's panic eased as she closed the door to her room behind her. She walked straight to her balcony and sat on one of the chairs by the table, not wanting to dirty the plush fabric on the hanging bed, though her body itched to sink down into it and nap in the midday sun.

Relaxing back into her chair, she thought about the events of the past few days. Had she really agreed to be Gray's? And what did that even mean? His to share her bed with, or his to love? It couldn't be to actually love. She'd only known him a few weeks—she was just a human whose life would be only a fragment of his as she aged and he remained young and beautiful. She shook away the thought, not liking the sourness it brought to the back of her throat.

"Lea." She jumped again, though rather than the whisper of the wind, this was the firm voice of a man she knew very well. She turned to see Thomas standing in the doorway to her balcony. Lea froze. She wasn't ready to see him, ready to look at him in the eye after he'd avoided hers during her attack.

"I had to see that you were okay. Last time I saw you, those bruises…" he trailed off.

"I'm okay. Gray healed me," she replied softly, unsure what else to say.

"That fucking bastard. I'll kill Evander for you one day, Lea. For keeping you locked in here… Alaric, too, for what he did to you." He walked to her and knelt before her, taking her head into his hands. She pulled away on instinct. The intimacy of him touching her felt wrong. Anger filled her belly at his words. "He's not who you think he is, Thomas. Gray saved me, fixed my broken bones and protected me against his brother. He did everything he could to keep me from even coming to Auropera. It's my fault we're both here... not his."

Thomas rocked back on his heels, looking at her incredulously.

"You're defending him?" he questioned, his eyebrows raising, showing his confusion and hurt.

"He's a good man, Thomas. No matter what you think; no matter what he thinks. He's nothing like his brother or father."

"He's exactly like them!" Thomas stood and shouted at her. "He wants to control you, Lea, own you, because you're beautiful, a challenge for him."

"And it's impossible to believe that he just wants me because I'm me? That there's no ulterior motive?" She stood, growing angrier.

"You know that's not what I meant. I love you. I love you because you're you." He walked back toward her, and she placed a hand on his chest, eyes sad.

"I love you, too, Thomas—of course I do. You're my best friend. But you never told me how you felt. Never gave me the chance to love you in a different sort of way... And who knows if I would have if I had known..."

His eyes hardened as his hands lowered to his sides. "You have feelings for *him*," he said angrily, and Lea sighed.

"I don't know exactly how I feel, Thomas. But I deserve some room to figure it out. They took me from my home and friends, all because I was trying to protect you. These monsters beat me to near death at your feet. Or have you forgotten?"

"Of course I remember. How can you act like that hasn't haunted me every second since I watched Alaric attack you?" He took another step back, clearly hurt by her words.

"Then why didn't you help me?" she cried, the hurt in her voice mirroring back at him. "I risked my life to save you, to keep you back in Bearswillow. I did it without thinking twice. Yet there I was, bloody on the floor, pleading with you to help me, and you couldn't even look at me." She realized how hurt she actually was by Thomas's inactions, knowing rationally that there was nothing he could have done, but believing if the roles had been reversed, she'd have tried to do something, *anything,* to help him.

Thomas stared at her for several seconds before letting his shoulders sag and walking to the chair opposite hers. "I'll never regret anything more than I regret not helping you. I didn't think... I didn't know what to do." He turned toward her.

"There are plans in place. I promise I will get my revenge against him, Lea. Against the entire royal family. Alaric mentioned he thought you were part of the rebellion. I know that you're not. But... *I am*, Lea." He grabbed her hand across the table, and her eyes widened in shock.

"The rebels are in every town, every city. They have been, for years, making plans. They're done with the evil rule of the Black King; of the whole Nestruir Family. The leader of the rebellion, the Eclipsed King, he's been laying down the groundwork to overthrow them all and rule fairly. I've been meeting with them. That's who you saw me with the other night. No more sending all our food and goods to the capital, or being killed for our magic."

Panic grew inside her at the thought of Gray being hurt by the movement, knowing he was nothing like his father and brother. But a better kingdom, one that was more free? The idea intrigued her.

"You need to keep your distance from Evander, Lea. I'm warning you, if you get too close, you will go down with the rest of them."

Lea saw shadows slither across the floor a moment before Thomas was suddenly ripped from his chair and somehow dangling over the balcony in front of her in the space of a blink.

"Don't you *ever* fucking threaten her again," Gray said as he walked forward, grabbing Thomas from his own shadows and throwing him against the floor. Lea winced as she heard his ribs crack against the stone balcony, but breathed out a small sigh of relief that he was no longer hanging fifty feet above the ground.

"It's okay! Let him go, Gray. He didn't mean it. He'd never hurt me."

Gray stared at Thomas, the anger on his face so fierce she wanted to walk to him and smooth away the lines of his fury with her fingers.

"I'd never threaten her! I love her!" Thomas said. "Even though you're warping her mind so you can control her. I'll *always* love her, and I'll save her from you."

"And yet, it seems that she is once again the one saving you. What you said was right. I do want to own her. Just as she owns me." Thomas's eyes widened in fear as he realized that Gray had been listening to their conversation. Panic filled Lea's gut as she prayed Gray did not hear him admit to being in the rebellion.

"You're a fool to speak of treason and rebellion within these walls. Do you not think there is magic to detect such things around every corner and in every room? Spells to alert the king to your treachery and disloyalty, triggered by certain words the moment they are uttered? You should pray that the magic finds you too inconsequential to detect."

Thomas turned white, his eyes darting around as if he could see the invisible magic that Gray was insisting floated through every inch of the castle.

"I gave you your chance, but you lost it when you didn't protect her. Further, do not believe for a second that I'm unaware of your *Eclipsed King*. I don't care if he's descended from the gods themselves. I swear to you, he is not capable of overthrowing *me*." He took one more step toward Thomas, towering over him on the ground. "And do not think for a second that I wouldn't destroy him, you, and every member of your foolish movement to keep Azalea safe. I would lie down on my own sword if it meant protecting her... something that you clearly don't understand."

Thomas looked up at Gray with a hatred so intense that Lea hardly recognized him.

"Please, Lea, please see him for what he is," Thomas pleaded.

She looked away. "Just go, Thomas. We'll talk later, when you've calmed down. I'm safe with Gray."

Gray turned to her and met her eyes for the first time, the tension on his face easing at her words. "Always," he told her.

Thomas stood, looking between her and Gray. "I'll prove I'm better for you, Lea. I love you, even if you're blinded by his lies right now. You'll see, and I *will* come back for you when you do." He turned and disappeared through the gauzy curtains framing her balcony doors.

"And I will be here," Gray replied, staring straight into her soul.

CHAPTER 37

Lea heard the door click behind Thomas as they stood on the balcony, Gray statue still as he looked at her with enough intensity to heat her blood.

"You were listening the entire time? Every single word?" she asked, already knowing the answer based on the tension in his posture. He nodded at her, but remained silent.

"I'm sorry." It was all she could say, conflicted between that tether inside her chest that seemed to pull her toward Gray while her rational thoughts pulled her toward her history with Thomas.

He stepped toward her, lifting her and carrying her to the swinging bed behind him. The ropes groaned slightly with their weight as he lowered her upon it and laid next to her.

"I can live with the fact that you don't know how to feel right now," he said, his deep voice rumbling through her as he crept his body over hers, caging her against the bed. "You already told me you were mine. Your heart knows it." He pressed a kiss above her left breast, causing her heart to rap erratically against her chest.

"You defended my character against Thomas's words. You said I'm a good man. Your soul knows it." He kissed her lips gently, barely touching hers as he tried to maintain eye contact.

"And I know, after last night, that your body knows it, too." He reached beneath her skirt and grabbed her hip, pushing her flat on her back. Lea gasped as his hand trailed down beneath her panties, pushing through her folds before he slowly pushed one finger inside her, groaning at finding her ready for him. She arched into his hand, desire filling her as he slowly began to move in and out. She grabbed his arms, closing her eyes against the sensation.

"I've waited this long to have you, Azalea. I can wait for your mind to catch up." He looked up at the sun, its rays falling on them, illuminating them in its soft afternoon glow. He scooped her up and brought her inside, walking to the attached bathing chamber rather than the bed.

A large oval bathtub sat in the center, bright white and large enough for even Gray to relax in. It was already filled, and she closed her eyes as she inhaled deeply, smelling the oils swirling in the water. She looked back toward the balcony, wondering why he had stopped what was clearly about to happen between them.

"I'll take you in the sun one of these days, Little Flower," he said, reading her thoughts. "Watch your skin glow as I touch every inch of it, your hair shining as I wrap it around my fist." She shuddered, wishing they had stayed on the outdoor bed.

"But I did promise to bathe you, and you know how I feel about promises."

He set her down on her feet facing him, taking off his shirt to reveal the powerful muscles beneath it. He grabbed another bucket that had been warming over the fireplace and poured the near-boiling water into the tub. Lea watched the steam rise as it warmed the water already in the tub and was taking a step toward it when he caught her arm and turned her to face him.

"I've wanted to take this fucking uniform off you all day. Even for someone so beautiful, you look ridiculous," he teased her as he reached both arms around her waist to untie her apron, letting it fall to the floor. He untucked her shirt from the skirt she wore, his thumbs brushing up against the sides of her ribs, her skin tingling as his fingers trailed upwards. She felt herself lean into his touch. With a flick of his fingers, he released the button on the back of her skirt, holding it around her waist, and she felt cool air hit her legs as it fell into a puddle around her feet.

"I never want to see this uniform on you again." Gray lifted the shirt above her head, then pulled her by the hand to step out of the pile of clothing. He knelt before her and untied her laces, looking up at her as he pulled the boots from her feet, followed by her socks. Setting them aside, he stood, grabbing the pile of her uniform from the ground. He walked across to the fire, throwing it all in unceremoniously, before turning back to her.

"You serve no one, especially me." He knelt before her, hooking her panties with his fingers and slowly dragging them down her legs. Standing, he led her to step out of them, pushing her toward the wall behind them. She felt the cool kiss of stone against her skin as he knelt once more, grabbing her leg and hooking it around his shoulder, a wicked grin across his face.

She tried to pull away, but he pressed a large hand to her belly, pinning her to the wall. "You serve no one," he repeated, "But I do. You will let me worship you." His words held no room for argument as she leaned back against the wall. He parted her with his fingers as he lowered his head, sending a jolt of energy through her as his tongue found her most sensitive spot. She whispered his name as he sucked and teased, his tongue moving slowly as he added a finger inside of her. All her shame of such an act melted away as she leaned back into the wall, grateful for her leg on his shoulder, as she could barely hold up her own weight. She ran her fingers through his thick hair as she looked down at him, the Night Prince of Desia, kneeling before her, between her legs. He licked and sucked like a starving man, and she cried out as pleasure built inside of her, so intense that her knees buckled beneath her with its release. He kissed her one last time before pulling her leg off his shoulder and collecting her in his arms.

"I'll fucking worship you every day, Little Flower." He carried her to the bath and gently placed her inside, the warmth surrounding her languid muscles. She was certain she'd never felt more relaxed in her life as she closed her eyes and sank deeper into the water. She felt him walk away and then return a few moments later. Gray had taken off his shirt, displaying the hard, defined muscles of his chest and arms. He kneeled once again behind her as he soaped up a soft washcloth. They didn't speak for several moments as he cleaned her, starting with her shoulders and arms before moving down along her body.

She studied him as he washed her in silence, moving her eyes from his defined jaw to the thick, corded muscles of his arms. She reached up to trace the tattoo across his chest.

"Gray?" she asked as her fingers moved along the black lines.

He didn't say anything, but turned his face to hers, waiting for her question.

"When did you get this tattoo? It looks fully healed. A little faded, even." He leaned into her touch before moving to the side of the tub to wash her legs, pausing for several seconds before answering her.

"I've had it for five years."

"But I thought—"

"That I got it for you? I did." He offered no further explanation, grabbing a pitcher from the floor and filling it with water to wet her hair.

"Are you going to make me ask for every single detail of your life? You tell me I'm yours, but you keep so many secrets, it makes me feel like you don't trust me," she said quietly, surprised by her honesty. He paused in his movements.

"That wasn't my intention. I'm so used to keeping secrets that—" he paused. "You remember when I told you that you had always been mine?"

She nodded. "I thought it was just your penchant for dramatic statements."

"If you think it's dramatic that I tell you how I feel, get ready for your life to be full of entertainment. It'll be like you're at the theater every day."

Lea rolled her eyes, trying to steer him back to the subject at hand. "So... I've always been yours somehow?" she continued.

"Do you remember when I told you I'd waited for you, wanted you from the first moment I saw you standing in the sun?" He poured a floral shampoo into his hands and lathered it up, then tangled his fingers in her hair.

"Yes, that day at the market." She lifted her head a bit as he continued massaging her scalp, slowly working the suds in between her strands.

"It was at the market, but not the one only a few weeks ago." He paused as if reliving the memory before continuing.

"I saw you years ago. You were much younger, only seventeen, and walking out of a field of wildflowers with a woman who looked nothing like you. I realize now that it was your mother." He rinsed her hair, needing several pours of water to rinse all the shampoo out.

"I wasn't lying when I said I'd never seen so much light before, or when I said that I felt I needed to protect you from the very beginning. Erik and I have visited hundreds of times and kept suspicions off your village for years." He began rubbing a sweet-smelling oil in the bottom half of her hair.

"How did you do that? I've never even seen you before."

"There's a cavern within the mountains. I carved it out with my shadows and created a home within them where I could stay when I felt the urge to find you, watch over you."

He'd lived within the mountains that she had always felt protected her? Had it been his proximity to her that had caused her to feel like something was missing her whole life? Lea turned to look at him, placing her hand on his chest above the dark lines.

"Is that why you chose this tattoo? Because you spent so much time there?" She met his eyes and saw a look of vulnerability on his face she'd never seen before.

"You were this little wildflower, thriving in the middle of those jagged mountains, in a kingdom that wants to extinguish everyone who is different, special. It reminded me that beautiful things can still belong side by side with something so harsh and unforgiving. That the things that surround you don't define who you must become." He rinsed her hair once more.

"There," he said, as if he had shared enough for the day. He stood and walked around the tub, stepping into the water with his pants still on and sitting on the opposite lip. He rested his arms on his knees, bent forward toward her as if he might launch on top of her at any second.

"Little Flower..." she pondered for several seconds. "I thought it was because you thought you could destroy me so easily... crush me under your overly large boots..." She gave him a small smile.

"They go with my huge nose," he replied jokingly, with a wink. He reached to the side and grabbed a towel before standing and walking toward her in the tub. She stood, letting him wrap her in the plushest towel she had ever felt, as he picked her up and carried her into her room. "You've never been more wrong, Little Flower. It's always been you who could destroy me."

CHAPTER 38

Lea had dressed in a soft set of pajamas, a pair of light pants, and a tank top, and was browsing the books on her bookshelf when she heard a knock at the door. Gray had just left for one of his mysterious "meetings," and she wondered if he had forgotten something.

She walked to the door quickly, then paused before opening it. Alaric hadn't found her since the... *incident.* Wouldn't he come to fulfill his threat at some point?

"Do I need to sneak up another balcony to get to you, or are you going to let me in?" Janelle asked, somewhat angrily, and Lea threw open the door.

"You're here!" Lea yelled, pulling her inside.

"And you're alive; thanks for making sure I knew you were okay. I had to hear everything from Thomas, who is not very happy with you right now." Janelle plopped onto Lea's bed. "Holy shit, this is comfortable," she said as she rubbed her hand along the fabric. "What is this thing made of? Angel feathers?"

"I haven't slept in it yet, so I wouldn't know," Lea replied with a laugh before freezing. She didn't want to get into it with Janelle and didn't need another one of her friends disappointed in her decisions.

"You slept with Prince Evander. Didn't you?" She stared at Lea, whose only response was the blushing of her cheeks. Janelle punched her in the arm, surprisingly hard for someone so tiny.

"And you didn't come to get me this morning? Holy shit! Was it amazing? Is his... you know... as big as everything else? Is it princely? Wait! Is it magical?" Janelle laughed at her own jokes.

"You're not mad?" Lea asked her friend, stunned at her calm reaction.

"Yes, I'm mad. I'm furious! I'm done with these secrets, Lea! First, you keep your plan to save Thomas from me—which epically failed, by the way—and now you hide that you're into the brooding, terrifying Night Prince? I followed you both here because I love you. And I'm a good friend, and I deserve better from you." Janelle crossed her arms, and Lea's heart fell into her stomach with guilt. Janelle had been nothing but loyal time and time again, and she realized that she'd been too self-obsessed to see that she'd been hurting her friend.

"You're right, you do deserve better from me. No more secrets. I'm sorry, Janelle." She reached out and touched Janelle's hand.

"Okay, then." Janelle nodded, accepting her apology and moving on. "Spill. Now," Janelle demanded.

Lea told her all the details of the last weeks: Thomas professing his love for her, her journey here, Alaric's unwanted attention, the attack, Gray saving her, and everything else that had happened between them, minus a few details.

"I'm happy for you, Lea. You have a good head on your shoulders and, except for Thomas's trial, I've never known you to make a poor decision. Not to mention, Evander is ridiculously attractive. We should shred all of his shirts. Like, does he work out? What does he eat? I'm not kidding. There's a chance that he might have entered my dreams once or twice in the past few weeks."

Lea shoved her friend backward against the pillows, and Janelle raised her hands in surrender.

"But what about Thomas?" she prodded gently. "That boy has loved you for as long as I can remember." Lea thought about her words, searching for anything that felt different from friendship for Thomas, but it just wasn't there.

"And he never told me. I love Thomas, but I don't feel what he feels for me. It kills me to hurt him. It really does. But there's just something that pulls me to Gray, like there's a chain between him and me that grows shorter every day."

"Okay," Janelle replied as she shrugged one shoulder.

"Just okay?" Lea said. "That's it? No lecture?"

"It's your life, Lea. I'll support you no matter what you decide, but that doesn't mean I'm going to go easy on him."

"I'd be disappointed if you did."

They laid back on the bed together and talked for what felt like hours, past when the sun sank below the horizon and the magic floated through her room. They were discussing Janelle's affair with Thomas's brother when a knock sounded at the door. Lea's heart raced as she felt a large, electric presence behind the door. Gray was here. Janelle, mistaking Lea's anticipation for fear, jumped off the bed and crossed to the door, wrenching it open to reveal Gray on the other side, a tray in one hand and a bottle in the other.

"Oh no, no, no. You're not coming in here and crashing my night with my best friend. I think you've had her enough, don't you?" Janelle wiggled her eyebrows suggestively, then put her hands on her hips and widened her stance, while Gray's eyebrows raised in surprise.

"I'd never dream of it. I thought you might be hungry." He looked past Janelle toward Lea. "You haven't eaten. I brought dinner and wine for you *both* to enjoy." He swung his gaze back to Janelle. "Together. Without my presence ruining the mood." He handed the tray over to Janelle as he turned to face Lea.

Janelle met her eyes with a smirk. "I like him," she mouthed.

"I hope it's okay, but I told Emma that you would be staying here tonight. I presumed you'd want to—"

Someone behind Gray cleared their throat, and he stepped aside to reveal Emma.

"I told him you both would not be having a sleepover without me there as well. I hope that's okay..." she trailed off, as if nervous to be inserting herself into Lea and Janelle's old friendship.

"If you hadn't come, I would have come to get you myself," Lea told her, jumping off the bed and walking to the doorway. She hugged Emma as she came inside, then stepped out into the hallway.

"Thank you, Gray," she reached up on her toes to kiss his cheek, and Gray was forced to bend down slightly to accept it.

"I have meetings most of the day tomorrow, but I'll be just next door tonight. I'll ward the door at the end of the hallway since you won't be with me." He grabbed her face between his hands and kissed her deeply, unwilling to let her lips go until Janelle reached out the door and grabbed her arm.

"You said she was ours tonight, Prince Oaf. Don't start lying to me now." She pulled Lea in and slammed the door in his face.

"Game on, Janelle!" he shouted through the door before they heard his close beside them.

"Was he joking? Does the stern, serious man next door actually have a sense of humor?" Janelle asked her.

"I'm honestly not sure," Lea said with a dramatic sigh, then walked to Janelle and grabbed the bottle of wine from her hand. "And tonight, I really don't care." She opened the bottle and took a deep swig, passing it to Emma.

They spent the next hours talking and eating, passing around the wine that soon ran out. Janelle jumped off the bed with a belly laugh and ran next door, returning nearly thirty minutes later with another bottle of wine and an armful of chocolate treats, refusing to tell them what she and Gray had talked about in her absence. They climbed into the enormous bed and talked well into the night. As Lea faded into sleep, she felt another piece of her life click into place, making her feel that much more like she was where she was supposed to be.

The next morning, they ate the breakfast Gray had sent over as they readied themselves for the day.

"Gray has no visitors for you to tidy after, and it feels weird to have you clean my room for me. I'll take the blame if he finds out. Please?" Lea begged, hoping Janelle would join her in the gardens today.

"I never planned on cleaning your room for you anyway, so let's go." Janelle linked her arm through Lea's, and the familiar gesture made her smile.

They hurried to the gardens, trying to avoid any unwanted attention, and as they cleared the trees, Lea noticed a large form standing between the rows of vegetables, eating ripened tomatoes off the vine.

"Erik!" She waved to him as they approached.

"Hey there, Sunshine!" He turned midway through taking a bite out of a juicy red tomato to walk over and give her a hug, lifting her off her feet and squeezing the air from her lungs.

"You haven't come to get me recently."

"Too many eyes, Sunshine. Alaric's been on a witch hunt since you stopped showing up to dinner service... Which is why I'm here. I placed wards on the path on the way in. If Alaric triggers them, we'll see a flash of fire shoot into the sky. That's our cue to run, and Gray will come find us. Got it?"

"Got it," she said confidently, even though the thought of Alaric chasing her like a game of cat and mouse made her nauseous.

"Don't worry. Gray entrusted you with me. That's not something that I take lightly. I will not let him, or you, down. Now, introduce me to your friend here." He turned and pointed an accusing finger at Janelle. "You're the one who snuck that magic into the house that allowed Sunshine here to escape. Got me in a massive amount of trouble with the boss, by the way."

Janelle smiled sweetly at him. "Guess you should have done a better job searching me, then." She trailed a finger down Erik's chest before winking and plopping down on the grass as Lea walked toward the first raised bed.

"You looked trustworthy," Erik grumbled. "I didn't think someone so small could be so deceiving. I've got my eyes on you, Purple." Janelle just waved her hand in the air as she laid back and rolled up her sleeves, letting the sun warm her skin.

Lea sunk her hands into the dirt, a sigh escaping her lips as she began tending to the flowers and herbs while Erik made a point of watching Janelle for signs of mischief, and she *pointedly* ignored his attention. Lea was tending to the roses that could be used in a tea for relaxation when a thorn cut through her finger.

"Gods!" she yelped as she jumped back and pulled her thumb up. A small trail of blood was running from a cut along the side of it, and she stuck it into her mouth to soothe the sting away. Erik walked over to her and pulled her hand back.

"Heal it," he instructed her, nodding toward her thumb.

"Erik, I don't know how, you know that. I've never had to try before when I've healed myself. It's always just happened." She looked at her thumb and imagined the small cut healing over.

"See, nothing. Why are you so sure I can do this?" Lea asked, confused.

"Because things have changed. Now," he clapped his hands. "Find that warmth in your chest, Lea. Imagine molding it, controlling it. Think of sending it down to the cut; really feel it travel down into your fingertips."

She did as he said, concentrating as she searched for the flicker of heat inside her chest. She could feel the thumping of her heart, the blood rushing through her veins. Lea pictured the warmth in her mind and sent it down her arms and into her hands. Peeking one eye open, she pushed as much energy as she could through her fingers. A bead of blood dripped from her thumb.

"It's not working, Erik. Maybe I have to be in danger or scared or something. Or maybe Joshua healed himself... maybe I can only do the fire thing. Give me a stick." Lea held her hand out, but Erik pushed it back down.

"You just need to focus, Sunshine. Think of your plants, their roots driving down into the soil to search for water. Even on the hottest day, roots will find every drop of water they can and pull it within themselves to grow stronger. Send out your roots. Search for that power that will help you survive."

Taking a deep breath, she focused inside herself, finding her roots and allowing them to search for any kernel of magic that might be hiding within her. She imagined grabbing it within her fist, taming it, then sending it traveling through her veins and down into her fingers. She jumped in surprise when Erik clapped her on the shoulder, her concentration broken.

"Well done, Sunshine. I knew you could do it." She looked down and saw smooth skin where the cut had been just moments before, no scar or indication that it had ever been injured to begin with. She turned her hand back and forth, inspecting every inch as she wondered how she hadn't felt this sooner.

"You actually have fucking magic? And you didn't tell me?" Janelle punched her in the back of her shoulder before spinning her around. "If there are any other secrets, you tell me now," she almost shouted, hands on her hips as she waited for an answer.

"No more secrets, I promise." Lea nodded at Janelle as Erik spoke.

"And you can't tell anyone unless you want your best friend executed."

Janelle's face turned white at Erik's words.

"She won't tell. Can I only do this during the day?" Lea asked, turning to Erik.

"For now, that's likely. But depending on the strength of your magic, you may be able to do it at night as well, though it will never be as potent as what you can do during the day."

"Gray seems to have no problem using his magic during the day. Does he have day magic as well?"

"Queen Emmaline was the last to be blessed with both types, but Gray has the most potent night magic I've ever seen. His magic is of the elemental line. He doesn't show the full might of it often," Erik hesitated, dropping his voice, "but his magic could destroy the world if he was motivated enough."

Lea walked back to the garden beds, considering this for a moment.

"You said that Queen Emmeline brought balance back, that she was the most powerful Fae ever born. A direct descendant of the gods?"

"Yes, she created the only peace this kingdom has known in almost a thousand years." Erik remained behind her, clearly still watching Janelle.

"Then how did the king overthrow her? He doesn't seem as fearsome as the stories I've heard. Honestly, Alaric seems far more bloodthirsty than he does."

"The king holds more power than anyone in history ever has before. It's unnatural, his power. Something one can't be born with. Don't be fooled by his lack of outright evil. He's called the Black King for a reason. Death follows him wherever he goes, Sunshine."

"He wasn't born with it? What do you mean?" Janelle piped up from the grass. Lea looked over to see her moving to a sitting position, clearly interested in the conversation she and Erik were having.

"That's a story that's not mine to tell and one that you likely don't want to hear."

"Seriously, Erik? Why tell me anything at all if you can't answer any of my questions?" Lea raised her arms up in the air. "Just tell me why—"

"What about the queen?" Janelle interrupted, chewing on her lip as her mind worked. "Is it true that she has no powers?" Janelle walked over to Lea's side, officially joining in on the conversation.

"She wasn't born that way, either." He gave them a serious look. "Now, no more questions about the king and queen."

"What about Gray? Can I ask about him?" Lea turned and looked at Erik and gave him a saccharine smile.

"No," he said, deadpan.

"But he told me you knew about the magic in our village, knew about *my* magic. I need to know more... like, who had magic? Was it the butcher? How many people were there, and how long have you known? Gray only told me that you both had been watching for a long time." She pleaded with her eyes.

"He did, did he? Why don't you ask him to tell you the rest?" He crossed his arms.

"Because it's hard to talk when you're sucking on someone's tongue." Janelle elbowed Erik, suddenly his co-conspirator.

"Because I'd like to hear it from you, Erik. That's the only reason," she said pointedly, though the color in her cheeks gave her away. Erik sighed.

"We've known for a while about your village. We still don't understand how you all remained undetected for so long, but we think it might have to do with the mountains. With so few people passing through, the risk of being detected was small. It's possible you were all just lucky."

"So you've seen me before?" Lea asked. "Knew who I was?"

"You feel like an old friend by now," Erik replied with a smile.

"What about me? Do you think I have magic? Have you guys seen me before?" Janelle asked, holding her hands out in front of her as if trying to blast Erik across the field. She scrunched up her face in concentration, pushing her arms out even further.

Erik stood there and crossed his arms, widening his stance as he turned toward her. He smirked as he remained firmly planted on the ground, and Janelle dropped her arms to her side.

"We knew about you. Called you Sneak. Always swiping things from people. Honestly, I'm not sure how you never got caught."

Janelle fished within her skirts, then held out her hand.

"You didn't catch me swiping this," she said with a grin, showing him the small silver dagger that had been at his waist belt earlier.

Erik looked toward his hip, then held out his hand, his face turning red.

"Trouble. The both of you," he said as Janelle handed his weapon back to him. Erik gave them both a suspicious look and pointed his dagger toward them, moving it back and forth between Janelle and Lea as if warning them he'd be watching as he turned and walked to a tree nearby.

Janelle leaned toward Lea to speak in her ear.

"He's cute when he blushes. I think he's going to be a fun one to mess with," she said with a wink before turning and lying down in the grass again. Lea returned to her plants, feeling warmth once again pooling in her chest. Could she use her magic for her gardening? If she could, maybe she could get the moonflowers to bloom in time. Maybe she could finally succeed at stopping the Lonely Death. With a new goal in mind, Lea imagined a warmth like lava traveling through her veins and into her fingertips. She pictured the heat flowing into the lavender she was tending to, filling it with energy like the sun and causing it to grow tall and strong.

She felt the warmth leave her fingers and looked down at the young plant to see it had grown several inches, purple blossoms at the top when there had been none before. She smiled to herself, a feeling of pride filling her heart as her eyes glittered with tears. Was this real? Could she really use her magic to help with her gardening? Her heart sang at the thought.

She looked toward Erik, then Janelle, to find that they were paying more attention to each other than her, their eyes darting back and forth as they pretended their focus was elsewhere. "Erik?" she called, his eyes snapping to hers as if he'd been caught with his hand in the butter rolls. "Do you know if we have any moonflower seeds here? Or where I could get some?"

Erik lowered his brows, tilting his head to the side. "Moonflowers? Hmm, I'm not sure I've heard of such a plant, Sunshine. But we can always ask Elise. If it's grown on these grounds, she'll know about it."

Lea felt disappointment settle in her chest, and she mentally kicked herself for allowing herself to get excited about the prospect of the moonflowers. Of course, it wouldn't be easy to find them. She'd only ever found the seeds herself from the wreath hanging above her bed.

Determined to not allow her lack of moonflowers to ruin her time in the sun and soil, she walked to the next plant, where a tiny sprout had just begun growing. She cupped her hands over the top of it and pushed her energy toward it, grinning as she felt the leaves pushing up into her palms from below. Chamomile, she thought, picking off a leaf and examining it.

She walked to a cart nearby that held different seeds, shovels, and watering cans. Lea plucked a seed at random from a small bag and carried it to an empty bed, examining it between her fingers. *Rosemary?* she guessed.

Digging a small hole and pressing her fingers into the dirt, Lea gasped when she felt roots burst from the hard shell. She looked around, letting the wind guide her on where to go next.

From plant to plant she went, pushing her energy into them as they grew and sprouted, budded, and flowered, until her body felt spent, and she had nothing left to give to the gardens in front of her. She laid back in the grass and looked up at the sky, feeling the sun replenish her energy and the gentle wind caress her face as if telling her it was proud of her.

CHAPTER 39

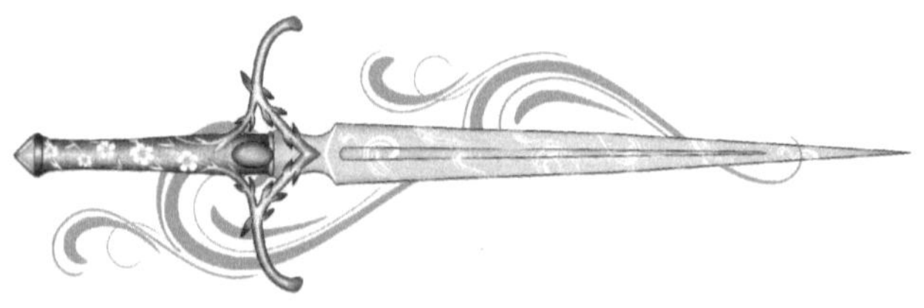

The swinging bed on the balcony called to her when she returned to her room after leaving the gardens. Erik had walked with them as they returned to the castle, his eyes darting about and his hand on his dagger the entire time. Janelle prowled around him as they walked, frequently changing sides or dropping behind them, and Lea had to bite down on her knuckle several times to keep from laughing at Erik's paranoia.

Lea lounged on her swing in the sun, considering how different her life was now compared to a few weeks ago, until she fell asleep. She woke to Gray pressing a kiss to her hair, more gently than she thought a giant like him would be capable of.

"Shhh, rest, Little Flower. Erik told me you used your magic all day. You must be exhausted."

She pushed herself into a sitting position, and Gray smoothed down her hair. "He knew what I was doing? Here I thought I'd been sneaky."

"He told me the garden had grown a month's worth by the time you were done with it. I'm sorry I missed it." He picked up her hands, kissing her fingers. "I'm sure it was a sight to see." He lifted his head, and Lea saw one of his rare smiles. Butterflies filled her stomach, and a grin crossed her face as she looked at him and laughed.

"At least my magic makes you happy. That's the..." she paused, "third smile I've seen?"

"It's not your magic, it's you. You make me happy." Gray leaned forward and kissed her. "The first thing that's made me happy in a very long time." He kissed her once more, slow, sensual kisses that made her crave more before pulling back.

"Unfortunately, I have to go. Duty calls at the most inconvenient times." He stood, suddenly turning serious. "Do you have plans tonight? I'd like to take you somewhere. There are some things we need to discuss, and I don't want to be within these walls when we do it." He looked nervous, like a young boy asking a girl on his first date, as if he was worried she'd reject him and go giggle with her friends about it.

She pretended to consider it. "I think I could spare an evening for you. Though I do have a very busy social schedule." Lea sat up straighter as she took in Gray's fisted hands, his shoulders raised in tension.

"Gray? You're worrying me. What's wrong?" she questioned, rising to stand. Gray opened his arms as she walked into them, needing the comfort as much as he seemed to.

"It'll be okay, Little Flower. But there are things that can't be said in the castle. Things too important to risk being heard by the wrong ears. I promise, I will tell you everything tonight," he whispered in her ear.

"Okay. Tonight. Can we be under the stars? I haven't been under the stars in so long." She thought of all the Fire Nights she had missed since coming to the castle.

"I think I'll need the strength of the stars to tell you what I need to tell you tonight." His demeanor had changed so much in the few minutes since that first kiss he'd pressed to her forehead as she'd slept, a sadness now embedded in his features that hadn't been there before. "I'll come to get you this evening, Azalea," he said sadly. She returned his concerned look and nodded, offering him an uncertain smile as he turned to walk away.

"Oh, and your friend has been lingering near this hallway all day. I think you should be expecting a visitor soon. Remember, you have magic now. You do not accept threatening words from anyone." He looked at her with an intensity that told her she needed to listen closely to what he was saying. "Thomas is angry that you have feelings for me. I can see it radiating off of him. Do not let him give you guilt for something that was never within your control to begin with." He leaned down, giving her a lingering kiss on the forehead before leaving the room.

Lea moved to the inside sitting area, not wanting to taint her outdoor sanctuary with what would likely be another argument with Thomas. Within a few minutes of Gray leaving, she heard a knock at the door.

"Come in!" she shouted, knowing who it was, thanks to Gray's warning.

Thomas entered sheepishly, giving her an apologetic smile, and the coldness she felt toward him eased a bit. She didn't stand as he waited in the doorway.

"I'm sorry. I don't know what else to say, Lea." He held his hands out, his voice cracking as he said her name. She sighed, seeing in the man before her the boy she'd caught frogs with in the stream, who'd bought her sweets when he could tell she was hungry.

"How did we get here, Thomas? We've never fought. We've always been each other's safe place."

"I don't know. I wish I'd done so many things differently, Lea." She turned away and led him to the moss-green chairs, the couch feeling too small to hold the things she knew they needed to talk about.

"You were right about a lot of things. I should have told you how I felt. *Feel*," he corrected himself. "I should have stepped in when Alaric was hurting you."

Lea winced at the memory.

"I should have found a way to protect you from even coming to this place with me. It's all my fault, every bit of it." Thomas shifted in his chair, leaning forward toward her. "But there is one thing that I wasn't wrong about, Lea. And I really need you to listen to me."

She nodded, willing to hear him out with whatever he needed to say.

"You can't trust Gray. He is every bit as evil as the Black King, as Alaric. He's just as much to blame as they are for everything wrong in Desia."

Lea stood, feeling more exhausted than angry. "Thomas. We've talked about this. I can't keep having the same conversation with you. If this is all you wanted to talk about, then you can leave."

"You don't understand. You don't know what I know, Lea! I have been your friend for twenty-three years! I think you owe me five minutes of a conversation when I tell you I'm trying to protect you!" he raised his voice, clearly trying to control his anger.

"Protect me? I have protected myself. Gray has protected me. Janelle has protected me. *Emma*, and *Elise*, and *Erik* have protected me! When have you protected me since we got here, Thomas? What you're trying to protect me from is another man who might love me!"

"I'm trying to protect you from the man who killed your mother!" Thomas screamed angrily, then froze, his eyes going wide.

Killed my mother? The words rang in Lea's head like a gong, ricocheting off her skull until a headache pulsed behind her eyes. It couldn't be true. Gray would never. He'd protected them, her entire village, for years. "The Lonely Death killed my mother," Lea said stonily.

"That's not how I wanted to tell you, Lea. I'm sorry."

Her knees buckled from under her as she fell back into the chair. Thomas was at her side in a moment, kneeling before her. "You're wrong, Thomas. Gray wouldn't... He couldn't have had anything to do with Mom. It was the Lonely Death, just like your father. How can you say these things?" Was Thomas lying? Simply mistaken? She'd known him her entire life. He wouldn't lie to her... but if he was telling the truth...

"He might not have directly caused it, but he knew it was happening. Evander didn't stop the murder of your mother, or my father, or the other thousands of innocent people who have died at the king's hand."

"Explain. Now." She felt seasick, as if the entire world under her chair was shifting. They'd seen the Lonely Death time and time again over the years, watching as it spread through their village, always claiming a few lives before disappearing for years. Thomas sighed, then moved to the couch and motioned for her to join him.

"This isn't something I ever wanted to tell you, Lea. I never want to hurt you, but with what seems to be going on with you and Evander... You should know what you're getting into." Lea rose numbly and sat by him, needing to hear what he was going to say and not believing it at the same time.

"The Lonely Death—the king created it, Lea. It's his magic, not a disease, that spreads through the kingdom with death following behind it."

"Why? What would he gain by killing innocent people for no reason?" Lea felt like she was going to throw up. This made no sense.

"He doesn't do it for no reason. Like calls to like. His magic finds others who hold magic, infects them and attacks their body until they can't survive it. Haven't you wondered why it only spreads to some people, while others are completely unaffected?"

Lea thought back to her mother's illness, how her father had been with her after her body had begun to fail without getting sick himself, but she had been barricaded outside the door, unable to say goodbye. How her father had washed so thoroughly after leaving her mother's room before touching her. Her note had hinted that they had both known about her magic and had tried to protect her from being found.

She suddenly couldn't breathe, her lungs unable to fill with air as what he said clicked into place. The room spun, and she closed her eyes tight against the dizziness washing through her.

"I still don't understand. Why? Why would he want to kill everyone with magic? They can't serve the kingdom if they're dead. Gray would never agree to this. You're wrong, Thomas. You have to be wrong." Lea was panicking. She could hear it in her voice, but couldn't stop it. She pressed the heels of her palms against her eyes as black dots spotted her vision.

Thomas placed a hand on her arm, forcing her to look into his eyes.

"Breathe, Lea. I need you to breathe." He inhaled and exhaled slowly, and she followed his lead. They did this for several seconds, until she gained some control over her breathing, before he continued.

"They take the bodies. We're not allowed to bury them, mourn them, or honor them. We're not allowed a place to visit those we love. Why do you think the king bothers sending soldiers of his to travel all over the kingdom to collect them?"

"So the Lonely Death isn't contagious? But... you're saying the king wants it to spread."

"It doesn't spread through their corpses. It's so he can take their magic, Lea. They bring them back here, and the king steals their essence, every drop of magic that runs through them. It's how he's so powerful. It's why his voice is so strange. He holds the magic of thousands of dead Fae and humans inside him."

Lea bent over as the dizziness clouded her head. It made too much sense for Thomas to be lying. The room spun around her as bile burned the back of her throat. Waves of nausea overtook her as she threw up onto the carpet, feeling as if everything she'd ever thought to be true was a lie. This couldn't be real, but it was. *It has to be.* The king. This was how he had been strong enough to overthrow Queen Emmaline, and why Erik wouldn't tell her how it had been possible.

Thomas jumped up and knelt next to her, rubbing her back.

"I'm so sorry, Lea. I'm so, so sorry. I wanted to protect you from this. I never wanted you to know how truly evil they are."

"Then why did you tell me? You said the king steals the magic, not his sons."

"Because Evander and Alaric knew, Lea. They know everything he does. What do you think Evander is doing when he is scouting the countryside for months at a time? He's finding those with magic, telling his father where to spread the Lonely Death next."

"No." She couldn't believe it. "It's not true. Gray wouldn't do that, Thomas. He wouldn't." But even as she said the words, she couldn't come up with another explanation for what else he had been doing for months on the road. He was clearly working for his father, reporting back to him. Gray had told her he wasn't a good man, that he had killed countless people. He'd warned her away from him many times, said that he'd been selfish for keeping her. She sat up and looked at Thomas. "Are you sure? How do you know?" she asked quietly.

"The group of people who want to fight," Thomas said, looking around the room, playing a word game to prevent triggering any magic, before dropping his voice to a whisper so low Lea had to strain to hear him. "I told you, I'm a member. This is why we're risking everything, why we're going to fight." He held his hand over his heart with his thumb tucked into his palm as he looked at her seriously, a frown crossing his still boyish face. "There are hundreds of us just within the palace. Lea, we are all over the kingdom. I'd heard whispers back in Bearswillow, but I didn't know the extent of the King's wickedness. We're going to overthrow him, the whole royal line. We just need more time. The Eclipsed King has traveled from city to city, growing our numbers, and opening peoples' eyes to the evil within Desia. We will win this war."

She nodded, numb. It was all too much. She'd just been taken from her village. Was she now expected to join a rebellion and fight to escape her new home? What could she even trust, if not her own intuition? "I need to get out of here, Thomas. I need some space."

"Don't you understand, Lea? I can help you. I can protect you from him. Let me be that person for you." He leaned forward to embrace her, but she held both hands up.

"I need to be alone, please," she said, scooting backward.

"I don't want to leave you like this. You need—"

"Listen to me! What I *need* is for you to stop telling me what is best for me! How long have you known about this, Thomas?" She stood.

"That's not fair, Lea. I didn't want to hurt you."

"Why do you get to decide what will hurt me? You're only telling me now because you know I have feelings for him!" she shouted, furious with Gray, but also furious with her best friend.

"But Lea—"

"No!" she said firmly. "No."

She turned and walked calmly from the room, closing the door behind her before breaking into a run. She cried out in pain as a searing wound opened up inside her. Fire bloomed behind her breastbone, a pain so severe it took her breath away, but she couldn't stop.

Lea ran like an animal escaping down its tunnels during a wildfire it knows will leave nothing alive. She fled into the depths of the castle—down hallways and staircases, down as the air became cooler and cooler until she found the room Erik had taken her to train in. She was furious. Furious with Thomas for trying to control her, furious with Gray for lying to her about her mother, for being the monster that he told her he was. She grabbed at the locks on the door and sent searing fire down her arms into her palms, melting the metal enough to rip them away. Hurrying inside, Lea slammed the door behind her, grateful to see piles of sticks and straw and buckets of water.

She walked forward toward the first small pile and threw her palm out toward it. It exploded in a blaze of fire that shot back into her, reenergizing her. Lea watched it fizzle out into a black pile on the floor, then held out both hands toward the larger pile in front of her, at least five feet tall. She watched as it incinerated, looking up to see blazing pieces of ash and small flaming pieces of straw floating through the air. Looking toward the pile of sticks nearby, Lea sent a blast of heat toward them, then turned toward the mat on the floor. Nothing helped the pain now spreading through her body.

Lea burned every inch of everything within the room until sweat beaded her skin and matted her hair to her forehead, and still, nothing eased the fury she felt bubbling in her stomach. She tried to pour every bit of her hurt and anger into the fires burning around her, not realizing that tears were streaming down her cheeks, running tracks through the soot across her skin.

Once there was nothing left to burn, she let herself sit, pressing her eyes into the tops of her knees. *How did I get here?* How had she been so blind that she missed what had been right in front of her? Gray had warned her, had given her every opportunity to see who he really was. Her pain faded, only enough to allow her to breathe deeply. She wasn't sure the pain would ever fade completely. Not when she was so completely shattered.

Lea was going through every moment in her mind since she'd met Gray, looking for anything that could redeem him, when she heard the door opening behind her. She reached backward, ready to turn whoever was behind her into ash, when she heard a voice.

"Sunshine." She lowered her hand, relieved it wasn't Gray. She felt the room cool as Erik doused all the flames with his own magic and came to her side.

"What happened? We couldn't find you. Gray is out of his mind. We need to get you back to him before his next lightning strike shatters every window in the castle."

Lea looked up at him, and he reached out to her, grabbing her arm gently.

"Lea, tell me what's happening. Was it Alaric?" He scanned her body, his eyes frantically darting across her skin as he searched for injuries, more serious than she had ever seen him.

"No." She sniffled. "It's Gray. Did you know, Erik? Did you know about the Lonely Death? About my mother?" Erik's face turned white, and he slumped down next to her, sitting with his knees bent and staring at her as if he wasn't sure what to say next.

"He didn't tell me he'd told you," Erik replied cautiously.

The crack in her chest opened wider at his confirmation, excruciating pain bursting once again behind her breastbone, so severe it took her breath away. "He didn't." Lea closed her eyes briefly before turning to look at Erik accusingly. "Thomas did!" she spat, her words filled with venom.

"That—Listen. It's not what you think it is. You need to give Gray a chance to explain." Erik's eyes filled with panic as he reached out to her.

"Did. You. Know?" she asked again, her voice even, furious.

"We knew. We know. But listen—"

She held her hands out to him, flames dancing along her fingers and spreading up her arms where he touched her. Erik jumped back, hissing in pain. "Then I don't want to hear another word from you," she seethed.

"Listen, we didn't know for sure that your mother had magic. We'd never have left—"

She cut him off. "I don't fucking care!" Lea tried to take even breaths. She needed to get out of Evander's quarters, move back in with Janelle and Emma. She needed someone she could trust, someone Evander would allow to take her things. "Did Elise know?" Lea asked Erik, hatred shooting from her eyes.

"No, she doesn't know. And you can't tell her."

"Bring her to me."

"I won't let you hurt her because you're angry with Gray and me." Erik stood, words firm, "If you'd just listen..."

"*Now* you care about people getting hurt? Too bad your empathy was missing the day my mother was murdered," she seethed, her fire reaching out toward Erik. "I'd never be like you. I'd *never* hurt someone who didn't deserve it, and right now, I'm not so sure you don't. So get me Elise, or I swear I will burn you like the fires of the underworld"

Erik took a step back, clearly hurt.

"I will get her, and I will give you some time to calm down. But there's an explanation for everything, Lea. We never wanted your mother to get hurt. We would have stopped what happened if we could have," he tried to reason with her.

"As opposed to everyone else who has died the same way? Thomas's father? The thousands of other parents, *children*, who have died, their bodies taken away and desecrated to give the king more power? You have three seconds to leave, or I swear to the gods, Erik—"

"I see there's no use talking right now," he said. "But I want you to know Gray's not the only one who loves you. I've watched you grow up. I've known you longer than you realize. You're like a sister to me, so someday you will listen, and I'm certain you will forgive me." He turned and walked from the room as Lea collapsed into a sobbing pile on the floor.

CHAPTER 40

Lea thought her tears had run dry by the time Elise found her, but as soon as her motherly touch ran across her hair, she felt them begin again. She could hardly speak with all the emotions running through her, her breaths shuddering between words.

"Can you bring my things back to Emma's room? Don't ask me why, Elise. I know you love Evander, but I can't be there, and I can't go back... Just... please?"

Elise nodded without argument.

"Anything you need, dear. I'll have them brought up and a bath drawn to clean you up. You will be okay. No matter what happened, you will be okay." She placed a hand against Lea's cheek, her eyes glassy, and Lea sobbed harder. "But I want you to know," she continued, "Gray loves you. I haven't seen life in him for years, but with you here..." She sighed, her voice trailing off. "He'd never hurt you on purpose. I'd rest my soul on it. But if this is what you need, I will help you."

Not Gray, she thought. *Evander. He is his father's son. The Night Prince above all else.* "It is," Lea nodded, too exhausted to argue further.

She sat for what felt like hours before standing and turning toward the door. Her feet moved robotically underneath her as she climbed staircase after staircase until she reached Emma and Janelle's room. *Her room*, she thought sadly.

Janelle and Emma were huddled on her bed, and both turned when they heard the door opening, their eyes widening in surprise as they took in her appearance. Janelle immediately stood, running over to Lea and putting her arms around her. She cried into Janelle's arms until she was wrung dry before she allowed her to pull her over toward her bed. She laid down as Emma and Janelle held her in silence, listening to the windows rattle with each boom of thunder, closing her eyes tight against each strike of lightning, shielding herself as if Evander could see her through that flash of light.

None of them spoke as they listened to the storm, the evidence of Evander's anger raging against the castle. Lea cried until her tears ran dry once again, until she couldn't decide who she was angrier with—Evander, or herself.

Hadn't he warned her several times? Hadn't he told her he was bad, that he had done unforgivable things? If she was being honest, she'd never really believed him. She'd convinced herself that if he had done terrible things, he'd had a good reason to do so. His father had been the one to kill her mother, sure, but if Evander had known... It was unjustifiable. The rain continued to beat against the window as Emma and Janelle drifted off to sleep beside her.

Counting fat drops of water as they rolled down the window, Lea tried to think of something positive for each one that made it to the bottom.

One: The new friends she had made...

Two: Elise acting as a surrogate mother when she needed her...

Three: The gardens she could now go to...

Lea jumped when lightning struck again, and she saw a reflection behind her in the window, surprised that she hadn't heard the door open. She quickly sat up and looked toward the door to see Evander, soaking wet with darkness surrounding him unlike anything she'd ever seen. His eyes were black, and shadows burst from his hands, his arms and legs, sliding along the floor and into the air toward her, as if unable to resist touching her. Yet Evander remained still. His chest heaved up and down, the desperation on his face causing her heart to stop for just a moment. The sadness in his eyes called for her to reach out to comfort him until she remembered why she was in this room instead of downstairs with him.

A few moments later, Erik ran through the door behind Evander, also soaking wet and with a bruise blooming across his jaw. The blood from his mouth mixed with the water on his face, dripping onto the floor.

"Touch me, Erik, and I will rip your spine from your body," Evander threatened.

Erik gave her a stern look and stepped back, holding his hands in front of him. "Give her space, Gray. She needs a night to process."

Evander shot his hand toward Erik and sent his shadows racing toward him, pinning him against the far wall. The noise woke Emma and Janelle, who stood up and rushed to stand in front of Lea as if they could shield her.

"Get the fuck out, you fucking waste of space. I swear, if I had magic, I would burn you to a crisp for what you did to her. You fucking liar!" Janelle screamed as she walked toward him, jabbing her finger in his direction with each sentence until she poked him roughly in the chest.

Evander looked down at her, not moving a single muscle other than his eyes.

"Janelle," he rumbled darkly. "I like you. I like that you protect her. But you misunderstand what has happened. I am the *only* person in this world that you will never have to protect her from. Now, if you can't tell, I'm having a difficult time controlling my anger right now, so I suggest you leave and let me have a moment alone with Azalea." His nostrils flared as he tried to wrangle his temper, his fists clenching and unclenching at his sides as his shadows danced wildly around him, trying to escape his control. Janelle stood toe to toe with him, as if she could stop the deadly Fae male from getting to Lea.

Lea stood, worried for her friend's safety. "I have nothing to say to you," she whispered, refusing to cry in front of him.

"You will hear me out," he said firmly, looking straight into Lea's eyes.

"Five minutes," Lea told him sternly. "You have five minutes, and then you are no longer welcome here, ever again."

Janelle turned toward Lea. "Are you sure? I'll kick this asshole out. You don't owe him a single second."

Evander never broke eye contact with Lea, taking slow, measured breaths as if he was a bomb and any sudden movement might cause a devastating explosion.

"Stay just outside. He won't be here long," Lea said pointedly.

Janelle nodded to her and then turned to walk around Evander, purposefully crashing her shoulder into him on the way out. Emma walked to the door, touching Lea's arm gently as Evander released Erik from the shadows.

"You should give her time, brother," Erik said solemnly to Evander. "I think—" A boom of thunder rocked the castle in response.

"I think you should keep your mouth shut on matters you know nothing about." Evander growled at him like a feral animal. "When you find her, the one who is fated to be part of your soul, then you can tell me how you should behave when you've hurt them. Until then, back the fuck off, Erik."

Erik patted his arm, conceding. Evander bristled at the contact, his shadows surrounding Erik's hand and pushing it away from him. Erik held his hands out in front of him.

"I'll come find you later, brother," he told Evander as he left, closing the door behind him.

The air left the room along with Erik. Lea could hardly breathe as Evander stood in front of her, statue still, as if he was afraid that the slightest movement would send her running.

"I'd never hurt you, Azalea," he breathed.

"Did you know your father killed my mother? Murdered her while I sat outside her room, knowing that she was dying?"

He looked at her for a long moment before replying.

"I wasn't there when she was infected. I'd have stopped it if I had known. You have to believe me.

"Did you know?!" she screamed, her blood boiling more with each word he said. "I don't care what you would have done! Have you known this whole time what happened to her? What your own father did to her?"

He looked down, his breaths ragged and eyebrows furrowed. He waited several seconds to answer, as if looking for the perfect words to say. "I knew. I was going to tell you tonight—"

"How convenient," she snapped back, venom dripping from every word.

He took a step toward her. "I swear it. The plan was to tell you tonight, tell you everything. I just needed time. Time for you to see who I really am, not who I have to pretend to be. I needed to know you wouldn't pull away from me when I told you. I needed to know that I'd done everything I could to show you how much I love you."

She laughed in disbelief at his words.

"You expect me to believe you *love* me? You love yourself, *Evander*."

He stepped toward her again, pain filling his eyes at her choice of words. She stepped back and held her hands up, flames dancing from finger to finger, her palms scorching with heat.

"You told me you were selfish. You said you were a dangerous man, that you had done unforgivable things." She stepped toward him as her flames grew. "Well, you were right. This is unforgivable. Allowing thousands and thousands of innocent people to be murdered so your power-hungry father can steal their magic is unforgivable. Scouting them out for him is unforgivable!"

"I didn't scout for him, Lea, I was trying—"

She pushed her fire toward him, the heat forcing him back into the wall. His eyes opened in surprise and awe as he looked at her.

"Lea, your magic."

"I don't care about my fucking magic! Don't you get it? That's why we're here, Evander. Because all your family cares about is magic. Unforgivable!" she screamed at him, the room growing darker and the windows rattling as the storm outside intensified. Flashes of light silver-blue lightning began to strike alongside the dark gray.

"Lying to me, taking advantage of me, unforgivable. Making me love you—unforgivable!" She screamed, her fire building before she dropped her hands, so exhausted. Evander stepped forward, tentatively.

"You love me?" he asked quietly.

"*Loved,* Evander. I loved you," she whispered. "Just like I loved my mother before you took her away from me, made it so that I can never love her again. Just like you made it so I can never love you again."

"Azalea, please. Little Flower, I can explain everything. If you'll just sit down..." He continued speaking, but the roaring in her ears blocked out his words.

"How dare you use endearments that you haven't earned!" Lea felt something snap inside her, the fire inside her fracturing, splitting in half inch by inch until she felt a chill take its place, something dark pooling in her chest.

"Get out!" Lea screamed as she closed her eyes and pushed the coldness out, imagining it creating a shield around her body, pushing it out toward Evander to keep him from coming any closer.

The room went silent, and Lea opened her eyes. Evander's ragged breathing intensified. She looked down to see a thin layer of inky black surrounding her body, floating in the air toward the Prince of the Night. Evander was frozen as he looked with wide eyes in shock and terror.

"Pull it back, Azalea. Pull it back now!" he shouted in a panic, locking the door behind him before walking forward and grabbing her arms.

"This is a death sentence if anyone finds out. Do you understand me? Pull it back!"

"Stop telling me what to do!" she yelled, throwing her arms out as flames and shadows shot from her hands at the same time. Evander went flying against the back wall, and she wondered in the back of her mind why he wasn't using his shadows to protect himself.

He held his hands up, speaking calmly. "I'm leaving."

She took another step forward, her rage pulling her toward Evander.

"I'm leaving," he repeated. "You won't be able to control this unless you calm down. And if you can't control it, the king will bleed every bit of your power from you. Do you understand the gravity of this, Azalea? Look at me."

The terror in his voice caused Lea to lower her hands, just a bit, and look up at him. Evander's voice grew deeper, quieter.

"That was night magic. Azalea, you just performed night magic." He said the words as if he didn't believe them himself. "No one in thousands of years has had both magic of the day *and* night; not since Queen Emmaline. I would die to protect you without a second thought, but if anyone finds out, my father will find a way to kill me to get to you, and no one will be able to stop him. Do you understand? I am leaving so you can calm yourself down, so you can pull back your magic and lock it tightly inside your chest. If you want to live, and I need you to live—" he said desperately, his voice cracking as he walked toward her, stopping before he could touch her—"then you have to control your anger. Don't trust anyone with this. Find me when you are ready to talk. I swear to you, Azalea, I love you. I have an explanation for everything. I promise you will forgive me when you know what I've been working toward. Please, be careful." He hesitantly leaned forward, and she allowed him to press a kiss to her forehead, his hands shaking as they framed her face. He lingered for just a moment until he turned and strode away, closing the door behind him.

Lea dropped to her knees, the realization of what had just happened crashing down upon her. The shadows—had they really come from her? She rubbed at her chest, trying to soothe the pressure she felt there, the burn of heat jutting up against what felt like a block of ice. She heard the door open and Janelle and Emma entered, followed by Erik, who cast his eyes around the room.

He looked at the singed curtains, then at her, knowingly. "Be careful, Lea," he nodded at her before rushing after Evander.

Lea looked up at Janelle.

"I need to find Thomas. Do you know where his rooms are?" Janelle shook her head no, speechless, but Emma touched her hand.

"I do. I helped my mother move his things in. I'll take you there. Do you want to go now?" she asked. Lea nodded, and let Emma pull her to stand.

"Please," she said, allowing Emma to take her hand and pull her through the doorway.

CHAPTER 41

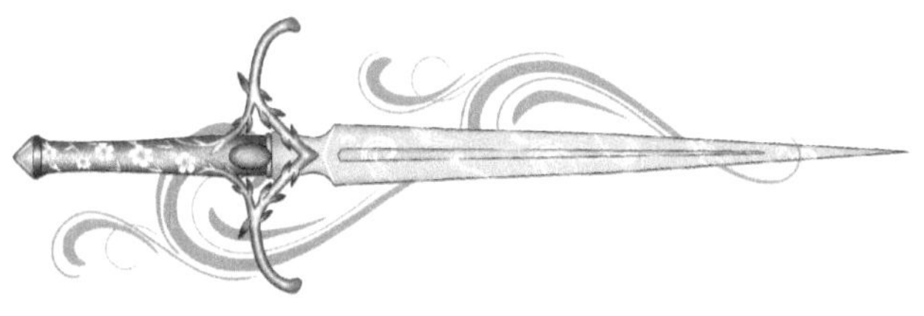

E mma pulled her by the hand through the dark corridors, further up than she'd been in the castle so far. She jumped with every crack of thunder, worried that Evander would somehow know where she was going and drag her back into his chambers, away from the man who had exposed him for what he was.

Away from the man who had ruined everything.

Lea was so lost in her thoughts that she didn't realize when they had stopped in front of a plain wooden door. Emma looked at her expectantly, then stepped forward when Lea didn't move. She rapped against the wood several times before taking a small step back.

Thomas pulled open the door, a small smile on his face when he saw who had knocked.

"Emma, what a nice surprise. I didn't think I'd be seeing you today." He stepped forward to give her a hug, but stopped abruptly when he looked over her shoulder and saw Lea.

He shouldered past Emma as he rushed toward her, placing his hands on her face and rubbing at the soot that she had forgotten was still there.

"What happened? Are you okay?" He turned to Emma, not letting go of Lea's face. "Is she okay?"

Emma looked at him for a long moment before giving them a sad smile. "She's not hurt physically, if that's what you're asking. Her heart, I'm not so sure." She walked to Lea and placed a hand on her arm.

"Do you think you can find your way back?" she asked kindly, and Lea nodded, though she honestly wasn't sure where she was even supposed to turn to get out of this hallway.

"Then I think I'll leave you to speak alone. Thomas." She nodded at him before turning and almost running down the hallway.

Thomas stared after her for a moment, then turned back toward Lea.

"What happened, Lea?" He pulled her into his room, closing the door firmly behind him. He led her to his bed and sat down, pulling her next to him.

"If he hurt you, I swear to the gods I will go kill him right now. Or was it Alaric? You're covered head to toe in ash."

"You were right," she said softly as she looked up at him. "About everything. He knew, Thomas. He knew everything, and he didn't tell me. I've been so stupid." She leaned into him as he brought his arms around her, whispering soothing words into her hair.

"I wish you didn't have to know. I wish I'd never had to tell you." He said her name over and over as she soaked in his familiar scent. "I promise you, we'll get our revenge. Every last one of them will pay in blood for what they did to our parents." His words were so filled with anger she had no doubt that he planned on following through with them.

"Something happened, Thomas. I don't know what to do next." She pushed back from him so she could look at his face. Evander's words circled her mind, his warnings to not trust anyone with the information she so desperately wanted to tell Thomas.

"Whatever it is, Lea, we will handle it together. I promise. It doesn't matter what you've done or what has happened. You know that." He looked so earnest, and she decided at that moment that she could trust him with her life.

"I have magic, Thomas."

He sat back, his eyebrows raising in surprise. "How long have you known, and who else knows?"

"Only since I've been here. Evander and Erik know... No one else that I'm aware of. But that's not why I'm scared..."

"You can tell me anything." He urged her on.

"I have day magic."

"Okay, were you expecting to have night magic or...?" he questioned, unsure why the type of magic mattered.

"It seems I also have night magic, Thomas. I think... I don't know. I just got angry and then it shot out of me like a reflex or... I couldn't control it."

Thomas paled before her. "That's not possible," he said, grabbing her hands and examining them as if he could find proof within her fingerprints.

"It is. I almost just burned Evander to a crisp while trying to suffocate him with shadows. I don't know how it's possible, but it is."

Thomas stood and started pacing the room, running his hands through his hair frantically.

"We need to leave, Lea. You're not safe if the Night Prince knows. He'll tell the king and you'll be dead before morning." He ran to his closet, grabbing a small bag. "No, this can't be happening. Okay, I'll grab what I can and we'll hide, run, whatever we need to do. I won't let him hurt you, Lea. They can't have you!" He was almost manic, as if his only purpose at that moment was to get them out of there, whether they had a plan or not.

She rose and walked toward him, stopping him as she grabbed his hand.

"Thomas, you need to stop. That's not why I'm here. We don't need to leave."

He looked at her like she was insane before grabbing her arm and pulling her back toward the dresser. "Of course we need to leave! We need to get as far away as we possibly can!" He continued shoving clothing into his bag at random.

"I know you won't understand this, but Evander won't tell anyone. We don't need to fear him. We can trust him with this."

Thomas looked at her incredulously. "You're still defending him? Has he poisoned your mind? You actually trust him after he had your mother murdered?"

"I don't trust him, but in his own twisted way, I know he wants to protect me. We're safer here with him close by than we are living on the run, Thomas."

"If you're so certain you're safe, then why are you here, Lea? What do you want from me?!" he yelled at her, his words so furious that she took a step back, shocked at his sudden outburst.

"I'm here because you're my friend. I need help learning to control my magic. I thought..." she trailed off, then turned to leave.

"Lea, don't go. I'm sorry, okay?" he sighed and rubbed the back of his neck. "I just, I can't listen to you defend and make excuses for him." His voice softened. "I'm trying."

"I'm not making excuses for anyone. I'm telling you I trust my gut. I am safer with Evander around. If you don't want to help me because of that, then I think we're done here."

"Of course I want to help you. All I want to do is to help you. I've been trying to protect you this entire time. Tell me what I can do and I'll do it." He went to sit on the bed, then held his arms out, begging her to let him in.

She walked to sit next to him, and he pulled her closer.

"Just teach me how to control it, help me stay hidden. That's what I need from you right now."

"Okay," he replied sadly, pulling them to lie down on their backs on his bed. They laid together looking at the ceiling, arms pressed together from shoulder to elbow like they had done so many times growing up, looking at the stars or watching clouds pass by.

"I still want that life with you, Lea," he said after a long time. "All the things I said, I still mean them. I don't care if you loved him. I don't care that you wanted him. We can move past that."

She reached down without looking and grabbed his hand.

"I'll never forgive him for what he did. Or what he didn't do, I guess. And I will always, always, love you, Thomas."

He turned to look at her as she stared up at the ceiling, wishing they could go back to a day in the fields, where he'd turn to her and tell her he loved her. That their love could have grown without so much pressure, without the threat of death hanging over her head at every moment.

"Things have changed, for me. I don't love him, I can't," she paused, tears filling her eyes as she tried to delay the moment she would break the heart of the boy she cared for more than anyone on Earth. "But I don't think I'm capable of feeling the same things you do right now. My entire world has been overturned... I'm here, I have magic... Let me figure out who I even am before I try to be something for someone else, okay?" Her voice cracked on the last word, and she turned to look at Thomas to see his eyes wet with tears.

He nodded at her before pulling her closer and kissing her hair.

"I'll be whatever you need me to be, Lea. If that's your friend, then okay."

She rested her head on his chest and let her tears fall, holding onto him as he cried silently into her hair. They stayed that way for a long time, both of them grieving what they might have lost, and what they may never be able to find again.

She'd stayed up most of the night with Thomas, trying to summon her night magic again, but it had remained locked away in a place she couldn't access. She could still feel it there, cool in her chest like after a sip of ice-cold water, but she couldn't seem to capture it, move it.

Somehow finding her way back to the room she shared with Emma and Janelle, she opened the door at the exact moment the morning magic rippled through the air. Her power seemed to grow in that moment, warmth and strength filling her in a way she had never noticed before as the change in magic had raced across the land. Did that mean her powers were growing stronger?

Emma entered the room just behind her, wet from bathing before her day began. She looked around and winced.

"I'm sorry, Emma," Lea grimaced as she took in the scorched room, the curtains in tatters and singed along the bottom. Small holes dotted the bedding on all three beds where sparks had burned straight through the fabric. The air smelled of smoke, despite the wide-open window and the breeze floating in.

"You have nothing to apologize for, Lea. Nothing that some stitching and fresh air won't fix, yeah?"

Lea wanted to cry, but Emma's forgiveness for trashing their room was a balm soothing her guilt.

"I'll help you with the stitching," she said with a sniffle, before turning toward her side of the room.

"Lea," Emma said hesitantly. "Prince Evander came by this morning. He left this for me to give to you." She held up a letter, a wax seal holding the envelope closed.

"You don't have to read it. You don't owe him anything. But he looked desperate and asked me to tell you to please be careful. He seemed worried."

"I'm sure he did," Lea mumbled, a flashback of his panicked face from last night filling her mind as she walked over and picked up the letter, the weight of it heavy in both her hand and her heart. Was she willing to listen to what he had to say, maybe try to understand why he had kept so much from her? She wasn't sure, but she knew she couldn't hold these words in her hand and not at least read them.

Lea sat on her bed and stared at the parchment for several minutes, taking deep, even breaths before turning it over and ripping open the seal.

She opened the folded pages, seeing a familiar scrawl across the page.

Little Flower,

I know you don't want to see me or hear from me right now, and that's far from fine, but I'll give you the space you need. I need you to know something. If I could go back in time to save your mother, at the cost of anything at all, my life included, I would do it without hesitation. I was not there when your mother was infected, nor did I know of my father's plans to target your village again. It's not an excuse for not telling you, but after finally believing you could be mine, after longing for you for so many years, I was afraid that this would be a wound I would open in you that I could never heal. I'm more afraid of that now than I have ever been.

I was being honest when I said I was planning on telling you everything last night, and unfortunately, there is still more that you don't know that I'd like to tell you when you're ready. I have waited for you before, and I will wait for you now. Love is not a strong enough word for what I feel for you, but it is the only one I have. I love you, Azalea.

I'm sorry.

Gray.

She didn't realize she had been crying until a single drop fell onto the paper in her lap, smearing the ink so that it bled down the page, reminding her of a trail of Evander's shadows. The words were so beautiful, so kind, and full of promise for the type of love she craved. Could she ever believe him? Believe these sweet words she held in her hands? She wanted to, but it didn't seem possible. She wiped at her cheeks and folded the paper up, putting it back inside its envelope and reaching down into her trunk to grab her mother's old wooden box.

She pulled out her other letters, the one from her mother, the one Thomas had written to her, as well as the few notes she had saved from Evander. Holding them all in her hands, Lea placed the letter from Thomas between the ones from Evander and her mother, feeling like nothing that touched his hand should taint her mother's last words to her.

She was about to place the letters inside the box to get ready for her day when the wind picked up suddenly; the curtains rustling around her. Lea leaned toward the window, expecting to see a breeze blowing the long grass. *Odd*, she thought, as she took in the completely still greenery around her.

Picking up the box, she opened the lid and set it on the bed. Lea was picking up the letters when the wind blew again, rustling them across the blanket so that the ones she wasn't holding scattered onto the floor.

Lea stared at the box. What was happening? She tentatively reached her hand out to close the lid of the box, when the wind blew through the curtains so hard the white fabric snapped at her hand, her skin stinging where the cloth had swatted her away. She looked up to see an open-mouthed Emma staring at the window.

"Did the curtain just slap you?" she asked.

"I was hoping I had imagined that," Lea mumbled in reply. The gusts blew harder, and she felt the wind wrapping around her arm, forcing it down toward the green bottle inside. Her hand closed around it, and she lifted it up, examining it. She felt the wind release her as she looked at the vial, tall and skinny, about three inches in length. She shook her head, not sure what she could possibly need protection from at that moment, and began to put the vial back into the box when the wind blew so hard through the window that it flew from her hand and landed on her bed.

"*Drink...*" she swore she heard the wind telling her, a gentle whisper that floated past her as the wind tousled her hair. She looked up at Emma to see her jaw had dropped further.

"I think I'm hallucinating," Emma said, sitting down on her bed and placing a hand on her forehead.

"If you are, then I am too." Lea picked up the vial, and the wind quieted a bit, as if approving of her decision to listen. Her heart fluttered, worry filling her gut. If the wind was telling her she needed one of the potions, then *something* was coming.

"*Drink...*" The whispers were softer this time, kinder. Lea looked out the open window, then opened the stopper on the bottle.

"Okay, Mom," she said, not completely sure who was sending her these messages but imagining once again that it was her mother who was guiding her somehow from beyond the veil, that it was her hand that had wrapped around her arm and helped her lift the vial. She tipped the rim to her lips and downed it in one gulp, the mystery contents washing over her tongue and sticking to her teeth. The mixture was tart, like berries that were not quite ripe, and her eyes watered a bit at its sourness. She put the vial, along with the letters, back into the box, then placed it in the bottom of her trunk.

"Do you have the energy to explain what just happened?" Emma questioned, always kind and thoughtful to a fault as she continued to dress, facing away from Lea.

"Honestly, I really don't," she shrugged.

"Another time, then," Emma said cheerfully. "Be careful today. I don't know what happened in this room earlier, but I know it is something that you want to keep close to your chest. I'll see you this evening." Emma tied her apron around her as she walked out the door, closing it gently behind her.

Lea felt a sense of doom as she walked to the gardens after changing clothes, her exhaustion driving her into the sun before she'd even had time for breakfast. She needed to be outside, to feel the dirt between her fingers and clear her mind... but was it safe? Something was coming. She could feel it in every breath. Why else would her mother, or the wind, or whatever it was, urge her to drink another potion? There was only one possibility. Danger was waiting for her...

Stop worrying, she told herself firmly. Erik had set a trap here. Surely, if Prince Alaric was coming, she would see the warning and could hurry back to the safety of her room. Yes, she decided. It was worth the risk if it meant she could feel the sun's warmth.

She tried to ignore the nagging feeling as she wandered the garden, hoping it might calm her anxious mind and racing heart. The sun beat off her shoulders as she moved from row to row, trying to use her energy to grow the plants, but very little magic was passing into them.

I must have used too much magic last night, she considered as she continued to work in her gardens the old-fashioned way, enjoying the ache in her fingers and exhaustion in her arms that distracted her from the pain in her heart.

She tried not to think of Evander as she worked, but she couldn't help but picture his face in her mind with each weed she pulled or plant she pruned. He'd looked so angry, then utterly terrified when she'd made shadows trail from her fingers. She thought about his letter to her, the words somehow imprinted on her mind after reading them only once, and she realized that she did believe that he'd been planning to tell her all along—that they either hadn't realized that her mother was in danger or that they weren't able to stop what happened. She could almost even forgive Erik for not telling her, knowing his loyalty to his friend was the only thing that could make him keep something so terrible from her. They clearly thought of each other as family, and Lea knew better than anyone that family came before all else.

Lea paused with her hands in the dirt, hanging her head. At the end of the day, it didn't matter to her what his motivations had been. Evander still hadn't told her possibly the most important secret he could have kept from her. He'd still allowed her mother to die by knowing what the king was doing and not stopping it. He was still allowing other innocent people to die by not exposing him.

Her magic dwindled into nothing as she continued to work, and she wondered if she should stop for the day to rest. Walking back to the tool cart, Lea froze as she recognized the outline of a man emerging from the treeline. Alaric, his face twisted in an evil smile, one that didn't reach his eyes. What had happened to Erik's spell? Did it need to be redone every day? Or had Alaric found a way around it?

Her feet turned before her mind could even comprehend the danger, panic filling her chest as she ran away from him, away from the castle. She screamed when a fireball the size of a horse flew over her head and crashed into the garden in front of her, lighting it on fire. The wind stopped at that exact moment, but even without it, the fire continued to spread through the dry grass surrounding them, blocking her path of retreat.

"If you take another step, I aim the next one at your head. You were foolish to think you could escape me again," he said with an eerie calmness to his voice. "And even more foolish to venture out here alone."

CHAPTER 42

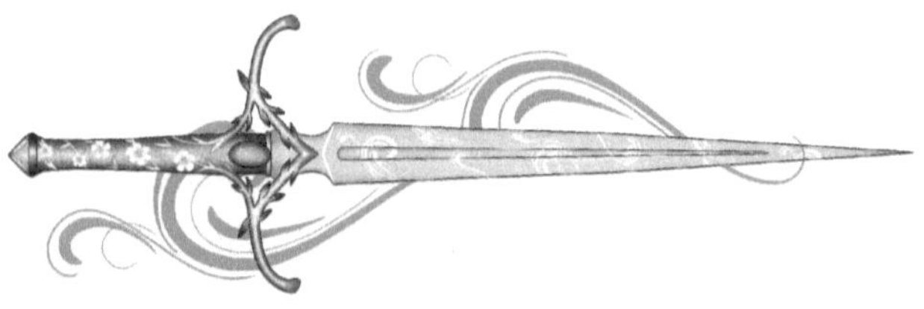

Lea slowly turned around to face him, schooling her face into a calm expression despite the fact that she was so afraid her knees were moments away from buckling.

"Prince Alaric." She bowed her head and was about to curtsey when he cut her off.

"Cut the shit, human. You're no more pleased to see me here than Evander will be when he finds your burned-out corpse smoking in this field. What a sight that will be to witness." He looked off to his right into the sky with a small smile, as if picturing Evander's discovery in his mind.

"You should leave. Evander will be here any second. He was planning on meeting me here five minutes ago," her voice shook despite her attempt to remain calm. *Shit*. She really needed to work on her lying skills.

"You're a terrible liar, you know. You were a terrible liar at the trial, and it looks like your time here hasn't helped you in that area one bit. Evander is in a meeting with Father, one which I was attending, but excused myself due to a headache. Or was it a stomachache?" he thought for a moment, tapping at his chin. "Doesn't really matter, does it? It doesn't change the outcome of this little meeting of ours."

"I don't understand. What did I do to you?" Lea began to shake, terror coursing through her veins, knowing that Evander wouldn't be coming.

He shook his head like he couldn't understand her confusion. "You're giving yourself far too much credit here. I don't care a bit about what happens to you. Live or die, it doesn't matter to me." He picked at his nails like he had all the time in the world to kill her.

"It's my perfect little brother, the one my father wishes could take over his rule, that I wish to see suffer. You see," he crossed his arms across his chest, "I could tell he was, if nothing else, intrigued by you when he stepped in to prevent your death at the trial. We have presided over hundreds of trials just like yours, and he has not so much as blinked an eye when I sentenced every last one of the accused to death. Then I learned from little Nora when I questioned her that he had been keeping you locked away, staying with you, and hiding you from standing trial yourself. Now, why would he do that?"

Dread filled her gut as a wave of realization hit her in the chest. He knew everything. He'd known all along. "Why let me come here, then? Why bring Thomas?"

"It gets so boring around here, you know. My father has all the fun, stealing souls and magic and whatnot. And what am I to do? Drink and fuck around? No, no, I have been far more entertained playing the part of puppet master over the last few weeks. My brother, competing with another man for the love of a human? Losing his temper in front of my father, showing him I'm not the only one who ever so rarely makes a mistake."

Lea looked around for a weapon but was too far from the cart to use anything from it. The only other thing around her was an open field, and with her magic drained... She tried calling it to her fingertips, but it was as if it had gone into a deep slumber, hibernating out of her reach completely.

"I saw the boy, the one I burned for helping you. I know you healed him." He looked directly at her, his eyes demanding that she answer him.

Lea froze, unable to breathe. "I don't... I told you I can't do that. Your brother was mistaken." She held her hands up as if offering proof.

He hurled a fireball at her, and she dove out of the way, but not before it brushed against her arm, searing the skin so deeply that it turned black in front of her eyes. She tried to call healing energy to the burn, to soothe away the pain enough to clear her head. To fight back. But nothing was there. Her chest felt empty, her fingers cold. Panic filled her as she tried again. *Nothing.* Her magic was gone.

Alaric walked over to her and stepped on her hand, pinning her to the ground.

"Defend yourself!" he screamed, spit flying from his lips and reminding her of the rabid dog who had once wandered into the middle of her village, foaming from the mouth and drooling until a farmer put the poor thing out of its misery. Lea covered her head with her arms as he lunged toward her, easily throwing her arms out of the way and grabbing her around the throat. She felt her neck burning in the shape of his hand, five searing fingers wrapping around the sides, his palm against her trachea, the skin blistering below it.

"Defend yourself!" he screamed again, shoving her back down to the ground and kicking her directly in the jaw. His kicks, easily finding their past targets, felt like searing reminders of their last encounter—his last attack.

"I can't!" She sobbed over and over as he continued to assault her. He crawled on top of her, straddling her waist and holding her arms down over her head, his hands burning away what skin remained on them.

"You fucking can! I know you can! Defend yourself or die! Defend yourself!" he shouted again and again, appearing more animal than man as his eyes went wide and his face reddened.

Lea continued to sob. She was going to die. Without her magic, she was a fragile human. An easy kill. "You're wrong, I can't!"

Alaric screamed at the sky, throwing fire above him in his rage, when the day suddenly turned to night. It happened in a single instant, with no warning before their world plunged into black. The wind picked up in a fury as lightning crashed all around them. The terrifyingly loud clap of thunder was the sweetest sound Lea had ever heard. Evander was coming.

"Oh look, little brother is on his way." Alaric laughed maniacally. A fireball grew in his hand and flames danced in his eyes. "I'll have to kill you now if he's going to discover your burning body, hmm? What a shame I have to rush."

CHAPTER 43

Alaric's words were calm, a testament to how unbothered he was by the act of ending a life. He crushed his fingers around her throat and squeezed, burning her skin and cutting off her air supply. Her vision turned black around the edges as she fought against him, her hands scratching everywhere she touched him in her effort to escape. She swore she could feel the inside of her throat burning, and her vision was tunneling when she heard a roar that shook the ground before Alaric went flying off of her, crashing into the fire he had started behind them.

Lea sucked in a deep breath, the air stinging her damaged windpipe and bringing tears to her eyes. She looked up to see Evander atop Alaric several feet away, his shadows wrapping around his neck and squeezing, just like Alaric had been doing to her, as Evander punched his face again and again. She felt someone touch her neck and hissed in pain before soothing energy eased the burn enough to halt the tears threatening to fall from her eyes. Erik kneeled next to her, trying to heal what Alaric had once again done to her.

"Not our best week, now is it, Sunshine?" He pretended to joke, but the fury on his face betrayed his true feelings. "Can you breathe?" he asked solemnly.

Lea tried to shake her head yes, but the pain from the burn along her neck was too severe. She noticed rain pelting against her face, the chill of it soothing her charred skin as thunder and lightning continued to crash around them. She watched Alaric throw Evander off of him, sending him flying as flames shot in his direction. Lea tried to scream in warning, but her hoarse voice barely left her throat.

Evander flicked his eyes to her in alarm briefly before dodging Alaric's flames and turning back to him. Shadows burst from his shaking hands, his nostrils flaring in fury. "I'll kill you! I will end you, Alaric, for ever considering hurting her again. I warned you what would happen."

"Oh, but don't you remember, little brother?" Alaric threw his head back in laughter before suddenly turning serious, his voice lowering. "You. *Can't.*" They continued to dance around each other, both holding their hands out in front of them as if mirroring the other.

Evander's eyes opened in shock, his movements pausing for only a moment. Alaric knew. Evander launched himself at his brother, his shadows traveling down Alaric's throat as if they would rot him from the inside out.

"ENOUGH!" The field vibrated as a flash of light that burned her eyes exploded between Evander and Alaric, throwing them both through the air before crashing them into the hard ground.

Erik cursed under his breath as he stood and stepped in front of her, trying to hide her from the king, who was now storming toward them as if he was about to scorch the earth they stood upon.

"Alaric!" the king's odd voice made Lea's hair stand on end. It had always made her uneasy, but it was so much worse now that she knew the origin of those voices. "Evander and I were in the middle of our meeting when he suddenly ran from the room. I followed him, and imagine my surprise to find you out here playing with a human rather than resting as you informed me you would be doing."

Alaric stood, walking toward the king. "I saw her performing magic, Father. I followed her to teach her a lesson. I thought you'd be proud," he told the king, lying so well it was as if he had studied it in school.

The Black King turned to her, but the pain in her body was so severe she could hardly pay attention to his stare.

"And is this what we do with those who have magic? Do we waste such gifts, Alaric?" he asked angrily, before standing in silence as he waited for an answer. Alaric did not respond as he dropped his head down toward his chest, and the king threw him backward with an impressive burst of magic. "Or do you report it, so that it can be taken?" The shadow voices of hundreds of *others* screamed along with the king's booming voice. "Do you bring them to me so that their magic can strengthen me and the kingdom you will one day rule?" He continued to use his power to hold Alaric down, and Lea noticed Evander using the king's distraction to inch closer to her.

"And you," the king turned toward Evander, throwing him through the air and erasing any progress he had made getting closer to her. "If you've known she had magic all along, and have been hiding it from me, you will not like the consequences of your deceit."

"She doesn't, Father. She's just a normal human. I was mistaken when I first met her—"

"She has magic! I've seen it. I've *felt* it!" Alaric countered, arguing like a child.

The king stood still for several moments before turning to her.

"One of them is right, you know. You either have magic, or you don't. And as disappointed as I am with both of my sons right now, it's easy enough to tell which is the liar."

He blasted Erik out of the way with a twitch of his fingers and pushed his hands toward Lea.

"NO!" Evander screamed in terror, raising his palms toward his father, running at him more quickly than her vision could track.

A bright light shot toward her before Evander could send out his shadows, wrapping around her and lifting her into the air. She heard her scream mix with Evander's as she cried out against the pain pounding into every inch of her skin. It felt like a million tiny hooks had embedded themselves into her and were all pulling her body in different directions. Her vision went black as another scream of agony tore from her mouth. She felt as if she might die right then and called out to the gods for help before she was roughly dropped back into the grass.

The king turned toward Alaric. "Not a drop of magic in her blood," he said sharply, stalking toward him furiously.

"That's impossible! She's hiding it somehow," Alaric stammered, clearly confused.

"Silence!" Another burst of energy exploded out of the king as the entire meadow fell completely still. The wind stopped blowing, and no one spoke. Even the fire around them seemed to stop crackling as it continued to burn.

"Are you implying I'm wrong? That I cannot detect the magic in others?" He stalked toward Alaric, power radiating off of him with every step, so intense it made Lea's stomach hurt.

"Your childish behavior deceives you, Alaric. My confidence in your ability to rule the kingdom," the king's lips *tsked* in disgust as he surveyed Alaric's rage, evident in the scorched earth around them, "is waning after this display of childish revenge against your brother. As for you." He turned toward Lea. "You have caused nothing but trouble since you walked into this palace. I do not believe for a second that Alaric followed you here for no reason at all, and even if that reason is only to hurt his brother, you are distracting him. I will not have my sons fighting over a foolish human girl, no matter how Evander feels about you. Erik." He turned toward the man next to her. "You'll take her to the dungeons to await execution."

A sob wrenched from Lea's throat as Erik took a step closer to her, his eyes shooting toward Evander as his hand went toward his sword.

A deafening crack of thunder boomed as lightning lit up the sky. She caught Evander's face in the flash of brightness, filled with fury as he moved unnaturally fast to cover her.

"If you hurt her, I will turn this entire kingdom to ruins. I will shove my shadows so deep down your throat that you will suffocate on my darkness. It will follow you to hell, slithering deeper inside you while you suffer for eternity. You will die at my hand, as will anyone else who attempts to hurt her."

"You dare threaten me?" the king laughed—a laugh filled with malice and hatred, a promise of death. "I think I'll kill her now and let you get on to your empty promises of retribution." He stepped toward her, and Evander pushed his shadows around them, creating a shield as he shot lightning directly toward the king. The Black King deflected the lightning with a flick of his wrist.

"You *will* move, son! I am the ruler of this kingdom. I *am* the law. There is nothing you can do to stop me. Do not make me take your life along with hers," he threatened.

"You've taken enough, Father. I wasn't strong enough once, but I will die before I let you murder someone I love again!" Evander roared as he continued to push his energy into the shadows shielding them, a misty black wall between them and his brother and father.

"Alaric told me you'd fallen in love with the human from the mountains. You forget, nothing is stronger than blood, my son. But if she is the family you choose..." The king threw his power against the shield, and small fissures appeared at the onslaught. It began to crack and Lea shuddered, curling closer into Evander to make herself smaller.

Evander looked down at her with a sad look on his face, then toward Erik, who nodded his head.

"I'm sorry I didn't tell you this sooner, but I promise, I will explain everything soon," Evander whispered into Lea's ear before kissing her head and standing, expanding his shield around them further with a burst of energy.

"I suggest you stop now, Father. You might think that you are the law, but there are boundaries that not even you will cross. The gods may turn an eye now, but I promise you, they will not if you harm her."

The king narrowed his eyes, trying to decipher the meaning behind Evander's words. "Even the gods are no match for my power! They don't care if I kill a human girl. After all that I have slaughtered, they have yet to punish me. They are not strong enough to punish me!"

"They will punish you if you kill the first mate they have blessed within Desia in a hundred years. Do you wish to risk their wrath?"

The king froze. "You do not expect me to believe—"

"I expect you to listen to me very carefully, and believe every word I say. She is my mate, the soul that matches mine in every way. Anyone who tries to take that away from me will suffer at my hands for every moment that I live. Without her, all I will have is time to crack each of your bones one by one, allowing you to heal as I carve into you with your own sword again and again. I will smother you in darkness until you're so starved of air you will beg for death. You will leave. My. Mate. *Alone!*" he roared, the words sending a shockwave straight into her chest as he sent the full might of his power toward his father and Alaric. The world before her exploded as dirt spewed from a giant hole in the ground next to the king, lightning crashing around them, creating holes wherever they struck.

Lea felt her vision grow fuzzy as flames rose in front of her. Explosions rocked the ground as the king's anger grew, and Lea had to cover her ears against the roaring fire and booming thunder. *Mate? It couldn't be.* There hadn't been mates since before she was born. This had to be a distraction, a way for them to escape.

The king raised his hands, locking eyes with her, his intention clear on his face. He was not deterred. He was not worried about retribution from the gods. He wanted her dead.

Taking a step forward, the king shot power out of his hands, crashing it into the barrier and causing it to fracture.

"Get her out of here, Erik!" Evander bellowed at him as he pushed more strength into his shield, his arms shaking in exhaustion as his magic grew weaker. "NOW!" Without hesitation, Erik lifted her from the ground and ran into the woods beyond and away from the castle, leaving her mate behind in a battle of fire and shadows.

CHAPTER 44

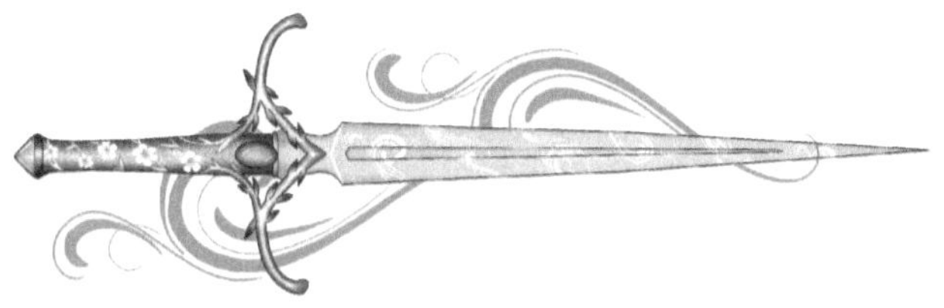

Erik paced back and forth in the meadow where he had laid her, his eyes darting toward the horizon beyond the trees where the sky was nearly black, lightning continuing to flash from enormous gray clouds. She looked back and forth between the bright sky above her and the dark clouds over the trees, her heart racing as she tried to wrap her mind around what had just happened.

"Erik?" she called out, shockingly calm despite her aching body. He paused in his pacing and rushed over to her.

"Hey, Sunshine. Are you okay?" he asked, as if he had forgotten her injuries from moments before.

She nodded. "I need you to tell me if he's lying. I need you to tell me what just happened back there," she said, trying to keep away the panic that was creeping into her chest. *Mate?* It wasn't possible, and yet, she'd felt more than once that being with Evander was where she was supposed to be.

"It's illegal to harm another Fae's mate. It's an ancient law, one even the king cannot break without consequences. He said it to protect you." Erik touched the bruise on her jaw, trying to heal it.

"It's not true then?" she asked, surprised at the twinge of disappointment she felt in her chest as the words left her lips.

"That's not what I said, and you know it..." Erik told her pointedly, looking straight into her eyes, before standing again and resuming his pacing.

Lea looked at her surroundings, trying to distract herself from the fear and worry gnawing at her stomach. She was in a large field, different colored wildflowers sprouting up in patches along a stream that was crossing diagonally through it. A pang of homesickness struck her heart as she listened to the water running across the small rocks, thinking about all the times she had walked in the mountain stream back home. She inched forward, longing to submerge in the cool water and soothe her burns, but the pain was too severe to get there on her own.

They remained like that for a while, Lea sitting in the tall grass listening to the stream, trying to make sense of this situation she had been dropped into, and Erik pacing back and forth. His heavy, repetitive steps wore a path into the ground beneath his feet as his eyes continued to watch the sky.

Mates. Her heart fluttered as she thought the word. It couldn't be possible... And yet, that missing piece she'd always felt inside her felt smaller somehow. She couldn't deny the way she felt when Evander touched her, the tether in her chest that pulled her to him. Could he really be her mate? And if so, had she really just left him behind to battle the Black King alone?

Her eyes scanned the woods, searching for Evander. Was he okay? *Neither his father nor Alaric can kill him, but what if he gets injured?* she thought as worry filled her gut. The anger and resentment in her mind faded as her fear grew. No matter how angry she was with Evander, her feelings for him still lurked somewhere deep in her chest. Feelings she didn't really understand or want to explore right then, but feelings nonetheless. Her chest ached as if calling out to him, telling her that without Evander, she'd never feel whole again. But that wasn't fair. She deserved her anger. Every bit of it.

He had known about his father's black magic for years, never tried to stop it from killing innocent people, but did that make it his fault? Could it even be stopped? She shook her head, trying to dissipate the argument she was having in her mind. Even if it couldn't be stopped, even if he couldn't have saved her mother, he could have at least told her the truth. They could have at least tried to work through it together instead of him keeping her in the dark about what he was trying to protect her from.

Lea shook away the thoughts, exhausted and worried, and focused her energy on healing her burns. While searching for the warm sensation of magic in her chest, she felt the meadow suddenly go still around her.

She froze when she felt eyes on the back of her neck, the feeling so similar to what she had felt back in Bearswillow as she had walked through the market. She slowly turned her head to see Evander, standing preternaturally still, black eyes wild and breaths ragged as he stared at her. Her body moved without thought, attempting to pull her closer to the savage-looking Fae before her. Her breath hitched, and she winced against the pain in her ribs as she twisted to push up from the ground. Evander was at her side in the blink of an eye, spatters of blood across his face and clothing, the cloth of his uniform scorched in several places. He lowered Lea back down to the ground as he pressed his hands into each of her injuries, the pain fading as if his worry was chasing it away.

"You're safe now," he said again and again, reassuring himself that she truly was. "You're safe. How are you safe? How did my father not rip the magic from your chest?" he whispered in disbelief, placing a shaking hand against her heart. "I was certain—"

Lea placed her hand atop his and he paused. "I'm safe now," she confirmed, smoothing the hair away from Evander's worried eyes. *Not Evander. Gray. Prince of the Night, my mate,* she thought incredulously. That is who he was, yet she saw nothing of the Night Prince in the concerned expression of the man kneeling before her. "I promise. I'm okay."

"But *how* are you okay, Azalea? I watched my father's magic search yours out. I've never seen someone with magic survive that." The anguish in Gray's eyes was so intense, Lea felt no choice but to explain everything, to make sure he knew that she hadn't been injured by the king.

Lea paused, unsure how to continue. "The wind, it speaks to me. Guides me."

"Follow the darkness..." he mumbled under his breath, his eyes narrowing as if he was reliving the moment he'd found her that night outside their tent.

"Yes. But, sometimes, it's more. I think it might be my mother. She left me a letter when she died, along with some potions. It's how your magic didn't affect me before the trial, and why my magic disappeared today."

"She left you more magic than I'd realized, then." Gray's lips turned up, some of the tension leaving his face as he reached beneath the neckline of her shirt and pulled out her necklace.

"What do you mean?"

"Your necklace... it protects you from the Lonely Death, Azalea."

Lea froze. *Could it be true?* And how could he possibly know that? "Gray, what's happening?" she asked him quietly. He stared at her for several seconds before settling down into the grass next to her, his hands never leaving her body as he soothed away her burns.

"I don't even know where to start," he said nervously. "Can I be honest with you?" he asked her quietly.

She nodded. "That's all I've wanted from you since the beginning."

"I'm afraid." He looked straight into her eyes as he confessed his first secret. "I've never been scared before, not like this." Lea sat up quickly, turning her head and looking around for the king and Alaric.

"They won't be following me."

"What happened back there, Gray? I thought they were going to try to kill you," she said, her voice cracking with emotion at the thought of Gray being harmed.

"Alaric tried to fight me, but they know it's not possible to kill me. My father tried to murder me for my magic long ago," he told her sadly. "But they can still kill you. That's why I needed Erik to take you. To keep you safe until I could *make* my father hear me, to ensure he knew that your death would cause an uprising. I told them I've been spreading the news that you're my mate amongst my soldiers. Soldiers that would only remain loyal to their king as long as he stays true to the oath he made upon assuming the throne. There would be no devotion from his army, or his subjects if he were to break one of their oldest and most sacred laws."

"Like killing your mate?" Lea whispered.

"Yes, Little Flower, like killing you," he said the words as if they physically hurt him.

"And you think that will be enough to keep him from trying?"

Gray's eyes turned harsh, angry. "He won't be able to kill you. He'll try to find a way around both the law and the curse to kill us both, but we won't give him time. You'll be safe, I promise."

"If you're so certain they can't hurt us, then what are you afraid of, Gray?" Lea didn't understand. What was there to be afraid of if he was truly confident that they were safe?

"I'm afraid of having this conversation with you. I'm scared I'm going to make things worse than I already have, and that you won't be able to forgive me."

Lea looked at him nervously, wondering if he was right. "It scares me too... That you might have to tell me things I would rather not have known... But I also think that honesty might be the only way out of this, Gray," she urged, still angry with him for the secrets he had kept, but ready for the last of them to be out in the open air. He nodded at her.

"I don't know where to start." He looked at her for a long moment. "Yes, actually, I do. I want to start with I'm sorry. I should have told you all of this a long time ago. I didn't tell you out of fear, but I swear to you, I will never keep anything from you again." She gave him a small smile, and his shoulders relaxed.

"I already told you that I have known you for a long time, watched you, and protected you from afar for years. Erik and I—" she looked around and realized that Erik was gone—"we've spent so much time keeping my family's attention away from your village. It's why the Royal Army visits so frequently. It's why I have remained the Commander of the army. I have always felt this deep need to protect you. It didn't make sense. If I'm being honest, it angered me. I didn't understand why I felt this draw to a human girl in a small village, why I needed to be near you. I hated that you consumed my thoughts, that even in the heat of battle, I worried only for your safety. From the moment I saw you, I needed to protect you like I needed to breathe." He took a deep breath, as if proving his point.

"It wasn't until I touched you the first time that I knew you were my mate." He touched her hand, and a familiar *zing* of energy ran along her skin. "It's not just my magic that makes you feel this. It's our bond, my magic calling to yours." He continued tracing his fingers up and down her arm, sending shivers through her body. "It's grown stronger every day since that first touch, and it's why I could feel your pain when Alaric was hurting you, how I knew that something was wrong."

"It's our bond? I've wondered why I don't feel anything when Erik touches me," she wondered. A rumble came from Gray's chest as his hand stilled.

"You don't understand the self-control it takes to hear about another man touching you and not rip their bones from their body one by one."

"It's only Erik, Gray. Your best friend. Your second in command," she reminded him gently, and he grumbled under his breath. "Why didn't you tell me this sooner? Why push me toward Thomas?" she prodded, worrying that talking about her relationship with Thomas might push him even further toward the edge.

"Because I love you, Azalea. I need your happiness more than I need my own. Because I didn't want my darkness to block out all the light you bring into the world." He placed his hands on either side of her face. "Because I carry your mother's death on my shoulders, and I knew that loving the man responsible for her death would hurt you more than my brother ever could."

She stiffened at his words, a sharp pain pushing against her breastbone. "You sent the Lonely Death there?" she asked, and Gray physically startled at her words.

"Of course not, Azalea. I've killed many people, but *never* an innocent one. Never someone so pure as your mother. But I knew she held magic. I knew she used her gifts to help those in need, that she wasn't secretive about her abilities, and it was only a matter of time before she was discovered. I just didn't think it'd be so soon. I should have taken her away, taken you all away and hidden you so deeply that my father's magic could never find you. I might not have sent the Lonely Death to your village, but I didn't act soon enough. Her death is a weight I carry with me every day."

Lea exhaled slowly, trying to keep the tears from her eyes. She knew in her heart that Gray would never have caused her mother's death intentionally, but she couldn't help but feel a kernel of resentment still inside her.

"I spoke with her, you know," Gray said, and Lea froze.

"My mother?" She felt an unexpected pang of pain when she thought about her mother knowing the man next to her. "When?"

"I was with her as she passed beyond the veil. I took away her pain, brought her peace."

Lea felt like the air was being sucked from her lungs, her mind racing.

"How is that possible? I'd have seen you." Lea's thoughts swirled. *He'd been with her. She hadn't suffered.*

"I came when your mother sent you away to see Thomas. I stayed with her, taking her pain as the Lonely Death took her. I could hear you, your sobs as you waited outside for your mother to pass—that sound still haunts my nightmares."

Lea grabbed his arm, grasping for something to ground her as she wondered what her mother had been thinking in her last moments. "You spoke with her?" she asked, desperately needing to know more about her mother's last days.

"I did, briefly, before the fever lured her to sleep. Before the hallucinations started." He placed his hand on hers. "Your mother loved you so much, Lea. She spoke of nothing else. She asked me to protect you, to help your father continue on, said you still needed him. I think she was concerned he would lose himself after she was gone. She wasn't worried for herself in death. She only worried for you."

Lea nodded. "That sounds like her. She was the best mother." Lea sniffled.

"She was. I promised her I would protect you. I helped her with your necklace... placed my own charm among the ones she'd worn for so many years. A piece of star from the day the Fe Fiada fell... filled with as much of my magic as the sacred stone could hold, every ounce of protection I could offer you. The Lonely Death can't touch me... and it can't touch you when you're wearing this." He fingered the sparkling black charm hanging from her neck.

"You're the reason I haven't caught the Lonely Death?" *I don't believe this,* she thought. But how else had she escaped alive when the king's magic had been inside her own house?

Gray nodded. "I still talk to her sometimes, you know. When I'm outside under the stars, I feel like she can hear me. Just last night I apologized to her for breaking my promise, for allowing you to get hurt."

Lea didn't feel the tear that was falling from her eye. *He spoke with her?* "Your brother is the one who hurt me, Gray. You saved me, more than once." She reached for his hand, squeezing it tight in comfort, her heart softening at his admission.

"I'm not talking about my brother, though he should never have been able to place a finger on you to begin with. I'm talking about the way I hurt you, for letting my fear of telling you the truth cause you so much pain."

They sat in silence for a moment, both unable to deny that his words were true. His lies had hurt her, and she still felt that sting of pain from their conversation the night before.

"I know I went about this all wrong, Little Flower. I know I should have told you everything from the very beginning, from the first night I slept in the room next to you in that cottage, feeling your sadness through the walls. I could have eased your pain then, told you I was trying to protect you, explained why I wanted to keep you safe. My honesty could have prevented this whole disaster," he said sadly, and Lea's heart ached to comfort him.

"I know you didn't do this on purpose, Gray. I know you were doing your best."

"So, you can forgive me, then?" His words were so full of hope, they made the ache inside her heart grow even stronger.

She looked around the meadow, focusing on the tiny purple flowers swaying in the wind near her feet. She needed time to think and space to breathe to figure out what she wanted, what she was capable of.

"It's okay, Little Flower." Gray's voice was soft as he pulled away from her.

"Don't leave. I want to forgive you. I know it wasn't your fault. But it will take time for me to be okay with this, Gray. You knew my mother had been murdered. You knew why her body was taken and that her magic had been harvested. How can I easily move on from something like that? Every time you touched me, you knew, and I didn't."

"I need you to know I'm trying to stop it, Azalea. I will stop my father *and* the Lonely Death, but I can see you need me to show you." He sighed, then reached out to cup her cheek.

"Marry me, Azalea," he said seriously.

Lea's lips parted. "Excuse me?"

"Marry me. It's the only way to keep you safe from my brother. The curse might stop the Nestruir's from killing each other, but he can still kill you."

Lea's pulse pounded in her throat at the words. "Then I'll have to kill him," she whispered.

"When the time comes, I will hand you my sword to plunge through his heart, if that's your wish." Gray's green eyes shone with pride as he reached out to caress her face. "But for now, we need to keep you safe. He can't hurt you if Auropera knows that you are fated to be mine. And he can't kill you once you are part of the Nestruir family."

Lea felt panic building within her as her hands began to shake. *Marriage? It can't be the only way.* "I thought it was illegal to harm another Fae's mate. I'll be fine, right? You just said he can't hurt me?" She could feel herself spiraling, her breaths growing ragged as she tried to suck in enough air.

"Breathe, Lea. It doesn't have to mean anything. Not if you don't want it to. It is illegal for him to hurt you knowing you're my mate, yes, but it also won't stop him. Without all of Desia knowing, there will be no consequences if he comes after you." He grabbed her hand, sadness creasing his forehead. "I know this isn't what you want. This isn't how I wanted you to become my wife, either."

He's thought about me becoming his wife?

"But if it's between this, knowing you'll be safe, or risking Alaric or my father killing you just to spite me, then the choice is simple. This is what we have to do."

Lea put her head between her knees as the world spun around her. She couldn't breathe, couldn't seem to clear her mind as her vision went fuzzy.

"We won't seal the bond, Lea. You'll still be free. You can do whatever you want, be with whomever you want. I won't stand in your way." His words were pained. "But this is the only way to ensure that everyone knows who and what you are to me. My brother will bow to the ancient laws regarding injuring another's mate. He would never be accepted as king if the kingdom knew he had harmed you after knowing what you are to me." He looked at her, and she wondered if it was her imagination or if he really had tears in his eyes.

Lea attempted to understand everything that had transpired over the past few minutes. From Gray's confession to her attempts to understand how to forgive him. Taking a deep breath, she spoke softly. "I know you never intended to hurt me, Gray. I know that every single one of your actions has been to protect me. But this is not how I imagined I would be married. It was supposed to be a love like my Mom and Dad had. It was supposed to be true and pure and honest." She glanced at Gray, seeing his attempts at hiding his hurt behind his tired eyes. "I can't marry you just because your brother hates you. That's insane, Gray."

His face fell, his body deflating as if her words had punctured his skin and allowed his soul to seep out through the small holes.

"I know. I can't make you feel for me the way your mother felt for your father. But I can tell you that I love you more than anyone has ever loved another. That I have done my best to protect you, to love you from afar, even if I have failed in every way. We don't have to seal the bond. I won't make you accept that I'm your mate. I won't make you live with me or talk to me, or love me. But I will make you listen to me." He pulled her to him roughly, as if he was worried she would disappear before his eyes.

"I will do everything in my power to make sure you are protected from this fucking family I was born into. I will make sure that you are safe, that you're happy, and that you *live*. No matter who you decide to live your life with. I can't exist in a world without your light. I won't exist in a world that you are not a part of. So, I will make sure that my brother can't hurt you, and to do that, the world will have to know that I love you desperately, and I will watch them all burn before my eyes before I live a life without you in it."

They went silent again, clinging to each other with their bodies as her mind urged her to pull away.

"I can't be with you, Gray, not right now. I just... I need you to understand why I can't."

"I do. I know you can't love me after what I've done. But you *will* protect yourself," he told her fiercely. "You have to, Azalea."

She took several steadying breaths, closing her eyes and letting the feel of the wind in her hair ground her. Tears pricked her eyes as it blew against her skin, wrapping around her and pressing against her chest before picking up her hand and placing it on top of Gray's.

Gray stared at their hands, his gaze fixed on her touch. *"Follow the darkness..."* the wind called again. *"The wind will guide you."* Her own mother's words...

"Okay," she told Gray simply. "If that is what I have to do to survive, then I'll marry you." She leaned into him, sensing his need for her contact as deeply as her own need for comfort, and Gray pulled her toward him quickly. Her face pressed into his chest as a sob wracked his body. She could feel his relief from the fear that she would prefer death at the hands of his brother to being bound to him in marriage, evident in the way his body shook.

"Thank you. Thank you, Lea. I will make sure you're happy, whatever you need, whatever you want," he paused, "whoever you want. For as long as you live." She wrapped her arms around him, feeling his love for her and wishing that her heart would thaw the layer of ice that still surrounded it, the reminder of her mother's life cut short.

Lea wasn't sure what was in store for her, what this marriage would mean, or if she would ever forgive Gray... but as they sat there in the heaviness together, she allowed him to hold her. They stayed there for what felt like an eternity, both taking comfort in the other as the sun sank below the horizon, unsure of what tomorrow would bring. As the wind blew around them, pushing them closer together, Lea wondered if the wind might help her find a way to forgive the man who clearly loved her more than the life running through his own veins.

CHAPTER 45

Gray decided that Lea would stay with him until the wedding, which he scheduled for the following evening at the chapel on the castle grounds. He wasn't willing to risk leaving her alone until the entire kingdom knew of their union—until it was clear to all that she was his and harming her meant certain death. After they returned from the field, Lea went through the motions of bathing and dressing in her room next to Gray's before wrapping herself in a soft robe and moving to the swing on her balcony.

She looked out over the garden, the bright-colored flowers and lush bushes, wondering if she could ask Gray to tend to this garden after the wedding. It would be easier to work with the moonflowers she intended to grow if the garden was within sight. Considering how to best approach the subject, she continued pushing herself back and forth with her feet on the sun-warmed floor. She would be marrying the Night Prince. These gardens must be his. There were no other rooms that overlooked the courtyard besides the ones in Gray's wing of the castle. Surely he could allow her the luxury of tending to them.

Marrying the Night Prince, she thought again—the Fae who's feared all over Desia for his brutality and dark magic. She knew better than that now, of course. Evander Nestruir was not the man he allowed people to think he was. She thought about the past few weeks, the many times and ways he had defended her. No, he was likely the only Fae in the kingdom that she was truly safe with.

Her heart fluttered when she thought the words, and she realized that no matter how angry she was with Gray, her true feelings for him were undeniable. Feelings she didn't want to explore right now, her mind going places she didn't want it to go. He had known about his father's black magic for years, never tried to keep it from killing innocent people, but was that even fair? He said he was trying to stop it, but could it even be stopped? She shook her head, trying to dissipate the argument she was having with herself. Even if it was unstoppable, even if it hadn't been possible to save her mother, he could have at least told her the truth. He could have told her what the Lonely Death was, that he had stayed with her mother so she hadn't suffered in death. They could have tried to work through it together instead of him keeping her in the dark about what he was trying to protect her from.

She jumped when she heard someone clear their voice behind her. She didn't turn around, continuing to look out at the gardens as Emma came to sit beside her, placing her hand on Lea's.

"Mates," Emma said with awe. "I had wondered, honestly. The way he looks at you, how he somehow knew when Alaric hurt you. His possessiveness, that need of his to keep you safe... It's amazing."

"Amazing? Emma, how is it amazing that I once again have no choice in my life?" Lea said the words gently, knowing Emma wasn't dismissing what she was feeling.

"I know you see it that way, but you do have a choice. You don't have to accept the bond, and even if you did, it's possible to break the bond once you're bound to each other. I know it's not what you want, but it's still amazing. Because there haven't been true mates in hundreds of years. No one has been blessed by the gods in this way in a very, very long time, Lea. And you have."

Lea shook her head. "It doesn't feel like a blessing. It feels like a trap."

"Perhaps try to think about why the gods chose you, a girl from a small mountain town, to be mated to the Night Prince of Desia. The god and goddess do not give mates without reason. I think... I have a feeling that something big is coming."

Lea turned to Emma and opened her mouth to speak.

"Before you argue with me, let me finish, please," she said the last word meekly as her fingers tapped against her thighs and she looked away. "I was wrong when I said that you needed to be careful with Prince Evander. He is the only member of the royal family with an ounce of humanity, and he clearly loves you, and... and I think you should forgive him." She nodded her head firmly. "If I had someone that loved me the way he loves you..." she trailed off. "I know he made a mistake, a huge, almost unforgivable mistake. But have you never made a mistake? Do you not think that you deserve happiness? Do you not think that your mother would want you to accept a bond that will bring you a love for the ages? One that will be written into history as a miracle? What is it that's making it so hard to forgive him?"

Lea thought for a moment, wishing it were as easy as Emma made it seem. "How can I ever look at him and not think of my mother, every single time?" she asked sincerely.

Emma paused. "I didn't know your mother. But I do have a mother myself, who I love very dearly. And I know she would give anything, her life included, to make sure that I was safe and happy. That is what Evander will give to you. Safety and happiness. I don't believe your mother would want you to sacrifice that for her memory. Just think about it," Emma told her as she patted her hand and stood to leave.

"Wait, Emma. The bond, how is it sealed? You said it could be broken?" Lea needed to understand, knowing little more about mates than she had yesterday when she wasn't aware they actually existed.

Emma blushed, shuffling her feet. "Erm... well... The couple has to... well... they have to be, um... *intimate,* under the element that holds their power. The sun for you, the stars and moon for Evander."

Lea thought back to the day Gray had kissed her on this very patio, the sun's rays falling over them before he took her and brought her back inside. "I will take you under the sun one day," he had told her.

"I'd have to have sex with him out in the open?" she exclaimed, a laugh bubbling up her throat as she watched Emma's face turn a deeper shade of red.

"More or less. It can still be private, but you must have nothing between your skin and the sun or moon above. Once the bond is complete, you'll be marked, here." She walked back over and touched just below her collarbone, above her heart. "A moon for you and a sun for him. A symbol for all to see that you are his, and he is yours."

"And to break the bond?" Lea asked.

"It's a very grave thing, to break the bond. Not to be spoken of unless it has to be done. I don't know how it works, only that it's possible. Once broken, the bond cannot be formed again. The gifts you are given as mates will disappear."

"Gifts?"

"If you accept the mate bond, your life force will be tied to Evander's. You would live as he lives, age as he ages. As mates, he can heal you far more quickly than anyone else can, faster even than a skilled healer. You can feel each other's emotions, each other's physical pain, if you open yourself up to it. You likely have these gifts to a degree now, but it's amplified if the bond is accepted. Anyway." She took another step back. "I have a wedding to prepare for. Your dress won't make itself, will it? Think about what I said. Promise me?" Emma gave her a small smile, bouncing slightly on her toes as she waited for Lea's response.

"I will," she promised. "Hey, Emma?"

Emma paused on her way out the door.

"You're a great friend… Thank you." Lea turned her face back toward the gardens, watching as the sun began to sink below the horizon. Could she forgive Gray? Truly move past her anger and hurt? She felt the wind stir her hair and she leaned into it, imagining it was her mother's touch, pushing her hair from in front of her eyes.

"Tell me what to do, Mom. Just tell me what I need to do." She placed her head in her hands.

"Follow the darkness," the whisper met her ears, unmistakable. *"Follow the darkness."* It said again and again. *Follow the darkness*—the darkness had to be Gray. Her mother had said the wind would guide her when she most needed it; was this what she had meant? Did she want Lea to forgive him? On shaking legs, she rose. She needed to talk to Janelle, needed someone who had known her mother. Lea had turned to go find her friend when she noticed Thomas standing in the doorway, still as stone.

They stared at each other for several seconds.

"Tell me it's not true. Please, tell me that the rumors of a wedding tomorrow are just rumors. Tell me you're not marrying him."

Lea had seen Thomas hurt before, but not like this. He looked like a trapped animal, wounded and unsure how to escape the danger.

"I have to," she whispered, so quietly she wondered if he even heard her.

"Why do you have to, Lea? Why would you marry him when I am right here? When I have told you time and time again that I love you… that I want a life with you." He stepped forward, and she held up her hands, knowing that if he touched her, she would fall apart.

"Alaric tried to kill me, Thomas. Again. He's never going to stop. Gray is protecting me."

"I will protect you!" Thomas screamed, fury etched in every feature as he walked forward and grabbed her arms. "I will protect you from Alaric, from Evander, from everything. I let him hurt you once, and I will never forgive myself for it. Is that what this is about?"

"Of course that's not what it's about. I know you wish you could have helped me that day. But no, honestly, I don't think anyone except Gray can protect me from Alaric."

"That's not true. We can leave right now, Lea. We can go south to Calir, cross the border, and be rid of this fucking place forever."

"That will never work, Thomas," she breathed, tears in her eyes.

"I will make it work!" he sobbed, dropping to his knees and pulling her down with him. He held her, his touch desperate as he rocked her back and forth.

"I will make it work, Lea. *Please* come with me. We can go now."

"Thomas, stop. I can't go with you," she said sadly.

"You can't, or you won't?" His words hit her in the gut, a stab so sharp she almost looked down to see if she was bleeding. She started to cry in earnest, knowing that her relationship with Thomas would never be the same. Wishing that she loved him back, that she didn't have to hurt her friend, the boy who had been by her side her entire life. She took a deep breath before speaking.

"I won't." She pried herself out of his arms as he sat frozen in shock.

"You still love him. That bastard who killed your mother, my father!" Thomas stood, his outrage etched into his face as he turned and punched the stone wall. The *crunch* of bones rang out and Thomas recoiled his hand, his human strength no match for the ancient stone. With a guttural scream, all of Thomas' pain, fury, and resentment echoed back to where Lea stood, frozen. "You love the spawn of the Black King, that evil man with the voice of thousands of slaughtered humans!"

"I don't know what I feel!" she yelled back.

"He'll destroy you, Lea. Just like his father has destroyed this kingdom," his voice echoed out over the garden as his screams grew unbelievably louder.

"He's nothing like his father, Thomas!" she screamed back at him, so tired of him judging her for things that were out of her control. "You know what?!" Lea shouted, shoving Thomas backward. "You're right, I do love him. I don't know if I can ever forgive him or if I can move past what's happened, but I love him." Lea paused at her admission, the pain she felt in her chest releasing her from its hold. In its place was a cool, soothing sensation, blooming just behind her breastbone. *Despite it all, I love the Night Prince.*

"I love him, Thomas. I can't give you what you want. You don't just want to take me from here to keep me safe, you want to take me from here to keep me from him. You want to build a life that we can never have together." Lea's chest ached as she watched her friend turn cold.

"We're coming, Lea." Thomas's voice was low, but she heard him loud and clear. The resistance. The word he didn't dare to say within these castle walls. "The Black King and your precious Night Prince. Their end is near, and I will watch as we destroy everything they have built, take back every bit of power stolen from our kind. If you are with him, then you are against us. If you marry him, then *you* are the enemy, Lea."

He looked at her for another moment, waiting for her to change her mind. But Lea just stared at the boy who had been her best friend for over twenty years, declaring her his adversary. She watched as he realized what he had said could not be unspoken, before he turned and walked from the room, the door rattling on its hinges as he slammed it behind him. Closing the door on their friendship, the line between friends and enemies etched in stone.

CHAPTER 46

Gray found her a few minutes later where Thomas had left her, sitting on the cold stone floor and staring absently at the door.

"Azalea, hey." He crouched before her and lifted her chin to meet his eyes, shaking her out of her fog of misery. "Are you okay?"

Lea nodded at him unconvincingly. "Thomas hates me," she told him sadly.

"I know. I heard everything. I wasn't trying to eavesdrop, I promise you. But I meant what I said earlier. I don't think it's safe for you to be alone until we are wed."

"I'm surprised you didn't come over and kill him for threatening you."

"I couldn't care less if he threatens me. But I did want to kill him for speaking to you that way." He lifted her from the ground and brought her to her bedroom inside, placing her down softly before coming to sit beside her.

"So you heard everything I said too, then?" she asked, embarrassed.

"I did," he nodded. "It doesn't have to mean anything. Whether you love me or not, it means nothing if you can't trust me. I know that. I meant everything I said. I won't force anything on you," he said solemnly.

"I just, I know you never wanted to hurt me. I don't know what else to say... or where that leaves us," she explained.

He put his arm around her shoulder and pulled her closer to him, pushing waves of calm into her skin.

"How about, for now, we're friends? After the wedding, once you're safe, we'll have all the time in the world to figure out how we're going to move forward."

"Friends..." She tried out the word, feeling surprised at the relief she felt at taking the pressure off herself to make a decision about her relationship with Gray.

He visibly relaxed. "It's nice to feel something other than hurt coming from you," he said with a sad smile. She returned his smile, letting her heart rate slow and her worries ease a bit.

"Feel something from me... Emma said we could feel each other's emotions if we wanted to. Is that what you mean?"

He nodded. "I can feel when you're happy or sad, restless or content. If it's an intense emotion or physical pain, I can feel you without even trying."

"Can you teach me? How to feel it, I mean?" she asked him hesitantly, not sure if he would want her prying into his thoughts and feelings.

"Of course," he beamed, pulling her back to lean against the headboard with him and grabbing her hand. Lea closed her eyes at the intensity of the sensation traveling through her hand and arm. "The bond, it tethers your magic to mine, your life to mine, and vice versa. Our magic is always connected, no matter how far apart we are. What does your magic feel like to you?" he asked her, tapping her chest.

Lea closed her eyes and took a deep breath, focusing on the ball of magic she felt in her chest. "It feels like... light. I don't know how else to explain it."

"Now imagine unwrapping it like a ball of yarn. My magic should be alongside yours. It will feel different from what you call on to heal yourself or grow your plants."

Lea focused on the feeling of light, trying to unravel it as she searched for Gray's magic. She jumped when she felt it, opening her eyes and smiling up at Gray.

"Cool water. You feel like the cool water from my stream back home. It's... soothing."

He smiled back at her, brushing his thumb across the back of her hand. "Good, now. Follow it. Let the tether pull your magic even closer to mine. Follow the path it takes, and really let yourself feel what it is trying to show you."

She laid her head back and closed her eyes once again, following the feeling of cool water as it traveled through her body.

"What am I feeling, Little Flower?" he asked quietly, not wanting to break her concentration.

Lea felt a swell of emotion building within her, foreign and familiar at the same time, and she let her magic pull her deeper into it.

"Love," she rasped. "You're feeling love." She swallowed, suddenly uncomfortable with understanding the depth of his feelings for her. It felt like a primal need—like craving air or water, but selfless, overwhelming. He'd said the words, said them many times, in fact, but feeling it from him was so different. Something she wanted to dive head-first into and run away from at the same time.

"For you, always." He leaned over and kissed her forehead before standing and walking toward the door.

"I need to meet with someone, but Erik is guarding the hallway. You're safe tonight. Get some rest. Tomorrow is a big day for us both."

Lea yawned as the door shut behind him, pulling back the covers and shuffling beneath them. She'd laid there for several minutes, waiting for sleep to come, when she felt a tug in her chest. She smiled as she closed her eyes and focused on Gray's cool magic, letting his feelings wash over her. There was love, all-encompassing and warm, as well as relief and contentment. Lea let Gray's emotions fill her, holding them tight and falling asleep as she thought that maybe being loved by Gray wasn't so terrible after all.

She awoke to a squeal and someone jumping on her bed.

"Janelle! She isn't even awake yet." Emma scolded in a half-whisper.

"Oh, come on, she can sleep tomorrow. Lea! Wake up!" Janelle cupped her hands around her mouth and yelled. "You are marrying a *prince* today! A very handsome prince with a giant di—oof." She doubled over as the pillow Lea had launched into her stomach hit the ground.

"I'm up, thank you. What a nice, calm way to wake me on the biggest day of my life. At least Emma has some manners," Lea teased.

"Emma also has your wedding dress!" Emma called from the window. Lea looked up to see her hanging the most beautiful dress she had ever seen from the top of the windowsill. The dress itself was white, banded at the waist with a waterfall of white fabric falling into a puddle on the floor. It had thin straps that attached to a fitted bodice, with swirling white patterns that reminded her of the wind embroidered into the bodice and skirt. Over the top of the white material was a sheer, almost silver layer, attaching to the straps at the top before billowing into loose sleeves that ended in a silver diamond studded cuff at the wrists. The sheer fabric gathered at the waist before joining the long white fabric at the bottom, the folds of the sheer silver and white mixing together. Moons and stars were stitched in silver into the shimmering top layer, and together the two layers of the dress seemed to tell a story of a windy, starry night.

"Oh, Emma. How? How did you do all this in a day?" Lea asked, shocked that Emma had created something so beautiful at all, let alone with only a few hours to do so.

"Mom helped, of course, but it was my design. Do you really like it?" she asked nervously.

"I love it. And I love you." She ran over and gave Emma a hug, squeezing her tightly before turning and walking over to examine the dress more closely.

"I've never wanted to put on a piece of clothing so badly in my life. Can I wear it now? Is it time to get married yet?" She looked to see Emma smiling at her.

"Does your lack of a sour attitude about marrying Gray today mean that you thought about what we talked about?" she asked hopefully.

"It means... that today I am getting married, and I will have to figure out the rest of it tomorrow."

Janelle and Emma helped Lea bathe, Emma putting oils and bubbles into the warm water. After she was clean and lathered in sweet-smelling lotion, they went to sit in the morning sun to let Lea's hair dry in the breeze.

Lea listened as Emma told her all about the sewing process, how she loved designing clothing and wished to create her own wedding dress someday. Lea sat contentedly as she listened to her friend, before reaching inside to find her tether to Gray. She followed it, wanting to feel the warmth of his love for her to calm her nerves, but... that wasn't what he was feeling. Nerves. Anticipation. And a hint of fear.

Her heart began to beat faster as she felt his emotions as if they were her own. Was he nervous about marrying her? Was this not what he wanted? She pulled back, not wanting to feel those emotions any longer. *I have enough nerves of my own*, she thought, as she stood to go back inside.

The day passed quickly as Lea spent time with her friends, and before long she found herself sitting in her wedding dress before the vanity, Emma expertly braiding her blonde hair from around her face. The braids twisted in intricate patterns until they joined in the back of her head, while the rest of her hair hung loosely around her shoulders.

Janelle applied more makeup to Lea's face than she had ever worn in her life, using kohl around her eyes and on her lashes and painting her lids a beautiful shimmering silver. She brushed a pretty rose blush across her cheeks, then covered her lips in a pale shade of pink that looked beautiful against her tanned skin. "Your necklace doesn't match," Janelle teased, removing it from around Lea's neck to clasp it around her own.

"It's fine," Lea protested.

"I will give it back to you after the ceremony. But it clashes with the beautiful dress Emma worked so hard on. You trust me, right?" Janelle questioned, eyebrow raised.

Lea looked at Emma, who, despite pretending to be busy, had a hopeful look on her face. She *had* worked hard, and it was true that her necklace was not nearly delicate enough to complement the gown...

"I trust you," Lea nodded, smiling to herself as Emma tried to hide her squeal of excitement.

Emma moved from in front of her with one last touch up to her hair, allowing Lea to look in the mirror for the first time.

Lea could not move, could hardly recognize the woman staring back at her. It was her, of course, but she looked so... royal. Confident but feminine at the same time. Strong, but delicate. Tears filled her eyes as she looked at Emma.

"No, don't. The black will run, and we'll have to start all over, Lea. We don't have time for that." Janelle reached for Lea's hands with tears in her eyes, holding them in front of her as Lea steeled herself for a sentimental moment with her best friend.

"The Night Prince is going to shit his pants when he sees you," she said with a sniffle, and Lea burst out laughing, doubling over as the three of them dissolved into a fit of giggles.

A knock sounded at the door, and Lea stood to answer it before it opened in front of her. She froze as Thomas stepped into the room, a sword strapped to his hip.

"Lea, you look... You look beautiful," he said sadly.

"Thank you," she said quietly, neither of them moving.

"I think we'll give you two a moment," Emma said, grabbing Janelle's arm and yanking her forward.

"Hey! That hurts! He's my friend, too!" Janelle whined.

"We'll be outside!" Emma singsonged, closing the door behind them.

"I can't argue with you today, Thomas. I can't, okay? So if you're here for anything other than congratulating me on my marriage, I will start to sob, and Emma said it would ruin my makeup and she'll be so mad at you—"

"I'm not here to fight with you." He remained standing in the doorway. "I just needed to tell you something. I wanted you to know that I'm leaving tonight."

"Where are you going?" she asked, fear filling her belly at not knowing where he was headed, or if he would be safe. Regardless of the tension between them, she couldn't imagine a life without Thomas in it.

"A group of us are leaving the capital this evening, after the wedding. I'm making weapons for everyone. I really think we can change things, Lea."

Heavy tears wet her cheeks as she watched the boy she'd grown up with turn into a man before her eyes.

"I will always love you, Lea. Every moment of my life, I will love you, and I will protect you, even if it's from those I fight alongside." He kissed the side of her head. "But I can't stay here and watch you start a life with him. I can't live here in this castle knowing that somewhere within these walls, you're together."

"Where will you go?" she asked, hating that she was the reason he was leaving.

"I don't know yet. I won't know until tonight when we're on our way. We *will* overthrow the King, Lea. We won't stop until we do. I truly hope that you're right about your prince. If he fights against us..." he trailed off.

"You'll have to fight back. I understand."

He unbuckled the sword around his waist, tracing his fingers across the sheath it rested in before handing it to her. "I made this for you. I remember how you looked at the one I'd made that day at the market. I could see how it called to you."

Lea took the weapon and examined the hilt, a beautiful pattern of vines and small silver flowers wrapping around it. In the center of the hilt was a hinge. She tilted the sword and noticed a small, undecorated piece of metal in the handle that opened to a compartment, similar to a locket and about the size of a thumbprint. She opened it, rubbing her thumb across the small indentation.

"What's this for?" she asked, her fingers exploring the smooth divot.

"I want you to place a moonflower there, when you learn how to harvest it. Because I know you're going to do it one day, Lea. You're going to cure the Lonely Death and find a way to stop your husband-to-be's father from destroying our kingdom."

Tears pricked at her eyes. He still had faith she would succeed, when all she had done time and time again was fail. She carefully unsheathed the sword from its sheath, gasping at its beauty. Beautiful swirling patterns ran down the entire length of the sword; the embodiment of the wind etched into the metal from the hilt of flowers and vines to the end of its razor-sharp tip.

Lea was at a loss for words as she took in the beauty of the gift her friend had made for her.

"It's amazing, Thomas. But why give it to me now?"

"Because I couldn't leave you without a way to protect yourself for when he eventually hurts you, Lea," he said quietly, tears choking back his words before he closed his eyes and turned away, closing the door on the most beautiful girl he'd ever seen.

CHAPTER 47

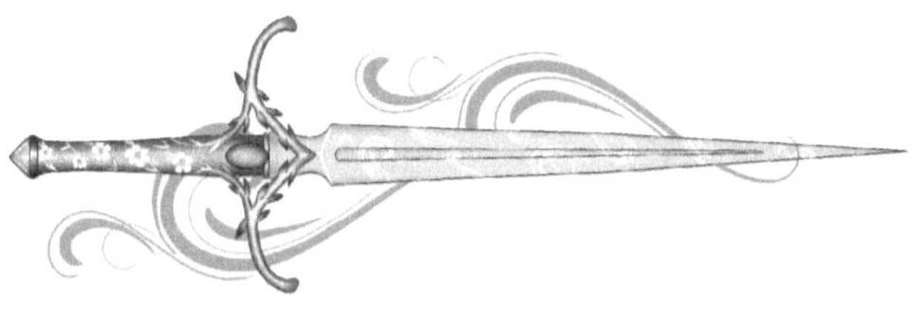

Lea's feet clicked against the stone floor as she walked to the church, her shaking legs carrying her down one winding hallway to another before leading her out of the main entrance of the castle and into the cool twilight air. The train of her dress trailed along the ground as she continued to walk toward the purple and pink sky until the spires of a church peeked out from behind the trees.

She paused as she neared the front doors to the stone church, trying to slow her racing heart. Inhaling slowly to calm her nerves, she studied the large wooden door in front of her, the portal to the life she was about to walk into. On one door, the god of the sun, the other, the goddess of the moon. Both held their palms forward as if beckoning her to open the doors and enter the sacred space. She paused, realizing that she didn't feel Gray's energy from behind the doors. *Where is he?* She reached inside herself to find his magic, following it until she felt his nervous energy filling her. More than nervous, actually. He felt terrified.

Dread filled her stomach. Everything is fine, she told herself. Maybe he was nervous his brother would come to kill her at the wedding, but surely he wouldn't be so bold in front of a church full of his subjects? Lea waited, distracting herself by studying the carvings on the doors, focusing on the goddess of the moon's long hair, not unlike her own. Except, the goddess's seemed to glow with the light of the stars themselves. She reached out to touch the carving and gasped as a strange silver-blue light began to illuminate the grooves within the wood, lighting the silhouette of the moon goddess. The wind stirred around her, words in an ancient language she didn't understand whispering in her ear as the light spread and grew brighter: "Faxo deae ante meos mala cadat pedes, et mors, quam tu juss, sequetur—"

"I've never seen anyone so stunning." Lea jumped in surprise as she turned toward the voice, the soft silver glow immediately disappearing as she broke contact with the image on the door. Lea met Gray's eyes as he stood behind her, the only soft feature on his masculine face. He was staring at her as if she had been the one to create the moon peeking out overhead as sundown approached. He wore midnight blue, his tattoo barely visible above his collar trimmed in gold to match the ornate pattern of golden stars on the cuffs of his jacket.

Lea felt her cheeks warm as she took in the Fae before her, her soon-to-be husband, in awe. There wasn't a more beautiful man in all of Desia, Lea was certain. "Emma made me the dress. She worked on it all night." She gave him a shy twirl, the dress billowing out around her legs. Gray walked to her and placed a hand tenderly against her cheek.

"The dress is beautiful, but it's not the dress, Little Flower. It's you. Everything that you are, every piece of you, body and soul. It's a beauty one dreams about but never actually sees, because it doesn't exist. And yet, in you, it does. Your loyalty to your friends and family, your heart, your courage, your light... Beautiful." He kissed her softly on the forehead before pulling back to look at her.

Lea allowed herself to reach out to Gray's emotions, her shoulders sagging in relief when she felt the sensation of his love wrap around her. It was calming, reassuring. But underneath, she felt a tinge of uncertainty... worry.

"Before we say our vows in front of everyone in that church," he interrupted her thoughts, cupping her face tenderly, "I have my own that I would like to say to you, out here, the goddess of the moon and god of the sun as our witnesses." He raised his eyebrows questioningly and she nodded at him, wringing her fingers as butterflies filled her belly. His eyes never left hers as he looked at her, the intensity in his stare making her legs feel weak.

"I vow to never keep anything from you again. Whether this marriage binds us together as friends or as husband and wife, or whatever you decide for us to be, we will be partners in this union. I will tell you all I know, the good and the bad. I will trust that you can handle whatever the truth is, because I know you are strong, and I know that without honesty, we have nothing." Gray's eyes shone with sincerity.

Lea blinked back tears at the intense emotion behind his words, nodding at him in encouragement. *I believe* you; she wanted to say, but the words were stuck behind the knot in her throat.

"I vow to love you fiercely, to protect you from anyone and anything that could possibly harm you. I will protect you with my words, my body, and my life. No one comes before you. *Nothing* is more important than you are to me." She took an involuntary step closer to him, opening up their connection to feel the passion behind his words. It ignited every inch of her body, wrapping around her heart and thawing the last layer of her anger. He meant every word. She would bet her life on it.

The wind blew Lea's hair around her shoulders, a familiar love wrapping around her along with the sincerity of Gray's promises. It smelled of her garden back home, and as Lea felt it caress her face, she knew without a doubt that it was her mother, speaking to her from beyond the veil—telling her to allow the man before her to love her. Urging her to forgive him. And so, with a deep breath, as she listened to Gray pledge his life to her, she did.

Gray's hand replaced where Lea had felt her mother's touch only a moment before. "I vow that whether or not you accept this bond, I will be yours until every last star falls from the sky. Just tell me what you need, and I will be that for you."

"Gray," Lea grabbed his arm. "I need to tell you—"

He looked up at the sky, stopping her. "We don't have time, we need to get inside... There's something...it doesn't matter. I just have one more vow." He pulled her toward the door, then pushed himself flush against her to speak into her ear, placing his hand in the dip of her lower back and sending shivers up her spine.

"I vow that I will find a way for my father and brother to die by my hand, and I will make them suffer for what they've done to your family, to you. For putting us in this position. If I have to set the world aflame to make it so, then that is what I will do." He kissed her head again before stepping away quickly with one more worried look at the sky and opening the doors.

The church was lit by candlelight, so dark inside she could barely make out the faces of those filling the hall. She strained to see Janelle and Emma in the flickering golden lights held by those inside, but couldn't find them among the mass of people. A man in a long black robe stood at the front of the church, the same soft blue light glowing around the book in his palms that she had seen in the carvings of the moon goddess outside. The king and prince were notably missing, their large thrones behind the priest empty, cold. Her eyes scanned the church, and she realized that everyone was dressed in black, women and men alike, without a single drop of color among the crowd.

Gray took her hand and squeezed, and she swore she felt a rush of calm push through his palm into hers. The sensation slowed her heart and gave her courage. *I need to tell him how I feel,* she thought as he guided her forward by the hand. This was happening too fast. She needed to tell him she was taking these vows willingly, that she wanted every part of him. No—needed him. Her mind continued to race as they stepped forward together, and everyone within the church stood, the wooden pews creaking with the movement. They walked down the center aisle toward the priest, the weight of their stares heavy on her shoulders. Gray made eye contact with Erik, who nodded at him as they passed, and Gray's shoulders sagged in relief. He squeezed her hand again as he looked at her, leaning down to speak into her ear once again.

"When I tell you, Azalea. I need you to run. Run to the training room Erik took you to. I will come for you."

She looked up at him in surprise, but his eyes remained focused straight ahead, serious and stern as they took the final few steps to the front of the room.

They stood facing the priest, Lea's hand trembling in Gray's as she waited for the words that would bind her to him forever when—*BOOM!* An explosion rocked the church. Gray folded his body around hers in an instant as the windows framing the large double doors exploded inwards, sparkling shards of glass raining down like stars falling from the sky.

"Now! Run!" Gray said in her ear before turning and drawing his sword.

"We're under attack!" Erik yelled to Gray.

He looked at Erik over his shoulder, "Summon the armies, block off the main gates. Do not allow anyone to enter or leave the castle grounds!" Gray shouted to his soldiers.

Lea froze as the church erupted in chaos. She couldn't move, couldn't think. What was happening? Everything moved in slow motion, men and women running and screaming in panic as the flicker of the fire growing closer danced in their panicked eyes.

"Thomas!" she heard Gray scream. "Get her out of here!" She felt someone rip her hand from Gray's and pull her outside of the church, the world on fire. She looked to the side to see the grove of trees around the church sending thick black clouds of smoke into the sky as she heard another explosion further away. Thomas was pulling her so fast her feet couldn't keep up, and she stumbled several times as he pulled her from the church.

"Thomas, what's happening?" She was terrified, the smoke around them so thick she could barely see ten feet in front of her.

"It must be the resistance; I was told there would be a distraction before we departed tonight, something big enough for all of us to get out of the castle in the chaos."

"I need to find Gray. I need to find my friends. And where the hell is Erik?"

"We have to get out of here, Lea. They'll find us, I'm sure of it." He continued to pull her forward.

"No!" She dug her heels into the ground. "I won't leave Janelle and Emma, Thomas. Go find them, please.

"We need to get you out of here, Lea!" He tried to pull her toward the castle again, but Lea held firm.

"I'll run if you will get them and bring them with you. I swear, I'll run as fast as I can. Gray said to go to the dungeons, that he'd find me there." She heard a scream from behind them as the roof of the church caught fire. Thomas's eyes flicked to the flames, then back to her.

"Straight to the dungeons, Lea, do you understand? You do not stop. Do not slow down. You get there as fast as you can and you stay there until Prince Evander or I find you."

Lea turned and ran toward the castle before he could change his mind, tripping and falling as her shoes caught in the dirt. She hit the ground with an audible *thud,* knocking her head on the packed dirt so hard she saw stars. Pulling herself to stand, she rubbed her sore head and blinked away the black spots from her vision, unable to tell which direction she had been running.

The smoke had thickened, so dark that she couldn't see her fingertips when she held her hand out in front of her. She coughed as the smoke burned her lungs, and she pulled her sleeve over her mouth to try to inhale clean air. She needed to move. She'd suffocate if she didn't get out of here. Lea took off, still unsure which direction she was running in as she fought to escape the blackness surrounding her.

She ran until her legs gave out, collapsing once the air cleared enough to breathe safely. She'd somehow found herself near the river Erik had brought her to the day before, and she ran to the water to wash the cinders from her face, to let the cold water soothe her throat.

"Shame we were attacked before you could marry my brother."

Lea stopped dead in her tracks, slowly lowering her hands that had been pressed to her face as she washed the soot from her eyes.

"Alaric." She stood and stumbled backward, feet splashing into the cold water as she took in the man in front of her. His green eyes filled with malice and murderous rage, his intentions written like the ending to a book across his face. "I'm still your brother's mate. You can't harm me." She held her arms out, trying to summon her magic.

"Except, who would know? With the fires and the attack, who knows how many will perish tonight?" He took another step toward her. "What is another human life in the death toll for the evening?"

Lea turned on her heel and ran, her smoke-damaged lungs straining to open wide enough to let oxygen in. She pushed her fear toward her connection to Gray, praying that he could feel her emotions, praying that he'd be able to find her.

Her feet pounded through the dry copper dirt as she ran further from the castle, kicking up tiny hard flecks behind her as her bare feet flew across the ground. She could still feel Alaric's presence behind her as she ran, feel the pressure across her chest like gale-force winds trying to halt her path forward. He was trying to stop her, using his magic to pull her back toward him, but she continued to struggle forward. His footsteps vibrated into her bones with each step he took closer to her. Fear gripped at her throat, but she pushed through, feeling his green eyes on the back of her neck, her legs, just a prickle of awareness breaking through the fear. She felt her pace slowing, her legs shaking, and she was unable to catch her breath. She couldn't keep running, she had to fight. Unable to push forward any longer, she turned toward him and raised her hands out in front of her, screaming as she carved out every bit of magic she held within her. The sky turned impossibly darker as a roar in the distance shook the earth, a madman's fury unleashing in a violent rage.

She felt the clouds racing toward her; the wind encircling her, blowing her hair and pushing against her tired body. Darkness built within her as she met Alaric's taunting eyes, his hands raised like he was about to deliver his final blow. She threw her magic outward along with her rage, thunder crashing around her as silver-blue lightning struck all around them. Alaric's eyes widened in fear as he jumped back from a bolt of lightning crashing into the dirt.

"That's not possible," he said before he was thrown forward, his knees slamming into the rocky ground.

"Azalea! *Run!*" Gray cried out as Alaric threw him into the air with a burst of flames. Alaric climbed to his feet and drew his sword.

"This ends now, Evander!" he shouted as he ran toward his brother, sword held high.

"Go, Azalea! *Dammit, run!*" Gray's bellow shook the ground as he blocked Alaric's strike with his sword before rolling to the side and standing. They circled each other like predators, both poised to strike. She ran toward him, unable to watch as Alaric jutted his sword toward Gray's neck.

"Go with Thomas. *Now!!*" Gray ordered. Lea swung her head to see Gray had brought Thomas with him, Emma and Janelle at his side.

"GET HER OUT OF HERE!" Gray roared, the terror in his voice causing her to pause for just a second. She rushed toward him again but felt firm arms encircling her waist, lifting her and dragging her away from Gray as he and Alaric continued to circle each other. Thomas threw her over his shoulder, and she looked up through a curtain of hair to see Alaric strike out, almost swiping Gray across his stomach.

"No!" she screamed, kicking and pushing at Thomas as he carried her away. "Let me go! Please, let me help him!" she sobbed, but it was no use. Thomas would not let her go as he ran, holding her tight, Janelle and Emma following behind.

Sobs wracked Lea's body as she collapsed against Thomas with words on her tongue she worried she'd never get the chance to say. "I love you," she whispered to Gray under her breath as she was ripped away from her mate. His head swung toward her, his eyes meeting hers with a look so filled with happiness and love that it would have brought her to her knees if she had been standing. A swell of Gray's emotion hit her chest as Thomas pulled her away. Lea could feel his urgency for her to leave, along with a desperate fear that she would be hurt—but beneath his worry was a feeling far stronger. A message he was sending her through their bond: he loved her, too.

CHAPTER 48

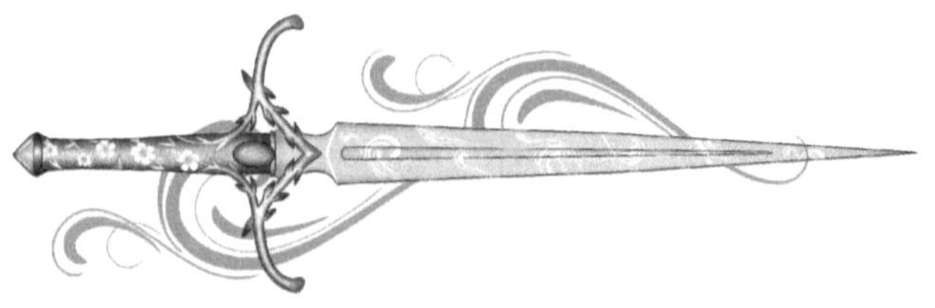

"What the fuck is happening?" Janelle screamed at Thomas as they ran. Thomas finally put her down, grabbing Lea's trembling hand and dragging her behind him as they raced toward the safety of the castle.

"Let me go! I need to go back!" Lea tried to pull away, but Thomas's grip was too tight. He turned around and grabbed her firmly by the arms, shaking her gently.

"You're a fool if you think for a second that I will let you go back there! And every second you spend fighting with me, you put them in danger! Do you not understand that?" He thrust a finger toward Emma, who looked at her with terrified eyes. He was right. She couldn't put her friends in danger again. Wiping the tears from her face, she tried to ignore the stab of pain she felt in her chest, nodding before grabbing Emma's hand and beginning to run again.

They ran through the main doors and down—down staircase after staircase, not pausing until they were deep enough within the bowels of the castle to feel safe enough to rest.

She stood with her head in her hands, each inhale sending sharp, breathtaking pains through her sternum, so severe she felt as if her heart was being carved out of her chest.

"Thomas, what's going on?" Emma asked him quietly, tears streaming down her face. "I need to find my mom. Are we really under attack?"

Thomas reached out to comfort her, pulling Emma close. "Your mom is the fiercest woman in this castle. She'll—" Lea let out an inhuman scream as fire tore through her arm and chest, tears springing to her eyes as pain lanced through her shoulder, so severe she felt as if her arm had been severed from her body. She drew her arm into her chest as dizziness overwhelmed her, causing her to fall to her knees.

"What's wrong, Lea? What's happening!?" Janelle screamed, running to her and kneeling by her side.

"I think it's Gray," she sobbed, rubbing her chest and searching for anything but pain through her bond. "I think he's hurt." She looked down at her arm, her chest, fully expecting to see blood pouring from an open wound across it, but found only her soot-covered wedding dress.

"We need to keep going. We need to get to the meeting. They'll know what's happening." Thomas bent over to pull her to stand.

"What meeting? What in the gods' names is happening?" Janelle shouted.

"I'll explain later. We have to go." Thomas grabbed Lea and Emma's hands and pulled them deeper toward the dungeons. Lea could barely stand through the pain in her shoulder. She tried to reach toward Gray's magic as she stumbled down toward the dungeons, but could not focus enough through the agony to find it. She needed to get to him, but the pain was so severe, the only reason she was moving at all was that Thomas was pulling her. Gray had to be okay. There was no other option.

Lea continued to search for him through the bond until they stumbled into the large training room with at least three hundred people standing inside it. Lea collapsed onto the floor in agony when the pain suddenly stopped. She looked behind her to see a shimmering veil across the doorway, one that reminded her of the magic that raced across the land to mark sunup and sundown.

"Where is he?" she screamed, her voice hoarse as heart-stopping panic rose inside her. "Gray!" She couldn't feel him. "Why can't I feel him?" she cried, the room growing quiet as sobs wracked her body.

"Enough!" a loud voice boomed through the crowd. She looked up through her tears to see the large tattooed man from the tavern standing atop a crate in the front of the room. His posture was tense, a warrior ready to fight. Several soldiers flanked him on either side, waiting for instructions from their leader, Lea guessed.

"We don't have time for any of this. We leave tonight. This is the beginning of what we have been planning for years. This is the beginning of the end of the Nestruir dynasty!"

The crowd cheered, shouts of "Kill them all!" merging with swords banging against shields and feet stomping against the hard stone floor. The air was thick with the passion of the men and women gathered in the room. They would not allow the king to continue ruling, and they were ready to die to stop him.

"For too long, we have suffered at the hands of the Black King! For too long, he has stolen our magic, our livelihoods! He has poisoned the land, so that magic can not flourish! He has killed our wives, our brothers and daughters! But no more! Our numbers are strong, but our hearts are stronger!" The crowd cheered again, and the man lowered his voice, his intensity almost deadly. "The resistance is ready. We have traveled the kingdom, grown our numbers, and now it is time to do what needs to be done to protect our people."

Lea felt shivers run up her spine at the leader's words, a pang of guilt mixing with her fear for Gray's safety. She wanted to join them. She ached to fight against the family that had killed her mother, that had killed little Anthony the day before her world was turned upside down... But what about Gray? No matter how much she wanted to fight against his father and brother, she couldn't leave him.

More shouts filled the room, fervent cries for justice. She noticed the tattooed man's eyes flick behind her head. He nodded before raising his hand and then bringing it across his chest, his thumb tucked behind his fingers. "Are you ready to pledge yourselves to the rebellion, at the risk of your own life, to ensure the downfall of the Black King?" the man roared, the crowd answering his call in turn.

"Then bow before your new leader!" he cried. "The one that will lead this kingdom back into peace! The Eclipsed King!" The room went deadly silent as Lea watched each man and woman present drop to one knee, bowing their heads solemnly with their hands over their hearts, thumbs tucked inside their palms.

She heard footsteps behind her and turned, wondering who had refused to bow. "Gray!" She jumped from the floor as she took in his appearance before her, blood soaking through his clothing, a rip across his black shirt in the exact place she had felt such severe pain in her own body minutes before. Her legs moved before her mind told them to, relief blooming in her stomach as she launched herself into his bloody arms, not caring for a single moment about the rebellion behind her, about the Eclipsed King the crowd knelt for behind her back.

"You're okay," she sobbed. "I felt you, I thought you were…"

"I'm okay, but later, we *will* be talking about your lack of ability to follow instructions." He squeezed her tighter. "You should have been safe here the whole time. That was the plan."

She pulled back to look at him. "The plan? I thought this was the plan of the rebellion?" she whispered, unsure what was safe to let others around her hear. "We need to leave, Gray. *Now.*"

"Long live the Eclipsed King!" she heard Vincent shout behind her, a war cry filled with so much hope, it sent shivers down her arms. "Long live the Eclipsed King!" soldier after soldier cried out in reply.

Gray bent down and kissed her softly, a whisper of relief in his exhale as he took a small step back.

"You're right. It's time to leave here." He lifted his gaze from her eyes and nodded behind her. Lea swung her head around to see the entire crowd still on their knees, heads bowed and eyes turned to the floor. Janelle and Emma stood wide-eyed beside Thomas, who slowly knelt as the truth crashed over him. His face turned pale from confusion and shock as he bowed his head and placed a shaky hand across his heart.

"I don't understand. Are you...?" Lea didn't have the words to ask what she was thinking. He couldn't be behind the rebellion spreading throughout the kingdom. But if he wasn't, why were hundreds of men and women kneeling behind him? Gray's eyes crinkled at her sudden understanding.

"Yes, Little Flower. Here's your proof. I vowed tonight to protect and love you until I take my last breath. And I vowed I would find a way to defeat my father and brother. But tonight is not the first time I have made that vow. I made the same one to myself long ago. I made a plan, a secret known only by myself, Erik, and Vincent, and we have kept that secret closely guarded for over a hundred years. But tonight, we set that plan in motion."

Lea's lips parted as the air was sucked from her lungs. "But I thought Vincent was their leader? I saw Thomas meeting with him. More than once..."

"Vincent may have been the face of the rebellion, but I have been leading from the shadows. We couldn't let my father and brother know I was committing treason. Not when my position as the Commander allowed me to watch their every move."

Gray reached out, cupping Lea's cheek with his palm, running a soft caress with this thumb over her jawline. "My love, believe me when I promise you that those monsters will die by my hand, and I *will* make them suffer." He leaned forward to speak in her ear, his rumbling voice settling deep into her stomach. "Now, stoke your flames and ready your shadows, Little Flower. We have a rebellion to lead."

ACKNOWLEDGMENTS

To everyone who read this book, thank you from the bottom of my heart. I hope it took you on an adventure, and I hope you look forward to book two of the *Magic of the Wildflower Series*, coming soon. If you enjoyed this book, consider helping me get the word out by leaving a review on <u>Amazon</u> and/or <u>Goodreads</u> and follow me on Instagram and Tiktok @meganshadeauthor

"Vulnerability is scary." Those are the words my wonderful sister-in-law, Leslie, said to me when I told her I wanted to write a book. She's right, letting the world read something you have poured your time and heart and mind into is scary. Thank you, Leslie, for the words you probably didn't even know helped me decide to write this.

To the greatest beta readers I could ask for—Brittany O'Barr, Molly, Tammy, Mindy, Dani, and Kenzie—the thoughts you gave me were invaluable.

Janelle, thank you for reading, for being a great friend, giving me feedback, helping me with my blurb, and encouraging me at every opportunity.

Di, thank you for your advice, proofreading, and support, even when busy working so hard on your own series. Check out D.L. Blade's Sea of Zemira and Blood of the Chosen series!

Bri, thank you for allowing your art to make my book more beautiful. Check out @busybri.art on Tiktok and Instagram!

And to all my family and friends, thank you so much for being my cheerleaders and supporting this crazy dream I had. I love you all!

9 798987 832400